Penguin Books
Madame Solario

Madame Solario

Penguin Books

Penguin Books Ltd, Harmondsworth,
Middlesex, England
Penguin Books, 625 Madison Avenue,
New York, New York 10022, U.S.A.
Penguin Books Australia Ltd, Ringwood,
Victoria, Australia
Penguin Books Canada Ltd, 2801 John Street,
Markham, Ontario, Canada L3R 1B4
Penguin Books (N.Z.) Ltd, 182–190 Wairau Road,
Auckland 10, New Zealand

First published in Great Britain by William Heinemann 1956
First published in the United States of America by
The Viking Press 1956
Published in Penguin Books 1978

Printed in the United States of America by
Offset Paperback Mfrs., Inc., Dallas, Pennsylvania
Set in Monotype Times

Part One

Chapter One

In the early years of the century, before the first World War, Cadenabbia on the Lake of Como was a fashionable resort for the month of September. Its vogue was easy to explain. There was the almost excessive beauty of the winding lake surrounded by mountains, the shores gemmed with golden-yellow villages and classical villas standing among cypress trees; and the head of the lake lay close to the routes that connected Italy with all the capitals of Western and Central Europe. Yet Cadenabbia itself was difficult to reach, which was an added charm. Long stretches of the lovely shore were without high road or traffic of any kind, and one arrived by the little steamboat that started at Como and shuttled back and forth across the lake, calling at one dreaming place after another in a journey of incredible slowness. It was wonderful to arrive. As no wheels ever passed, there were no sounds except human voices, the click of the peasants' wooden pattens, and the lapping of waves. One heard from balconies, 'Isn't this stillness delicious?' 'Ah, que ce calme est exquis!'

In the gay scene that met the eye during the season, women's clothes were the dominant note. And in the year 1906 women wore long skirts that moulded the hips and just escaped the ground; waists were small and tightly belted; busts were full and bodices much trimmed. Voluminous chiffon veils were the summer fashion. A veil would be thrown over a large hat and float over the shoulders, down to the waist or below it. So much clothing and embellishment turned each woman into a sort of shrine, and where there is a shrine there is a cult. The social atmosphere of that epoch was particularly loaded with femininity.

A young Englishman called Bernard Middleton, who had just arrived in Cadenabbia, was responding to the atmosphere, prepared to admire and to enjoy himself. He had expected to be joined there by a friend and was met by a telegram instead that told him his friend had been taken ill at St Moritz and could not come yet. Bernard was a little lonely at first, but by the second day he could see patterns emerging out of the first bright impressions of crowd, and was hoping that he might be included in a pattern – which one, he could not yet say. Looking on, he was amused and interested also by the cosmopolitan character of the company. He was still alive to the interest of being abroad, and indeed much was novel to him, for he had little experience of the world.

On coming down from Oxford, he had been sent abroad to prepare himself for the Foreign Office examination, but his parents changed their minds within the year and decided on another career for him. An uncle, his mother's brother, who was a banker, had offered to take him into the family bank. It was not at all what Bernard wanted, and as a slight compensation for his disappointment he had been allowed to spend the rest of that summer doing as he liked, and had been given what was to him a large sum of money with which to do it. After some mountain-climbing in Switzerland he had come to Italy; in a few weeks he must return home, and this short period of time had the urgent quality of the last of holiday.

When he had stepped off the boat on to the landing-stage in front of the Hotel Bellevue late on a September afternoon, he had thought he saw on either hand groups of people of bewildering attractiveness, but they seemed to dissolve as he went forward between them, rather as the reflections of the mountains and of Bellagio in the mirror of the lake had been dissipated into sunset-coloured waves by the prow of the steamboat. The groups formed again for him during the evening with a general character of awe-inspiring elegance, and it was not till the next day that figures began to acquire some precision and individuality. He had studied the visitors' list and found a number of English names among the foreign. The men who would be Lord H— or Mr V— or Colonel the Honourable Algernon Ross, and the ladies who would be Lady H— or Lady Victoria B— or Mrs Ross, stood out obviously. It was not so easy to place the label of nationality on everyone else. There was a middle-aged woman of commanding beauty – whose long veil thrown over a wide-brimmed hat was of fine black lace, as in a picture – who was closely attended by a mincing young man with a pointed nose and by a distinguished elderly man with a pointed beard . . . Her grown-up daughter ran up to her and kissed her, for no apparent reason, and was kissed back lingeringly as if they were meeting after a long separation. They spoke English to each other, but they were certainly not English. There was another middle-aged woman, whose presence had another sort of command, who had a stony face and talked in accurate French to several people who sat with her in a corner of the hall. She might be very important, but she was not French.

The older people moved in various and, he could see, separate orbits, but the young people flowed together in a single stream. Its most flashing point was the girl who had run up and kissed her mother; there was a stir wherever she went, and some young man was always with her. As the young men were none of them English, they remained vague to Bernard, simply alien in their self-possession.

In the afternoon sunlight a girl's voice suddenly said, 'Yet all the same we shall go – yes, Kovanski, yes?' – as Bernard was coming out of the front door, and he almost collided with a pink dress. 'Oh, pardon,' she said in French, but she hardly looked at him. She looked at a man who stood outside with his hands thrust into the pockets of his jacket, as though he did not intend to move.

'What do you say, Kovanski?' asked the girl, and when she got no answer she quickly entered the hall. As Bernard walked past the man who stood with such a curious stolidity he saw that his prominent eyes had a disagreeable stare, and he knew at once that he did not like the man or the stare. A little later he saw this man walking away, slowly and alone, with his hands still in the pockets of his jacket. The girl had seemed – in that fleeting glimpse of her – very slender and pale.

A motor launch was rocking on the little waves that heaved against the posts of the landing-stage, and two boatmen in white sailor suits were trying to keep it steady. A party of people was preparing to embark, but there was so much talking and laughing that they could not get themselves off. Someone began calling, 'Ilona!' And then others of the party looked up at a balcony of the hotel, and all shouted together, 'Ilona!' Someone also called, 'Kovanski!' But neither appeared, and the motor launch filled at last and got away.

Bernard was walking on, wondering if he would have liked to go too, when a puppy dashed out of an arbour that overhung the lake and almost tripped him up. There was a shriek from the arbour – 'Catch him!' – and after an absurd chase Bernard caught him, and handed him to an American girl who had followed breathlessly, accompanied by two men. She was American from the word go, and Bernard was swept up in her train and taken to the arbour, where they had been washing the puppy. A bucket of soapy water was on the ground, and the girl dropped on her knees and tried to re-immerse the struggling puppy; the water was splashed about, the girl was serious in her determination and yet kept on giving little shrieks, her two friends teased her, the puppy was delightful.

At last the older of the two men said patronizingly – as though he liked to take that tone with her – 'Come, Beatrice, that's quite enough. Go and change your skirt. What do you look like!' He had a French accent and a conceited drawl.

The girl got up; her white piqué skirt was indeed wet and muddy. She was not pretty, but she had a sort of exaggerated chic; the smallness of her waist was exaggerated, and so was her pile of ash-blonde hair. Appealing to them all to assure her that the puppy was 'perfectly sweet' and of course she must keep him, she took them all with her back to the hotel. There she asked Bernard how long he was staying, hoped she would see him again, and said, 'I'm Beatrice Whitcomb!' – while kissing the puppy, which the conceited man was holding in his arms. She was very jolly, and the first acquaintance that Bernard had made.

Much later in the afternoon, after a row on the lake, Bernard found himself standing beside the tall Englishman who wore a yachting cap, at the desk where the concierge was sorting out the post. The concierge addressed him as Colonel Ross, and Colonel Ross spoke to Bernard rather as though he had already been intending to do it; and very soon he was saying as they took up their letters, 'Middleton! Are you by any chance ...?' And that led to the discovery that he had been at Eton with Bernard's father, and that Lady Louisa Middleton was Bernard's grandmother, which was interesting, as she was a connexion of Mrs Ross's.

So the society of Cadenabbia was opened to Bernard. While waiting for dinner he walked up and down in front of the hotel with Colonel Ross, who told him – without being asked – who everybody was. The commandingly beautiful woman was Marchesa Lastacori. She was an Englishwoman by birth but had lived all her life abroad. Her husband was a rich Italian industrialist who had only lately received a title, said Colonel Ross a little regretfully, but they were a charming family. They, like others, came here every year. And the stony-faced lady was the Austrian Ambassadress, who had a daughter, added Colonel Ross, adapting himself to Bernard's age – 'a nice girl; but Countess Zapponyi's girl is prettier. Ilona is a very sweet girl.'

'Ilona!' said Bernard.

'Yes, do you know her?'

'No, but I heard some people shouting her name. Is she Austrian too?'

'No – Hungarian, as a matter of fact. Countess Zapponyi has been a very pretty woman; in fact she's had a great career, what?' And Colonel Ross dropped his voice into a pleased cackle. Then he called out, 'Good evenin', did you enjoy your picnic?' And Bernard recognized some of the party that had gone out in the motor launch.

'They are Italians,' continued Colonel Ross, dropping his voice again, for they were close by. There were several villas owned by Italians across the lake, and there was 'a lot of visitin' between here and there. Princess T— has a villa – you can see it, that big one all alone.' And he mentioned other romantic-sounding names, and feminine figures stood gracefully talking under the trees in the light that had faded to dove-colour. And Colonel Ross was as cheerful as if he were to be personally congratulated on all the good points of the place and its society. He was now responsible for them because he was here for the third year running, and he would have been hurt if they had not been appreciated.

The attitude of Mrs Ross was quite different. When Bernard was introduced to her he thought he was being deliberately snubbed, until he saw that this was no special treatment of himself

11

and that in her presence Colonel Ross was like a dog with a drooping tail.

Through the kind offices of Colonel Ross he was asked after dinner to join a party in the Salon de Lecture, and to his initial shyness the company seemed more numerous than it really was, and Beatrice Whitcomb appeared as someone he had known for a long time and was fond of. She greeted him as an old friend but took no notice of him after that. A game he did not get the hang of was in progress. Later Marchesa Lastacori's daughter went to the piano and sang, accompanied by the conceited man, and that was a remarkable performance. Music gushed from her throat, which vibrated like a bird's, and her voice was as free and pure as a bird's, but her expression and restless dramatic manner contradicted the quality of her voice. She had black hair and a naturally high colour, narrow hips and a full bosom; her bracelets jingled with her nervous movements; she broke off in one song and then sang another so that she brought tears into her own eyes. When she had done this there were 'Ahs!' of admiration, but the man at the piano said, 'Missy, what a cabotine you are!' and she stamped her foot. There was no more music, and Miss Whitcomb was seen to be doing tricks at the other end of the room. She bent over backwards in a hairpin bend and kissed the wall at about the level of her waist, and there were the same 'Ahs!' and hand-clapping, and Missy rushed into the night alone.

Feeling out of it, Bernard strolled over to the open window and sat down on the broad window-sill at some distance from Miss Whitcomb and her audience; and in a few minutes a girl had drifted towards him and stood as though she too had come to look at the starry night. It was Ilona Zapponyi, with whom he had collided at the front door that afternoon.

'It is very pretty here,' she said, pronouncing her r's in her throat in the foreign way.

'Yes, very pretty.'

'Are you often coming here?' she asked. 'Or is it the first time?'

'The first time – the first time I've been in Italy at all. Do you know Italy well? Have you seen the famous things – I mean, Venice and Florence and Rome?'

As he spoke he took in how pale she was, and how unhappy

she looked. One could see at once that she was unhappy. But while they were exchanging little phrases about Italy her manner was suddenly galvanized into animation, and, sitting down on the window-sill beside him, she said brightly and rapidly, 'I am always wanting to go to England because England is the nicest place. The life of the country in England must be so nice, like the life in Hungary, only I think it should be nicer, because in Hungary it is sometimes very lonely. The hunting in England must be so good. I was in Rome last winter, and there was hunting there too – but it isn't good. They make a great deal of it, but really it is rather – well, they are all tearing about. It is really rather ridiculous!' And she forced a little laughter.

Bernard had cautiously turned to discover the cause of all this, and there it was. Standing outside, near the window, was the man with the unpleasant fixed expression; and Missy Lastacori, recovered from her tantrum, was composedly talking to him.

'Are you fond of hunting?' asked Bernard.

'Oh, no, I am not very fond, but Hungarians must always pretend that they are.' She laughed again, but this time drearily. 'Are you fond of it?'

'It's the same with me – in my part of the world we must pretend that we are.' And they both laughed, quite naturally.

'My mother is very fond of hunting. She liked it very much in Rome.' She glanced out, as if by chance. 'Ah, there is Missy, and she is in a good humour again!'

'Who is she talking to?' asked Bernard. He thought it would make it easier for her to look, if he asked.

'He is Count Kovanski, a Russian.' She took the help that Bernard gave her. She looked. That made it possible to talk about him. 'He was in Rome; he is a military attaché. Last spring other Russian officers came for the riding at Tor di Quinto – that is the Italian Cavalry School. The riding there is wonderful. Officers from all other countries are coming to it, and they join in the Concours Hippique, and this year at the Concours Hippique the Russians won.'

'They must ride wonderfully well,' said Bernard.

Her slender arms in their white sleeves were crossed over her bosom as if she were cold. She continued to look; her glance followed someone.

'Shall we go out?' asked Bernard, and she gave a start.

She looked at him with gratitude. 'Yes, let us go out.'

There was no door on to the terrace in front, and they stepped into the shadows of an avenue that stretched from the side of the hotel as far as the water-gates of the Villa Carlotta. Even in the day-time this walk had a kind of mystery, for huge pollarded plane trees in a double row made a ceiling so low and dense that the sun never got through it, and the shade was damp from the high, mossy wall of the villa gardens that went all the way on one side. On the other was the low lake wall. There was a lamp where the lake wall jutted out and the arbour was, and Bernard and Ilona turned towards it. The avenue was dark and anyhow Ilona wanted to face in the other direction.

Almost at once they saw that Missy was talking to someone else, and that Kovanski was standing alone in the area of light by the embarcadero. He was smoking a cigar. And Bernard and Ilona stood side by side where the darkness began, and were silent at first. She was relieved; he knew it. She was having a few minutes of calmness now that Kovanski was alone and she could gaze at him, and Bernard felt even closer to the emotion of love than before. A realization of love had come to him through someone else, for he had never felt anything like this – like this that Ilona was feeling. As he was thinking this he was looking at the lake water where it lazily moved under the light, and, scarcely knowing what he did, he watched the light slide up and down on the tiny swell, sink into it a little way or shiver into fragments. At the same time he listened to the sound the water made, gurgling in the corner of the wall. But the silence had to be broken. Another sound had reached his ear: a faint tinkling that came from the lake, from all over the lake, and was really unearthly.

'Am I dreaming, or do I hear little bells?' he asked Ilona. 'What can they be?'

'They are on the fishing-nets,' she said. 'I also was asking that when I came. The nets are out on the lake all night – ' And her poor little voice failed, as though the effort of speaking were too great.

'Oh, I see, and the bells give them away.'

'Give them away?' she repeated, and then they both laughed because she was puzzled and he could keep her so.

'I don't know English very well. You could often laugh at me. And you have thought you were dreaming?' she asked as a little joke.

'Yes, of course – I think we're dreaming. Both dreaming.'

'Yes, I think we are both dreaming,' she said. With one accord they started to walk back.

Bernard didn't know what to hope or fear for her – whether it would be better to meet Kovanski or not. He was conscious of Kovanski where he stood, as in mountain-climbing he might have dreaded a difficult bit ahead of him. And his heart did the sort of thing it would have done if he had stepped on a loose stone in a tricky place, when Kovanski threw away the cigar and, just as they came up, walked into the hotel.

Bernard and Ilona stood still again. She smiled gallantly and said, 'It was very nice. Thank you so much – so much nicer than the hot room where there was so much noise.'

She lingered, bracing herself. There, under the lamps at the front door, they could see only a foreground – the landing-stage and the little white steamboat moored to it, and the trees in whose shadow Missy and two other people sat on a bench and talked in murmurs.

'Isn't it funny?' said Ilona, of the steamboat. 'It looks fast asleep.'

'So it does.'

She smiled again, and they went in.

In the big hall, in which there was a loud buzz of talk, the various groups of guests were sitting in their accustomed places, for each family had appropriated a particular combination of chairs that had become their own as much as a private sitting-room. Bernard did not yet know to which party Ilona belonged, and which lady was Countess Zapponyi, and it was with a slight shock that he learned she was the lady with yellow hair.

She might still be considered pretty, but she was unnaturally youthful and vivacious, and – Poor little thing! he thought as he saw Ilona lean over the back of her chair. The Countess put up a hand and patted her daughter's cheek affectedly, and went on talking to her circle, which included two Italian cavalry officers in uniform, and Colonel Ross, who had his chair drawn close to hers and was evidently very well pleased with himself.

15

Compared with her mother Ilona looked so pathetically young in her elaborate white muslin dress, whose frilled bodice could not disguise the lack of fashionable roundness.

After a few minutes she bent down and whispered good night, and as she went up the central staircase her mother said complacently, 'Le climat d'Italie ne convient pas du tout à Ilona. Elle dépérit à vue d'oeil!'

'Mais vous, Comtesse! Il vous convient à merveille! You must never leave us!' And without actually hearing it all, Bernard could guess what silly talk it was, and it disgusted him.

He thought he would look in again for a moment at the party in the Salon de Lecture, and on the way he passed the open door of the Salle des Jeux. There several games of bridge were in progress, and he saw that Mrs Ross and Kovanski were playing at the same table. As there were people standing in the room and looking on, he went in. He wanted to have a good look at Kovanski.

The Russian had a cigarette in his mouth while he played his cards, and he was making a grimace to keep the smoke out of his eyes. His composure was such that it gave the impression of his being alone – of his playing by himself. His way of throwing down a card and taking up a trick was that of the gambler, but his expression did not correspond with the action of his hands; it betrayed no interest. And yet he was a young man – that is, much younger than the people with whom he was playing; about thirty, thought Bernard, who could not but envy his extraordinary assurance. He had a round head with bristly dark hair cut very short, and a small dark moustache. His features were not particularly harsh or noticeable, except for those prominent eyes like marbles, yet the head was somehow brutal. When the game was over, Mrs Ross, his partner, began to find fault – as if it were a habit of hers; one could imagine she would always do it – and Kovanski did not answer or even look at her. It was his turn to deal, and he pointed to the pack beside him without a word; it was cut for him, and Mrs Ross stopped criticizing. After he had dealt and had picked up his cards he put them down without arranging them, lit another cigarette, and, not looking again at his hand, declared trumps in such a hoarse voice that he had to clear his throat and repeat the declaration. And then, as he took up his hand again, he looked up, the hard gaze of his eyes travelling over the room. They reached the door, and those eyes met Bernard's suddenly and fully, and with an odd sense of perturbation Bernard removed himself.

Chapter Two

The evening took another turn. He had got to know all the girls by the end of it, and the one he thought he admired most was an American girl, Miss Leroy, who lived in a villa near by, he was told, and was called Belle. She was a real Gibson Girl – the dark one who laughs out of the corner of her eye – and, however gay, was more reserved and sophisticated in manner than Beatrice, who was rather too rowdy, he began to think. And before they all separated he was invited to come on a picnic the following afternoon.

As this party assembled in front of the hotel he remembered the day before, when he had been alone and had tried not to look too obviously as that other party was setting off, and the re-collection made his present inclusion seem still more satisfactory. That everything was so 'foreign' pointed the charm. The girls – even the Americans – called the men simply by their last names, and he was just 'Middleton' to them. And these girls seemed to like this Middleton. Bernard was a very pleasant-looking young man, of a good height, with reddish hair that, if it had belonged to a woman, would have been called auburn. He had the quality of skin that goes with red hair, but not the light eyelashes, and he had a very nice smile. It had been taken for granted that, being English, he was what they called 'timid', and Missy, especially, made a joke of it. She had a very direct approach, and, going straight up to anyone she wished to speak to, she would laugh at whatever was said as though she had her own reasons for laughing, and her laughter vibrated in her throat as her singing did. She talked to Bernard and laughed – playing with her watch-chain, on which hung a score of little charms – all the time that the party was collecting, and he admitted to himself that she was rather fascinating. And when he turned and saw Ilona – saw that she was coming too – he felt a sort of reluctance and regret, as if there were something he did not want to remember, and knew he was disloyal to feel it.

It was, just as it had been the day before, almost impossible to get them started. Miss Leroy was of the party, and he formed a definite hope that he would go in the same launch as she; for there were two launches. One belonged to a German family that had a villa at Tremezzo. That launch got away first – with Belle sitting beside the young man at the steering-wheel. There was then a sudden move to go aboard the second, to which Bernard had been allocated, but they were held up for another few minutes because Missy and one of the men of their party had stepped aside and were engaged in such deep conversation that they did not hear; one might have thought that they were alone on a desert island where they had just found each other.

At last the launch was cleaving through the water; the air freshened, the land receded, and Cadenabbia became a string of little houses along the shore, with a mountain rising steeply up behind. And they were making for more beautiful shores, seeing mountains all around them like moving processions of shapes that kept changing their positions in relation to one another as the launch sped towards the middle of the lake. Mountains behind mountains majestically moved in their own rhythm, while under the launch the water rushed gaily away in two high waves from the sharp prow. A light spray flew up; it was pleasant on that hot day. The shores were basking in the rich sunshine of early September. That was the scene, and for the young people it served to heighten their enjoyment if they were getting the companions they wanted, or to deepen their dejection if they were not. Bernard was feeling only a little dissatisfied, just enough so to think that the more amusing company was in the other launch, and, in his own launch, that it was in the stern, while he was forward. Ilona was sitting in the cabin. Among those forward with him was the condescending man, Guimard, who seemed to enjoy snubbing the girls and pricking their conversational balloons, and whom Bernard now knew he disliked. But when they had all disembarked at San Giovanni – the two parties numbering more than twenty in all – a sort of collective enjoyment took possession, and as soon as it established itself it was bound to increase in a gathering momentum.

Bernard was so reassured by the way Ilona welcomed him that he had the impulse to believe he had previously been mistaken about her. There was nothing to make her different from or less happy than the other girls; she was charming, too; they were enjoying themselves. They and some others perched on the lake wall, and the rest sat on the launch cushions that had been spread on the ground for the picnic. The fun was general. Cakes and fruit and drinks were handed round, and in handing them the young men went to and fro and jokes were carried about and got called across the circle, and as two of the young men – one of the Germans and one of the Italians – were born buffoons of different types, they were able to start and spread a wild hilarity. Everyone began to feel that he had never laughed so much. And as happens when a number of people are all together infected with gaiety, a mysterious *other one* was added to their number – the spirit of gaiety itself. There was each one of them – and something else, made up of all of them. It was like someone else – who, which one? – at the elbow of each, and Bernard looked round, not knowing what he looked for. It was Ilona who was on his other side, and it made him happy – each time happier – to find her laughing too. As time passed and one had to think of going, the genial spirit withdrew, leaving them all more aware of one another, each turning to someone who had felt the spirit and felt it passing.

Behind Bernard and Ilona were the landing stage and watersteps of the little fishing port, and before them the two huge cypress trees in front of the church. Bernard said, 'This spot stands out particularly. I look at it from my bedroom window across the lake. I know these cypresses well, from over there – and now we're here.'

'It's like your English Märchen, *Through the Looking Glass*,' she answered, and when she asked him why he laughed he said – and now he laughed at her affectionately – 'Because you called *Through the Looking Glass* a Märchen.'

'But it is – and a very nice Märchen. I liked it very much. I read it when I was a little girl. Didn't you?'

'No, because I was a little boy.'

'Don't little boys like Märchen?'

'Not that kind.'

'What do they like?'

'Something quite different.'

'They are always liking something quite different from what little girls like?'

'Nearly always.'

When they got into the launch, as young people do who know nothing about each other except that they are pleased to be together, they went on making the most of their first joke. They kept it up: 'What do little boys like?' 'What do little girls like?' 'This?' 'That?' Remembering that the evening before they had spoken of dreaming, they added that too: 'Do they like dreaming?'

The launches had been turned not towards home but westwards, and the sun was sinking. They were going against the breeze. Ilona had light-brown hair that blew about prettily, and a powdering of freckles on her delicate little nose. The slight roll of her r's made what she said even more attractive. As they skirted the sombre shore, with a mountain looming over them, she pointed to the single house upon it at the foot of the gorge.

'That is a spot where they say the sun is never shining in winter nor the moon in summer. That is like a Märchen. Would you like that?'

'I would. Little boys like to frighten themselves. They could make something creepy out of that.'

Under the mountain the air was suddenly cold.

'What is *creepy*?'

'Don't you feel it? Very cold.'

'Yes,' she said in an altered voice. 'It's cold . . .'

'That is another kind of story,' she said as they were coming up to Balbianello.

'What is that story?'

At the point of a long and narrow promontory that almost divided the lake in two, rising to high ground from the water's edge, was a group of buildings, towers, cypresses, and statues, composed with indescribable fantasy. On the wooded crest an open arcade let them see between its columns through into the sunset.

'There was a beautiful actress who married the last owner of the villa – an Italian, a count – and when he died she went

21

away to Paris, and now she is living there and is never coming to see it. But the old gardener is keeping it beautifully because he thinks that one day she may come. I have been up there. We spoke to him. He said, "I am waiting for years for my padrona" – that is the Italian word for owner. "I want my padrona to see it beautiful, as it always was. But I am old, and she is never coming."'

'But doesn't somebody see it?' asked Bernard. 'Can't he have the pride of showing it at least to other people?'

'No, the public cannot go. One must have special permission. He is there all alone, with no one to see how beautiful it is. But I don't think he would want the public to see it. It is not for the public.'

'No, it is for –' But Bernard could not bring out the word 'lovers'. He fell back on their joke. 'It would be a good place for dreaming!'

'Yes, a good place for dreaming.'

They rounded the promontory, and he glanced back at the villa, seeing it now with the sunset upon it. That balustrade where one could lean and look ... Such romantic beauty of place, would one ever find it again? And had it any memories for Ilona? He felt sad. Ilona is a very sweet girl, he thought.

She asked him a question, a simple question: Where had he learned German? He answered, and then he told her a little more about himself. She was the first person to whom he had expressed his disappointment that the plans for his future had been changed, and he confessed how much he had wanted to go into the Diplomatic Service, and how very dreary he thought a bank must be. As he was telling her he remembered what he had heard, that to Austrians and Hungarians – of her sort – banking and business were outside the social pale. He would have been only amused if she had shown surprise at his destined career, but, though at first she looked sympathetic, she said, 'Yet I think it will be nicer for you to live always in England.'

'Then you meant it when you said last night you thought England was nice!'

And she answered, 'But of course I meant it!' She had been there once and knew what she was talking about.

He asked her where she lived. They had a place in Hungary,

but also an apartment in Vienna. Might he come some day to Vienna? He wondered – well, perhaps he might. The launches were making a wide sweep that announced the return journey. 'What a pity. Why must we go back?'

Everything the eye could see was lovely. And the church bells were ringing. It was Angelus. The bells answered one another, some close to the water, rather loud and clanging, and others far away. There were different voices, and which voice came from which church-tower? Which church-tower looked as though it had the loudest voice?

'That one isn't fair,' he said. 'It has the fattest church and it's the nearest.' And for a moment that one drowned all the others, and they could see the bell violently swinging to and fro. But they were carried past, and anyhow that bell slackened and grew languid, and in a sudden quiet they heard a faint one among the hills. On the hills were scattered little white churches with their campanili.

'Which one said that?'

'That one,' said Ilona, 'over there. Doesn't it look innocent?' It seemed certain that it was that one, the most innocent-looking of all, that they heard before another arose.

As they came again to Balbianello the speed of the launches was reduced, and they moved close inshore. The dense woods of the deserted place – all mystery and silence – plunged down to the lake, and a wall, crowned here and there with statues, followed the line of the shore round the tip of the promontory. At one point the wall ran out a little way in a breakwater protecting a flight of water-steps, and the slender baroque statue of a monk, his stone habit as if slightly blown by the wind, faced inwards, with his hand raised in an airy gesture; and probably everyone in fancy stopped there and went up those steps into the secret gardens of the love-haunted villa, which stood above them, a symbol of the love-haunted imagination of youth.

The boatmen put out their poles and steadied the launches for a few minutes at that point, and during those minutes no one in the company spoke but only looked, while the wash broke against the walls and swirled round the breakwater, and the last wave could be heard falling back from the water-steps. Bernard felt a longing for which he had no name, but

23

which was like happiness – he could not have said why, except that now he knew there would be other days like this one. The engines started up again, the voices too, and Missy was heard beginning to sing. She sang, she broke off, and that was tiresome; but after a little while the thrilling voice rang out and did not stop, and once more no one spoke but only listened.

Bernard and Ilona listened side by side. It seemed to him that she must be feeling as he did. Happiness and sadness pulsed together as the shore approached, with the moment when it would all be over. Lights twinkled in front of the hotel. Missy had been singing simple songs, Neapolitan love songs and *stornelli*. The intensity with which she finished one of these was able to give Bernard a sense of the words:

> *Già suona mattutino, lento, lento,*
> *Ritorno a casa e non veggo la via.*
> *Gli occhi lasciai teco e il sentimento!*
> *E ne portai con me la gelosia –*

After a dramatic burst the last words were almost spoken, in a throaty whisper, as though they could not be sung.

Bernard was startled by the effect of this; and then he was startled to feel Ilona shudder. She turned. They had arrived. He saw her face; and something took place within him that was like the sort of shifting which changed the position of the mountains in relation to one another when one's boat was crossing the lake. His position in relation to her changed. He still felt drawn to her, but they were on parallel courses – not meeting, as during that last half hour he had thought.

As those who lived elsewhere said good-bye to the Bellevue people Miss Leroy asked Bernard if he would come to a dance at her house the following week.

'We've got to do everything about it ourselves,' she said, 'and we'd be very glad if you'd come round that afternoon to help us make the cotillon favours.' It seemed like a particular invitation to himself, which was gratifying.

Ilona must have at once gone upstairs, but he thought that after dinner he would see her, as there would certainly be something going on. And then after dinner there was the effect

24

of another shake to the kaleidoscope. All the young people disappeared – all, that is, except the Austrian Ambassadress's very plain daughter, and she didn't count as young. It was mystifying, and rather sad. And as Countess Zapponyi was holding her court near where he sat with the latest romance by H. G. Wells, he listened to what was being said in the hope of hearing where Ilona had gone.

'You will hardly believe it,' said Colonel Ross's voice, 'but the hotel at Fontainebleau has, I consider, a better cuisine than any restaurant in Paris.'

'But the *ambiente* will not be so agreeable,' said another man's voice.

'I have been in Fontainebleau,' cried Countess Zapponyi. 'But I was not noticing the cuisine –'

'Oh! Oh! What were you noticing?'

So it's true, thought Bernard, after listening a little longer, that when one is old one talks about food. Without any reason for it, the fear of Kovanski shot into his mind.

Kovanski wasn't in the hall. Mrs Ross was absent too, and they might be playing bridge. He went to look. In the Salle des Jeux Mrs Ross was playing, but not Kovanski. Bernard returned to his place in the hall and heard Colonel Ross say on the other side of the column, 'Madame Solario is coming back tomorrow.'

'Ah, vraiment?' Countess Zapponyi replied, a little sharply.

Chapter Three

On the morning after the picnic Bernard went for a long walk up into the hills. Some of the lower slopes were covered with chestnut woods, and others with vineyards so steeply terraced that the cobbled path between them turned into steps and became a staircase going up and up, like Jacob's ladder. He had something to eat, with a flask of red wine, sitting outside a *trattoria* in a village that had barely showed at a distance, it was so much part of the mountainside, and he then briskly started homewards. The upper floors of some of the Cadenabbia houses were attached to the hillside, and suddenly he was coming down the sides of the houses like a fly, and there was the now familiar road, and there the space in front of the hotel, with the people strolling out after lunch to sit or walk in the shade.

Missy was the first to hail him, and when he answered her questions as to what he had been doing she appeared to think there was something behind his long walk that he would not confess.

'Have I presented you to Mama?' she said and turned to her mother. 'This is Middleton, Mama, that I told you about.' And she went into another peal of laughter.

The Marchesa's manners were gracious; she addressed some polite remarks to him, and said, 'You are a cousin of Mrs Ross?' He had been asked that before, and it made a flat beginning.

Bernard sat down with them under the trees. The party included what to himself he styled 'the hangers-on', of which there were a few around each one of the great ladies. Deriving from Marchesa Lastacori all the society she got, was an unmarried woman of about thirty, Signorina Petri, and the young man with the pointed nose was also a hanger-on and not an accredited admirer of Missy's. They waited for some rover to come up to them, one of those independent persons who went about choosing their company, and it was Wilbur who on that occasion joined the Marchesa – a middle-aged American, talkative and glossy, who started gossiping without the slightest preliminary pause. The Marchesa inclined her gracious smile upon him and soon was taking the words out of his mouth; and then they both broke off, but not too perceptibly, while the Austrian Ambassadress went by. Bernard found her such a repellent personage that he followed her with his eyes, and as she and her ugly daughter passed the door of the hotel he saw coming out a lady he had not seen before. She was not a girl, not young in his sense, though he knew she could not be more than twenty-seven or -eight, and his eyes stayed on her – not with the interest that a girl might have aroused, only contemplatively, but stayed, because he at once thought her beautiful. Her figure was a little above medium height and very graceful; she was fair, and she wore a hat trimmed with velvet pansies in shades of mauve that deepened into purple. After she had walked out into the sunlight she stood and opened a white silk parasol, and Bernard saw a tall Italian called Ercolani go quickly up to her; she turned round to him, and they stood talking – that is to say, she stood very still with her parasol resting on her shoulder, while he did the talking.

Bernard said to Signorina Petri, beside whom he was sitting, 'Do you know who that lady is?'

She looked that way, and then at Bernard more observantly than she had yet done. 'That is Madame Solario,' she answered.

Missy, who was usually restless and disconnected in everything, stopped in the middle of what she was saying and with a gesture that set her bracelets jingling made a sign to someone, got up, and went away. Madame Solario and her companion directed their steps towards the Marchesa's bench, and there were cordial greetings.

'Welcome back to us,' said the Marchesa. 'Did you have an amusing time?'

'Yes, thank you, quite amusing.' And, as it was so shady, Madame Solario closed her parasol. 'But I am glad to be back,' she said after a moment. 'This lovely view –' And she glanced across the lake.

'Only the view?' asked Ercolani, and with a little laugh she turned her eyes on him, and then upon the others sitting together. Bernard thought he should get up.

'Let me present Mr Middleton,' said the Marchesa, and Madame Solario bowed, and, with the faint hesitation that seemed part of her manner, she looked at him. Her eyes were of a violet blue that might have been taking a little reflection of colour from the pansies in her hat, and just as she had hesitated to look she hesitated to look away, so that it was impossible not to look back at those beautiful eyes.

'You haven't been here long?' she said to Bernard. 'You were not here when I left.'

He told her what day he had come. He could not but feel flattered by her notice of him.

'Now let us be going to see a little more of the view,' said Ercolani, and Madame Solario took leave of them and walked slowly on.

Everyone looked after her in a moment of silence that lasted till Wilbur picked up an anecdote where it had been dropped. Then Missy returned, with her quick, petulant step, her chiffon veil floating out behind her.

'Natalia Solario is back,' said the Marchesa. 'Did you see her?'

'Yes, and I've won a bet. I bet with Raimondo that she would come back, and now he must give me something funny we saw in the window of the shop.' And she laughed a great deal.

Bernard had been struck by the entirely foreign name because Madame Solario had spoken as an English-speaking person, not as a foreigner.

'What nationality is Madame Solario?' he asked Signorina Petri.

'I think she is by origin English,' she answered.

The others were talking about her, and the young man with the pointed nose – who was called familiarly Pico, short for his nickname of Pinocchio – after twice putting the question to them and getting no answer, said to Signorina Petri, 'She is American, isn't she?'

'I think so,' she replied.

'But you said she was English!' said Bernard, and she appeared surprised, as though he had been rude, and also uncomprehend-

28

ing, and he realized that there was no difference to her between the one thing and the other.

'Her stepfather was South American,' the Marchesa was saying.

'It is therefore probable she is American,' said Pico.

'But what kind of American?' asked Bernard, and Signorina Petri again seemed to think he had been rude. 'I mean, she doesn't look South American!'

'It might be North American,' she said with dignity.

'A very rich South American,' the Marchesa was saying to Wilbur, 'who lived in Paris. Monsieur de Florez – did you know him? No, the Solario wasn't born de Florez. I don't know what she was. I'm told the Florez' had a superb apartment.' Her emphatic manner made it truly superb. 'Such pictures, furniture, tapestries! But he died some years ago. I met Natalia in Venice last year; she is a friend of great friends of mine, and we lived through a terrible time together when our friend was taken ill. My dear! It was a drama!'

The distinguished elderly Count Mosca was lifting her hand and kissing it. 'Marchesa bella!' he said.

Beatrice Whitcomb had come up with her puppy in her arms. 'Look at them over there!' she exclaimed. 'They're all making a fuss over Count Greppi and thinking he's sweet because he's a hundred years old. I don't think it's a bit sweet to be a hundred. Come and see what it's like.' And she drew Bernard to where a group of people were surrounding a little shrunken figure dressed as a dandy of thirty years before, with a white flower in its button-hole. A young woman had her arm in his on either side, and the bleary eyes in his toothless little face showed the pleasure of an animal.

Bernard agreed it was a horrid sight, but he was distracted from it by seeing Countess Zapponyi making an appearance with her two cavalry officers and her smiles, her yellow hair looking very dyed in the sunlight. Ilona was behind her, and he soon manoeuvred himself away from Beatrice, for, on seeing Ilona, he knew that she was the person he had been hoping to see.

'That is Count Greppi,' she said, finding something for them to speak of. 'He has come here to lunch from Urio. He is a hundred years old.'

'That's what I'm hearing on all sides,' said Bernard. 'Do you think one should admire him for being a hundred years old?'

'Why should one admire that?' she answered. 'I think he cannot have much heart or he wouldn't be living so long.'

'Oh, I see. You think the heart wears one out –' But, while trying to add another joke to their store, he noticed that there were dark rings, like bruises, under her eyes.

'I imagine so.'

'I'm still feeling awfully strong,' he said, wishing she would smile.

She did.

'I see very well – you are feeling awfully strong.' And her 'r' rolled in her throat.

He asked, before he knew he was going to do it, 'Won't you come for a walk with me? Just to the Villa Carlotta?'

'Not now. I must go on a little excursion with my mother in the launch – but later I could come.' And they arranged to meet when she returned.

After she had left him he had another glimpse of old Greppi and thought: He couldn't have had a heart.

She was later getting back than she had expected; it was already six o'clock when he saw the launch approaching. He had placed himself where she could see him waiting, and sure that she had understood he walked expectantly away in the direction of the Villa Carlotta. Under the pollarded plane trees he turned, and saw her a little way off; and an uneasiness he had felt seemed justified, she was coming with such a wavering, hesitating walk. She seemed blown by a wind, but not blown straight towards him – blown a little to one side, so that he had to go to her or she might never have reached him.

Her little face, which could be so charming, was drained of colour and life.

'What is it?' he asked. 'Has anything happened?' He almost hoped to hear that there had been an accident.

'Oh, no, nothing – nothing has happened. I am only tired. I am very tired.'

'Then you should go in, not come for a walk!'

'It was being with people all the afternoon. So many hours

I have been sitting with people! So many hours trying to smile, trying not to cry!'

'How hard it must have been –'

'So many hours with people who must not see – I must not let them see! And I did not know how I should bear it.'

No, she must not be seen if she cried, and he led her to the inner side of the double row of trees. He thought that with this protection she would burst into tears, but she said, 'This is so good – so good – that now I won't cry.'

She repeated with a sob as they walked on, 'Now I won't cry!'

What was strange was that, after the first moments of amazement, it was natural to be receiving her confidence; and his vanity did not suffer from it, the only use to which she could put his interest in her. Just then only she existed, and that made everything simple.

'You don't have to pretend any more. You can cry if you want to.'

'I thought that if I could it would make it all right, but it wouldn't – it doesn't make it any better. It is silly –'

'No, not silly –'

'Little girls are silly. Little girls cry,' she said, picking up their joke with a fleeting gleam at him. 'Little boys don't cry.' And she sobbed again.

'I suppose they don't.'

'They are having nothing to cry about. Why should they cry?'

'They might do it inside themselves when you didn't know.'

'Why, why? Everything is different with them – you know, you said it. For them it could never be like this.' Feeling resistance to her idea, she grew more vehement. 'They can fight. They can always go where they like. They are never lost – are they? But I am lost!'

'Lost?'

'Yes, lost in a dreadful pain!' And she stood still and looked about her.

'What shall I do?' she whispered.

If he had answered he too would have hushed his voice, so great was the sense of disaster. No means of helping her were to hand.

'I love someone,' she said.

'I knew it was that.'

After those words had been said they started walking again.

'And I don't know what I should do.'

He asked, 'How do you mean – what you should do?'

'He may never speak to me again!'

She stopped and put her hand for support against the trunk of a tree.

'Why do you think so?' said Bernard. 'Don't you know each other very well? But in that case, perhaps in time –'

'He liked me very much – once. We were great friends – once.'

'Then mightn't he –' began Bernard.

All the time he was trying to keep Kovanski out, and not let the round, brutal head come into his mind. How could one associate this with Kovanski? He tried to see only her as she stood beside him, a fragile figure in a pink linen dress and a hat swathed with a white veil. She had her head bent, and her fingers picked at the bark of the tree.

'Last spring in Rome he liked me very much. When he went away he said we must meet in September at Villa d'Este. We were there, but he didn't come.'

He would not give in. He searched for some hope for her. Before he could find it she went on. 'My mother was wanting to come here. So we came here, and one day – a few days ago – I saw him –'

'He may have heard. He may have followed you!' said Bernard.

'He will not speak to me. He is always walking away!' She had to lean her whole weight against the tree. It was as if everything had deserted her.

'What can it mean!' exclaimed Bernard.

There was a movement of desperation on her part, of turning this way and that. After a few moments she said, 'I thought one day he was coming with us to Balbianello – and he didn't come!'

That was most pathetic of all. And the pang that Bernard felt was for himself too.

'I thought we should go there together,' said Ilona, hardly audibly.

'Perhaps you will.'

'I am still sometimes thinking we will.'

Suddenly she broke away, out of the invisible bonds in which she had been held, and – so unexpectedly that it was a moment before he caught up with her – she began to walk back to the hotel. It seemed to Bernard, after that pang of regret, that he had been told something definite, cancelling what had gone before, and that it was certain that she would go to Balbianello with Kovanski. He walked beside her, his sympathy confused by a change in the whole aspect of the case. He could almost have wondered why and what she had confided in him. And this new aspect was strengthened by her saying with a bewildering formality, 'I am so sorry I have been so foolish. We could have gone for a nice walk.'

He would not reply to this, and they went the last part of the way in a constrained silence. It was then that he heard the sound of a church bell coming across the lake, a single bell, tolling slowly. He wanted to say, 'Do you think that is the bell of San Giovanni?' but he did not speak, and she said low and hurriedly, 'I will not go in the front of the hotel. I will go in here.'

He understood – she was ashamed! – and he struggled for the right words and could not get them. He had never actually seen her tears falling, but they had fallen; they had been washed over the pallor of her face.

'Thank you so much – thank you so much,' said Ilona.

The avenue came up so close that the door of the room looked like the opening of a cavern between the trees. Ilona's light figure stepped into the cavern and disappeared.

The evening steamer was just coming in, and everyone was out in front to see what new arrivals there might be. It was one of the events of the day, a social event, a 'meeting'. It was by this steamer that he, too, had arrived; and he remembered the bright, mysterious impressions of the people who then were perfectly strange to him, whom now he saw as people that he knew at least by sight and name, among whom he stood, looking outwards at a different view from the one seen by those who were coming in. The archaic little white steamer had a paddle-wheel that churned up the water with a lot of noise. Ropes were thrown out, and the nooses caught the posts of the landing-stage, and passengers came down the tiny gangway. Someone on shore recognized an

33

acquaintance, and there were greetings. Everybody seemed to be talking and smiling, and it was all very gay – it was almost like opera. But he was feeling sad, and very soon he went upstairs.

He had letters to write – one to his parents to tell them that he was staying at Cadenabbia till Charlie Trevor, who had an illness that put him in quarantine, could join him – and this made him late for table d'hôte. The table that had been assigned to him was by the wall, not far from the door, and two columns hid part of the dining-room from his view. At a table at this end of the room – just beside a column – was Madame Solario, also dining alone. He saw her after he had sat down, and he wondered what was the correct thing for him to do. Should he bow first? It was impossible always to look away, and the moment came when he met her look. She inclined her head with a slight smile, and he felt relieved. That was over. But it was astonishing that she should be sitting alone. She must have been the only woman in the room to be by herself, and it gave her singularity in more senses than one. Nearly all the other tables were like dinner parties – he could hear if he couldn't see them all – and why was she not at one of them? She was as elaborately dressed as any other woman. She wore a large white hat – what was called a 'restaurant hat' – with a transparent brim and a huge pink rose in front, and the same kind of rose was fastened to the belt of her white lace dress. His glance had to be swift and could not rest on her features; it gathered only that her face met the challenge of white-and-rose with equal softness. He wondered if she felt any self-consciousness in dining alone, but this was a passing thought, for his mind was occupied with Ilona. He was young enough for all experience to be in some way new and surprising, and everything about Ilona's confidence, even its naturalness, even his own pity, had come to him with surprise. He wanted her to be happy; he wanted it to a surprising degree; and as his opinions about what she had told him were conflicting, there were moments when her happiness seemed possible to imagine, and the oppression lifted.

He could not see Ilona, because her party had their table in an inner room, the restaurant, and he had never seen Kovanski in either dining-room. To try to make out if Kovanski were there that evening he moved his chair a little, and, soon after, the two men who were at the table next to his, to whom his back had been previously turned, got up to go, and he glanced round as they did so. Then he saw that Kovanski was sitting at a table in the corner; he must have been there all the time. The moment of seeing him became a flash of revelation. Kovanski was gazing at Madame Solario.

A waiter offered Bernard a dish; he helped himself. But he felt rigid and restricted in his movements, as though something physical had happened to him. Those strange eyes were fixed on Madame Solario with an expression that no one could mistake, that was intended not to be mistaken. It was not the vulgar ogling of a woman that Bernard had often seen abroad. There was a concentration in the whole face, and a force of emotion behind it, that was not the ordinary tribute to a pretty woman; it was not a vulgar or conventional, but an extraordinary message that was being conveyed. And Bernard intercepted it in a moment that was like the click of a photographic shutter. He turned his back to Kovanski again, but the picture remained.

There was no hope for Ilona. It was all over. He went on dining, and at the opposite table Madame Solario was doing the same, and in order to see what Kovanski saw, Bernard, too, gazed at her. He observed everything she did, to guess, if he could, what she herself was feeling. Now he was sure she was self-conscious. She was too much unaware. She was not quite facing Kovanski, and her faintly smiling attention was directed altogether away from him, but not to anything in particular – to some chance focus for her secret musing. And that musing look, which lent shade and subtlety to her loveliness, was like a *coup de grâce*. There could be no hope for Ilona, no hope if this woman were her rival. The light sometimes fell on her face, which had a sort of impersonality of beauty, and sometimes, with a bending of her head, it fell through the transparent brim of her hat, and then the upper part of her face was slightly veiled and her mouth had for a few seconds a life of its own. It was full, but it sank in a little at the corners, which gave it an expression difficult to define. The softness which was one of her first effects was not only that of colouring. There was softness in everything she did, and even the prosaic act of eating was invested with grace. Once she rested her elbow on the table while drinking her wine, and the column against which she sat and the large open window beyond – with the sky in it, a little less dark than the trees – composed themselves into a background for her attitude. Bernard could watch her openly, because his position between herself and Kovanski made it certain that she would not see him look: but it was because of Ilona that he watched. Before the moment when he knew how her existence affected Ilona, she had been only a beautiful picture without meaning, and it was not until he had a reason for it that he learned so much about her.

He was conscious all the time of Kovanski, sitting a few yards behind him, and of the sort of triangle that they made – almost absurd, he felt, the three of them fixed there during the long dinner. When there was a new stir in the room, with people rising to go out, he looked round again. The impression he got then was of Kovanski's rough disregard of appearances, for he was peremptorily dismissing a waiter, with his eyes still intent on their object, and that undisguised anger and intentness together were primitive – intimidating. Kovanski was intently listening as well as watching. Two people on their way to the door had stopped to speak to Madame Solario. They were exclaiming on discovering her behind the column.

'Comment! Vous dînez seule?'

She answered in French, and to Bernard's ears her accent was perfect.

They had hardly left her when Colonel Ross drew jauntily up. 'What! Dinin' alone?'

'My friends who were coming from Salsomaggiore didn't arrive. They were prevented at the last minute.'

'This mustn't happen again, what?'

She gave her little conventional laugh and raised her eyes with hesitation and without coquetry, and nothing more was required. Colonel Ross seemed enchanted and said, 'We will see you after dinner?' before he went away.

Bernard thought it would be better to wait till the animated hour after dinner was over before attempting to speak to Ilona, and he went out on to the terrace and then started walking along the lake road. A warm wind was blowing and raising up little waves, and pale lightning played over half the sky, bringing out the details of a range of mountains and giving a sense of movement there in the north, while in the east there was a steady silveri-

36

ness, and the mountain in front of that was terribly black and still. The lightning showed up, too, the cypresses ahead of him at every bend of the road. It was Italy. And the scene was so unreal to him that the unwonted agitation within himself became in an odd way part of it, as though they were two aspects of the same thing. He felt that he had been away a long time and must hurry back to the hotel.

The various groups were settled in their accustomed places, and Ilona was not in the hall. He wondered where he could find her. A passage led to the Salon de Lecture, and as he came into it from the hall he saw at the end of the passage what of all things he had not expected to see: Kovanski and Ilona, alone. They were pausing. Ilona, he saw, was being led to an interview that could only be anguish – but there was nothing he could do. Kovanski opened the door of the Salon de Lecture, they both went in, and the door was shut.

If he had come back a little earlier! If he had not gone out until he had seen her and warned her! What mercy would she get from Kovanski? He walked past the windows of the Salon de Lecture, but he could not too obviously look in. At first glance the room was empty, but the second time he passed he saw them, at the far side of it, standing. The third time he went by they were in exactly the same positions as before. Kovanski was standing squarely in front of her, with his hands thrust down into the pockets of his dinner-jacket, and Ilona was bending a little away from him, her hand grasping the back of a chair. She was perfectly motionless. If he had been mistaken about the situation she would not have stood as she did, shrinking away and almost inanimate.

Bernard had to leave her to her fate, and he walked on as far as the angle in the lake-wall where he and she had stopped on the night of their first meeting. How strange – only two days, and it was as if he were related to her, as if someone he knew most intimately, his own sister, were crying. The water was gurgling in the corner of the wall while he felt what she must be feeling in that room. He returned to the window and looked in again. They were gone! He could hardly believe it and went on looking for her – for her figure, which he had expected to find again and which in a sense was still there, there at the spot near the piano where a chair

37

had been pushed out of its place in a row. She had been grasping the back of that chair, and the chair was left queerly awry on an empty floor. And her figure was more touching than ever to him – there, and yet gone.

Chapter Four

He knew he would not see her again that evening, but the next morning was full, for him, of the expectation of meeting her, and he stayed near the hotel, with the front door constantly in view. He formed no idea of what he should say to her. That would be decided by what she said to him. He would see her – and her face and all that was she, Ilona, was already before him in his mind – and he would say – yes, that much he knew – 'Let's go for a walk, the one we didn't have yesterday.' After that, he had no idea. Missy met him and took him shopping, and that suited him very well because, while going in and out of the little shops, he could look back at the hotel. The lake sparkled from shore to shore and was reflected everywhere; even inside a shop, where, by contrast, it was dim, sudden quivering patches on a white wall or a copper surface would repeat exactly the quick motion of the water. It was enchanting, but he was waiting for someone, and by the end of the morning there was strain and emptiness beneath the surface dazzle. He went in to luncheon. Madame Solario and Kovanski were not where they had sat the night before, and the question sprang up like hope – had they left? After luncheon Bernard went out again, and very soon Colonel Ross spoke to him.

'Very surprisin', the Zapponyis goin' away like that. I saw you talkin' to Ilona yesterday. Did she tell you they were leavin' for good?'

'No,' said Bernard. 'I didn't know. When did they go?'

'While we were at luncheon, by the half-past-one-o'clock boat to Como. Very sad, what? But the little Countess never thinks twice – though I don't know what she was thinkin' about this time!' And he laughed.

Bernard saw him stop the next person and heard him say, 'Countess Zapponyi went off by the half-past-one-o'clock boat. Did you know?'

What had happened had been more dreadful than he knew. By expecting to meet her – here, quite ordinarily, as before – he had proved how little he understood. It had been much more dreadful. She had turned and fled without being seen again, without a word, and to have missed her by his stupidity, by not understanding well enough, hit Bernard very hard. For a few minutes he could not adjust himself to this news. Of course he would see Ilona again! No, he wouldn't see her again, and what should he do now? There was a boat just leaving – going in the direction opposite to the one that had taken her away – and, because he had to act quickly if he were to get it, he acted and found himself on board, with the ropes being thrown back from the shore and the paddle-wheels beginning to churn. What a silly thing to do! he thought when he had done it. But he was glad to be alone. He sat on a hard wooden bench against the deck-rail and thought with a sad heart of Ilona on her journey; she was still on the lake, and she too was on deck, seeing the mountains move and hearing the wash of the water. It would be a terrible journey for her, while on the far side, as it were, of the chasm of tragic happening that had come between, was the long afternoon of the picnic, which he remembered with another kind of regret. It had been delightful at the time, but he realized even better on looking back how very delightful it was. He wondered that he had not felt it even more than he had, as a sort of essence of the charm of that afternoon was distilled into recollection.

The steamer had called at Bellagio and crossed back to Menaggio and then started on a long cut across the lake again. Plans for leaving began to take shape in his mind. He and Charlie Trevor had meant to stay in Paris for a week or so at the end of the month that had been ahead of them, but had not decided what to do with the whole of the intervening time. What was certain was that he could not stay at Cadenabbia now.

He was composing in his mind a telegram to another friend of his who was abroad, and was meeting him now at Stresa and now in Venice, when he heard half a dozen voices shouting, 'Middleton!' Mid-dle-ton – long-drawn-out. He could not have been more astonished. And there on the landing-stage at Varenna were some of the young people he knew – girls in white dresses, with their young men – and the first person he recognized was Belle Leroy. Beatrice Whitcomb was there too.

'Where are you going?' called the girls as he got up and waved to them.

'Nowhere!'

'Then get off here. Come back with us. Be quick!'

The gangplank was already being pulled up, and he vaulted over the deck-rail and landed on the jetty. They applauded him for that. He replied to their questions that he was 'seeing the lake', and they told him they had just seen off a friend; Varenna was on the railway, the only place on the lake, except Como, that was. Their return boat was in the offing. Wasn't it lucky they had caught sight of him? In another minute he would have been carried off! Belle introduced him to her 'little sister Martha', who was taller than herself but evidently not grown-up, for her hair was tied back with a black ribbon and she appeared to be shy. They boarded their boat, and Bernard could admit to himself that this was better than the long, solitary return that would have been his. No effort on his part was required. He could look on. He had noticed before that with these people there were either deep, mysterious conversations for two, or uproarious general entertainment, and on this occasion it was the latter. Something started them doing imitations, and much was 'excruciatingly funny', for the young German who had been the buffoon at the picnic had a great gift for mimicry. The whole incident took on a dream-like quality – the dream in which one steps through a hole in the wall, or a door in one's room one has never seen before, into a new country. He had been alone and absorbed in something so different, and with perfect unexpectedness he was in the lightest-hearted of company. And the peasant faces of the other passengers – only a little puzzled by what was going on, the faint expressions suggesting the last ripple from a very remote centre of existence – were also incongruous, like something in a dream. The 'little sister' Martha had less part than the others in the fun and both he and she were outside it; he liked her. And when the sailors began to shout, 'Cadenabbia-a-a!' there seemed to be no connection between his departure and this return. Even the face of the lake had changed. It was glassy and brooding.

'Middleton, don't forget,' said Belle as they moved to the gangway, 'you are coming to our dance on Tuesday.'

He was about to tell her he would be gone by Tuesday when he was jostled from her side by a fat woman with a basket. He went up to the two sisters after they had all got off the boat, to tell them he was leaving and to say good-bye.

'You'll come early, won't you,' said Belle, 'and help us?'

'Oh, will he?' said Martha.

He hesitated, and then, though not thinking it out, merely said, 'Thank you.'

He could not keep on changing his mind, and he must stick to the decision to remain that was implied by his acceptance of their invitation. He would stay till after the dance, but he thought he would have been happier if he had been preparing to go away. He sat by himself during the evening, trying to read. It no longer interested him to observe what was going on around him. There would have been a bitter curiosity in seeing Madame Solario, but she was not there. That did interest him – to know if she had left. Before going to bed, he studied the list of visitors that was framed beside the concierge's desk. He had studied this board before, and knew the place of the card on which – in the marvellous script with ornamental capitals that was universal to foreign hotels – it had been possible to read *Madame la Comtesse Zapponyi*, and, below this, *et sa fille*, and, below this again, in smaller, plainer type, *avec femme de chambre* – with, in one corner, the numbers of the rooms, and, in the other, in ornamental type again, *Hongrie*. In its place there was now a plain white card. To find this blank, where Ilona had been, was like some cruel enchantment in a Märchen – yes, a Märchen. He looked further and came upon the sinister power in the Märchen. There he was: *M. le Comte M. A. Kovanski*. Below him was *avec domestique,* and, in the corner, *St Pétersbourg*. Bernard still remembered what he had come for. He hoped he would not see it, but in vain; *Madame Solario* pressed itself upon his sight. The name stood alone, without a maid, very clear on the card. In the corner was *Paris*.

The next afternoon he went on a walk that started in company with some of his new acquaintances but ended in his going farther than they and returning alone. He came down through chestnut woods, which the sunset was gilding, and for the last, steep stretch entered a narrow gorge between high walls; a little brook ran down the gutter; stone and cobbles were damp and the air extraordinarily chill. He emerged from this and saw in front of him the piazza that made a bay beside the water-steps of the Villa Carlotta. The piazza was shaded by pollarded plane trees like those of the avenue, and in it was a small, classic building, a temple. A solitary figure – a woman's figure – moved into view by the door of the temple as he was passing. The figure was in white, with a sky-blue veil falling round its shoulders, and under the trees had almost the aspect of a vision – till he recognized Madame Solario.

'I wondered if one could go into the chapel,' she said. 'But the door is locked.'

'It looks as though no one ever went in,' said Bernard.

'Perhaps it isn't used any more,' she said, but lingered.

'Did you want to go in?' asked Bernard, not knowing what to say.

'Well – yes, I would have gone in. It is called the Cappella Sommariva,' she said, as if that were the reason.

The syllables of the name had a romantic fall but were no help to a reply. He did not know whether he should leave her – to be the apparition beside the Cappella Sommariva to some other passer-by – or remain. She seemed to guess his uncertainty.

'You were walking very fast,' she said. 'You were in a hurry.'

'Not especially. I was just getting back. Aren't you?'

'I must get back too,' she answered, and her eyes rested on his with what might have been a question. Was she asking him what he wanted to do – accompany her or not? But whatever it was, there was nothing condescending, nothing to put him at a disadvantage. She did not make him feel young and stupid, and for that he was grateful.

He said, 'Perhaps we had better – ' And so it was decided. They were going to walk back to the hotel together.

But it was an ordeal to be faced – conversation with a woman of the world, older than he, and the woman who already had a painful interest for him. The conversation, however, did not begin at once. She walked slowly, not as though 'getting back' were her purpose, and at the gates of Villa Carlotta she paused and looked

43

up the long flights of steps, yet made no comment. Instead of wondering what he should say, he wondered what she was thinking as she looked up. And as he wondered she met his eyes and, going slowly on, said, 'Do you like Cadenabbia?'

It crossed his mind that – indirectly though it was – because of her he no longer liked it.

'It's a gay sort of place,' he answered. 'Not that it's only that,' he added, feeling the silence and the beauty.

'Are you here alone?' she asked.

'For the moment. A friend of mine was going to join me, but he hasn't come.'

'I too was expecting friends who haven't come.'

What she said was very simple, but he had to look at her because what she actually said did not seem to be all. And he had time to think about her. Her almost visionary appearance beside the chapel under the trees was changed into a fashionably-dressed figure with a pale-blue chiffon veil falling back from her hat, but the oval face, and especially the eyes and brow, might indeed have belonged to a vision. To recognize how beautiful she was, in a way to do a service to Ilona, for it explained her defeat.

'Did you know any of the people here before you came?'

'No, but I've met a few of them now.'

The path followed the baroque curves of the wall – and at the turn was so narrow that they could not go abreast – and there ahead was the plane-tree walk where he had walked with Ilona. He had not seen it since. It was the same hour, with the same mixture of gold and dark – glow on the water and shadow within the cloister of trees – and the same solitude and atmosphere of mystery. But this time his companion was alien to him. An enemy, he felt her to be – unwitting, perhaps, but an enemy: the enemy of youth.

'You've been making many friends, I could see that.'

They were to pass near the tree where he had stood with Ilona, against which she had leaned when her strength failed her. He knew which one it was. No human being was in sight, but, just there, rapid steps came into hearing. An unseen person was approaching along the inner side of the walk, and as Bernard listened he guessed what was about to happen. It was because it was

44

so strange – just there! – that he knew who was coming towards them. And he was right. In a few moments Kovanski had stepped into the path ahead.

Kovanski ignored Bernard; he turned him into thin air by looking straight at her, conveying that message again, that extra-ordinary appeal. Bernard thought he could leave them – escape, and neither would notice him go – but he found that Madame Solario wished otherwise.

'Do you know Count Kovanski?' she asked, as casually as if he were not there and she were talking about him.

Kovanski held out his hand. 'I think I have seen you before,' he said, with his stare.

They shook hands.

'Do you know if the Lastacoris will be back in time for dinner?' Madame Solario asked Bernard. 'Or will they stay for dinner at Urio?'

This was astonishing. Bernard had no idea what the Lastacoris were doing. But something prompted him to answer. 'I don't think they had made up their minds.'

'Will you allow me to walk back to the hotel with you?' asked Kovanski. He spoke English with not much of an accent.

She must have given an assent, because the three of them proceeded together after that. To answer Madame Solario, Bernard had to face towards the trees, behind which Ilona and his double walked.

'What other places on the lake have you seen?' she asked.

'We went on a picnic the other day,' said Bernard. 'But we stopped only at San Giovanni; and yesterday I went to Varenna.'

'There are much prettier places than those. You must see them before you go.'

'Did you make an expedition this afternoon?' asked Kovanski's hoarse voice at Bernard's shoulder.

'Yes, and on the way back we stopped at the Cappella Sommariva, but it was locked. We should have found out who had the key,' she said to Bernard so deliberately that he caught the significance of her words.

We should have . . . Was it possible? This was strangest of all.

'Who could have told us?' he asked. Hatred of Kovanski sharpened his wits. But he watched her face to make sure she was really giving him this incredible opportunity, as he went on, feeling his way. 'We might have asked the hall porter.'

She smiled at him. He had noticed it before – her smile seemed only to hover over her mouth.

'Hall porters are supposed to know everything,' she answered.

'I will put him to the test at once,' said Bernard with a boldness and assurance he had not known he could possess.

'And then we may find it was not worth seeing after all,' said Madame Solario.

Bernard laughed out. It was avenging Ilona. Everything was changed because of this. He turned with his new boldness to Madame Solario, who was so close to him that he was aware of the scent that emanated from her, the texture of her sleeve. In the radiance from the water which suffused her face she was smiling, approving him, and he smiled back.

Just here, where he had tried not to think of Kovanski, they were side by side, and he, Bernard, was helping to inflict torment upon him. That it was torment was certain. One heard it in the tone of the hoarse voice. 'As you said, there are prettier places than that,' the voice put in.

'It has a special charm for me,' replied Madame Solario, not even glancing towards Kovanski. 'Yes, do ask,' she said to Bernard.

'Of course I will,' he said.

But he saw the open door of the Salon de Lecture – in the gloom of the trees, as before – and he felt he had accomplished enough. Whether it was rude or not to take leave of her so abruptly, he said to Madame Solario, 'I will try to get the key for you tomorrow. I hope I can. Good-bye.'

As he drew near the spot where – he now knew – Ilona had spoken to him for the last time, he thought in a rush of remorse that during the last minutes of their walk he had been aloof and cold and had even wondered why she had made her confidence. She had been left with the shame of having made it, and he had never put that right. Before he took leave of Madame Solario it had almost seemed he must be going to meet Ilona again on the threshold of that door; and when she wasn't there he looked back at those other two. They were not far off, and Madame Solario was in the act of leaving Kovanski rooted to the ground.

'Natalia!' said Kovanski in a deep and terrible voice.

Bernard felt that Ilona must hear. Madame Solario made a gesture, quicker and more impulsive than anything he had seen her do. A moment later new voices broke upon them; she responded to a greeting, and walked quickly on. Bernard went up to his room.

Chapter Five

That evening he came face to face with Kovanski in front of the concierge's desk.

'Oh, *Mister* Middleton,' said the Russian. 'Now I know your name!'

His manner of announcing it was disagreeable, to say the least. Bernard could not expect him always to look as when he had last seen him, but this recovery was disconcerting. And he saw a smile pass over the concierge's face. Bernard addressed him at once. 'Has anything come for that name?' he asked, though nothing could have come in the evening.

'There has been nothing for you, Mr Middleton,' answered the man, immediately official.

He felt sure that the man started to smile again as soon as he turned his back, and to have to turn tail and be followed by those two smiles, the insolence of the one and the impertinence of the other, was very unpleasant.

A little later in the evening he saw Madame Solario sitting in the circle of Marchesa Lastacori, among those mature, sophisticated people enjoying as usual their worldly talk, and she was not out of place among them. But he no longer felt that she was the enemy of youth. While he was still tingling from the rudeness of Kovanski's manner she could seem an ally, an avenger. Kovanski was a frightening man, hard as nails; he was perhaps the kind of man who, strange as it might seem, is cruelly successful with women. But he could be humbled! How pleasant to think of it! And there she sat, she who had done it, indifferent to what she had done and with another adorer at her side, and her large black hat, which had a fine black osprey slanting right across it, was mixed up in his admiration of her power to humble a man like Kovanski. Ercolani – not so interesting a conquest, but very good looking in a conventional Italian way – had his chair a little behind hers and kept leaning forward, trying to engage her in talk. Sometimes she didn't even answer. Sometimes she let fall a few words, barely turning her head. She was wearing earrings of round single pearls, which gleamed under the sweep of her hat.

But something was said that caused an outburst in the circle. Voices and laughter suddenly shot up like a fountain. Bernard was impelled to look again, and in the middle of the general excitement, to which he had no clue, he saw Madame Solario overcome by what the French call *un fou rire*. He saw how it started, how a tremor passed over her face and a defence seemed to go down. It was as great a surprise as he had yet had. Her laughter, as it became uncontrollable, was noiseless – and secret, for she did not share it with the others; she tried to conceal it. Bending her head and biting her lips, she hid, as it were, and silently laughed. This mirth of hers, the unexpectedness of it and its peculiar air of secrecy, so fascinated him that he couldn't take his eyes off her. Ercolani, too, was amazed. He drew his chair forward till the tip of the black osprey brushed against his cheek, and began murmuring in her ear. She went on laughing by herself but trying to stop. At last she appeared to hear what he was saying. She had put her handkerchief to her mouth, and when she took it away she was no longer laughing. She was smiling curiously.

Bernard got up under a sudden impulse; then, for something to do, he went to the billiard room and watched a game of billiards, which Colonel Ross won.

As it turned out, when he went up to bed – going two steps at a time up the staircase – he came on Madame Solario at the top of the flight to the first floor, standing with her hand on the stair rail, looking down into the hall.

When he paused a few steps below her, she smiled down at him and said, 'You seem to be always in a hurry!'

She glanced over the rail again and drew back, and Bernard involuntarily glanced down too. Kovanski was below, looking up. Then Madame Solario leaned against the stair rail once more, so that she too could be seen from below.

'Was your book interesting?' she asked.

'It didn't interest me as much as it should,' said Bernard and had the sensation of blushing.

'What was it?' she asked, still leaning.

He told her.

'Yes, it should have been interesting.' And then she turned towards the landing, saying very kindly, 'Good night!'

He said, 'Good night!' and went his way to the floor above at a great pace.

Two mornings later he met her strolling with the French couple who had spoken to her, he remembered, in the dining-room on the night of her arrival. And when he saw her – still at some distance from him, but approaching – the various impressions she had already made upon him were, every one of them, present, arousing so much interest and curiosity that he became self-conscious. What degree of acquaintanceship was there between them? Would she speak to him? Should he speak to her? What about that piece of information he could give her? And, as if she guessed from his bow that he had something to say, she stopped, and he had to speak.

'I asked the hall porter about the Cappella Sommariva,' he said. 'And he knew all about it. But the chapel belongs to the Grand Duke, and that seems to mean one can't get in.'

'It doesn't really matter,' she answered. 'But thank you so much for asking.'

'But if you wanted to go in –'

'There are prettier places,' she said, and smiled, establishing acquaintanceship. 'We keep on saying that, don't we?'

She looked towards her friends and saw that they had been joined by someone else and were not waiting for her. This seemed to throw her and Bernard into each other's company, and she moved hesitantly to the parapet above the lake.

'Everything *is*, I suppose, prettier than anything else!'

'It's true – one could say it everywhere one goes.'

'What other places ought I to see before I go away?'

She rested the tip of her parasol against the low parapet and said, 'It depends on how you want to go. You like taking long walks? You had been a long way – up there – the other day?'

The details of her appearance and the recollection of their previous meetings were impressing themselves upon him more and more. The Kovanski incident – how amazing! There had actually been a sort of conspiracy between them. Was she remembering? The short scene on the staircase had been several times

50

gone over in his mind before he had fallen asleep that night; but it was her fit of secret laughter that now seemed most mysterious of all. Seeing her in her present thoughtful repose, he found it hardly possible to imagine her laughing uncontrollably.

'Only up to San Martino, and back by the longer way.'

He almost felt he shouldn't have seen her laugh.

In those days the great, equalizing power of cosmetics and beautifying inventions had not yet been let loose, and Madame Solario's complexion and colouring, and the arc of her eyebrows, and the wave of her hair (that morning under a hat made up entirely of crisp, pleated frills of lilac muslin) were not being counterfeited by everyone who wished; they were rare, like noble birth. The high rank of her beauty had to be met with something of awe.

'You are not going for a walk today?'

'This afternoon I have an engagement. Do you know the Leroys who have a villa here? They are giving a ball tonight, and I promised I would go in the afternoon and help. I believe there is to be a cotillon.'

'A cotillon – how amusing.'

He would have liked to hear whether she was going. She gave no indication either way.

The vivaciousness he had been seeing on all sides since he had come here brought out, by contrast, the simplicity of Madame Solario's conversation and manner. That vivaciousness took all one's surface attention, but it was a deeper attention that was held by the simplest things she said and did. He forgot to fear that he might be unequal to the occasion, he was so occupied in wanting to know more.

One could tell at once that she was English-speaking by birth, but yet there was at times a faintly un-English flavour to her speech that pointed to the probability that she had lived most of her life abroad. She was, of course, married to a foreigner; the name sounded Spanish. Was her husband going to join her here? Where was he? What was he like? And just then Bernard's attention was attracted to her hands, for with the tip of her parasol she was startling a lizard that had been basking on the wall.

'I think lizards are so amusing,' she said while it whisked off.

He noticed first the tall handle of her parasol, which was a carved ebony cat realistically arching its back – and this he thought amusing – and then, as she brought her left hand over the right upon the arched black cat, he noticed that there was a ring with a large round pearl on her fourth finger, but not a wedding-ring. But she certainly was married.

'You say you have an engagement this afternoon?' she asked after a little pause.

'Yes.'

'I would so much like to go out in a row-boat.' She was standing with both hands resting on the arched black cat. 'I would like to see the shore from a row-boat.' She looked in the direction she might like to take; it was westwards. There was another pause. 'Would it bore you?' she asked after that, and with a sort of candour she turned her eyes to his.

The beauty of her eyes was offered to his gaze. And when she gave her little laugh – she often gave this little laugh – it had nothing to do with the expression of her eyes. It did not disturb the effect of pensiveness.

He almost stammered, 'I would be delighted. Would you like to go now?'

'Not now, it is too hot and sunny. I would like to go in a row-boat some afternoon, rather late. But of course it may not be possible. You may always be doing other things.'

'Of course I won't always be doing other things. When you want to, won't you let me know?'

'It's something I've wanted to do.' Her friends were now quite near. 'And it might happen that you had nothing else to do and wouldn't mind.'

She left Bernard with this further amazing fact: while she could undoubtedly have been taken in one of those private row-boats that were such a smart sight on the lake, with a house flag and boatmen in immaculate white suits with red or blue sashes, she had asked *him* to take her out, in what would be an old, hired boat. And alone. After standing lost in this prospect for a few minutes where she and her friends had left him, he went off in the opposite direction and in another moment came face to face with Kovanski. This time he felt that it was not by chance, and that Kovanski had deliberately walked out right in front of him.

'Oh, *Mister* Middleton,' he said with the same offensive emphasis. 'How do you do? How are you?'

He was laughing. He had very regular teeth, of an unusual squareness and evenness, the blunt edges a little stained with tobacco.

'Very well, thank you,' said Bernard, to provide himself, too, with a little offensive emphasis. 'How are you?'

Kovanski was laughing in a way that hardly affected the muscles of his face. 'Do you like this place?' he asked. 'Were you thinking of staying for some time?'

'I'll stay as long as I like it here,' said Bernard, 'or, if you prefer, as long as I like.'

Kovanski's height was rather less than his own, but he was broad, with a look of such vigour as he stood there, squarely planted, that the thought leaped – Not easy to take on.

'Oh, *Mister* Middleton, that isn't polite.' And, suddenly abandoning his position right in Bernard's path, he walked away. He hadn't gone far when he turned round, and, thrusting his hands into his coat pockets – a characteristic attitude, it would seem – he laughed again, showing the even line of his teeth. Someone spoke to him, and a few moments later he was talking imperturbably.

Would they have to knock each other down? And it had been a mistake, that made the situation so ridiculous. How Kovanski would laugh if he knew that it was because of Ilona – only because of her, for if there hadn't been that reason for hating Kovanski, Bernard would never have fallen in with Madame Solario's intention; he would have got out of the way. I won't get out to oblige him, he thought, as he stood, apparently looking at a race between two sailboats. If he went now Kovanski would think he had been frightened off. And now Madame Solario had asked him to take her out in a row-boat. Perhaps Kovanski wouldn't be making so much of a mistake – But that wasn't possible.

There had been no further encounters when, in the afternoon, not at all in the mood for it, he betook himself to the Leroys'. Their villa was one of those on the lake road, and it looked out of its lush garden from behind tall iron gates and two palm trees that stood like sentinels, one on each side of a steep wide

53

path. There was no front door, and he walked from the veranda through a French window directly into the large drawing-room and into a gay commotion. At once he was asked to run to the shop and buy another twenty yards of white ribbon two centimetres wide, and when he got back he was put to making cotillon favours in a circle of 'helpers'. This 'helping' was in a way an excuse for a party, but the Leroy girls and Beatrice Whitcomb and one or two others were carrying out what had to be done with sustained energy and competence; Missy and the rest – who included Guimard and two of the Germans – were only pretending to be useful and always stopping to laugh and talk. Bernard attached himself to the workers.

Belle set the unserious ones to hanging Chinese lanterns in the veranda, and out there a guitar was produced and there was strumming as well as talk. The other workers were in the room next door, and for a time Belle and Bernard were alone in the drawing-room. He was fastening streamers, which would be needed for a figure in the cotillon, to the chandelier, and she was handing them up to him as he stood on a step-ladder. She spoke of the room and the villa. 'Isn't it hideous? We simply adore it,' she said. They took it furnished from a Milanese family and came every year, but only for one month, for September. This year was being the greatest fun – didn't he think so?

Then Missy called from the veranda: 'Belle, darling, I forgot to ask – may we bring Natalia Solario this evening? Ercolani begged us to get an invitation for her.'

'Of course,' said Belle, and, as Mrs Leroy came into the room – 'Mother, the beautiful Madame Solario is coming tonight.'

Mrs Leroy said, 'How nice. Sweetheart, I need your help in here.' And they both went out of the room.

Bernard was still on his step-ladder when he heard Missy say, 'Did you know Natalia in Paris? Oho, you never told me, but I can see you did!'

'I didn't know her,' said Guimard's voice with its French accent.

'But there's something you know – I can see! Now, Guimard, tell us! Do tell us!' she said. 'What is it?'

'Missy, only carps should open their mouths like that' –

54

which did not surprise Bernard, for he had heard Guimard before be as rude as this. He made a point of it. But Missy would not desist.

'Il y a longtemps de cela,' said Guimard. 'But there was a great scandal. Have you never heard? I thought, as you knew her, that you must –'

She denied that she had, avid to be told, and Bernard was suddenly afraid to hear.

'Her stepfather was in love with her!'

'No, really? What happened?'

'That, one doesn't ask,' said Guimard with his drawl that always sounded like a bid for importance. He passed his hand over the strings of the guitar.

'No, but really – tell us everything!'

'You know her stepfather was Monsieur de Florez – and what a lot of noise his money made. They were très en vue. At first all was well, but afterwards there was a great deal of sympathy for Madame de Florez; her position was intolerable. The part that scandalized was, the girl was so young – not sixteen, I believe.'

Bernard began to come down from the step-ladder, clattering as much as he could.

'Do you mean to say – Not really?'

'Oh, all of it may never have come out, but a great deal, I'm told, hit one in the eye.'

He meant to go away, and yet he stopped in the middle of the room, from where the people in the veranda were just out of sight; the two palm trees and the shimmering lake were a picture with figures, framed in the open door. There had been an interruption by other voices, and then Guimard's dominated again.

'But that wasn't the whole! There was a brother!'

'Natalia's brother?'

'Yes, who made the scandal much worse. He tried to murder Monsieur de Florez!'

It was their frivolous cynicism and Missy's shriek of laughter – brazen to laugh like that. And what they took so lightly, for some reason profoundly depressed him – not as merely an ugly story about someone he knew, but as something ominous. Yet whom did it concern? Why was it?

55

Missy was asking, 'What happened?'

'Monsieur de Florez nearly died of his wound, he was shot, and the young man – he was only eighteen, I think – was sent to the other end of the world. One has never seen him again. Monsieur de Florez had been very good to him, so people maintained he was very ungrateful.'

While picking out a few notes on the guitar, he went on, 'When she was old enough to be married they married her to a friend of Monsieur de Florez, as old as he was, who took her away, but la fin du drame was that Madame de Florez died of a broken heart! But all that was ten or twelve years ago.'

And then he fitted his words to an accompaniment on the guitar. 'And now la dame has come back – sans mari. Without a husband – ah oui! Sans mari! Et tout est comme si rien n'était ni ne fut.' And, with Missy laughing, he finished with a sweep over the strings.

Belle and some of the others came in and filled the room with bustle, to which those on the veranda were eventually attracted, and when Bernard saw Guimard he wanted to be rude to him. All the scandal seemed to come from him. But the excitement was mounting – whether everything would be ready in time. The cotillon favours were being piled upon trays, favours for the men on some and those for the girls on others – buttonholes and nosegays, hoops and wands bound with ribbon, and objects bought at the shop, such as hats, large or in doll's size, and Roman scarves, and little replicas of Canova's 'Cupid and Psyche', of which the original was at Villa Carlotta. Bernard's depression found a new cause; he did not dance very well, and he had never been to a cotillon. One had to have a partner for it, and if all the girls were engaged it would be an excuse for not coming. And then he asked Martha to be his partner. He and she could feel out of it together, he thought. Her face expressed almost simultaneously delight and consternation, for she had been provided with a partner, somebody rather elderly and kind, so as to be on the safe side, and now the precaution was proved unnecessary but she was committed. Or was she? All this was made plain by the consultation that took place with her mother and Belle while he stood by. Mrs Leroy said finally, 'It will be all right. I'll tell him, and I'm sure he'll understand.'

Chapter Six

The atmosphere of the ball, with the sound of waltz-music, met one already in the road. The night was warm, and so still that out-of-doors was like an extension of the house, which one seemed to enter at the tall gates, leaving there the noise of arrivals by launch and row-boat and the little crowd of boatmen and lookers-on, to advance with one's fellow guests through the garden turned conservatory, lit by Chinese lanterns and with the ballroom opening out of it. The row of French windows revealed the dancers, the bright light, and the colours, and the beat of music was the heart of the ball throbbing in the night. The still night and the throbbing heart were as mysterious one as the other.

Bernard's expectancy was not at all pleasurable. He looked at once to see if Madame Solario or Kovanski were there, but neither had come, nor had Guimard. The dance was only at its beginning. What was nice was that his little part in the preparations had given him a personal interest to be shared with the workers of the afternoon, and the girls gaily offered in turn to try his dancing and were lavish with encouragement and advice. Belle was even prettier than he had thought she would be. She wore a yellow dress, and a butterfly made of golden sequins was perched in her dark hair. Martha was in white, not quite grown-up and rather touching.

The crowd quickly grew, and with it the assurance of success, but Bernard was outside the vital current. He kept looking into the throng of dancers, which might be concealing someone he was just about to see. When he first caught sight of Missy, in scarlet, he thought for a few seconds that she was what he was looking for and fearing. Then a little later he had a glimpse of Guimard, and it happened that immediately afterwards he saw Madame Solario as she was entering the room.

Seeing her and her detractor in almost the same moment brought his indignation to a head and her unconsciousness of what Guimard had said about her made her seem the unprotected victim of his malice. Bernard felt that he must go at once to speak to her – to show Missy and Guimard, though they could not possibly deduce it, what he thought of their scandal – but he was dancing, and he could not get near her just then. As he went round the room the story came back in its entirety, and it was more like Elizabethan drama than like anything in real life. Because she was unconscious that it had been told again, and that he had heard it, there was an obligation to go and speak to her. His eyes sought her out, lost her, and found her once more. Her fairness and the silvery blue of her dress gave the idea that she was moonlit among colours seen by day, and, fastened by two diamond stars, flounces of blue tulle rose up from her shoulders like wings. In spite of her appearance there, in a ball-dress, he was relating her to her story. He saw her with the whole of the drama in his mind. The mother died, he remembered. But when he drew near enough to bow, Ercolani was placing his arm about her; her arm in its long white glove was rested upon his, and they yielded together to the languorous strains of 'Valse Amoureuse'. After that he could not see her without seeing, too, Ercolani's straight back and flat shoulders, and his head turning a little to right and left over hers – the minimum amount for looking and guiding, which he did without a fault. Everything else faded before this spectacle, because this was the perfection of waltzing. One shouldn't waltz at all if one couldn't do it like that!

Bernard's own shortcomings were borne in upon him. He and his partner, who was Beatrice Whitcomb, stopped by common consent, and she said cheerfully, 'They don't reverse in England, do they?' While they were standing out the other couple waltzed past. Madame Solario's lips moved in an 'Ah!' of greeting, and she glanced back at him as, without effort or even volition, it seemed, so instinctive and graceful was her motion, she was carried away on a wave of the music. This friendly recognition and the very thought of what he had meant to do filled him with alarm. For if he spoke to her he would have to ask her to dance, and if he did he would make a fool of himself. He could see that now. And he wouldn't! She expected him to ask her to dance, and so he must avoid her, and that meant spending the whole evening in keeping at a distance. There was no engaging ahead; the dances weren't numbered, and of the two or three would-be partners who were waiting, it was the one who reached her first who was able to claim her for the next. As time went on he saw that it was not likely he would have got the chance, but he was so little enjoying himself – so much the contrary – that he could think only of predicaments while watching those wings of blue tulle that he must never go near. Above the wings the lines of her neck were lovely – especially the nape of her neck and its curve with her shoulders – and it was these, and the fairness of her hair, which was dressed high and simply, that he was always seeing in the crowd, rather than her features. She danced every moment, and most often with Ercolani, who, Bernard imagined, danced better than anyone else.

Those two had just gone by again when suddenly the climax was reached, the great moment arrived. A man's voice rose above the music, above all else, in a ringing shout of '*Cotillon!*' – so commanding that everything stopped and everyone turned. A general on the battle-field could not have had a voice of more authority nor been more instantly obeyed. There was a storm of clapping. Bernard had been told that the best cotillon-leader in Rome, the Marchese Guglielmi, was staying at Villa d'Este and was coming to lead the cotillon for them, and he saw a man with a merry face standing in the middle of the room, receiving the applause. This man shouted out another command that Bernard didn't catch, and there began a sort of scramble, to get out of which Bernard stepped back into a doorway – where he found himself beside Madame Solario.

She was without her partner; she was alone; but she never noticed him. He need not have been afraid! She was evidently waiting for something that would happen, holding her feather fan open but hardly moving it at all. At first glance she might have seemed as impassive as she had ever done, as guarded, but at once he saw, he felt, her deep enjoyment as though it were breathing from her, and the smile that didn't part her lips gave to the corners of her mouth a mysterious look of greed. How was

59

it, when she was so beautiful, that he could think of greed? But each of the other men was busy bringing two chairs from the next room, and Belle, in passing, cried, 'You must get your chair and find a place!' Before Bernard had started to obey, Madame Solario saw Ercolani approaching with their two chairs, and, closing her fan, she bent a little sideways to sweep up the train of her pale-blue satin skirt. With that movement she was about to go straight towards pleasure and triumph, and he did not wonder that, though he was so close to her, she failed to see him. In his humility he could have believed he wasn't even visible.

From then on she seemed as far away as if he were looking at her through a telescope. He and Martha were in a back row, and she and Ercolani in the front row of chairs on the opposite side of the room. The noise, loud music, laughter were deafening to one not sharing the spirit of the carnival. When he had to take part he was as leaden and clumsy as he could possibly have feared. But he did not have to exert himself much as a partner, because Martha by very reason of her ingenuousness was reaping a little harvest of affectionate attention, and most of the time he could sit and look on. The favours were brought in by the leaders and handed or snatched and tossed about, all in an uproar, and the hoops and wands and streamers were used in pretty or ludicrous figures executed with infinite zest. There was never a pause, as the music never stopped for a minute. Bernard had no clear explanation to give himself why he could not recover his spirits. But when in a race one starts to fall behind, the distance between one's self and the others is soon doubled and trebled, and this became an interminable race in which he had started last, and the difference between himself and the rest kept increasing till he was quite alone.

Time, too, was in the race; that is, after doing odd things and stopping altogether, at some moment it had got so far ahead that he could not imagine how long he had been there, and everything that had happened was already long ago. As Madame Solario held up a hand-mirror and several competitors rushed forward to be the one whose face over her shoulder she should see first, it seemed so long ago that he had heard Guimard telling her story – out there on the veranda, while he himself stood under that very chandelier – so long ago that he could not remember why he had been shocked. It had nothing any longer to do with her when she turned and with simply a smile handed the mirror to the victor. Other women made play with the mirror, but not she. She looked and moved and smiled without a single superfluity of action and effort, as though it were enough to be what she was and she need add nothing more. Belle was leading the cotillon with Guglielmi, and doing it delightfully, and Bernard's eyes sometimes followed her golden butterfly with pleasure, glad that everything was going so well. But whether he was in his inconspicuous seat or dancing himself, he was positively haunted by the wings of silvery blue, by the masterly, flat shoulders of Ercolani, and by the perfect grace of those two dancing together. He got to know the look of her chair, heaped with favours, when she was away from it. Fatigue inseparable from the noise began to give a sort of double aspect to what he saw, a hollow echo to the medley of sounds. As Madame Solario's success drew more partners to herself it left fewer for the others and he seized the falsity of the other women's smiles when they were included in the same figure with her, and the actual sneers on the faces of two Italian girls who, he knew, were Ercolani's cousins. One of the Italian men who belonged to the same group as the cousins, which always went about in a body and sat together in the hall, called out something to Ercolani, who flung back an answer, and as if this had focused a still more general attention on her, when Madame Solario returned to her chair three or four men made towards it. Guimard was among them. Her vogue was such that it had become a matter of pride to dance with her, and what Bernard had disliked from the first in Guimard was in that instant revealed as underbred bluff. Guimard affected being rudely frank with attractive girls, but before a success like Madame Solario's his vanity showed itself in another way. He ran eagerly. He could maliciously repeat scandal about her, and he could exclaim, 'Ah! je n'ai pas de chance!' when he was too late and another man took her hand to lead her on to the floor. Bernard gloated over Guimard's failure; this was the first moment of satisfaction he had experienced that night. A few minutes later he realized that, whatever the evening had been, the worst was still to be. For Kovanski had come at last and was standing in the door.

He appeared in a new guise, that of a man with a particularly courteous manner, for nothing could have exceeded the politeness with which he made his excuses for being late to Mrs Leroy, and evidently also declined to dance. Bernard was acutely aware of everything he did. When Kovanski was left standing alone he surveyed the scene, looking as Bernard remembered him when he was playing bridge – picking up the cards with his gambler's face. Madame Solario was dancing with Ercolani, but Kovanski looked at everyone but her. His prominent eyes, hard and blank, roved over the room, singled out rather especially Missy and her passionate style of dancing, and skirted, without ever fixing, that other pair. What would one think if one didn't know how often they had danced together? Mightn't one know just by seeing them now? Kovanski, looking round the room, eventually found Bernard in the back row. He contemplated him for a moment, and then he grinned.

The day had to come when one or the other would get knocked down. That grin meant one thing only for Bernard – that tonight he was nowhere. He was sitting and looking on, and Martha was his partner. Poor little Martha, so beaming and proud – she was a schoolgirl, and she must make him look like a schoolboy; an older man like Kovanski might quite well class them together. And it was true, he had not dared go near Madame Solario, and Kovanski this time would draw the right conclusion. There was nothing he could do. He had to go on sitting there, never having danced with her, exposed to Kovanski's seeing that he had got put in his proper place.

Kovanski did not long stay in view, but Bernard could not be sure he had gone home, and with this the wretched evening became intolerable. When Martha had left her seat to dance, he edged his way to one of the French windows and out into the garden. There were a few figures in the veranda, and he lit a cigarette and casually strolled on; the Chinese lanterns had gone out, and the darkness of a thicket of trees engulfed him. Oh, the comfort of being alone! But why had he not been able to enjoy himself like everyone else? Could it have been different? He thought of Ilona. But if she had been there she would have been watching all the evening for Kovanski, and that fell upon him like another stone. If only there were someone who would have come out and stood with him here; and he heard the trees faintly stirring in their darkness, the stirring of the night air, through which came the muted lilt of 'Elixir d'Amour'. The bushes were exhaling an ineffable fragrance that belonged to this beautiful, strange place where nothing, not even himself, was familiar. If he were given a wish, if he could have what he wanted, what would it be? Only that he shouldn't be seen, and should never see Kovanski or any of these people again. For that very reason he must return to the ballroom; the longer he delayed, the worse it would become. On his way he passed between the two palm trees, and he looked back from the veranda and saw them standing like sentinels with, between them, a broken moon.

He was buffeted on the threshold as much by the hectic atmosphere as by the dancers. A favour was being distributed, a little *bersagliere* hat with a tuft of cock's feathers, to be given by the ladies, and he watched the trays being carried above the hands, the faces, and the little hats reaching like a shower to all parts of the room. Before he knew it he was looking at Madame Solario, and she was only a little way off, just receiving a favour. She glanced around to decide to whom she would give it – several men clamoured for it, laughing – and then she saw Bernard. She checked herself in the act of making a choice and changed her direction, yet so smoothly that he could not be certain until she was actually there in front of him, holding out the little hat . . .

'But I can't ask you to dance!' he said before he could think.

'Why not?'

'I dance so badly!'

'I am sure you don't.'

'I know quite well that I do. Must I give it back?' And he began to screw up his courage.

'No, but then you will be owing me a favour.'

Her smile had something more direct and personal than anything she had yet given him.

'So I will! And I can't go without paying my debts, can I?'

'Of course you can't.'

'Shall it be the next?'

'Let's say the last.' She had only to turn to get another partner. 'I will expect the last favour, just before the end.'

'The last favour!'

He went back to his chair as to another ball on another evening. He met Martha with smiles and conversation and stared boldly about in search of Kovanski, whom he soon forgot. He was not impatient, and the end seemed to have come suddenly when Martha told him that the last favour was being brought in. It was those little replicas of Canova's 'Cupid and Psyche,' which that afternoon he had thought were rather charming in their dozens. He secured his and waited for his chance. The last figure developed into a frenzy in which no one but himself heeded anyone else; for him, as he waited, everyone – Beatrice, romping to excess; Belle, whipping up her exhausted vivacity; Missy and a young man, revolving in a narrow space with that effect she could produce of being alone with her companion on a desert island; and others he knew in the room full of movement – had an oddly intensified reality. The rowdy figure did not suit Madame Solario. The moment came when Ercolani was obliged to let go her hand and was pulled along and away from her as she stood aside and the whole line rushed on. Bernard went up to her; she withdrew to the protection of the wall, and he followed. They were out of the whirlpool, the only quiet ones in the room.

She took the little statuette, evidently pleased by it, the thing itself.

'I haven't had one – the figure started before I was given it. But what a pity, I don't think we can dance. Not in this.'

'It's really better. I told you the reason,' said Bernard.

'But I don't believe it. Haven't you been dancing all evening?'

'No. Very little. I didn't want to.'

'I am afraid it will break,' she said. 'Do keep it and give it to me when we are out of this.' And she handed him back the 'Cupid and Psyche'.

He was nearly sent flying by the last man in the line, and Madame Solario seemed to think he was about to leave her.

'Tell me,' she said rather quickly, to bring him to her side again, 'you are not going yet, are you?'

'Not till it's over; one can't, I suppose.'

'Why do you say it like that? Don't you think it has been nice?' She saw that Ercolani was coming for her – she saw, one might have said, without looking. 'Are you going to have supper? Or were you taking your partner in to supper?'

'She doesn't seem to be thinking of it at the moment.'

Paper streamers were being hurled about, and Ercolani was held up by his Italian friends, who wrapped him round and round with the streamers, jeering at him. Madame Solario put her hand on Bernard's arm, and on the way to the dining-room he was conscious of it all as a truly fabulous turn of the wheel.

On going in she hesitated – perceptibly – and he felt with a start that she was *making sure*. He, too, hastily made sure. There were few people and nothing to fear. It was not really supper, no tables to sit down to, and they stood at the buffet – the wings of blue tulle and the diamond stars beside him that had been so far away. Her face was pure and unflushed as though she had not danced at all.

She held a glass of sherbet and asked, 'How is it that you say you haven't danced much? Why? What were you doing? You won't let it be broken, will you?' – meaning the 'Cupid and Psyche' he was holding, and she gave her little laugh.

'You can't really want it!'

'Yes, I do. I would have loved it once; that's why I like it now. I've collected little china figures that are given to me ever since I was a child.'

The signs of nervousness were not enough to have been noticeable in another woman, but were in her.

'I've kept them all.' She put down the sherbet, having barely tasted it. 'I have been given some very pretty ones in porcelain, but I like the others just as well – especially the one that started the collection.'

'What was that?'

'Two lizards walking arm-in-arm and holding up their tails!' Her laugh seemed genuine.

A number of people came in from the ballroom, Ercolani topping them by half a head. One saw him at once.

'I think the music has stopped at last and you will soon get your wish,' she said to Bernard.

Ercolani was coming towards them.

'But do wait a little,' she said, 'because I too would like to go soon.'

Bernard gave place to Ercolani, who came full of confidence, but he had a few moments of delight, waiting for what would happen next. She opened her big feather fan to its full width and swept it slowly to and fro upon her breast, and what passed between them did not take very long. It left Ercolani bowing ironically – a formal, yet supple Italian bow, bringing the feet together with a slight swaying of the whole body. Suddenly Bernard's delusion dropped from him. This was no triumph for himself. There was too much that wasn't clear.

Ercolani went out, and she turned to Bernard with her limpid look. 'You haven't gone,' she said, but her little laugh was so absent that he did not reply.

The tension he felt in her involved him, too. He had her in sight until the end. He believed that she had asked him to go home with her and that she would summon him when the moment came – but it never came, for eventually they all went away together. The company went, laughing and talking, carrying the atmosphere of the ball into the night outside, filling the road as it had filled the ballroom. Launches were waiting for those who lived at a distance; there were boatmen and shouts, and coloured lights rippling on the black water, the chunk-chunk of engines and splashing of waves, and good-byes growing fainter as the boats got away. Those who lived at the Bellevue and beyond walked on down the road in the black shadows thrown by trees and unlighted houses, the men singing and calling out, the women rather shrilly chattering. Madame Solario did not join in their talk. She was altogether silent, as Bernard knew, for he was only a few steps behind her; in the midst of the babble they both walked in perfect silence. Her white lace mantilla glimmered even in the darkest patches, and it was in those that he was on the alert for a man's figure that might approach her. None did. He believed she knew he was always close behind, and in the light of the hotel door she turned and looked. But he kept in the shadows; he let them all go in ahead of him.

Chapter Seven

Colonel Ross asked Bernard the next morning if he would go on a day's expedition with them, and there was no excuse he could offer; he had to go. He felt desperate, but Colonel Ross was all hopeful kindness, for they were to have luncheon with the D—s at Villa d'Este, and the D—s were charming people. It seemed even to add to Colonel Ross's pleasure that he had to go such a distance to have luncheon with them.

The compatriots of Bernard's who were staying at Cadenabbia were much older than himself, and everyone – except Colonel Ross – ignored him because he was young. They were like the people he had known all his life, if they were not the same people – his parents' friends – and he had never so consciously rebelled. What on that day and in those surroundings he especially disliked was to hear the same conversation and the same tones of voice that he would have heard at home; any other kind would have been preferable. Other people would have been a little affected by the change of environment, but these remained intact because they were not capable even of curiosity about anything outside their own superior world. The difference between himself and them was not merely one of age.

The large luncheon party was only another kind of boredom from that of getting there. He was calculating the whole time on how soon, with any luck, they would get back, and he was banking on five o'clock when he discovered that his party, together with the D—s, intended to go to Urio for the regatta. He had the sensation of being a captive, dumb, and dragged about in chains. But it would still have been possible to get back for dinner if it had not been decided to dine at Urio, and then hope vanished. On the return journey, which had everything of romance but the essentials – gigantic black mountains under the stars, mysterious shores with little lights that beckoned and then were left behind, never to be answered – in the last phase of that dreadful expedition, he remembered Ilona's sob: 'All those hours . . .'

He could not be sure that Madame Solario was still there until he saw her the next day. She might suddenly have decided to leave. In front of the hotel before luncheon there was a centre of interest for nearly all the men in the place. There Missy and the liveliest young women were making their stir, and Marchesa Lastacori was holding forth as usual; she talked with great emphasis always, as if she were relating something startling, disastrous, or merely incredible, and her listeners would look at her as if they were hypnotized. And there Madame Solario, wearing the hat trimmed with shaded velvet pansies, was standing and leaning lightly with both hands on her closed white parasol, listening. Mosca was talking to her.

Because of that interminable previous day, it was like a return after a long absence. Things might have happened, might have changed, and he knew nothing. Farther on was the other group of Italians, that of Ercolani's relations, who as usual had the arbour as their own, but what was not at all usual was that Ercolani was there too, sitting in the bosom of his family. Kovanski was not about, but the idea of meeting him was already oppressive. Bernard turned at the end of the terrace, just as Madame Solario began to walk towards the front door. Acting almost without thought, he went into the hotel after her.

She was crossing the hall alone, and when she saw him she spoke.

'You were away yesterday,' she said. 'I looked for you.'

'Yes, I went to Villa d'Este. The Rosses took me with them.'

'Was it amusing?' she asked, but her eyes asked him another question, or so he thought.

'I might be overheard,' he answered, 'so I'd better not say.'

'That must mean that you are always bored! It makes one afraid to ask you –'

'Ask me – Were you going to ask me something?'

The hall was about to be invaded. The first to enter were Ercolani's cousins, and Madame Solario turned so as to face away from everyone but Bernard.

'Do you remember you said you would take me out in a row-boat one afternoon?'

'Of course!'

'It's something I have wanted to do and haven't done yet.' She did not appear aware of Ercolani as he went by behind her. 'I think it would be just the afternoon for it, don't you?'

'What time would you like to go?'

They agreed upon the time, prolonging the discussion until those others had gone into the dining-room.

'I would like it very much,' she said.

It was the most beautiful hour of the day when he saw her appear and had his moment of disbelief that it was towards himself that she was coming, and that it was for her he had been waiting. There was no one in front of the hotel as he handed her into the boat, no one to see them go.

She settled herself in the cushioned stern. 'I shall steer,' she said with a pleased look, a holiday look – but why should she be pleased, why was it a holiday? – and took up the steering ropes while he adjusted the oars.

Soon they were slipping along under the arbour.

'Are we going to keep close in, or go out into the middle?' he asked.

'Not far out – about like this.'

They were passing the plane-tree walk, and next they came to the water-gates of Villa Carlotta, and a little farther on he thought of saying, 'Capella Sommariva'. But it was all too dream-like.

Past that jutting-out spur of the hills the lake broadened, and the mountain range, in drawing away from the shore, opened out the sky as well. It was another and wider prospect, steeped in mellow light. Enormous clouds rested on the shoulders of the mountains, not white and cold, but apricot-coloured, and the reflections of villages in the water had the same warmth; it might have been clouds and it might have been houses that the oars dipped into. To the quiet dipping of oars the boat went evenly forward. They were alone, where nothing ominous could intervene, nothing would hurry them. He would have liked to think about it, and he could not because she was there. He could not even look at her – that is, not fully. She was dressed in white, with a hat of natural straw shading her eyes, a light-blue cape thrown over the back of the seat; he knew that much, and saw her

69

face for a moment when they exchanged a laugh about her rather erratic steering. She spoke of the people who had villas there when they were passing Tremezzo, and said no more for a time, leaning back but looking with interest towards the shore.

A faint hum of life reached them from within the arcades at the water's edge, and then the sounds died away and they passed beyond the limit of where he had previously been.

'It's different here,' she said, at last breaking the silence. 'There are no hotels, no foreigners. You can see the villas here have never belonged to foreigners.'

'They do look different – but they're all shut! That may be why.'

Her steering brought them close inshore, and they could see and feel desertion and decay; the several villas within sight had every window shuttered, and in the gardens the paths between the oleanders had almost disappeared. Going by, she peered into a forlorn little stucco pavilion flush with the lake, and at dilapidated statues in a thicket of magnolia.

'Let's go slowly,' she said. 'Let's look.' And he rested his oars and looked with her.

Here was an entrance guarded by cypresses, but the fine white villa stood, some way back, against a bare slope. He knew she was right; it had never belonged to foreigners – which meant to anyone like themselves – and it was closed to them not only by its shutters, which were pale as eyelids. This decaying backwater, which the tide of modern fashion hadn't reached, though not so beautiful, fell in with the most romantic places in his memory.

The oars dripped; the boat creaked a little.

'Let's go on,' she said, and he resumed his rowing.

He did not particularly want to look across to the side of the lake that held the picnic, but he could not prevent himself, nor from seeing in the ravine at the foot of the mountain the little speck that was the house that Ilona had pointed out to him. For a few moments he held back the words, and then they came out.

'That house over there – the only one on that mountain – they say the sun never shines on it in winter nor the moon in summer.'

She gave it her consideration, but her answer was a mere slight lifting of the brows. 'Can we get as far as those woods?' she asked.

He looked over his shoulder. She meant the wooded promontory of Balbianello.

'Yes, of course, if you would like to.'

He had to manage the boat when the wash of the steamer caught it, and it was at that moment that he asked himself point-blank: What had taken place that she and Ercolani should now be avoiding each other? She must be under a threat; and the sense of menace was as strong out here on the lake as it had been during the last half-hour of the ball.

'Have you been up to those woods?' she asked, and he made out which she meant. He took in the character of the shore – that tranced stillness – while he was answering. 'Not as far as that – only up to those above Cadenabbia.'

He was thinking of her secret anxieties, but she herself was certainly not thinking about them then. She was relaxed in her whole attitude, turning her head to see the woods he had spoken of.

'Are they big ones, those above Cadenabbia? Can one walk for long in them?'

He answered mechanically. 'There are some fairly big patches, that I suppose take about an hour to get through. But from that pass up there one looks down on a great mass of woods, between that mountain and Lugano.'

She was taking pleasure in what they were doing, drifting along in the golden afternoon. He rowed slowly, and the motion and sound were as soft as could be. His curiosity was now aroused – not by what must have happened, but by her faint smile of gratification, with its background in his mind of all that he might guess.

'I could never get there.' And he had to cast back to what they had last said. After a moment she added, 'I dream so often about being in a very large wood. I dreamed it again last night.'

After another moment she added to this, in the same casual, absent way, 'It must be because of the woods when I was a child.'

'Where were they?' asked Bernard.

Whatever she said, whatever it was, it must come as a surprise.

'In America – in the very north.'

'Then you are American!' he exclaimed.

'No.' It seemed she was going to leave it at that. He had almost

71

given up hoping to hear more when she said, 'I was born in England. My father was English. But we went to America when I was a child.'

Some peasant women, kneeling on a strip of shingle, were washing clothes in the lake. Their heads were bound with dark handkerchiefs, and their full, stuff skirts were a rusty black; there was no colour about them. They were vigorously scrubbing the clothes with soap on a board, and then wringing them out, and Madame Solario steered the boat in close to watch them.

'See how well they do it,' she said, 'how thoroughly they rinse.'

The older women never looked up, but a girl waved. Madame Solario did not wave back.

'Bella come la Madonna!' the girl called out.

She did not show that she heard. 'It's a pity the water isn't cleaner,' she said.

They went on; it was a rather sad corner of the lake.

'Where do you live in England?' she asked next, and smiled.

He told her the county and wondered where she had been born and had lived before going to America as a child.

'Is the place like a scene on a china cup – cows by a river in front, and a square white house in a park at the back?'

'No, the house isn't white or square, and there's no river. It sits in a valley, with a lot of trees around, and rookeries in them.'

'And are you always going to live there?'

'Oh no, I'm going to live in a town. I'm going to be a bank clerk.'

He enjoyed saying it. And he didn't miss her expression; he saw it chill a little.

She inquired no further.

The scene changed with their course, because they reached the promontory and turned into the shadow of its banks; the water there was an extraordinary green.

'These aren't real woods,' he said. 'They are just a tangle. What sort of a wood is it that you say you often dream about?'

'Sometimes they are great spreading trees,' she answered. 'Perhaps they are oaks – I don't know. But where I am is more often like the woods I knew in Sweden and America.'

'Sweden!'

'My mother was half Swedish.'

72

When she said 'my mother', remembering the story he had heard he could not look at her. She went on. 'She took us to Sweden when my father died.'

'*Us?*' Bernard repeated.

'My brother and I.'

'You have a brother. But no sisters?'

'No. And I haven't seen my brother for nearly twelve years.'

He raised his eyes to her at that. There was just a momentary tightening of her lips, and her violet-blue eyes calmly met his eyes.

He asked no question, which might have seemed strange to her, considering what she had told him, on which some sympathetic comment would have been natural. She supplied an explanation – 'He was always very adventurous' – but not as though it were much needed, and returned to her meditating.

It came to Bernard then that she was as good as alone in the row-boat, and that in his youth and shyness she found simply an absence, welcome for a time, of the attentions that pursued her. It had kept recurring to him – why had she asked him, him of all people, to take her on the lake? He felt that he understood when he saw how his lack of comment went unnoticed and she did not have to say one word more than she wished. It all fell into place after that. She had wanted an hour on the lake, left to herself, and he gave her what she wanted. For he left her to her thoughts as perhaps no other man would have been willing to do.

A reminder of the terrible drama in her life had come as a shock to him, and that passed into another kind of shock. But he kept on with his even strokes; the click of the rowlocks was the only sound between them. Then, leaning back in her position of repose, loosely holding the steering-ropes, she began to talk as if she were thinking aloud.

'We went in the summer always to the same kind of woods, with the same big lakes. Many things were the same. In Maine we knew that Indians were still living there, and in Sweden there was a colony of Lapps hidden in the forest – we knew they were there, but we never saw them.'

A smile of reminiscence hovered over her lips, and he gazed at her, fascinated by the incongruity of these memories with her name and all that he had seen and heard of her.

'The lakes up there are only lakes. If there was more than sometimes a few houses or a sawmill – if there was just one beautiful
building on the shore, a church, or a castle – it would be a scene, a
picture – something else. There is nothing.' She mused about it.
'But here –'

He looked with her. He saw it as never before.

'We are coming to Balbianello,' she said presently.

'Yes, I know.'

'Let us go out into the middle to see it, and then we must go
back.'

He did as she said, and the villa appeared to them, with the
open arcade on the height, and the haunted gardens coming down
to the towers and the port and the breakwater.

'Have you been there?' he asked.

'No,' said Madame Solario.

He had no impulse to tell her the story that had been told him
about Balbianello. The boat gently rocked, as he had stopped
rowing. With the sun beginning to set, strong shafts of light were
slanting through a gap in the mountains and striking like swords
across the foothills and the bay. It was tremendous. But she was
looking up at the villa, and he observed her. Her face was somehow baffling in its beauty, but that might have been because its
shape and the unbroken line of nose and brow – that classic
sweep of the brows from the straight nose – and the large orbits
of her eyes belonged to a conception of beauty itself. When she
next spoke the mood of these contemplations was shattered by a
shock of still another kind – that, at first, of absolute surprise.

'Kovanski meant to buy Balbianello,' she said.

He caught himself hearing it open-mouthed.

'Is he going to?'

'No!' And she showed impatience. She added, 'The price
would be fantastic! You can imagine.'

Bernard abruptly began to turn homewards. What had there
been . . .? And if she knew this much about him, why now did he
and she . . .? And Ilona was saying, 'I thought he was coming to
Balbianello with us.' But he was trying to buy Balbianello to take
Madame Solario to it. There it stood, waiting, it would seem.
Ilona had been there alone – that is, without the one who should
have gone with her – and he himself had never been, and Madame

Solario would not go with Kovanski. None of them would ever go.

She moved, changing her position to draw the folds of the light-blue cape about her shoulders, and this movement coincided with a change in her expression, which was like a still surface catching the light, and in her attitude towards him, for it was with a livelier recognition of him than hitherto that she said, 'Now tell me what other people you have met here. Where were you before, and what were you doing?'

He told her, and that he had been doing some mountain climbing in Switzerland, and she asked which mountains he had climbed, and then how the parties were organized. The silence and the brooding within it were banished. One subject led to another – he had no time to think how it could be, but there it was, they were talking. She drew from him that he had one brother, older than himself, and two sisters, younger, and that he had gone to Oxford. And she was no longer relaxedly leaning back; she was sitting more erect, keeping the steering-ropes taut, her head slightly tilted as if she were bending her attention upon him.

'Now you must tell me why you didn't dance at the ball – as you say you didn't,' she said.

'For a very obvious reason. I told you – '

'Then do you never dance at any ball you go to?'

'That sounds somehow – well, too interesting! As though I went to a lot of balls and stood in doorways and glowered!'

'But what do you do?'

'Oh, it's all right when I am with people who are no better at it than I. Besides, I haven't been to many balls.'

'But you will go some day, and enjoy them.'

'Will I? Do *you* like dancing very much?'

There was then what was like a correspondence between her and the rays that were striking from the sky, for when she answered – 'Sometimes!' – a ray came from her, too, and travelled straight. It struck him. She added, 'One enjoys it when one has a good partner.'

She knew he was remembering the ball. That was in the ray. But then she said, 'I don't do it very often, only sometimes.' And the ray was extinguished by reserve.

'You may be a good partner,' she said next. 'I'm sorry I don't know! But there are things you like better. You row very well.'

'I shall say, "Not in this old tub. You should see me!"'

'Oh, I'm sure,' she said. 'When?'

He really hadn't known what he was saying, and then found that they had laughed.

'Of course I didn't mean it.'

'But it may be true!'

He stopped rowing for a few minutes. They had come up to Tremezzo, and that was an excuse, but his reason was that they were almost home. In the pink arcades whose foundations went down into the lake the hum of life was louder than it had been. Fishermen were getting into their boats to go out and throw their nets; children were swarming about and screaming at their play. The steamer that was churning on ahead, with its lengthening wake smoothly parting the rosy water, was the last one of the day, the one from Como. These were the sights and sounds of sunset, but this hour had more than ordinary brilliance. Madame Solario asked her questions. From her attention upon him, her smile, there were subtle emanations. All regret was now centred in the thought that they would soon be home; but he was having to go on.

Their talk was inconsequent. She saw three hotel guests walking in the narrow path along the shore and hinted that she thought them silly. Seen from below, they were cut off at the waist by the lake-wall, and Bernard said, 'They're like moving targets in a shooting-gallery.'

She said, 'Oughtn't they to bob up and down?'

She had the carefree, holiday look that was in delicate, not obvious, contrast to her usual thoughtful calm. Hers was not the gaiety of other people – not outwardly demonstrated, more like an atmosphere about her.

At the water-gates of Villa Carlotta just that little bend of the shore diminished the gorgeousness of the sunset. But when they passed along the plane-tree walk the shade meant only that the last minutes were speeding away and there had not been a word to suggest that this would ever happen again.

A hotel boatman ran down the water-steps to pull them alongside, and by the time Bernard had lifted the oars out of the water and got up she had put her hand on the boatman's arm and, sway-ing gracefully, had stepped out of the boat. She did not wait for Bernard to help her. The perceptions of the moment were very acute, even the physical ones – of the dank mossiness of the lake-wall and the smell of the water.

Before she could speak to him again – as she must have done – a voice called down from the terrace above. It was Colonel Ross, and Bernard caught his surprise at seeing them together.

'What – out for a row?'

He seemed to be there on purpose to receive her, and to prevent anything more from being said.

Chapter Eight

Kovanski was so seldom to be seen, taking no part in the social
life of the hotel, that one could sometimes have doubted that he
was staying there. Bernard never again saw him at the *table
d'hôte*; he had occupied the table in the corner only once, on the
night of Madame Solario's arrival, and after that night Madame
Solario had never been alone but had sat at the Lastacoris' table
or with the French couple. Where Kovanski ate, Bernard didn't
know. His room, Bernard found out by consulting the visitors'
list, was on the third floor. His own room was on the second floor,
in the passage to the left of the staircase. Madame Solario's room
was also on the second floor, but round the corner at the end of
the passage on the right, and not in all the times he had come in
or out of his room had he met her, and only twice caught sight
of her in the distance.

On the evening after their expedition he was drawn into a
group of young people who were entertaining themselves in the
Salon de Lecture, but when an excuse offered itself in the game
they were playing he went out and up to his room, in order to
come down the central staircase again to survey the whole hall
from that vantage-ground. And just as he was emerging on to the
staircase from the passage he saw Kovanski go past, coming from
the floor above. They had missed each other, but the effect on
Bernard of simply seeing him was a rage that was the very repetition of what he had felt when Kovanski grinned at him. Kovanski
now would always make him feel young and ridiculous. He had
not known he could hate as he did when watching the other, who
was unaware of him, go down the stairs. He noted Kovanski's back
and shoulders as he went, and the character of the round head
covered with short, dark hair – for the very pleasure of hating, to
get to the bottom of it if he could.

The next morning he saw Kovanski again where he least expected it. Bernard had gone to Bellagio with Missy and the others, knowing very well that he wanted to stay where he was in the hope of meeting Madame Solario. That was a weakness and folly he wouldn't yield to, but the desultory sort of shopping that the girls liked to indulge in, if it wasn't fun was the exact reverse. He got away by saying he had left his watch at the watch-maker and would fetch it and come back, and he walked along the front alone. There had been rain earlier, and the morning was steamy and grey. At the end of the arcades he did not stop but went farther, the foreign crowd suddenly left behind. What was he going to do with himself? he was thinking. He was more than bored, he was depressed; and yet, far off, as it were, not quite belonging to him, was a throb of excitement. Turning a corner, he saw a man sitting on a bench half concealed by the wall of a small piazza in which there was no one but himself. Bernard's path was leading upwards, and he had to take a few steps to look down and be sure – though there was no need; he was instantly sure. Kovanski was sitting there with his elbows on his knees. The bench was facing the opposite shore and the long line of houses at the foot of the mountain that composed Cadenabbia. He was watching Cadenabbia as if he could see into it, and what she was doing could not escape him. So it seemed to Bernard. He was too much interested to think that Kovanski might look round. And there was a solitariness about that figure that was permanent; he wouldn't look round. He had meant to buy Balbianello, and here he was sitting alone in this shabby little piazza, looking across the lake, which was as near as he could get. Bernard noticed the slump of his back and shoulders under the blue serge coat, together with the strong set of the dark, bullet head. Kovanski dropped a cigarette and ground it with his foot, still leaning forward with his arms resting on his knees, and Bernard retraced his steps and was soon among the shops again.

The shopping party got in just before luncheon, and almost the first people that Bernard saw were Madame Solario and Ercolani, standing under the trees and talking to each other. She was at her stillest, her eyes raised to her companion's with their most reflective look, and it was her way not to appear to see anything but the person who was speaking to her. Ercolani's tall figure was a trifle inclined, in the Italian attitude of extreme respect. It would have been difficult to find a more romantically-handsome pair—except, one liked to think, his good looks were rather too conventional.

It was odd how the hotel guests could evaporate in the hot afternoons, leaving the hall and the road and the terrace empty. There would not be a soul in the plane-tree walk, and Villa Carlotta and its approaches were a picture of baroque beauty without life. But at the 'meeting' before dinner Bernard had a chance to bow to Madame Solario. She stopped as she went by and said, 'It was so nice yesterday!'

After dinner he saw her established in the circle of Marchesa Lastacori, with Colonel Ross beside her. Rather than sit in a corner with his eternal book, he directed himself to the Salon de Lecture, but on the way saw the door of the Salle des Jeux half open and heard bursts of noise within. He looked inside, and his eyes at once found Kovanski. There were two or three tables at which quiet bridge was going on, and a knot of people collected in front of *his* table, where merriment was unrestrained. Several spectators must have been interested in the game itself, for they were watching it closely, but the players were putting up another performance at the same time, which had a separate audience; they were behaving as though they were drunk. Kovanski's chair was against the wall; he was the most in view from the door, and for Bernard, the focus of the scene. He was not making as much noise or ragging as the other three were, but he was laughing even more. They all had glasses beside them, and the others stopped to drink between tricks. Kovanski wasn't drinking at the moment; he was laughing and talking in the same breath; he was almost incapacitated by laughter. Yet his features had very much their usual immobility. His strange eyes, and that blunt, even edge to his teeth that, while the muscles of his face hardly moved, could make his expression so unpleasant, did not – and that was the surprise – belie his mirth. Bernard looked on with the rest, standing next to an Englishman called Blake, who had arrived that day and with whom he had already exchanged a few words. The other three players were men he had never seen before, and they were all four talking incomprehensibly – talking in Russian. The stakes must have been very high, or there would not have been so much outside interest in the game. There was a sudden murmur among the spectators when a card was slammed down.

Then one of Kovanski's adversaries, who was as broad and squat as a primitive idol, placed a full glass of brandy on top of his own head, and, having become as grave as an idol, kept the glass perfectly balanced while he continued to play. There was such an outbreak at this that someone at another table said very loud, 'C'est insupportable!'

The game having ended, Kovanski picked up a card and said something to the idol, who, with the glass still balanced on his head, also picked up a card. They threw down their cards, and Kovanski gave a shout strangled by hoarseness. The idol removed the glass from his head and emptied it, and jotted something down on the score-card, while Kovanski swept all the cards in front of him sideways on to the floor.

'Extraordinary, aren't they?' said Blake.

An intuition had pieced things together in Bernard's mind. He left the room and went straight to the frame containing the visitors' names that hung beside the concierge's desk, and the place where he should have read: *Don Ascanio Ercolani – Montefeltro*.

It had become a blank.

The atmosphere of the hall was one of decorous enjoyment, and there had been no change in the circle of Marchesa Lastacori. Bernard now knew that Ercolani had left by the half-past-one-o'clock boat, and that he and Madame Solario had been saying good-bye to each other that morning.

After a while he went back to the Salle des Jeux. The group, some sitting and some standing, around the Russians had grown. Blake was still looking on, and Bernard joined him and stood there with conscious defiance.

Blake said, 'Now he's talking about the Russo-Japanese War.' He might have been speaking of a public performance to someone who had come late. 'Two of them seem to have been in it,' he added, very much interested, but obliging to the newcomer.

Kovanski was talking, not to his friends but in French to his listeners in general. And he was still bursting with his peculiar hilarity – his face and eyes as if made rigid by his effort to contain it. Laughter from his audience punctuated his talk. The idol was good-humouredly adding some comment or explanation to those nearest himself, and one of the other Russians, a long and very

81

narrow man with a small head and a dissolute-looking face, was morosely sunk in his chair and not speaking – or apparently listening – at all. The fourth was a boyishly fair young man who had his eyes fixed on Kovanski.

The gist at least of what he was saying – in fluent but harshly accented French – soon became clear: he was relating experiences of his own in the war, as a staff officer, and they were entirely ridiculous. Farcical ineptitude at the top – that was the theme. And what was so repellent was the mixing of comedy and horror, absurdity and defeat: men running away, carnage and panic thrown in as background to a ludicrous order impossible to execute. There was a general who always took his cows with him, as he had been ordered a milk diet and there was no milk in Manchuria, and during the retreat from Wa-fang-Kou Kovanski had attended the general's cow – 'la vache du Général Stackelberg' – all the way to Liao-Yang. But he had returned to report without waiting to hand over the cow, and the next day, in the midst of the catastrophic confusion, a retreat in seas of mud, he received a field-telegram: *la vache du Général Stackelberg* was lost. The story went on and on, of how he got out of the stream of retreat, of his return to Liao-Yang, phrases succeeding one another in short barks, the tempo accelerating, *la vache du Général Stackelberg* always lost, always coming back as a refrain, his voice growing hoarser and everyone laughing more and more. The scene became a railway station; the commander-in-chief was expected; the divisional staff was on the platform, around them inconceivable disorder – extreme tension, for the train was late. It came at last, but overshot the mark, and instead of the carriage of the commander-in-chief a strange-looking wagon stopped directly in front of the assembled staff. There was an opening in it, and a head peered out. ' *C'était la vache du Général Stackelberg!* '

He drank as soon as he had finished. He had brilliantly brought it off, but that seemed to Bernard no reason for telling – or inventing – the story here. The laughter and a few questions were getting him started again when the talk took another turn. Someone knew about a certain battle, and to what was asked the idol replied. But Kovanski interrupted. One evening during that week, he said, while he was trying to find the commander of the 14th Division, for whom he had a message – and suddenly what

82

he was saying became perfectly clear to Bernard, whereas before everything but the highlights had been a good deal befogged; it was because what had just gone before had launched Kovanski into English – an officer galloped up to him in the dark, shouting, 'Victory! San-de-Pu has fallen!' This officer stopped long enough to direct him there and galloped on, and Kovanski, after having delivered his message and received further instructions, caught up with the colonel of the regiment that had taken the position as he and his staff made their triumphal entry into the village. It was the key point for which a battle had been raging for two days. Troops that had, he supposed, stormed it, were lying exhausted on the ground, but they struggled to their feet and cheered when the colonel stood up in his stirrups and cried out, 'God bless you, my children, you have taken San-de-Pu!' Kovanski was told that when the troops had burst into the village they had found it empty: the Japanese had not waited to be attacked.

In a strange silence all around (just his way of saying it started ripples of amusement) the officers crowded into an empty *fantze*, or Chinese hut; a table was set up, but before they began to write out a report of the victorious day a bottle of champagne was produced, and with great jubilation they drank a health to the Tsar. The colonel announced with emotion that this was the happiest day of his life. They had all sat down around the table when an adjutant hurried in and said a few words in the colonel's ear. There was a sudden, then a long and terrible pause. The colonel half rose from his seat and said, 'Gentlemen, I regret that there has been a mistake. This is *not* San-de-Pu!'

Kovanski had himself half risen to illustrate the story, and, exploding with laughter, he said to the idol, 'My orderly, Pavlusha, was at the door and heard. He's upstairs now, and you shall hear how he says it.' And he repeated the sentence in Russian, in that posture of apology, and the idol shook his head, speechless with delight, and wiped his eyes. As if quite unaware of all this – and there was noise enough – the long, lank, dissolute-looking man took out a small pocket mirror and examined his teeth, drawing up his lip and turning his head this way and that to get a side view. The youngest of the four Russians had flushed and was glancing from one face to the other.

Everyone seemed to be talking at once as Blake said to Bernard, 'Can you beat them?' – looking with a sort of admiration at Kovanski, who was being baited to go on.

There were now only men in the room; the voices were loud, and the air was thick with smoke. And, like two pictures back to back on the same page, there was, for Bernard, the one of the circle of Marchesa Lastacori, urbanely gossiping in the hall, and, among the feminine figures, Madame Solario. When he had last seen her, with her elbow on the arm of her chair, she had been resting her cheek on two fingers of her left hand. He had seen the pearl on her fourth finger, the pearl in her ear. In actual space, only the width of the hall and a short passage separated her from this masculine world.

Here Kovanski, who previously had not allowed a serious conversation, was being drawn into one by the persistent questions of an Englishman who was a professional soldier. Dropping his former line, he began to meet straight questions with brutally straight answers, and the extraordinary absence of hesitation and reticence that he showed had an unpleasant effect. Neither regret nor loyalty existed for him. There seemed to be no brake upon Kovanski, nothing that he was not willing to say. Then, when once he paused to drain off his glass, the idol again took up the thread. Though he was quite another thing, he too betrayed an attitude – good-humoured in his case – that was astounding towards disasters that had so recently occurred. The presence of a companion like the dissolute-looking man lent a sort of rottenness to these exhibitions of cynical indifference. The only one for whom Bernard felt the smallest comprehension was the youngest of the four, who was about his own age, which was anyhow a bond in that company.

Kovanski abruptly said something in Russian and started to sort out the cards that had been scattered over the table, and at a nod the young man picked up those that were on the floor. The idol said to him in English, 'Vanya, ring for the waiter!' – and that, too, he obeyed. Another bottle of brandy was ordered, and the four cut for a new game, the bystanders closing round the table to watch.

Bernard stayed a little longer, seeing the players between the heads of two men who were having a side bet. He stood with folded arms, feeling that a knell had been sounded. It was a fact to face that Kovanski might force him to leave, in the way that Ercolani had been got rid of. He didn't know how it had been done, nor how it would be done again, but, as he looked at Kovanski, it seemed probable that it could be done. Madame Solario would wish it, to save herself embarrassment if she were remaining on; that was the point. He might have no more than a few words with her after this – if he got as much as that. As if stung by the thought, he returned to the hall, but everyone there had gone up; it was much later than he had realized. He went back once more to the card-room, just to have a look. Kovanski had a cigarette in his mouth, and with a hard and abstracted expression was screwing up one side of his face to keep the smoke out of his eyes. The idol looked like a primitive idol, the long narrow man seemed to be playing in his sleep, and the youngest was getting drunk. He had become flushed, excited, and talkative, and was greeting the fall of the cards with wild, shrill exclamations. Kovanski, his partner, was ignoring his behaviour and his foolish play, but the spectators who were interested in the game had begun to be annoyed.

Bernard went for a walk down the road to get some fresh air, and when he went up to bed he heard even from the staircase the now familiar noise, and came upon the Russians in the passage on the second floor. They were standing before a half open door, the four of them surrounding a fifth figure, obviously a servant ('My orderly, Pavlusha'?), a man with a broad, simple face and a head that had been shaved, who kept bowing while they all talked to him. Kovanski had hold of his shoulder and was shaking him jovially, and every time he shook, the man beamed and bowed. Bernard was held up for a minute or two, and during that time the shaved man said something in the incomprehensible language which raised a shout. Kovanski gave him a still more violent shake, and the fair young man with his wild, flushed face fell against the door, which opened wide so that he nearly fell to the floor.

Chapter Nine

Bernard was out in the morning before any of the ladies had appeared, and was glad to meet with Blake and to sit on the parapet, talking about the previous evening. Blake said that the Russians were a rum lot, and no wonder they hadn't won their war, as they didn't care if they lost it. He had been in the South African war, and he told Bernard what he thought about that; it was very prosaic compared with the reminiscences of the night before. Bernard felt that Blake might know more about the newly arrived Russians than he himself did, but it emerged that Blake knew only that they were expected to leave that day.

'But not the lot of them?'

'The ones that came yesterday.' He didn't know their names, but had heard that the long, narrow man was a prince.

Colonel Ross stopped to say good morning to Bernard, excluding Blake from the short conversation, which he brought to an end with 'Aha!' as the first ladies to be seen came out of the front door. It was remarkable what a difference a few large hats, a few hour-glass figures in pale colours, a few high voices, made to the scene. Some rovers and hangers-on were very soon added to it – Wilbur the glossy American, Pico, as yet without his owner, the Italians belonging to Ercolani's family, the little Argentine. The day had begun. There had been no day whose outline was so sharp for Bernard, but whose issue was so uncertain. At any moment Kovanski might step into his path as he had done before, and something concerning her be used that he would not be able to resist.

Some time later, looking down the road, he thought he saw her figure between the row of oleanders and the line of shop-fronts. He started towards it, and it was indeed she, walking slowly, Colonel Ross beside her, glancing into the shop windows.

Bernard came up to them from behind, went past, turned, and said, 'Oh!'

Colonel Ross said, 'This is the young man who had the luck to take you out rowin', what? What had he done to deserve it?'

She was wearing a straw hat trimmed with sprays of natural-looking lilac.

'Now, let's see, what did you want to get?' asked Colonel Ross. 'Is this the shop? The ladies always seem to find somethin' to buy in here.' And they stopped before the lace shop. It was perfectly easy for Bernard to stay with them – more natural than to walk on.

'Don't those little mats tempt you?' asked Colonel Ross humorously. 'They're very nice. Can't I make you a present of them?'

'You're too kind, but I don't know where one would put them.'

'What an extraordinary woman you are! I thought women bought for the sake of buyin'–' But then the metallic voice of Mrs Ross called 'Algy!' behind them. She was shopping with Lady Victoria and desired change for a hundred francs, and Colonel Ross obeyed the summons.

'Do you see –' Bernard said to Madame Solario. 'Let me show you –'

He led the way to the next shop, and then on, and found her compliant. A path into the hills came between two buildings, just before the corner where the lake road bent out of sight.

'The woods are up there – not far. Do you think you would like to go up a little way?'

'Yes, I would like to go.'

There was danger ahead – the corner with its clump of dark-green bushes looking varnished in the sunlight, and some white figures coming round it. But they reached the turn on their left before there had been a meeting with those in front or any hailing from Colonel Ross in their rear. It was done, and yet he could not altogether lose the sense of pursuit. She went up the cobbled steps less slowly, rather more energetically, than she usually walked, and when they had got above the houses he glanced at her face in the hope of seeing her holiday look, which would have allayed every uneasiness. It wasn't there; the surface was still.

'Those roofs are the Bellevue, aren't they?' she asked when they paused and looked down.

'Let's get away from them. I'd like to forget them,' he said quickly. He had to restrain himself from walking fast. 'Now one can't see them any more,' he said after some minutes, looking back.

The wood lay around them, great chestnut trees throwing a light shade, and the sun sweeping, golden, into every clearing.

It had all been accomplished, but what he had schemed for evaded him. He was alone with her, yes, but he didn't know what he could say to her. And by this walk he was probably forfeiting every chance of seeing her again; this would indeed be the last time. He had unhappily searched and found nothing with which to begin when she observed, 'These woods are silent too.'

He noticed the silence.

'There aren't any birds,' he said. 'In England there would be birds, of course. All that one hears in Italy are the crickets.'

'And nightingales,' she said.

'I haven't been here at the right time. Are there lots of them?'

'In early summer one hears them night and day.'

He thought: She's been in Italy in summer – it may have been last summer. She heard them last summer! And with whom?

'There is a cave!' she said, while he was still, after a long time, hearing her say, 'and nightingales'. 'I hadn't seen it before. We must have come by another path. I wonder if it is very deep.'

The rocks of the hillside broke here and there into the wood, and at the foot of a crag there was a large opening. Madame Solario stood still.

'Shall I go and see?' said Bernard. He investigated and came back. 'Yes, it goes quite far in.'

'One could hide there!' she said.

That started him thinking again of the woods of her childhood – in Sweden and America, which was so surprising – and he was framing a question – 'Did you like to hide?' – when she said, still looking towards the cave, 'A hermit may have lived in there. A monk in a brown habit.'

'Well, long ago, before the Bellevue and the Villa Carlotta.'

'The little churches came first,' she said; and they walked on.

'I believe there is a Madonna del Buon Soccorso on this mountain that is very old.'

'In your woods –' he began, trying to return to what was after all the only thing she had told him, except that she collected little china figures and had a recurrent dream about a wood. 'In your woods, do you remember a cave where a hermit might have lived?'

'One wouldn't have thought of it up there, but in Italy it has been done for one. St Jerome sitting in a cave like that, with his red hat hanging up and the lion at his feet –' The inflections of her voice were vague. 'That has been seen for one. Nothing has been seen for one up there.'

'You would have liked to hide in it,' he said, pressing for some personal, childish recollection of those places.

'Ah, yes, that –' she murmured.

'Would you like to go back there?' he asked, seeing little of her face, for she was walking without looking round at him.

'Where? To Sweden?' He thought she wasn't going to say more. 'My grandmother is dead, and her house, that was a house that belonged to her family, has gone to a relation I don't know. There is nothing to take me back, and I am used to other places now.'

He waited. He must learn as much about her as he could on this walk, but it was clear that she talked less about herself than most people do.

'Do you ever go to England?' he ventured.

'Not now. There, too, nothing takes me back.' She added – more, it seemed, from a polite obligation to talk than anything else – 'Since I have been grown up I have lived only in Latin countries, in Catholic countries.'

'You are a Catholic!' he said out of an instant conviction.

'Yes,' Then she made another concession to conversation. 'Yes, I became a Catholic when I grew up.'

He felt his youthfulness. This step, which implied so much thought and decision, she must have taken at the time when he was still at school – her voice put it years ago.

'I wonder where the church is that you spoke of,' he said, escaping into something simple. 'What did you say it was called?'

'It is a Madonna del Buon Soccorso – that means it is a place of pilgrimage, because it is connected with some special event.'

'I may have gone past and not known it was that.'

'If you had gone in you would have seen it was a shrine.' The depths of the sunlit wood drew her attention still further away. 'There would be votive offerings, and perhaps little paintings of the miracles that have been worked. Sometimes those things are so amusing.'

The sequence was unexpected and nonplussed him. He did not try again, and it was she who made the next remark.

'You said you had gone on a picnic the other day. Who went? Were there many of you?'

It needed an effort to enumerate the names, to which she said once or twice, 'Ah, yes!' Then: 'I'm sure with those people you were very lively!'

He did not pronounce Ilona's name. The reason for omitting it was a passing explanation of the dejection that he felt. Now this was disappointing, ordinary talk, even – as it began to range further over their common acquaintance – mere gossip, and what she had earlier let fall had echoed within his imagination. She, on the contrary, grew more animated; she appeared to enjoy discussing their acquaintances. There was a little malice of a light and, one might say, unmalicious sort, in some of her comments. She found Colonel Ross diverting.

'Do you often think what he says is funny?'

'Yes, because he is so English.' And she smiled charmingly at Bernard.

'Indeed he is!'

He would not make too free with his middle-aged compatriots; nor she with Marchesa Lastacori. Keeping out Ercolani and his cousins, they spoke of the Italians who lived in the two large villas across the lake. The heir to the beautiful historic villa, who was so much sought after, never came over by day, and sometimes, haughtily, would not even come into the hotel.

'Last night,' she said, 'he stood outside in a black cloak' – and she sketched with a slight gesture a cloak being flung over a shoulder – 'and spoke to no one. He reminded us of le "beau ténébreux", the character in the story of Amadis de Gaule, but only as a copy. We called him le *faux* ténébreux!' And she

90

offered him this for his own entertainment, sure that he could appreciate it. He responded as convincingly as he was able, and was seized by an idea. It had not occurred to him that he could speak to her of Kovanski, but suddenly it seemed that he might.

'I didn't see him last night, I was in the card-room. There were great goings-on there. Count Kovanski and his friends made everyone roar with laughter. Did you hear about that?'

She said on the same note as before, not less but not more interested, 'What was there to hear?'

'Oh, just that four of them were playing bridge and playing the fool at the same time, with people looking on and laughing. They were all of them Russian, and they seemed very different from everybody else.'

He hoped for – he needed – a little inducement to say more; but the going was rough just there, as the path rose sharply, and that acted as an interruption. This made him the more determined to go on when he could.

They reached a shelf of rock above the crag, and there a bench had been placed and he could ask her if she would like to rest. Instead of sitting, she stood looking from the edge down into the wood, through the spreading branches of beautiful foliage to the great spreading roots that gave a sense almost of motion below as they appeared or sank in the open spaces of sunlight. Bernard watched her and waited. He felt he had a purpose in speaking of Kovanski, though he wasn't sure what he was leading up to. But merely to say and hear the name was preferable to leaving it unspoken.

She turned from her momentary contemplation to sit down.

'They talked about the Russo-Japanese War,' he persisted doggedly.

'Ah, yes?' she said.

He was on his feet beside the bench, and, as he was above her, it was the lilac in her hat that he saw, and even at that juncture it shared his preoccupation. It was so exquisitely real and fresh – double-petalled, mauve and pinkish-mauve – that he imagined the fragrance of lilac and even that he had a memory of spring.

'What gives you the idea that Russians are different from other people?' asked Madame Solario.

He could hardly believe it; he had got his chance. He sat down on the bench beside her.

'I've never met any that I can remember, but those last night made an astonishing exhibition of themselves. Some of it was what in England would be called a rag – pretending to be drunk, for I don't believe they were drunk to begin with – but it was rather out of place. And then they started talking about the war.'

'How many did you say there were, besides Count Kovanski?'

'Three others. They made their own four for bridge. You didn't see them at any time?'

'No, I didn't see them, and I believe they have gone away.'

'Only three have,' said Bernard. 'The three strangers.'

She accepted this with her inscrutable expression.

'I particularly asked if they had *all* gone,' he said.

There was a moment of silence.

'And you say they talked about the war?'

'Yes – that is, two of them, who had been in it: Kovanski and a funny sort of a square man.' This didn't convey the idol in the least, and he wondered how it could be done. 'He was in the Russian Navy, I think. It was very odd the way they talked in front of foreigners – as if it was all the same to them and they rather more enjoyed seeing their own people making fools of themselves, or running away, than otherwise; they made everything ridiculous, and everyone, high and low, a laughing-stock!'

The four faces round the card-table were returning to his mind, so vividly that he forgot he was trying to explain something to Madame Solario. Kovanski's face while he was telling those stories – it was there again, and for a few seconds he was talking and exploding with laughter soundlessly and uncannily in Bernard's retrospection, as in a peep-show, an action that one can see but not hear.

'Kovanski said the most,' he resumed after the brief pause. 'He didn't hold anything back, and it was all just a huge joke to him.'

Stillness was usual with her. One had no clue to what she was thinking.

'There was nothing he wasn't willing to say.'

Bitterness had got into his voice; one might have thought

that he bitterly resented the aspersions on the competence of the Russian high command. She was surprised, perhaps, and with the point of her parasol she traced one and then another small figure in the dusty ground.

'That's why I said they seemed different from other people!'

But, interested, mystified, by everything she did, his eyes noted what she had written on the ground. It was a letter, the letter C repeated three times. Then she interlaced two C's together, but after that she glanced up.

'Is this cabalistic writing?' he asked.

She gave her little laugh and effaced the C's.

'I didn't know what I was doing. I was thinking of something else – of what you were saying.'

'His stories were extremely amusing,' said Bernard, the bitterness gone out of his voice. 'There was one about a cow. A general had been ordered a milk diet, and during the campaign he took his cow with him –'

'Ah! la vache du Général Stackelberg!' she murmured, looking down at her parasol, which was obliterating all trace of the C's.

'You have heard him tell it! He does it very amusingly, doesn't he?'

'Yes, very amusingly.'

Bernard could see her mysterious smile of reminiscence, and he was tormented and fascinated at one and the same time.

'Do you think it's true?'

She just perceptibly shrugged her shoulders.

'He told other stories too. I wonder if you've heard the others.'

'He talks a great deal about the war,' she said in a tone he didn't know how to interpret.

Her knowledge of Kovanski made her still more fascinating.

'And what is he doing now? He isn't out of the Army, is he?'

'No.'

'Then why is he here?' And at that point he realized that though he and she were talking like this, no one left at the hotel had probably any idea that she and Kovanski had ever met.

She was not unwilling to answer. 'A good many officers made themselves unpopular when they got back from Manchuria. They talked too much, so they were given reasons to go abroad.'

'Reasons?'

'Opportunities. Now Count Kovanski is staying abroad as a military attaché.'

'If he stays any longer in this place,' said Bernard, discovering his purpose and taking the plunge, 'I may have to leave. I don't know how it will come about, but yet I can't but think it may.'

She turned to him, and in suspense he saw her face, her face in the softness of its colouring, for a whole moment before he was aware of something more: her expression, which was of an unusual inquiry.

'It sounds very conceited, I'm afraid. Why should anyone pay me the compliment of asking me to go? You must think me –'

'No, not conceited,' she said. She added, 'I'm sorry.'

'Then I *may* have to go!'

He had the feeling of a swinging downwards, a big drop.

'I don't see why you should,' she answered, with so little stress that his exclamation became rather too dramatic. 'Why I am sorry is that you should have thought so, even for a moment. I'm sorry that there should have been anything disagreeable.'

'There hasn't been – please don't think that! Only it couldn't but occur to me –'

'I don't see why you should go,' she repeated, which had the effect of a little phrase used while she was thinking of something else.

'If you tell me I need not,' he said, with a wonderful reversal of feeling, a swing upward, 'nothing would matter in the least.'

'It depends upon you,' said Madame Solario. Her smile rewarded him already for his resoluteness. 'But what made you think –'

'Well, you know,' he answered, his voice giddy with delight, 'in the stories about Africa that one used to read, a man finds warning signs put in his way by his enemies – a branch pointing in a particular direction, or a little heap of bones.'

Her laugh had a genuine sound. For the first time that morning he had inspired her laugh.

'Don't notice a little heap of bones or whatever it may be.'

'A dead carrion crow. It might even be something quite nasty!'

'Would you find it too disagreeable?'

'No. Not if it was of no consequence to you.'

She evidently decided that they had been explicit enough.

'At least don't go away –' Instead of him, she now regarded a horse-chestnut leaf as it came slowly, spirally, floating down to the ground. 'Don't go away without letting me know.'

'I can promise you that!'

'And let me know also if there is anything disagreeable,' she murmured, so vaguely that her words were like the ghosts of words.

He resisted this in silence. Then: 'Can I ask *you* something? I wonder if you would promise me –'

'What?'

'Not to go away without telling me first.'

'I promise,' she said, smiling at him directly, indulgently. 'I promise you.'

He thought: No more of *that* anxiety. He lost himself in relief.

'And it isn't just yet?'

'I am still waiting for news of my friends.' This sounded more intimate and confidential than it would have done a little time before. 'I won't go until I hear from them, as we might miss each other, and then we might not be able to meet again.'

'Your friends –' A new anxiety was created. The term could conceal something, someone, that would come as a shock. 'Is it a party of them?'

'There are two of them – an old gentleman, an old American gentleman who was a friend of my father's, and his niece.'

It was another surprise – an old American gentleman! – and again relief.

'And you – are you free to stay as long as you like?' asked Madame Solario.

'I still have nearly a month in which I can do, really, just as I please.' And he explained his circumstances to her.

She listened closely all the while; then she rose and they started off again – not onwards, but downwards. But though they were on their homeward way, he was not on his way to the end as he had been at the beginning. Going downhill they did not talk very

95

much, but there was harmony in everything, in their easy movement and their silence within the larger silence of the wood. And the wood, with its glades and depths pervaded by sunlight against which the foliage looked transparent, was like a painted wood, more beautiful than real, like the lilac in her hat. He almost saw themselves from without, two figures in the painted scene – a feminine figure full of grace, and a bare-headed young man in white flannels and a blue blazer.

Even so, Kovanski wove in and out of his thoughts, and at one such moment, as if she were with him there, Madame Solario asked, 'What did you say the other three were like?'

He described them as best he could, and enjoyed doing it. She laughed over the glass of brandy that the idol had kept balanced on his head. She had never met the three, and it was fun to talk about them; but when he was trying to give an idea of Kovanski's conversation he found difficulty for himself and met reticence in her. At one point she paused and said, 'Listen!' and he thought that she had heard a voice, that Kovanski was upon them.

'What is it?'

'Don't you hear a stream?'

It was true; some way off water was falling.

'We didn't hear it on our way up. I wonder why not.'

'What is his Christian name?' asked Bernard.

It was a second or two before she told him. 'Mihail,' she said.

'And then I saw them again upstairs,' said Bernard. 'They were all of them in the passage on the second floor, surrounding someone and making him talk, and laughing and shaking him at every word.'

'Ah, yes!' she said, comprehending at once.

'Do you know –'

'It might have been a servant,' she replied indifferently, not as though she had been taken off her guard. But the suspicion that she knew 'my orderly, Pavlusha', halted him, and, then she remarked, 'It would be like them, and if you don't know who it was – With their servants they are very despotic, and very familiar.'

It was part of her knowledge of him.

With a glance of significance, amusement and invitation to

96

him to be amused, she asked, 'You didn't find a dead bird afterwards in the corridor?'

'I'm not sure that I didn't!' he said, eagerly answering that glance. No matter now, but, when he was trying to pass, Kovanski had moved farther out into the passage so that Bernard had been obliged to go close to the wall; the lack of recognition of him was characteristically insolent. 'I'm rather sorry it wasn't a bigger one!'

'Sorry! Do you like such things? But we are joking. And I am glad we have had this talk. I wouldn't want you to go away with a wrong impression.'

'I'm not going away!'

By chance the unevenness of the ground just there – a straggling root to be stepped over – brought them to a pause, face to face.

'How will I know when you'll want to go out for another walk with me? May I come to ask you?'

'Do it –' she said. 'Do it when – Or rather wait; yes, wait till I let you know.' He saw that he mustn't hang about her, that there was need for caution. 'There's always a way,' she added, smiling. 'You will see!'

'I'll wait for a sign,' he said as they walked on.

'What! More signs! You must be collecting them! What shall it be?'

'A flower, of course. Couldn't you drop an oleander flower when you would let me come and speak to you?'

'There are red oleanders and white –'

'They could mean different things. The red that I can come at once, the white, within the next hour.'

It was another occasion on which he was showing a self-confidence that he didn't know he possessed.

The roofs below came into sight; they were passing the spot where they had looked down at the Bellevue. The cobbled steps began, and the first intruder disturbed him here. It was an old peasant woman with a hod on her back, coming down the mountain, clop-clop, on her wooden pattens.

'Would you let me take you to Balbianello?' Bernard was about to ask, when the old woman pushed past them. One might have thought she didn't see them and wasn't conscious of pushing past, and as she went on ahead, not having even raised her eyes, she was so dismally drab in her dark stuff dress and black headkerchief that one saw her belonging to the sad earth-race for whom they had the intangibility of celestial beings – or hotel guests, which was the same thing.

Bernard was again about to ask the question that was charged with meaning for him when Madame Solario said, 'I have no idea what time it is.'

He put off asking. He was so full of hopes that he felt he had only to wait a little, a day or two, to ask her.

They parted in front of the shops; she went into one of them, and he walked alone to the hotel. He walked on air.

That afternoon he was drawn into a party whose object was tea at the German villa beyond Tremezzo. He was not averse to going, but he was entirely absent-minded; he couldn't fix his attention on anything. The girls seemed very young and rather silly, even Belle Leroy, and he had never liked any of the young men. Coming home, they passed the last steamer of the day as it was leaving Tremezzo, and the sight of it made him remember it on another evening, remember in every detail the return in the row-boat. This was a different sort of evening, without flame, all pale, the lake like aquamarine, but it was the same hour, the hour that kept bringing different experiences. The very hour increased the intensity of his desire to arrive.

As soon as he got out he looked up at the terrace. There were the groups as usual awaiting the steamer from Como, that daily event that he now never missed. Madame Solario was standing with the Lastacoris, and she didn't look in his direction when he came up the water-steps. But Missy provided him with an excuse; he followed her, and, being welcomed by the Marchesa, he stayed beside them.

The high-pitched voices around him were merely noise. Then someone said, 'There aren't many people on the boat tonight.'

The little white steamer nosed up to the landing-stage, and there was the usual scurry, shouting of sailors and throwing of ropes, with luggage being deftly handed overboard. A small crowd of dull figures, disappointments, got off first, and after them a single passenger of another sort stepped on to the gangplank and came ashore. He was a man of about thirty, rather tall, rather slenderly built, wearing a brown suit and a brown Homburg hat, and carrying a light fawn overcoat over his arm. At once he became a focus of feminine interest, for he was well dressed and very good-looking. His moustache was golden-brown and brushed up from his lips. His eyes, which were brown, scanned the faces nearest him on his way to the hotel, slipped over several, and then rested for a moment on Madame Solario. He stopped to look again, to stand in front of her.

'Nelly!' he said.

Madame Solario stood still as a statue till he put out his hand, when she gave him hers, which he clasped in both his. Then as he looked aside at the faces, obviously interested, of her friends, she laughed – her little laugh repeated two or three times. Singling out the Marchesa among the on-lookers, she said to her, 'This is my brother. Let me present my brother, Eugene Harden.'

Part Two

Chapter Ten

The brother and sister turned away together after the introduction and hand-shaking.

'What are you going to do?' she asked as, under acute observation, they crossed to the door of the hotel.

'I am in your hands,' he said in a suave and pleasant tone. 'You must tell me, Nelly.'

He held the door open for her, and they went in. She looked around, but there was no one in the hall to provide any intervention or postponement; instead, the clerk of the *Récéption* sat as if waiting for them at his desk.

'Have you got a room engaged?' she asked, looking not at her brother but about her, with a smile for those who were not there but who would have been observing them.

'No,' he answered pleasantly.

'Will you ask for one?'

He made a deprecating gesture that was half a bow. 'It is for you to say. I am your guest.'

She went up to the desk with her unhurrying step, told the clerk that her brother had arrived unexpectedly, and asked if there was a room.

The clerk consulted the framed list of visitors; he opened a ledger and ran his finger down the page.

'On the same floor as Madame's – the second,' he said in French with his Italian accent.

She looked at her brother then, and he made another little bow.

'Cela va bien,' she said.

The clerk opened the visitors' book, and Harden put his overcoat down on a chair in order to sign his name. Like his sister's sometimes, his smile hovered without fully declaring itself, but this, on his mouth, produced an expression different from hers. A white scar notched his cheek just under the cheek-bone.

'Ah, la même adresse que Madame,' said the clerk, betraying a little surprise as he took back the book.

'C'est pour le moment une poste restante pour moi, je suis beaucoup en voyage,' answered Harden blandly, and she confirmed what he said with her smile.

People were coming in on their way to dress for dinner. Her brother said in her ear, 'I will see to my luggage,' and left her, and his overcoat lying over the arm of the chair. It was quite new and of the best quality, and after a downward glance at it she raised her eyes to Colonel Ross, who was exclaiming, 'I didn't know you were expectin' your brother!'

'I didn't get his telegram to say he was coming today.'

But this was an occasion when a look from her violet-blue eyes was not enough.

'You know I was expecting friends. I thought he would come with them, but he has come a little sooner.'

Colonel Ross's curiosity was, plainly, still unsatisfied.

'It is a pity I didn't receive his telegram, because I would have been more ready to meet him. I haven't seen him for many years.'

'Ah!' said Colonel Ross, as though the target had been hit at last.

'It has happened like that, that we have lived in different countries and haven't seen each other for a long time.'

Harden now entered the front door, followed by a porter carrying two suitcases.

'What did you say his name was?' asked Colonel Ross with a new sort of inquisitiveness.

'Eugene Harden.'

'I've always been proud to claim you as a country-woman,' he said, pumping for information, and she gave him the silence that admitted what he claimed, but nothing more.

He at once spoke to Harden, as from an established friendliness that could dispense with the formality of introduction. 'I hope you have come to stay and not to take your sister away from us. We couldn't forgive you for that!'

'If she wanted to leave I would try to persuade her not to,' said Harden. 'I've never been here before. It seems a charming place.'

'One thinks at first there's nothing to do, but it's surprisin' how pleasant that is. They're talkin' of makin' a golf-course above Menaggio, but I think it'd spoil the place. It'd bring too many people.'

'Ah, yes,' said Harden with a natural, easy manner. 'One would like to keep it away from the crowd.'

Colonel Ross's expression was naïvely puzzled because he was trying to put Eugene Harden into a class. Though without a foreign accent, Harden didn't seem quite like an Englishman. He was not, according to Colonel Ross's conceptions, either the right kind or the wrong kind of Englishman. Not quite English, yet too English to be foreign – one couldn't tell, in short, where he belonged. During these exchanges Madame Solario stood beside Colonel Ross, and her brother was in front of them; it was as if they two were together and he were by himself. And during this time her eyes casually passed over the two suitcases, whose fine new leather had not been defaced by a single hotel label.

'Well, I hope I'll see you after dinner. Will you both be dinin' with the Lastacoris?'

'No. I wonder,' she said, 'if you would tell the head-waiter to give us a table to ourselves?'

And on his assuring her he would go at once to do her bidding – and while her brother was engaged with the concierge, who had come to speak to him – she stepped to the lift and was taken out of sight.

They were given a table in the middle of the dining-room, and when they came in, when he was handing her to her chair, they were looked at. He was impeccably turned out; she was wearing a *demi-toilette* of mauve chiffon *plissé soleil*; no hat that evening covered her fair hair. The fact that they were brother and sister and that there was a resemblance between them, in features and build, made this extraordinarily good-looking pair still more interesting. The obvious affinity that was there seemed to enhance the total effect; because of it they were even more striking together than either would have been alone. When they were waiting to be served she rested her elbow on the table and he leaned forward with a look of intimacy. Yet it was impossible for anyone to catch a word that the brother and sister were saying; possible only to deduce at the beginning from his gesture to call the wine-waiter that he wished to order something festive, perhaps champagne, and that she demurred. Their talk was inaudible even to their neighbours. He too sometimes rested his elbows on the table when waiting for her replies, to which he would respond with amused astonishment, with raised eyebrows or a laugh. He looked at her the while with great insistence. She sometimes looked down, and when she was looking down, her smile was like a faint reflection of her state of mind. She helped herself to the dishes, one after the other, and delicately and deliberately she went through the motions of removing the bones from the trout, of cutting her meat, of raising the fork to her lips; but almost nothing passed her lips. And the over-deliberate motions without practical result, the graceful attitudes and the soundless conversation, could have suggested a shadow-play, some highly polished form of evocative illusion.

There was this artistry on the one hand, and, on the other, a rather crude manifestation of impertinent curiosity. It was displayed at the Lastacoris' table, with Missy laughing and talking her most, the very personification of malice. The older ones were not overtly looking, but when Harden glanced that way he could guess from the faces who was the subject of talk. The Lastacoris' table was in front of a large open window, and Harden's glance dwelt for some moments on the window, which framed the night outside and trees made visible by little coloured lights. Then he spoke to his sister with a broader smile that caused a sudden twitching of his scarred cheek. She serenely met the eye of someone at the next table and bent to catch what was being said to her. She answered, and it was all done to perfection.

Soon after the first move had been made to leave the dining-room, the brother and sister rose and went out. A table for one behind the column near the door had already been vacated.

The night had an air of fête. Coloured lights were hung in the trees along the front of the hotel, and a local crowd had gathered on the road by the embarcadero. A rocket rushed up into the sky from a point on the right and exploded with a hissing sound into a rain of stars. The fireworks, having started, continued spasmodically for a time, and the hotel guests came out good-humouredly to see. The brother and sister went out too. On her way through the hall Madame Solario, though it was still so warm outside, took up the lace wrap that she had left before dinner on one of the chairs that were reserved for Marchesa Lastacori's party; she might have been withdrawing from the circle. Outside, her brother took the wrap from her and placed it on her shoulders. Bernard was standing under the trees, and as she received the light flounce and adjusted it she looked straight at him, without apparent recognition and without a smile, and he answered her look in the same way. Then she and her brother – it seemed vaguely, and with no set purpose – moved apart from the company.

They reached the arbour at the corner. There was a choice to be made – to return or to go on beyond the last lamp. After a moment they went on, into the unlit plane-tree walk.

When they had gone a little way – 'Where have you been all these years?' she asked.

'I don't think I will tell you that.'

It was so quiet that one could hear the rustle of a silk lining that accompanied her steps.

'You knew I was here?'

'But of course! Do you think we have met again by accident?' He divined her question and answered it. 'It was quite easy to find out!'

'I never knew where you were,' she said.

'And I always knew where you were. Not always exactly at the moment; but sooner or later. When I was ready to join you I was able to come almost straight.'

'Why wasn't it before?' And, as though it were an effort to say it, she stopped beside the lake wall, half turning from him. 'Why is it here – and now?'

'For several reasons, and you shall know every one.'

They both were looking outwards. The shape of the opposite mountain had a liquid, absolute blackness like that of its double projected across the lake; one could see no difference between the two. For the night was perfectly still. There was not even a whisper of water against the wall.

'And for several reasons I haven't come till now. Sometimes, I admit, it was force of circumstances, but sometimes my own free will.' His intonation had a remarkable lightness and lack of emphasis; his words seemed to float from him. 'I stayed away while you had a husband to be embarrassed, but now you are separated from your husband and I need have no scruples. I have none, I must tell you, Nelly.' He gave her time, but she made no answer. 'Why should I? You were the cause; I blame only you.'

By a sort of crystallization in the atmosphere of her silence his words gathered weight.

'And you were the only one who never suffered. You didn't even shed tears, though you might have been sure your tears would be becoming. I won't speak of a broken heart – that can't be seen – but a ruined life is demonstrable. My life was ruined, or you would have known where I had been all these years.'

She moved then, away from the low wall.

'I didn't come back when I would have been paid to go away again. And I hoped I might come back with a little glory – at one time it seemed possible. I used my little bit of Harden money in a grand attempt – that failed. As it is, I have come back with nothing but the sense of what is owing to me.'

'Is it quite simple?' she asked, and it had an effect that she had spoken at all.

'No, not quite simple. A great deal is owing us. *Us*, I say! You know who I mean. But something is quite simple. We'll speak only of that.'

'What is it?' she asked without haste.

'I take it as owing me – *me*, I say now – to share everything you have.'

They were walking past the huge trunks of the plane trees, which were pale in the darkness.

'I have been here for several hours already. You are not being surprised!' said Harden.

'What do you think it is?' she asked then.

'What am I to share?'

The rockets suddenly soared up again from a point beyond Villa Carlotta, and music came into hearing from the same direction, the music of guitars and singing out on the lake.

'Let's say your life, the kind of life I was deprived of.'

'That's not so simple,' she said.

'You think not?'

'It would have been better for you to come back before – when there were others.'

'Better for you!'

'Not only that. You could have got something more substantial if you had come sooner.'

'Whatever I get now, it will seem riches to me.'

With the music and voices that were approaching like an interruption – and in the green glare of the fireworks, which exposed the place where they were, which before had been deep in shadow – his tone changed; it, too, came out of its shadows. He returned to what had gone before, which he then had let pass.

'You said you never knew where I was, but you must have known when you went to South America that I was still there. I wonder you took the risk! The Plata was between us,' he added with a kind of laugh, 'but I could have crossed it!'

He looked at her, while she seemed to heed only what was coming towards them.

'I didn't cross it, because I wouldn't so ill repay the chivalrous gentleman who had married you. I don't think money was everything to him. He married you on the assumption that the scandal could be forgotten. I was the walking reminder of it! I'm still inconvenient – it must be very inconvenient to have a forgotten brother rise up as through a trap-door at your feet – before everyone – but now I am not inconveniencing the chivalrous gentleman, but only you.'

'What is there now to share?' said his sister, going to meet what was coming.

'Your chances. With a woman the last word is never said.'

A festal procession that had been screened by the trees of the point emerged into full view, and the music swelled into fullness with it. The musicians were in the leading boat, which was lit by Chinese lanterns and propelled by two gondoliers, and a man's rich voice was singing an operatic air. The boats that followed in single file were surmounted by arches covered with flowers and hung with lanterns; garlands of flowers were trailing out in each wake, and little lights closely studded the gunwales. Ladies in

109

light gowns and cloaks and their cavaliers in evening dress were being rowed by smart boatmen in white sailor-suits. It was a pretty sight; the boats looked like costly toys drawn over a black mirror. A dark crowd of people and children was keeping abreast on the shore path. Their voices rose with each explosion of the fireworks.

'Your chances,' said Harden, speaking faster. 'And you may do much more brilliantly yet. It wasn't very brilliant the first time. Even with the walking reminder at your side you can do better!' The crowd came round the corner just ahead and burst into the avenue. 'I mean to share your future, as well as your fortune now.'

'I have very little fortune,' said Madame Solario.

'Come, now!' said her brother.

'Where should it come from?' she asked.

'Where from?' His irony was malignant. Running children bumped into them. 'Do I have to tell you?'

'I am separated from my husband.' And as if people, strangers, around them could make her speak more naturally, she said with actual bitterness, 'Why should I be rich?'

'What about that fortune that was considered fabulous? Wasn't most of it left to you?'

People of no consequence were hurrying past and even coming between them.

'Carlos had his own children. What of them?'

'Carlos!' he exclaimed with a loud laugh that visibly pierced her armour. 'We used to call him Papa!'

She betrayed an impulse to draw away, putting out her hand to get clear of a little boy.

'There at home, where we were like his children!' He was at her side again. 'We were a family, I respected him – and she – And you going to school, with a governess – in schoolgirl clothes with your hair not up! How did it begin? What was the first step? *Where?* And you could carry it on, saying, "Bonjour, Papa!" "Bonsoir, Papa!"' His voice shook when he was imitating an innocent 'Bonsoir, Papa!' 'I try to see through it all, through the wall into the room. But what drove me to do what I did – or tried to do – How terrible,' he said, as about something he was thinking, not saying. 'How terrible. You don't know what the remorse has been, nor why. You felt nothing! And now – for you it's all so long ago. But not for me!'

He suddenly and suspiciously glanced around him. The crowd and the louder sounds were receding towards the hotel, but a few figures were discernible stopped beside the wall, quite near; they were talking low. The rockets only occasionally went up.

'And yet – at the same time as remorse – you speak of his fortune,' said Madame Solario in the tone of a mere observation. She was watching the procession that was floating past in front of them.

She seemed indifferent to the risk of his violence, but instead of being roused to it again he answered calmly.

'There are several aspects to the situation, my dear sister. Many aspects have presented themselves to me during these long years. There were the relations between one and the other of us four, all those relationships, that tortured me when I could only think about them and do nothing else. What is left, all that's left, are the relations between you and me. That's outside the tragedy. For there is one injustice that can be put right.'

The boat that came last was the prettiest of all. It was a bower of white roses, delicately lit, a little porcelain scene enclosed by the night, and a lady in white was leaning back alone against green cushions, while her companion seemed to be sitting at her feet.

'Do you see?' said Harden. 'It is you! That should be you! I could believe I had seen this before – I have seen you in that boat!'

The procession glided on with the motion of swans.

'There you go, though I was cast out!'

A peasant boat with the top that looks like the spine and ribs of a whale followed soon after, a man standing up and gondoliering as the peasants do. Closer in shore than the wake of light, he and his boat were a silhouette that was slipping by.

'Look!' said Harden. There was no doubt what he meant. He turned to her, and his voice shook with triumph. 'Look! *Do you remember how I used to like stories about shadows?*'

'He'll go on and fish,' she observed.

He changed his meaning easily, with a laugh. 'That may be. But have you heard of the children of light and the children of darkness?' The peasant boat did not seem to be within range of

111

the music; it gave the impression of going in darkness and silence. 'There they are. My sense of brotherhood is strong with the children of darkness. But I mean to be in the other boat, with you.'

The procession was disappearing round the next point. 'I wouldn't have accepted it from him,' he said, referring without explanation to their previous subject, 'but I will take it from you.'

'But it has gone elsewhere,' she said.

'I'm not so sure!' he answered, gripping her arm. 'We'll see!'

When he released her she made a movement to go back to the hotel. But then she saw that only one person was there where before there had been half a dozen; the others had walked on. This man was standing alone, as if lost in contemplation of the lake. She checked her movement.

'Do you know who that is?' her brother asked in a low voice.

Even in the dusk it was obvious that the man was not a peasant.

'We won't go back yet,' said Harden when the man had started to walk away. 'You and I, Nelly – isn't it strange? Don't you think it is very strange?' That urbanity of his was the suitable mask for a cat-like cruelty. 'There is so much to say that I don't know where to begin. Who – how many – But it's too soon to ask you that. Well, let's go back; it will all come out gradually. Now about that fortune – I have no delicacy in speaking about it. So much has been trodden down, down into the mire.' After a moment – 'Weren't you left a good part of it?'

When she didn't answer he peered at her, and he saw that just then she could not, rather than would not, answer – fatigue or lassitude, she was physically unable. Their steps came almost to a standstill.

'Weren't you?'

'It was not what you thought,' she said, forcing herself, 'not fabulous.'

'How one can never foresee!' he said with humour and nothing else. 'One is always following a twisting, turning track! But still I am not convinced. I hadn't heard this story of yours. It may be true. There were some things I couldn't find out or hear. Now, of course, I can. But in any case I find you in this fashionable, expensive place, beautifully dressed, and so far it's all as I imagined

112

it would be. And you see I am not disgracing you – on the contrary. I too am beautifully dressed. And I will let you at once into my confidence. I sold the very last asset that remained from my last effort to make my own fortune, and I stopped in London on my way to Paris and equipped myself. My clothes are English – the very best, you see. I have already tipped the porter here handsomely, and am established in the hotel as a guest of importance. A new life, your kind of life, has begun for me. But from now on I am entirely dependent on you.'

They were walking back slowly, and in the dark Harden was talking, inclined towards her ear.

'Tragedy is behind us. We have stepped into another story. And yet, of course, nothing is simple. Your position is not secure, my poor sister! It may look so on the surface, but you are still at the mercy of *incidents*. Incidents! That's what one has to fear when one hasn't a family behind one – which is what you and I haven't got. From force of circumstances – force of circumstances,' he added hastily, dropping into sincerity as if it had been a snare. He disengaged himself from it. 'The protection of family – it's needed even in the pampas! Here we are – here I am, and I have reached one of my goals, and it's very nice for me; I am very pleased. But everything isn't quite simple. Not for you and me.'

He again came to a stop.

'Nelly,' he said, while she continued evenly – and in his voice were several shades to make up the sum of its malice. 'At dinner I saw – and you must have seen, too – they were talking about us! What do you think they know?'

He caught up with her.

'Those people – the lady to whom you presented me; the name was Italian, a Marchesa – why were they laughing so peculiarly? Of course there was that little moment of suspension when we met – things were evidently not quite ordinary. But my highly trained instinct tells me there was more than that. What do you suppose –'

'I don't know. I met them only last year.'

'Were there any French people at that table?'

'No.'

'Are there any French people at the hotel who might have

heard of our family history?' He pressed his questions with enjoyment.

But her readiness now to reply gave her answers the sound of indifference. 'There were some French people here, but they have left – one yesterday and two the day before.'

'Who were they?'

'They were a Monsieur et Madame d'Antin, and a young man called Maxime Guimard.'

'The name is unsympathetic, but otherwise says nothing. But, though we may never have heard of them, they may have heard of us, because there is more to hear. Let's wait a minute and think it over.'

They were reaching the first lamp.

'Nelly, what shall we do? Here I am, the walking reminder, at your side, and they looked at us very significantly.' He still spoke with enjoyment – as it were playing with his manner. 'Shall we *not* give these particular people the chance to whisper about us? Shall we go straight into the hotel, and leave tomorrow morning?'

'If you like,' she answered.

She had come into the light of the lamp, and the purity of her expression was unmarred – the eyebrows raised a little thoughtfully.

'Your nerves are under iron control, I see, as they always were.' He spoke out of hatred. 'They need to be. This evening must have been a trying experience, but not so trying as some you have passed through.'

At the same time they went forward, and he could feel that it was not only composure, but a restored, mysterious inner rhythm that was carrying her so smoothly.

114

Chapter Eleven

With the little lamps dyeing their leaves in different colours, the row of trees, in which not a breath stirred, had a charmingly unnatural aspect; the company was assembled under them, and evening gowns looked exotic in that setting out-of-doors. When the brother and sister were in front of the hotel door they paused. They were by themselves, and all the others together.

Then Colonel Ross saw them and called out, 'We've decided to award a Bellevue prize. Come help us judge' – which tipped the balance for Harden. And as they came forward Missy Lastacori detached herself from somewhere and put herself directly in their way.

'Oh, Mr Harden,' she said, laughing and addressing him in her own particular style, 'we are so glad to meet Natalia's brother! But why didn't she tell us you were arriving?'

'You must ask her,' he said. 'Perhaps she didn't think you would be interested to know.'

'Of course we would be interested!' Her chin was tilted up, her laughter gurgled, she shook her hand to send her tinkling bracelets over her wrist. 'And where have you come from?'

'From Turkey,' he answered promptly, returning her bold look.

'Turkey!' she cried. 'Have you been for many years in Turkey? We wondered where Mr Harden had come from, and he has come from Turkey!' she said to one of the hangers-on. 'And what have you been doing there?'

'I was a very private secretary to the Grand Vizier.' And as she laughed more and more he added blandly, 'And you have no idea what goes on upon the Bosphorus!'

'No, really?'

'I assure you!'

'We must hear. We must hear, mustn't we?' But her mother sternly called, 'Missy!' and the girl turned away from him, obeying a warning.

'What shall the prize be? Who will offer something?'

Colonel Ross was saying confidentially, '*I* knew she was expectin' him any day.'

Some distance out, the boatmen were resting on their oars; the procession had broken up into a haphazard formation of boats whose lights undulated like serpents over the water. The music came softly across. On the terrace, a little apart, were those guests who were not in hotel society, and farther away the villagers had congregated. Madame Solario had been alone for a minute when her brother was engaged by Missy Lastacori, but only for a minute. Count Mosca approached her and asked if he could present the Marchese di San Rufino, who had arrived with his wife the day before. San Rufino was there, waiting. He had a goat-like length of face, ending in a pointed, jet-black beard, and he wore a single eyeglass. His expression – which, like that of goats and unlike that of sheep, was not in the least vacant – did not change when the introduction solicited by him had been effected, and this frigidity suggested a perfectly conceited consciousness of being who he was; of what *she* was conscious was the enigma of her beauty.

He said, 'Vous êtes ici depuis quelque temps, Madame?'

Colonel Ross was asking various ladies if they could suggest a prize, and he asked Madame Solario, 'What would *you* like, if it were you?'

'Do you think a fan would be nice?' she said.

'A fan! What a capital idea. Who would be willing to give a fan?'

'Un éventail?' said San Rufino. He took out his eyeglass and replaced it with an effect of suddenly intensified concentration. 'Pour qui?'

'Dites, votre voix pourrait être décisive.' Stepping indolently to the parapet, she indicated the spread-out galaxy of boats.

'Ce n'est pas ça qui m'intéresse,' said San Rufino.

Colonel Ross was announcing that the Marchesa San Rufino had kindly offered a fan of her own as a prize. The pattern changed. The boats landed their occupants, who were received

116

with great animation; the prize was awarded to the lady of the white rose bower, who was known to them all.

Madame Solario and Mosca were sitting on two little iron chairs while this was going on. He was informing her *sotto voce* that San Rufino was the nephew of the powerful minister and was Chef de Cabinet, and there were other relatives in the ministry. These great Sicilian families held together like medieval clans – into her listening came a gleam of some ironic thought – and when one of them got into power this became serious. San Rufino's wife was perhaps English, of very ambiguous origin, but had brought him an enormous fortune.

'Her fan was exquisite,' she said.

She saw, then, her brother sitting on the parapet of the terrace at a point just opposite to her. He was striking a match to light his cigarette, and when he protected the flame with his hands his face was for a few seconds intimately illumined against the background of night: the golden-brown moustache brushed away from lips whose cut it was that gave the illusion of a smile, as in certain classic statues; the rounded, cleft chin; the pale tan of his complexion. The fingers outlined by the flame were long and fine. His sister's eyes were not the only ones that were fastened by this glimpse of a face. Missy, moving rapidly as always, came to sit on the parapet near him.

San Rufino drew up another little iron chair and established himself on the other side of Madame Solario. He and Mosca exchanged phrases while her eyes roamed over the figures within her view. The young people were sitting in a line on the parapet, and she said, 'They look like swallows perched on a telegraph wire.'

Because she had spoken to Mosca, San Rufino at once claimed a corresponding attention for himself. She turned her head – only a little, not her full face – to him.

'Vous n'avez pas trouvé que c'était joli?' she said.

Among the young people, but in a way not of them, was Bernard Middleton. An unhappy absence of mind put him quite outside the general gaiety. Madame Solario regarded him for a few moments but didn't catch his look.

The musicians' boat with its Chinese lanterns was moored to the landing-stage. 'He has a pretty voice,' she said of the singer.

'C'est l'Italie pour les étrangers,' San Rufino said to her.

'Accordez-nous cela,' she answered, her face, above the lace flounce that one hand held in place, turning to him now.

The song had come to an end, but the guitars were still being thrummed when Missy's voice was heard. It was at first a trill in her throat and a burst of melody; then, when she saw that Harden was surprised, from that humming she began to sing the words of a Neapolitan song; the guitars took up the accompaniment. Harden's surprise and admiration were subtly conveyed. He looked only at her lips and didn't appear to be aware that she was singing just for him. At the end of the song she laughed, and her laughter, too, vibrated in her throat, and he rather slowly looked higher, from her lips to her eyes. She spoke first to him, not he to her, and she took the lead impudently, but also beguilingly.

There was a dreamlike moment of time when the figures under the lighted trees and those sitting on the wall with the darkness behind them seemed touched by a spell into stillness. Then Marchesa Lastacori exclaimed, 'Missy!' again, on the note of exasperation that, to her family, boded nerves and 'scenes'. Missy quickly got up, and Harden was left by himself noticeably in isolation. But it happened that soon Madame Solario and San Rufino got up too, and San Rufino introduced his wife, who wasn't far away.

The Marchesa San Rufino's ambiguous origin could not immediately be detected under the stamp of her smartness and her own kind of conceit. Her technique was to be very cordial when and if she was polite at all, and she narrowed her eyes as though she wished to see better, and spoke with short rushes in a husky voice. The Lastacoris were close by. Madame Solario met the cordiality retiringly, almost in silence, and, having rounded off the business, said, 'Eugene –' But the Marchesa San Rufino detained them by asking to have him presented to her. After that the sister and brother separated themselves from the company and went indoors.

She entered the lift, and he followed her; they went up together and walked along the passage on the second floor. His room, giving upon the front, came first; hers was at the end of the passage.

118

As she was going past his door he said, 'Won't you come in?'

She went in. He switched on the light, shut the door, and said, 'No one can be surprised if you come into your brother's room.'

She stayed near the door, and he walked over to the window and let down the venetian blind – slowly, looking at the scene below until it had been shut out.

'That was a situation saved!' he said. It was a moment or two before he looked round.

'For their benefit you said, "Eugene" – and the last time I heard you say it was the night you said, "Good-bye, Eugene".' There was a spasm, soon over, in his scarred cheek. 'You didn't stay to see me taken away by the two family friends, who came like policemen, though they were preventing an arrest. *Papa* was in his room, bandaged, in a high fever!' He kept to this form and only laughed. 'I wonder if we'll ever quite bury our past? You saw – the mother!'

He seemed to expect humorous agreement.

'Adventurer that I've had to become, I can appreciate the finest shades of a situation. Sometimes luck depends on time, a minute one way or the other. Tonight was an example, a case of *time*. It was awkward when I was left high and dry! When such a thing happens there must be a diversion – if it comes one thinks one's had a miracle – or one is marked.'

His self-repeating laugh, though so differently meant, had a sort of resemblance to hers.

'Once or twice I've been marked.'

He came to stand in front of her. Her attitude would have been the same had she been listening to Mosca.

'I was left high and dry – planté – and can one believe it was accidental? Even here! I'm almost flattered. But then – you!'

He looked her up and down as if in admiration alone. '*You* made the miracle! And I'm sure you always will. The diversion was so inevitable, it was like a piece of music. That's what I'm going to enjoy – being carried along to music!'

He smiled, with nothing sinister appearing in that subtle and yet natural smile.

'I see you again after nearly twelve years! And you were barely sixteen when *all that* happened on account of you. I've

119

so often wondered – would you have passed your moment of perfection when I saw you again? *Have* you passed it? When was it, do I think? Was it then – or is it now?'

He continued to look at her. 'Would you like to hear what I think?'

She bore his scrutiny as though she didn't feel it.

'As Nelly Harden – Nelly Harden! – or Natalia Solario? Nelly, it makes no difference! I watched – and it's always the same. It's what you are. And you were that at six, at dancing-class in Cincinnati!'

He wouldn't have allowed her to leave, and she did not try. There was no chair close to her, and she sat down on the bed, by the foot-rail, letting her wrap slip from her shoulders with a seductive leisureliness.

'I've no anxieties. I'm safe with you!'

'But *you* are the same as you were,' she said.

'What does that mean?'

A little motion of her brows had significance.

'What was I?' he asked threateningly.

'Very dramatic,' she answered. 'Always that.'

'And why was I?' he asked, violent at once, without transition, 'Because I could feel, and all that happened to us hurt me, hurt me to the soul!'

'It was not only then,' she said.

'You can take it as far back as you like. My first memory is of being hurt because she was. I was dramatic and was laughed at when I tried to protect my mother as a child. Was that absurd?'

'It was not always because you were hurt,' she said.

He had passionately embarked upon his own train of thought. 'I was utterly unlike you, that's why I could suffer for her. How absurd to have had the feeling for my mother that I had, and to tell *you* that when I was a child it was like agony! But that's why I was dramatic, as you say – I had *that* to make me so!'

She observed, 'I think in any case you would have been dramatic.'

'It was that alone. And it was when I saw the supreme hurt that I was driven mad. I wasn't avenging your honour, my dear sister! I would have left your honour to take care of itself!'

She gave no sign to show that he had attained his object.

'That could drive me mad, what I saw in *her* heart and soul. But now nothing can, any more. It's all over.'

He had gone, unconscious of what he was doing, to the dressing-table, to touch something, occupy his hands; then he noticed and picked up one of the new brushes for her to see, and pointed to the two suitcases on the floor, open and half unpacked. He did it with his laugh.

'All that's over now. No reason any more – no reason to go back on what I said, that I'll be safe with you!'

'If you are the same, will you ever be safe, Eugene?'

'There's the deadly, practical woman you always were, even as a child! It wasn't practical to take the matter as I did, was it?'

'What was the result?' she asked, and because of the beauty of her eyes she did not seem to need courage to say it.

'Greater suffering for her,' he answered with extraordinary calmness. 'The last station, perhaps the worst. My remorse for that. That was the only result. But wasn't there cause? To see such anguish, such humiliation!' He was able to express the very taste humiliation had of bitterness.

'I felt everything that she must feel. And did you never – never for a moment?'

She looked down, impassive; her hand smoothed the lace that was lying on her lap.

'How could it happen! *Where did it happen?* You are going to tell me! I have to know!'

There was another oscillation, towards fury.

'When will you tell me?'

'What would it undo if I told you?' she asked.

'It would make everything more horrible. But that's what I want! That's what I must have! The treachery, the sensuality – all that was depraved behind the respectability and the innocence! There was all that on the one hand, and, on the other, pure grief.'

It was the last descent into feeling. That was over. He pushed a chair nearer to her and sat down on it astride, facing her, with his arms folded on the back, and he began to speak with his conversational lack of emphasis, his baleful lightness of tone.

'I've thought about it so much – I shall never rest until I know all. I used to think – in circumstances that I won't describe now – of the house in the Avenue Hoche, and go through all the rooms which I remembered, and still do, very distinctly, and the life as well: the huge dinner parties – at which you and I were too young to be present – on some nights, and then our four selves in our family life. And I used to try to get – I used to try to get it by intuition or a dream – the scene, the scene! And when I have the scene we will all four sit together again – in the blue room, in the evening, as a family.'

He merely smiled.

'Were you an unwilling victim at first, my poor sister? You were certainly seduced, as you were not yet sixteen. Didn't it come at least as a surprise – *Papa*, a man of forty-two? But you ceased to be a victim; you became an accomplice in the long-drawn-out, absolute treachery! And it's the whole story that I want to hear!'

She made a quick, spontaneous gesture – his voice had been suddenly raised. He understood what she meant and stopped; at once he had been put on the alert. He reverted to cynicism.

'Anyone on the next balcony! Or passing by. They would ask themselves!'

He got up, went to the door, and listened; they could hear good nights being said, footsteps, and also a pleasant hum downstairs. The place – that impersonal hotel bedroom, aridly lit by a pendant light from the ceiling – became equivocal and secret when he listened at the door and she turned her head towards it.

'I didn't know for a long time,' he said in an almost low voice, going back to his chair and to the subject. 'She hid it from me. She covered everything. One day I *overheard the servants talking*. Do you understand? The horror seemed for a time to be all in that – that it was like that I heard. Then there was no more concealment.'

He drew his hand over his eyes. 'It's because I didn't know for so long that I'm still pursued by what I still don't know – what I was never told.'

She had put her elbow on the bed-rail and her hand up to her brow. When he saw that, he opened a line of quiet persuasiveness. Someone passing the door would not have heard perhaps even the murmur of a voice. They sat without movement in the hard light that fell from above, she at the foot of the bed and he with his arms folded on the back of his chair. No sort of light could be unbecoming to her, nor indeed to him. In the pauses in which he got no answer he made it seem that he was not yet expecting an answer, only preparing the way for it to be given him, that his patience was infinite. Though the ominous glitter came back now and again, his voice he kept low; its rising inflection on a question had at times a peculiar note of cajolery. But nothing prevailed against her intangible defences. The pauses grew longer. And at a certain moment the realized silence outside was added to the quiet in the room. The room was compressed and isolated by a silence all round it. He listened again.

'No one is about any more. They've all gone to their beds.'

He got up. 'Has your admirer – But you may have several. Have your admirers been thinking about you, do you suppose? However much they may have tried to imagine what you were doing, they won't have arrived at this interview!'

He had gone to the window to pull up the venetian blind. 'Even they may be asleep,' he said as he was doing it.

She rose from the position in which she had been so motionless. Standing, she swayed a little. The blind went up on the sapphire blue of the night sown with stars.

'Not a soul,' he said, gazing out. 'Only ourselves. And those two little lights, opposite.'

The two little points of light at Bellagio were the only human presences in what lay – mountains and dark or silvery, winding shores – beneath the panoply of the sky. But in the air was diffused, as if from near and far, a tinkling sound.

'What is it?' he said, still in an undertone. 'Do you hear? Tiny bells.' And after another minute: 'Are we really here – up here – suspended in this lighted cage, just you and I?'

While he was at the window she said, 'Good night, Eugene.'

He turned to watch her but didn't otherwise stir, as with a pensive languor she picked up her wrap and moved to the door. His expression conveyed: Let's see how you do it! And when she was opening the door he said, 'S-sh!' and laid his finger on his lips.

Chapter Twelve

Madame Solario breakfasted in her room and left it when the morning was well advanced, wearing a light-blue dress and a straw hat trimmed with marguerites. Her brother's door was open – seeing which, she paused on the threshold. The radiant day now filled the room, and reflections from the lake danced in little waves of light on the ceiling.

'I hoped I would see you go by,' he said affably, coming to the door. 'I waited to go out with you. I wanted to do it to music!' he added as they proceeded together.

A number of people were already out, and the brother and sister merged into that number; the young people were the centre of interest at the moment. Bicycles for hire had been discovered, and there was going to be a long bicycle ride to see a ruined castle. But the machines were mostly ancient and dilapidated and were being tried before the start; performers, including some of those older ones who would stay behind, were riding up and down in front of the hotel and sometimes crashing, to great amusement. After a little while Madame Solario took a few steps with the deliberate purpose of speaking to Bernard Middleton, who wasn't performing on a bicycle.

'You are going too?' she asked him, and her look questioned rather specially.

He could say no more than 'Yes.' His mood was too grave to be dispelled, even by her advance. He met her with a sort of searching gravity.

'I think it will be nice,' she said; she could give with her slight utterances the impression that they were not nearly following her thought to the end. 'Where will you go – a long way and not come back till late?'

He tried to fathom her look. Plainly he asked her, had there been anything she wished him to understand?

'I don't very well see them staying the course. I don't think we'll be back late. Supposing we were – It doesn't mean you will be leaving today, does it, before you think we'll have got back?'

'Not today,' she said.

'But it may be soon? That's what I thought. Sooner than you thought yesterday morning.'

'Yes, it might.' She saw his reserve yield to dismay and so she added, 'I said I would let you know.'

'It might be tomorrow?'

For answer she asked, 'Do you remember the oleander blossoms? I forget what the red was to mean, and what the white!'

'How jolly it would be,' he said, trying to suit his manner to the words, 'if one found an oleander flower in one's path!'

'Then it really must be like that,' she said with even a kind of wistfulness.

'So you think I'll get a sign?'

'You see, my brother has come,' she replied more formally, 'and I haven't seen him for a long time.'

'I know, you told me that.'

In this moment there was something he could connect with the confidence he thought he had received the night before.

'We will say, if you don't see the oleander blossom you will know I'm not leaving.'

'Not leaving,' he repeated, as if he were learning a lesson.

Her attention was taken from him then. The Marchesa San Rufino had got on to a bicycle, and was making more of it and being applauded more than anyone else because of being who she was. And Harden was her conductor. The front wheel was wobbling, and he caught hold of the handlebars; he walked beside her, steadying her, and instead of turning when they had gone a little distance she dismounted. A young man had to go and fetch the bicycle, which proved to be the one intended for Missy, and Missy laughed a great deal.

The start was due. The ten or twelve of them got away, passed Harden and the Marchesa San Rufino on the road, and disappeared round the corner, chiffon veils fluttering in the breeze, young voices floating backwards.

Before Bernard had departed from Madame Solario's side

San Rufino had reached it. He came with his eyeglass in his eye, looking inhumanly intelligent.

'Les plaisirs d'une villégiature vous paraissent drôles?' he said.

Eventually they sat down on two of the little iron chairs that were under the trees. His conversation was not abundant; it confined itself to remarks whose object was the focusing of his eyeglass upon her, and these sometimes found her, and left her, glancing reflectively elsewhere. But sometimes they received a little laugh, or a response that curved her lips and even when her lips were closed seemed to linger in the corners of her mouth. Friends of the San Rufinos, who had arrived on the same day as they, were clustered near, with the Marchesa and Harden somewhat apart, her voice emitting a succession of short bass sounds, and his, a baritone, coming rarely but agreeably. All these people were sitting as the Marchesa Lastacori and her entourage of Signorina Petri, Mosca, and Pico strolled past, now walking and now standing still. The two groups continued to be separate.

A little while after that there was a move to do other things, and the Marchesa San Rufino invited Harden to come too, but he thought he could not. He said to his sister, 'Shouldn't we send off that telegram, this morning?'

It was managed suavely and with the proper regrets, and after the feint of a little conference in the hall they went up. He was leading her back to his room.

'I can't bear it!' he said when he had shut the door.

As though their talk had never been interrupted – that talk in which he had failed to get her to tell him what he wanted to know – he burst out, 'How could you do it when you knew she loved him? She didn't marry him for money! Though we were poor she didn't do it for that – you know it. And he wasn't younger than she; he was older. There might have been excuses, but there were none!'

Actual physical pain, or it seemed so, made him lean heavily on a chair.

'It drives me mad when I think of it, still. I've lived ever since with the consequences, *in* the consequences. They caught me like a trap. But there's more! There's my remorse for making her suffer more. And there's the humiliation! Hers, and so differently mine. I can never get over it! She was humiliated, and so was I.'

His emotion vitiated his good looks, which lessened the resemblance between the two faces, for in hers beauty was inviolate.

'I feel my humiliation most when no one else is thinking of it. I felt it this morning. That wasn't what I was born to, to be flattered by the notice of people! And it wasn't what I was born for, to be here without a franc, dependent on you!'

'You said there was an injustice to be put right.' And she made it a simple statement of fact.

'What can be put right? When I thought of you unpunished and rich it was one thing. When I see you it's another. The unnaturalness of what you did!' he said with his ability to give horror to a word. 'To take your mother's husband from her! Our stepfather, who was like a father to us!'

A flush came into her cheeks. He saw it. With his spring the chair was knocked over. She freed her hands from his, and as he scanned her face, letting her go, he knew he had already lost his advantage.

'When you look back what is it you see, of all that happened?' She remained perfectly inaccessible to him.

'Did you hate her because I was her favourite?'

'No!'

He studied her for a time, and then, knowing that he would get nothing, that he had failed once more – 'Did you like him?' he said.

The smile and the ignoble inflections in his voice were back again. 'A South American, blue-shaved and showing his age. An odd fancy for a young girl! But he was clever, he had charm. Or was it the triumph? A triumph – your mother's husband! A sense of power. You could have used your power not only for destruction, but prettily, by helping your brother, let me point out. I could have been brought home in a year or two – but no. He wouldn't forgive. But if you had asked, though it might have taken more than asking – besought, gone down on your knees! *She* will have done that, but that couldn't move him!'

Because he saw that he was defeating his own purpose, he

127

broke. 'I never saw her again, do you understand? I had said good-bye to her in her room that night, before you said, "Good-bye, Eugene". And I never saw her again!'

'Eugene –'

'There's something that touches you! What is it?' He waited, haggard. 'Can one be like you, the cause of tragedy, and feel none of it? You know it was a tragedy, for all of us. She died. Isn't that tragedy?'

They were still standing in the middle of the room. 'I must go,' he said. 'It isn't as I imagined.'

'But why?'

'I was wondering what you had become. Now I see. You have become not quite someone else to me, but almost.'

'Do you think so?'

'Have I not become almost someone else to you?'

They looked at each other, but it is impossible to sustain a reciprocated gaze for long.

'Now I see. I can't share your life. I can't live on you as I had meant to do. I'm going.'

He turned away with resolution. In doing so, he stumbled over the chair that had been knocked over and just saved himself from sprawling. It made an absurd anti-climax, and he laughed. In the sudden snapping of tension she laughed too. She put up her hand, the back of it, to her face, pretending to hide behind her fingers but looking between them.

'What does it mean?' he asked when the senseless gust had passed.

It was beyond their own understanding, but it had been a dividing line. All was different on the other side. For a moment he would not admit that it was. Then, in a new tone on the other side, he said, 'Tell me more – what you think I always was!'

'Oh –' She deprecated this.

'How am I the same? Let's hear again. What did I always do?'

There was the hint of a threat at the possibility of resistance, but she replied with a smile so undisturbed that it had a flash of mischievousness in it. 'Talk beautifully!' she said.

He was entirely surprised.

'As a little boy you could talk on any occasion – so well, such

128

language, it was wonderful. Don't you remember how you were admired for your wonderful phrases?'

He hadn't recovered from his surprise.

'You talk as beautifully as ever, Eugene.'

The memory of tragedy had been banished; it did not belong on the other side of that dividing line.

'Never as much to the point as you!' he answered.

She allowed herself to be distracted by sounds that rose to the window, recalled to the fact that they were still standing in the middle of the room, a room brimmed with light from the scintillating lake. She walked to the window and looked down on the glossy row of dark, clipped trees.

'Don't you think we might go down again? It may be nearly lunch-time.'

He was taken aback, in spite of the change. He gave in by saying, 'What time is it?'

He went over to the dressing-table and opened a drawer, and after a brief conference with himself he took out the gold watch he had consulted and showed it to her. 'Do you remember? Grandmother gave it to me when Uncle Eugen died. The arms on it are Grandfather's.'

She looked at the watch, but not with the interest with which he showed it. In his voice there had been a curiously ingenuous note of satisfaction. He said as he shut the watch up again in the drawer, 'It's too big and old-fashioned to carry always.'

She was close to the dressing-table, and they both together saw him, in the tall looking-glass on the wall, give a brush to the shoulders of his well-fitting brown coat. And it was certainly at the pristine smartness of his brown coat and silk shirt, and of his whole appearance, that their reflections smiled with meaning.

'They'll come in useful somewhere else, Nelly! You'd be glad to have me go, wouldn't you? Have the hindrance removed?'

'I don't think you were a hindrance this morning!' her reflection with a pointed gaiety said to his.

He was pleased, and then checked by pride. 'It's a game,' he said, not so pleasantly. 'One knows how it can be won, but one isn't always in position to make the winning moves.'

There had been a deterioration, and she said, 'I'll go to my room, and we can meet downstairs.'

Chapter Thirteen

In that era of triumphant femininity a manner like Madame Solario's was very individual. She appeared in public with none of the brilliancy and assurance that were the rule among women of any looks or charms. Claims to admiration were generally blazoned, but in her case were never made. A sort of modesty, an exquisite doubtfulness, characterized especially her entrances, her advance into the public eye. It was with this manner that she came out of the front door after luncheon and crossed the road towards those already assembled and talking under the trees. Her brother accompanied her, slowing his steps to suit hers. Mosca and San Rufino at once got up, and that circle opened to receive the pair.

There had been a few introductions that morning; they were completed. But the topic then under discussion among the ladies was not to be interrupted. It was the men who were, and remained, responsible for Madame Solario's inclusion, and also, by sitting on each side of her, protected her from what she could have no share in. The women were too self-confident to resent this sponsorship of beauty, and accepted it of one about whom nothing was known, except that here there seemed to be no absence of *usage du monde*. The same was true of the brother, and a present of him was allowed to Georgette San Rufino.

Then Colonel Ross drew up a chair, and the conversation became general. It was perfectly insipid and lazily pursued, but to anyone not in that world it might have had a certain unadmittable interest. Harden was beside the Marchesa San Rufino – she had indicated the place – and he listened reposedly to what she said to him and to what they all said to one another. It was the repose in which one saw that a smile lay in the actual shape of his mouth; and when the surface had been suddenly shivered, for his scarred cheek had twitched, his face after that brief disturbance appeared even to have gained. His smile was accentuated.

The talk rolled on the competitive merits of the places where one could spend the month of September. A few people still persisted in going to Lucerne. But Lucerne was getting completely spoiled. Villa d'Este, too, was getting spoiled; too many people got in. Cadenabbia, last year and this, was really ideal.

'It's almost like a house-party,' said Colonel Ross, trying not to boast.

Harden saw that Missy Lastacori's restless movements, with a young man in tow – returned from the bicycle ride – were bringing her closer, to the very edge of this circle of chairs.

'Were you here last year?' the Marchesa San Rufino asked Harden.

'No. I wasn't even in Europe,' he said, with Missy quite close. 'I have only just come back from –'

The Marchesa was interested. 'From where?'

'From Japan!' he answered, not having given the girl a sign of recognition since she had 'planted' him, but now looking her, mockingly, full in the face.

She didn't laugh.

'Japan!' said Colonel Ross. 'Had it anything to do with the war? Were you in Manchuria at any time?'

'Oh, not exactly,' answered Harden.

'How – not exactly?' the Marchesa brought out in two rushes.

He said something to her that she had to lean sideways to hear. She laughed, but they couldn't go on just then because Colonel Ross said to him, 'There's a Russian here who'd be quite willin' to discuss the campaign with you even if you'd been on the Japanese side. That's Count Kovanski. He'd cap anything you could say. A peculiar fella.'

Only the name was picked up by the ladies. One of them cried, 'What, Misha Kovanski is here?'

'Do you know him?'

'Kovanski?' said another – who was dark and majestic – in a grand, drawling way. 'He was in Rome last spring.'

'I knew him before,' said the first, a pretty princess. 'We are a little bit cousins. My grandmother was born Apraksin.'

'He led the Russian équipe at the Horse Show last spring. What riders!'

'But why doesn't one see him?' asked the first. 'Where was he last evening?'

'An odd sort of fella. I don't know what he does with himself. But he plays bridge sometimes. And the other night there were some friends of his here, and they made rather too much of a row.'

'Some of them were very wild, in Rome.'

'Surtout when he is wild, Misha can be very amusing.'

One of the men spoke. 'Not so amusing when he kills one in a duel.'

'Dear me!' said Colonel Ross. 'Does he fight duels?'

The ladies started to talk exclusively among themselves. An argument sprang up, and Colonel Ross tried in vain – even though they were speaking on the whole in English, out of politeness to him – to understand what it was about. He wanted to know if it concerned Kovanski's duels. The man who had launched the subject was already bored with it and only shrugged.

At last someone answered, 'He has fought several duels. C'est un homme très dangereux.'

'Ma non è vero!' said the pretty princess, who was a little bit his cousin. She was called Vivina by her intimates. 'That may have been just invented.' The man who had been bored was of a sudden not too bored to make an allusion, which she disregarded. 'And now he will marry and keep quiet.'

The other man, who was her *cavaliere servente*, said, 'Then it is true he is marrying the little Zapponyi?'

'Little Ilona Zapponyi?' said Colonel Ross. 'Oh, I don't think so!'

'Yes, they were saying it last spring. He was making her very much court.'

'But the Zapponyis were here up to a week ago, and I never saw Ilona and him even speak to each other!'

'Biba Zapponyi was here?'

One of them knew she had intended to come, the others knew that she hadn't, and Colonel Ross tried to place what he'd got straight from the horse's mouth.

Madame Solario with her protectors, Mosca and San Rufino,

looked as if they were miles away from all this. At one point in it San Rufino asked her if she ever went to Rome.

'No, never.'

'You do not know Italy?'

'A little. I spent a month in Florence last spring.'

'You should not visit only the provinces.'

'Do not listen to him!' said Mosca.

After another half-hour, as the shade was ebbing away, the ladies thought that they would go in and up to their rooms. The big hotel launch was chugging in the drowsiness, about to put off, which gave them an idea, and the Marchesa said, 'Go and engage it, someone, quick. For five o'clock.'

Harden would not accept the invitation that was extended to him to go out with them at five. This patronage had become valueless to him. He wanted another interview with his sister. She had been allowed to escape him, and he must re-impose the domination over her that was justly his. He tried to get her to come with him to any place where they could talk alone – a public room that had been deserted, or outside the hotel – but she was able to resist. He tried, when they went upstairs, to make her stop at his door, but she proceeded to her own room. As she had not refused the invitation to herself, he was downstairs before five o'clock to prevent her from going; but then a small discovery engaged his attention. She found him in front of the framed list of visitors in the hall, reading it.

'I see,' he said in an undertone, raising his eyebrows, 'that most of the ladies are with *femme de chambre*, but Madame Solario is without *femme de chambre*. Why is that?'

'Can't you guess?' she asked in the course of her progress to the front door. 'After what I told you?'

'Do you mean she can't afford it? No, it is not as I imagined!'

He had not held her back, and it was taken for granted that he was coming after all.

The lonely little *latteria* hidden in an indentation of the shore pleased the company. They liked sitting round a rustic table in the rather gloomy shade, developing appetites with much display of juvenility, and they had the woman who kept the place running backwards and forwards with their orders for tea and more

133

cream and more and more toasted *panettone*. Ercolani's cousins, who were of the party, behaved with the most decorum, being young girls.

There were a number of people on the terrace who saw them return, and the Lastacoris were closest to the water-steps; Madame Solario stopped to speak to them and was enfolded in friendliness.

At dinner, at their table for two in the middle of the room, Harden analysed the social situation for her. It was a way of giving her pain. He had observed the people they had been with so well that he could guess at the attitude each one would develop on further acquaintance with themselves. He had seen the coldness of the young girls towards her, but when he asked her what was the reason of it he received a limpid look of non-comprehension. The point was, he said, that their situation would always be changing. Already the Lastacori mother and daughter had fallen into the most elementary pattern of behaviour. To see his value alter in an unexpected combination was like watching a chemical experiment – a red liquid turn blue under your eyes – and his bitter humour had a second source: bringing out what one would normally keep to one's self.

'Now it's a favour to them,' he said, 'as they see we can do so much better. But I'm willing; they could have their uses. For my success this afternoon in high society might not be repeated. The lady with the raucous voice has things to forget behind her – not things like yours and mine, but worse, you might say. Her cradle. *That,* one soon understands. And she'd understand sooner than any of the others what it is I've become. There's too much in common between us, and she must be careful. And she would remember to be careful if – It will be another experiment in values!'

He seemed to like being forced to speak discreetly low and to cover his bitterness with an air of pleasantry.

'It isn't as if you and I had committed our indiscretions in the Faubourg. Ah, then! Nothing, not a rumour even at the time, would have got through.' He looked towards those tables at the inner end of the room. 'How lucky they are who don't have to take care of themselves!'

She was keeping established the effect of harmony.

'But home in the Avenue Hoche was a stronghold too – of another sort – and we should have stayed in it, my poor sister, not broken it up. Now we are out in the open – as we are at this table: right in the middle of the room, no wall anywhere near.' He conveyed, as he glanced around, a sense of dizziness.

When he filled her glass he looked hard at her. 'We both lost our supports in the same catastrophe, Nelly. And we are *together* out here in the open – different from everyone else.'

They both at the same moment felt that they were being an object of interest. It was no one person, no one markedly, but several people in various parts of the room somehow made that table for two in the middle seem particularly noticeable.

'One would say that they knew it,' he murmured, pressing on his point with enjoyment.

The struggle between them – to have, and not to have, further explanations – continued to produce in him alternations of mood that his sister had to watch, lest they become too visible in public. She let him lead her away once when sarcasm was uppermost. At times he played for social success, in order, it would seem, to ask her if she did not feel safer now, but at no time could he tempt her into saying a single unconsidered word.

At the end of a day that had seemed very long he gave her to understand that he would wait for her in the Salon de Lecture and expected her to join him as soon as she could, and his intention was to walk with her in the avenue where they had had their first talk. San Rufino had found a chair for her after dinner in the corner of the hall acquired by his friends, whose number had been increased by new arrivals, and she did not come to the rendezvous, which was galling. The Salon de Lecture was not being used, its lights were not fully turned on, and by himself there, hearing the steady buzz of talk that came from the hall, Harden waited in limbo. He felt it so, yet could not bring himself to renounce his intention.

A door connected the Salon de Lecture with the Salle des Jeux, and while he was pacing up and down a man strayed in from the next room. It was like straying in, for the man was not in evening dress and did not appear to belong with the other guests; Harden had certainly not seen him before.

'Forgive me if I am making a mistake,' he said in English, with not much of a foreign accent, 'but weren't you on the Irish Mail last spring when – '

Harden's cheek had strongly twitched on being spoken to. 'The Irish Mail?' he answered. 'No, I wasn't anywhere near it last spring.'

'I have made a mistake. I thought we had seen an accident together – in fact that you were one of those who helped – '

'What was the accident?'

'We rammed a fishing-smack a little way out,' said the man. 'It had lost its tiller in rough weather.'

Harden regained what for a few seconds he had lost. 'And how was my double able to help?' he asked.

'That was afterwards, when the men had been rescued.'

'There were no casualties on the smack?' asked Harden with mock concern, seeing that the other was now ready to drop the accident.

'No, the three men were fished out of the water. No one was drowned.'

'I am sure the unknown was more useful than I would have been,' said Harden, and the other gave a short laugh and then brought out as an afterthought, 'Two other Russian officers and I had gone to Ireland to buy horses.'

He stood stockily there as if, unsuccessful though his opening gambit had been, he was willing to try again, or let Harden now try, and Harden asked about Irish horses because he was wondering what this nocturnal visitor had come for.

Before long, in a burst of voices, the door was thrown open, all the lights were turned on, and the young people crowded in, headed by Missy. She was surprised and delighted to find Harden in the room, and then noticed his companion.

'Kovanski, why does one never see you? You are a bear!'

She had been asked to sing, which was the reason they had come, and she swirled to the piano and opened it. Signorina Petri had been brought to accompany her. Harden felt at first the intense irritation of having been balked – he would not be able to carry out his intention – but a part to play had been thrust upon him. To play it, he leaned one shoulder against the wall near the piano and watched her. It was a case of watching as well as listening, so much of her personality was in evidence when she sang and was the prophetic explanation of why her voice would never triumph. Its wonderful natural qualities had been partly trained but would never be fully trained; she herself was incapable of going that far. And sometimes her voice in lovely notes of purity and pathos seemed to be expressing the sadness of its destiny, which had given it to this wayward being who would cheat it of fulfilment. Harden watched and listened with a look of subtle perceptions, but when after several songs she was feeling quite sure he had been enthralled by her voice he smiled – a smile to tell her that if she thought she was going to get compliments from him she was mistaken. She took a quick step forward and soared to the high notes of the waltz-song from *Roméo et Juliette* in answering provocation.

The singing was attracting attention and drawing people from the hall, and among them appeared the Marchesa San Rufino. She looked on, narrowing her eyes in her way that was more calculated effect than myopia, but Harden at the end of the song walked away from her over to the piano, and there was much banter and laughter from Missy.

At the other door, too, faces looked in, and Kovanski, who was standing close to it, was espied. But to an exclamation from the pretty princess of 'Misha! que faites-vous là?' he replied without evincing the smallest pleasure at being discovered, 'Je suis simplement ici.'

When she showed him to those who were behind her he conformed a little better to the social exigencies and explained that he had not known of their arrivals, as he had gone to Milan to see a colleague who had been with him at army manoeuvres. It was suggested that they should now go back to the hall and that he should come with them, but he excused himself on the grounds that he hadn't changed and wasn't fit for their company.

The singing continued intermittently till the general good night had begun, which that evening was prolonged with particular liveliness.

Half an hour later Harden was sitting, bowed, with his forehead on his clenched fists. They had not turned on the light, and his room was dark but for what reached it from the tall lamps on the terrace; it was a ghostly illumination, making shadow-patterns stand on the wall up to the ceiling. She sat withdrawn into the darkness of the corner, but he was in front of the window, and she could see him. On his shutting the door they had entered into the atmosphere that was theirs, that of their place of privacy where they were as no one in the world knew them, and for him that meant entering, comparably to entering the room, into the drama of the past. Her silence was not any longer that of her inviolability; it had a kind of receptiveness. There was not so much emotion even as sympathy, but there was no resistance, and he could feel his confessions penetrating, not being turned away by her silence.

'It wasn't only the revelation – and I had to hear in the coarsest words before I could have any suspicion – it wasn't only that that was unbearable and that I had to bear. It was another moment, and you could never guess which!'

He beat his forehead with his clenched fist. 'That moment stayed – it's something by itself, and I can always see it, never less clear.'

'What moment, Eugene?'

'You'd never guess! I see it as though I were looking, seeing us far away and small in a brightly lit room at the end of a long, dark tunnel.' He broke into what could be called laughter. 'I see myself firing – from the door – but he doesn't fall! He's across the room, but how many yards can it have been? He isn't falling, just staggering back. I had only winged him!'

There the strident sound actually had the nature of laughter.

'The ignominy! I should look back as a man – but I've never got out of that moment when I was a boy whose hand trembled. A criminal boy, not a serious murderer! What I felt when I was rushed at from behind and the revolver taken from me – and I knew I had missed – has me at the end of a tether. Strange, isn't it, Nelly?'

His face was now in his hands. 'God knows I've had better reason since to feel humiliated, but I've never felt as I did then. Or rather, I feel *that* all over again. Even a little thing brings back the whole feeling. I can't get over it. I'm a fool. And at the same time – there's no sense in it – it's the reason of my remorse. The remorse I felt when I said good-bye to her, because of what I was making her suffer.' He couldn't go on for a minute or two. 'That is

138

the other moment that I can always see, never less clear – when I said good-bye to her in her room. That was just before you said, "Good-bye, Eugene," and I was taken away. I wish I hadn't missed, and I wish I hadn't made her suffer.'

He raised his face out of his hands. 'What drove me mad was seeing her humiliated. Can you imagine a greater humiliation for a woman than to see it happen, there, in her house, where there was no escape from it?' He jumped up, as if to escape himself. 'A woman growing older and less beautiful, watching the effect of beauty she couldn't compare with, knowing that everyone else in her house was watching too! She couldn't leave – she was caught by circumstances.'

He walked through the shadow-patterns while his shadow moved over the pattern on the wall. 'It was her own daughter.'

Coming back, he passed through the shadow-bars again. 'I can barely see you,' he said in a hard, new voice, 'but I see your diamonds flash. Don't think I haven't recognized those stars. You are capable of wearing her jewels! But they were given by him, and I suppose that made them almost yours!'

'She left you her jewels,' she said, speaking as much as that for the first time, 'all except the two stars. Did you get them?'

'What are you made of that you can speak of her jewels? But you are so practical! "Did I get them?" Yes, I got them in the end, and I sold them all. They saved me, I can tell you. But for that I wouldn't have kept them, because of where they came from. I would have dropped them in the sea. And you can talk about them! "She left *you* her jewels!"'

'You can speak of his money,' she said, and in the manner of that comment there was no apparent desire to goad him; nor did she seem to regret it when she saw his fury.

'Do you make no allowance for the difference between us – you the cause and us the victims? I have the right to say everything! And where *he* is concerned, without delicacy! Any kind of getting back at him – I have all the rights, do you hear, and you have none!'

But he knew by this time what led nowhere. Either to gain his ends, or because he was really inclined to softness, he made a bid for another kind of reply. 'Nelly, Nelly, it's different now that I've seen you. There isn't the same difference between us now.'

He sat down by her in her darkness and took her hand, bringing it with his against his brow. Bowed like this, not looking up, he said, 'We could understand each other now – don't you feel it? We have seen each other. I never dreamed I would let you say so, but I'll let you. You can tell me that before the end half the blame was mine.'

Keeping her hand in his belonged to the admission of partnership, when he took half the blame upon himself. But he could not leave the blame at that. Before long, yet in the same soft tone of his admission, he was laying it full on her. His deed had been the direct outcome of hers, and but for her there would not have been that good-bye. There could be no doubt of the agony of that; and no doubt that there was an easing of the agony, an evasion of remorse, as soon as he could go behind that moment, further back in the chain of events. To be caught in that chain was to be loosed of all responsibility for the suffering he had caused, and to have no part in the tragedy except as a victim.

'But why, why did it have to be?' he exclaimed, suddenly abandoning the argument. 'Why, when other people are happy, couldn't *we* have been happy?'

He felt her stir under this. She had let him keep her hand till then, but now she took it away.

'I was happy – I respected him – that's why the world fell round me.' These were the phrases that sprang of themselves, almost unbidden. 'I was even proud of all we had – the money and the fine things we had never had before – the advantage it gave me, and I wasn't jealous of him. That never occurred to me. One might have thought I would be, but it was like a fairy tale, what he took us to – and a fairy tale with a good stepfather, not a bad one. Nelly, *how can it have happened*?'

He waited, but this question did not produce a start, as had the other. This, like a setback, made him grow more agitated. 'It can't have taken you unawares, in a way to horrify you. Then it would have been known, it would never have happened again. Nelly, *what was the beginning*?'

All at once she found it intolerable. She got up with a suddenness for which he was not prepared, and the effect was overwhelming. He believed that at last he had attained his object, and the small control he had over himself gave way. There had been on every occasion up to then a conscious exercise of his resources, and, even in his most violent expressions, nothing beyond what he thought would suit his purpose. It could be seen that there had been no more than that when, in the surprise of attainment, his emotion ceased to be exploited. Then it became so abnormally uncontrolled as to be like a fit of illness; he could hardly stand up.

'How did it begin?'

He knew she would not resist him any longer. She was going to speak, but was not yet speaking, and he groaned as if he could not bear the suspense.

'Was there a beginning? Or perhaps not – nothing till it came upon you.' Then he said in a tone of cajolery, 'It just came upon you – was that it?' He went on, still more coaxingly, tenderly low, 'You had not known it was coming – but yet, it did not horrify you at all?'

She was in one of the ghostly squares of light, and he saw her expression.

'No, not that,' he said for her.

'One day –' She spoke as simply, as unhurriedly as always, and what twisted her mouth was not in the inflections of her voice. His breathing was audible, but not hers. 'One afternoon I was doing my lessons in the schoolroom; I was preparing for my class the next day. Mademoiselle was in the next room, and that door was a little open. He came in by the other door.' Even his breathing was stilled. 'He asked me how I was getting on with my composition, and leaned on the table to look. He saw a spelling mistake I had made and corrected it. I looked up, and he leaned over a little more and kissed me. Then we heard Mademoiselle coming, and when she came in he pretended to make another correction on my cahier. His hand was pressing my shoulder. She said, "Comme votre papa est bon pour vous!"'

It had come to an end, as if there were no more.

'That was the moment.' He again made a sound as though he could not bear what he had to endure, but this was of understanding too acute – of participation. '"Comme votre papa est bon pour vous!"'

No denial came from her when he said, 'You were as good as taken there and then!' What he was obliged to master was his own participating. 'The rest came of itself.'

Seeing by the perceptible convulsion of her lips that he had touched the springs of the past, he proceeded with the matter-of-fact. 'Where actually was it? In what room?'

She told him.

'I always came back to that room, in my mind,' he said. 'It was the farthest from the servants, and it would not have been too suspicious to be seen coming out of it. Was it always there?'

He observed that there was no resentment to his questions. There was something else.

'The supreme experience,' he said, comprehending, accepting, jeering, and not judging, 'and it was Papa!'

His understanding had brought him an appeasement both physical and moral. He was no longer outraged; he no longer even blamed. What had seemed so unnatural to him was explained as one of those vagaries of the senses that are in nature and for which the human being cannot be held responsible. He observed with a sort of kindliness the symptoms of unrest in her, a disturbance of the usual harmony. When he turned to watch her moving, pausing, moving again, their two shadows on the wall seemed to be executing movements different from their own in the architecture of still lines that divided up the light. He had gained his victory in getting her to speak, and for the first time could study her from a position of vantage, not thwarted and merely watching his chance. A few more questions that he put to her later were left as statements of fact, and he obtained a final confession when they were standing together near the window, in whose light he could see her face well enough. Now he did not jeer, but said with sympathy, 'Poor Nelly!'

Chapter Fourteen

His victory changed his manner to her; the good humour of it was unfeigned, instead of being an aspect he wore while speeding his arrows. At lunch the next day he began, as though nothing more serious than his mistake had ever been between them, 'I haven't told you that I gathered almost at once, of course, that you can call yourself Natalia now. The Spanish-American influence on your destiny – very suitable. And I've repaired the mistake I made in my ignorance by explaining I couldn't pro- nounce "Natalia" as a little boy.'

He then confided his impressions of Missy, who had taken him to pay a morning call, as if that were all that was in his mind. The girl was so spoiled and vain that she was silly, and yet there was a hint of something – though that might be an illusion created by her eyelids.

'You know, don't you,' he said to his sister, 'that any beauty of the eyes lies in the eyelids?' And hers dropped – meditatively – while he spoke of Missy's. Missy's did not have the classic fullness, but their shape gave her regard a certain eloquence when she wasn't laughing. He then asked his sister about her own morning. He did it in a way that insisted on the change in their relationship, forcing his good humour upon her as before he had forced his bitterness: all tension, he implied, was relaxed, and they must be happily intimate with each other now. Her way of replying as he required was an indication that she knew their positions had been reversed. Before, it had been she who always returned them to everyday life, and now it was he. While sub- mitting to his tyranny, she answered – when he asked her particularly about San Rufino whom he called her Satyr – with a minimum of words, but it seemed enough to amuse him, and there was no venom in his speculations.

'But tell me, Nelly,' he said, 'I heard today that friends of yours are arriving here. Who are they?'

'Do you remember Mr Jefferson Chase, a friend of Father's?'

'Of course – an old gentleman in Cincinnati.'

He was struck by the fact that she had so naturally referred to their childhood; she, however, believed that he was struck by the recollection itself.

'We thought of him then as very old, but he can't have been. *Now* he's very old, but still quite active. I met him in Paris last June. He remembered us perfectly! He was a great friend of Father's.'

There was in her voice now – as on the first morning there had been in his – a quickening of satisfaction, and he paid attention to it.

'Mr Chase is a great philanthropist. He came to Europe on his philanthropic schemes, but he was advised to take a cure this summer, and he wrote to me soon after I saw him that he and his niece would come here from Salsomaggiore; and he said he would be very glad if I were able to meet them here.'

'You came here on purpose to meet old Mr Jefferson Chase?'

'Yes.' As soon as she saw that, inadvertently, she had aroused his wonder, the flow of speech was checked. She didn't wish to proceed.

'And why isn't he here?'

'He was taken ill at Salsomaggiore. Twice I expected them, that very day, and then had a telegram.'

'But why do you want so much to see old Mr Chase?'

'He is very charming. One feels such kindness and benevolence.' But the vagueness had come back, the spontaneity was gone.

'Are you still expecting them?'

'In a way, yes. If not, I would have left last week and you wouldn't have found me.'

He gave her a sharp glance, but her remark appeared to be perfectly simple. Yet he laughed, as though it couldn't be.

He now took for granted that he and she would stay on and make the most of what this society offered them. Even the young people interested him and were already recognizable to him, with their places and personal chances in the world. He had nicknames for some of them, – Beatrice Whitcomb was "the blond Wild Indian", Pico "the perfumed snipe", and so on.

'Who is the young man with rather red hair whom you talked to before they all went bicycling? He's by himself near the door – so English and pure.'

'His name is Middleton.'

'Just Middleton?'

'I don't think I know his first name.'

'I hoped he was Lord Middleton. He keeps looking at you.'

'He told me he was going to be a bank clerk,' she answered, positively with malice.

'Really, Nelly!' he said, making his exasperation comic. 'Do you know nothing? Haven't you seen your Colonel Ross being paternal to him? Would that yachting-cap be paternal to a bank clerk? I wonder how you get on, my poor sister, if you have learned so little!'

'I wonder where you can have learned so much.'

'You think I must have got out of those consequences that caught me like a trap, because I've been able to study the social shades?' The change that had taken place was manifest in his indulgence – mentioning those consequences without fastening them upon her. 'One notices much more if one is outside the charmed circle than one would if one were in it. Inside, they act by reflex and don't see themselves; it's only we who are outside who can see them and what they are doing.'

'Didn't you ever get out of those consequences, Eugene?' she asked, with reluctance, but impelled to ask. Everything was reversed; she spoke of his ruined life, and he was disposed to make light of it.

'Well, they had me for a long time.'

'How?'

It was that night at dinner, and he was talking easily, with the look of intimacy.

'If one is reduced to earning one's living in the Latin world – and unfortunately it was in that, Papa's world, that I was made to expiate – one must have qualifications; you know, all those *papers*. And when I lost the position I was sent out to – "lost" is putting it mildly – there I was, without recommendations or papers! I was like Peter Schlemihl, the man without a shadow. Do you remember my reading *Peter Schlemihl* at Gössefors? It made such an impression on me, Peter's terror when he finds

145

what it means to be without a shadow, which is something that everyone else has got – I thought of it when I was trying to get along without those papers. What, no papers? What, no shadow?'

He laughed out. She was looking at him with intentness, disconcerted by the facts now that he presented them like this, whereas she had been impenetrable when he tried to put them tragically.

'But I didn't figure in just one story. That little bit of money came to me, and that was another story – and that landed me in another, when I was believed to have made a fortune and believed it myself. I must tell you about that period – very baroque and brief. And now here I am, here we are, in another story. But now I come to think of it, Nelly, Peter Schlemihl has been in all of them, and still is!'

When they were again alone together, next day in the middle of the hot afternoon – the hour of the siesta, to which he did not let her retire, guiding her away from the door of the hotel towards the plane-tree walk – he said, 'Now you and I seem to be parting company, Nelly. I heard you are going in high society to Urio, and you saw I forfeited my chance to go too. But I'll better my chances. You'll see! At least I hope you will. And at least you won't see me the victim of a caprice, as you might have if I had allowed myself to be too easily flattered. I am going to take the girl out rowing. She's all out for a flirtation, and thinks it's a feather in her cap that the raucous lady is annoyed. But the mother won't be so pleased with me then, and my value may alter again. Well, as I say, we'll see!'

They were sauntering. All life in front of the hotel had ceased; there was no sound behind them.

'There are always such a lot of things to be kept in equilibrium,' Harden went on, maintaining his jovial mood even in that languorous scene and with her own languor beside him, 'and if one of them drops, then all the rest may come tumbling down.'

'You don't always succeed in keeping them in equilibrium?' she asked.

'Of course not. If I always had, would I be here in my present situation – in other words, dependent on you? But the curious part is, I always know how it *could* be done. It isn't for lack

146

of knowing how. But *you* don't know the moves in the game, that is obvious! Events have proved it,' he said.

'Do you like playing this game?' she asked without criticism.

'Of course not. It is a malign fate that has made it necessary.' He fell into sombreness. 'I am ashamed to have to do anything for myself.'

The great high wall, adorned with statues, of the Villa Carlotta gardens looked pale and baked by the sun, and the trees of the bay beyond leaned over glassy water. They had said nothing more when they turned the corner of the wall and were upon the water-steps, but there they paused, though in full sun, to look through the great gates and up the many flights of steps to the villa. At that hour the grandeur and the somnolence were together rather overpowering.

'Now, Nelly,' he said with restored geniality, 'when you see that, what do you think? Does it suggest anything to you?'

'What does it suggest to you?'

'That it belongs to the Grand Duke, and that I might have been the Grand Duke and it might have belonged to me. Why wasn't *that* my fate?'

'There were too many chances against it,' she answered.

'I can't blame *you* for that, can I? And now, what does it suggest to you?'

She deprecated having to say so much and said it with her little laugh. 'A fête, perhaps, two hundred years ago – with the musicians hidden behind the charmilles, and the company coming down all those steps, to the music of Lully.'

'But Nelly, you have imagined something, and I didn't think you had any imagination!' They walked on past the gates. 'Even if one got possession in a break-up of society – which is possible, you know – it would be nothing. One must be the Grand Duke. I don't want another to have it rather than he, understand; I'm not that kind of revolutionary. *I want to be he.*'

They sat down on a stone bench in the shade of Piazza Sommariva.

'Those people' – and he made a movement of the head to the left, towards Cadenabbia – 'they have the superiority of owing their good fortune to something they themselves had nothing to do with. And that is the superiority I envy! To be born with

147

a sort of super-self, for that's what rank is, a super-self that planes over frontiers – to be *born* thinking one has the right to look down – hasn't that got more charm than anything one can do for one's self?'

He left it open as to whether he were joking or meant what he said. She smiled, as at a joke, but vaguely.

'Now if we were Grand Ducal would we be different from what we are now as we sit here, do you think? *I* think so. I don't believe human nature is as universally the same as they say. We wouldn't be at all the same as we are now. But we would be together in that too. We would still have everything in common.' He could see only her profile, for she was looking out at the lake, not enough struck by what he said, even with the emphasis he put upon it, to turn her head to him. 'We have everything, every ancestor in common; all our beginnings – they are the same for both. I don't believe there is any absolute equality except between brothers and sisters. The individual differences don't count by comparison with the equality that one can have with no one else.'

The quiet was heavily settled upon that spot, but sometimes the tiny splash of a fish could be heard. They listened to the tiny sounds. After a little while he said with humour, 'Don't you think so, Nelly?'

She then began, hesitating, 'You mustn't feel you are dependent upon me for every franc –'

'Oh, Nelly, why are you so practical! Is *that* what you pick out, of all I've said to you?'

'You once spoke of injustice, and there was an injustice, I think, because Grandmother left me some money and it should have been divided between us –'

'Then why wasn't it?'

'Grandmother would have wished to divide it, I'm sure, but at the time of her death –'

'No, it wasn't because I had disappeared. She was put off by my having tried – and failed by an inch – to murder my step-father!'

He had so banished all tragic tones that he could say this as if they were playing comedy. She neither flinched nor conformed but simply persisted with her theme.

'I wouldn't want to keep more than my share. There wasn't very much, because most of the money went with the property – '

'If you tell me the amount in kronor I shall have hysterics,' he said.

She laughed then.

But as though the word had just come to his ear – 'Grandmother! Grandmother and Gössefors! Why couldn't we have stayed there? If only we had! If we had, I wouldn't be talking as I do now. We were looked up to there. Grandmother was born Baroness Stjerneld. We were the manor family. – But doom might have come upon that too.'

She got up quickly, stung by the word, and he kept her waiting a little, observing her, before he too got up and let her direct their steps past the Villa Carlotta again.

'Well, what is this idea of yours?' he asked.

'You must consider that I had some money that belonged by right to you, and here you are spending it – your money, not mine.'

'That is very delicate of you, Nelly. You think I don't like being your guest. But I'm already thinking beyond that, and my hotel bills are such a small matter after all – and the few hundred francs I'll need for pocket-money. I thought only of arranging myself through you, but now I see a positive duty: to arrange *your* affairs for *you*. When that's done the little sums that came to you or to me – and we must remember that she' – his tone altered for a moment there – 'did all she could for me, which was at your expense – they'll seem laughable. They are, anyhow. Isn't it absurd that you and I should not be rich?'

Sauntering back, he asked her to give him the details of a situation she so far had treated only broadly. The change in their relationship appeared very obvious now. He had become irresistible, and she was telling him what he wanted to know, what till then he had not been able to get out of her. The *dot* settled upon her by M. de Florez had not been conspicuously large – and with deceptive simplicity she spoke of their stepfather as 'Carlos', while he did not once say 'Papa'. He merely commented that a larger *dot* would not have been in good taste. But she was to have inherited a substantial part of the fortune – and at this point her brother was all attention. There was then a great surprise: the fortune was barely a third of what had been expected; certain financial disasters had been kept secret.

'All this I never heard.'

When she spoke of what was subsequent to their stepfather's death she did it with some effort, and he was, as it were, respectful of her feelings. Because of the shrunken inheritance and of a legal quibble, the two de Florez children of a former marriage had been able to take nearly all that there was, and there had been almost nothing for her. She did not express regret or resentment, she stated, and her brother made the sympathetic sound 'T-t-t!' quite simply.

'Have you at least kept the whole of your *dot*?'

'Yes.'

'The chivalrous Señor Don Luis Solario allowed a separate property arrangement?'

Her silence was affirmative.

'He had money of his own, I understand, but even so, considering the circumstances . . .' He then asked her if, given the nationality of Don Luis, it was impossible for her to get a divorce. Not very readily, she replied that she could get a divorce in France.

'The chivalrous Señor agrees to that too?' He stopped dead on reading another affirmative. 'What a treasure, that man!'

Obliged to walk on because she wouldn't stop – 'But Nelly, then there are no difficulties in our way! You can marry again! As soon as you like! I thought you might have to wait – Well, I didn't know. Now we have a clear run ahead of us!'

She seemed to be quite strongly of the opinion that it was not so, but he went on exclaiming over his plans for her. They entered the hotel by the side door into the Salon de Lecture, and she wished to pass straight through and go upstairs, but he detained her, not wanting to break off.

'A few more words before parting – let me tell you what you should do this afternoon!' It was to be the most gay-spirited advice. 'The lady is annoyed with me and would take it out on you over her husband's attentions to you. So don't let the Satyr advertise what's in his mind – not yet; wait! If you keep him at a distance today, as I've done her, there'll be nothing initial to be said against us, but anything too rapid and it's "Beware of people you meet in hotels!"'

150

This held her attention.

'Don't let those other men, the two young ones, I mean, even speak to you. Leave them nailed to the masts they adorn. Content yourself with Fine Mouche, or sit with the unattached ladies, even the raucous lady herself. *That* would be a master stroke!'

'And you,' she said, 'what will you do?'

'My course this afternoon is straightforward.' And for the first time that day there was the unpleasant laugh that was very nearly a cackle.

She would not be delayed any longer, and he did not see her again to speak to, but he was in the hall, watching, when her party set forth. During the preliminaries to departure Madame Solario, drifting as will-less as a sail on a ripple of water, left San Rufino, who had been at her side, and came to rest with those ladies who were ready to embark. With her almost diffidence she engaged in talk with one of them, and was about to step right after her into the launch when she remembered something she had forgotten in their talk. Mosca caught this, and at her request went back for the light-blue cape that had been dropped on a bench, and, having followed her forward to consign it to her, he sat down with her and Donna Virgilia in the bow.

Missy came down while Harden could still see the launch speeding away, dark in the general whiteness of the glaring afternoon, and he was laughing when they met. There was no one but themselves in the hall.

'What do you want to do with me?' he asked.

Standing facing her, he began to play with the long gold chain she wore, on which were hung at regular intervals little charms of all sorts. He took hold of a tiny bell and shook it, and then a coral amulet in the form of a twisted horn, which he pressed against her neck.

'What does one do with this?'

'Nothing,' she replied in her usual gale. 'It protects one against the Evil Eye.'

'How does one know who has the Evil Eye? Do you know I haven't got it?'

She shrieked and backed, making horns with her forefinger and little finger.

151

'No, no, I haven't got it.' And as she no longer backed away he took hold of her chain again and touched her lower lip with a ruby heart. 'No, on the contrary, I am susceptible to it. You must give me one of these to protect *me*.'

'Oho, you have no courage!'

He dropped the chain. 'What do you want me to do?' he once more asked. 'Shall we sit in the arbour in front, in full view of all the balconies, either very far apart to surprise them or very close together to shock them?'

'What are you thinking? One of the balconies is Mama's!'

They walked out and did go into the arbour, where they leaned on the railing at just the proper distance from each other and appeared to look down into the water. He went on doing so after she had begun to fidget, to hum, to strip leaves off a bush, and to exaggerate her gestures. Finally she got him to move, and they went down the water-steps to wake a boatman who was lying asleep in one of the hotel row-boats. They did not take him with them, for the girl insisted on rowing and grasped the oars while Harden leaned back on the cushions in the stern. She pulled far too vigorously to be able to keep it up for long – her bracelets jingling, her bosom pushed forward by her exertions and anyhow prominent and firm in its inner casing under the muslin and lace of her blouse. The boat wobbled on for a time, and then he made her change places with him, and her 'Ohs!' and 'Ohos!' echoed in little volleys of sound. The boat progressed more swiftly and regularly, and soon it was but a dark streak in the whiteness.

Chapter Fifteen

Harden met Missy again, with her family, before dinner, and while he was making himself agreeable to all, even to Signorina Petri, she called out, 'Kovanski! You have come out of your cave! Come and let us look at you!'

With her bold readiness on every occasion she was more like a married woman than a young girl, which gave her a great prestige among her contemporaries.

'Now you don't look as if you were running away' – for he was in evening dress. 'So you will spend the evening with us?'

He gazed stolidly and said, 'I haven't made my plans'.

He kept his manner, as a rule, uniform, and it was the intention behind it that varied its effect. As he was not now wishing to be rude, his words and his stolidity gave an impression contrary to themselves. Then Harden and he recognized each other. Harden was just saying he was surprised that 'they' had not returned, as nothing had been said about being late for dinner.

'But they started for Urio too late to get back in time for dinner,' said the Marchesa, almost as though she had told them so.

'Who?' Kovanski asked of Harden.

'A party that went off in the launch this afternoon' – and Harden turned his agreeableness upon the other man – 'for some distant spot, it appears. My sister is with them. That is why I am concerned.'

'Concerned?' said Kovanski. 'Has there been a storm on the lake?'

'Concerned in the matter of dinner, I mean. I don't know how long I'll be kept waiting, or if it would be better not to wait and dine alone.'

'Come and dine with us!' cried Missy.

'I couldn't do that, because it might end in Natalia dining alone.'

153

'But of course she would join us,' said the Marchesa.

He would not be persuaded, and with the Marchesa saying 'I don't think they'll be back before nine o'clock,' the Lastacoris went into the hotel, leaving Harden outside, like a watcher who must scan the distance for a sign.

But Kovanski too stayed outside.

'You are not going in either?' asked Harden, whose suspiciousness had been awakened at their first meeting.

'No,' said Kovanski. 'I don't dine in the table d'hôte. I dine when I want to.'

'Do you know when you will want to tonight?' And he added, 'But I heard you say you hadn't made your plans.'

The other's short laugh was appreciative of the way he had been quoted. 'I meant that I never announce them,' he said.

'That is wise in feminine company,' said Harden, 'but not so necessary among ourselves.'

Kovanski looked simply wooden.

'Well,' continued Harden, 'I will announce mine. I won't wait any longer.'

The lights in front of the hotel were already strong in the September dusk, and if one looked as far as one could the spark of the launch was not to be seen upon the lake.

'But,' Harden said at the front door, 'I would like to suggest that, if you are inclined to dinner now, we should dine together.'

Kovanski, who hadn't moved, now turned towards him. Under the bright lights of the entrance Harden saw his indecision, greater than the occasion seemed to warrant.

'D'accord,' he then replied.

At the table for two in the middle of the dining-room he took the place usually occupied by Madame Solario. The head-waiter came up to say, 'Monsieur le Comte dîne ici ce soir?' and to inquire if he wished to order à la carte. He answered that he would take the first part of the table d'hôte dinner.

'You will excuse me if I leave you before the end of it,' he said to Harden. He then consulted him about wine and ordered for both of them.

When he started the conversation, for Harden would not, he asked, 'Are you staying here till the end of the season?'

'That is the question that everyone opens with – not with a

remark about the weather, because that's always fine.' And Harden said it as if it were an accepted humorous return of the ball. But Kovanski didn't seem to appreciate this.

'I say that it depends on the whim of my sister, and that I hope she will stay.' He already had the sense that the other man was at some disadvantage, that he himself was inexplicably in the superior position. 'But you – from what Mademoiselle Lastacori says – you don't seem to like the place for the reasons that we like it.'

'What are those reasons?' asked Kovanski.

'All this sociability –'

Kovanski surveyed the scene. In his eyes the irises were very dark, and what should have been white was sallow. Those eyes were directed – not at once, but as if they had been drawn there – to the door and to the young man sitting alone at his table near it. Then he suddenly smiled, with a broad and obvious, even brutal smile.

He answered Harden with the last of the smile on his mouth. 'I have great friends who have a villa at Tremezzo. I spend much of my time with them.'

'I see,' said Harden.

Something had restored Kovanski to what one must think was his natural self.

'Do you live in Paris?' he suddenly and arrogantly asked.

Always made cautious by an unexpected question, Harden thought a moment. But under his name in the list of visitors was *Paris*.

'I do now, but I've been away for some years – until this summer, in fact.'

Kovanski looked so hard at him that he must have been interested by this information.

'I was brought up mostly in France – at least from the age of about thirteen.' Harden allowed himself a little pause in which to gather an impression. He came to the conclusion: He doesn't know; but one can't be sure – with him. 'Oddly enough, as I am English, though I went to an English school it was not in England.'

'And I went to school in England for a year.'

'You speak English uncommonly well.'

'Before that I had an English tutor called Mr Winterbottom,' said Kovanski, beginning to laugh. 'And my sisters had a French governess called Mademoiselle Delierre. We called her Mademoiselle Derrière. What a chance, that brought those two together!' He was laughing and coughing together. 'Yet they didn't marry.'

He did not seem to want Harden to share his mirth, which was brief. 'And you have been away for some time?' he asked.

'Yes, and I've been in a number of countries; but never in Ireland,' answered Harden.

He was sure that Kovanski didn't like him, and also that he did not normally put up with people whom he didn't like; and what interested him was to see that Kovanski was putting up with *him*.

'You told me that, and that we could not have met before.'

'Unless it was on some other occasion,' said Harden. 'But it was not that one on the Irish Mail. We may have run into each other somewhere else.'

He looked as if he thought Kovanski might supply him with a clue, and on his side Kovanski waited, frowning.

'Well, where could it have been?' Kovanski asked.

'Well – South America?'

'No. Why does one go to South America? What does one do there?'

'There are horses in some parts of it,' said Harden.

Kovanski gave a laugh, with a lifting of his frown. 'I didn't find you knew much about horses,' he answered.

'My particular activities didn't take them in, except to bet on them sometimes. If I knew yours I might be reminded – What have been your activities?'

The frown came back, and much more heavily. 'Those I belong to,' Kovanski said.

'How do you mean?'

'It's enough to know where a man belongs. Then you know everything about him, except the details.'

'So you think there is a nice little labelled box for every man?'

'It may not be nice, but it is a box,' said Kovanski.

'It would be nice to be in a box,' said Harden – reflectively, but as though he were meaning to be witty. 'It wouldn't be so nice to have to try to get into one.'

Kovanski obviously suspected that in this there was something that made game of him.

'I assure you that you are fortunate,' Harden went on, looking at him with candour, 'et je parle en connaissance de cause. I am not in a labelled box – at least, not the kind that *you* mean.'

To that Kovanski listened intently.

'It was force of circumstances – mixed nationality, my father dying when I was very young, and that sort of thing. Anyhow, my career was not mapped out for me, as I imagine yours was.' He went straight on. 'The other night I didn't know your name, but I gathered you were a Russian officer. And you are now on leave?'

'On short leave from my present duties. I am at present at the Embassy, an assistant to our military attaché.' His laugh showed the blunt, stained edges of his teeth. 'My career has had an interruption; I was indiscreet; but it would never have been taken seriously. For us everything leads back to the same rotten place, and, especially if one has a relation in favour, one sometimes gets advanced, and then he loses favour and retires for a time to his estates – or for some other reason one's advancement is stopped – but who is in favour, and what service one is in, and what one is doing at the moment, those are the details. It's all the same life.'

'Couldn't one say something of the sort about mankind in general?'

'I don't philosophize,' said Kovanski.

'And I am not interested in mankind either – only in particular classes of people.'

Even that might have been too much like philosophizing for Kovanski. He asked, 'You are staying here a little longer?'

'Yes, I think I may say that much.' But Harden, too, pursued what interested him. 'As you have spoken so frankly of what you belong to, I may ask, have the unfortunate events of last year brought any change to the good old life?'

Kovanski plainly liked him less than ever at that moment, and with a general contempt that included, by look, his questioner as well, he answered, 'The more the house is rotten the more things are running about in it.'

'Not a pretty picture. But I am thinking – I told you I was

interested in particular classes of people; and for some any change must be for the worse. Perhaps you don't follow what I mean when I say I think any change for you will be for the worse?'

'No, I don't follow,' said Kovanski. The conversation might have been killed by this and, as if he feared that it would be, he made an effort, though he scowled, to keep it alive. 'It is a change for me that at the moment I have to play the monkey abroad; but I don't think it is very different from what I would be doing at home.'

Harden's contempt was not concealed by a lightly sketched sympathy. He did not have to consider what he said; with a man of such limited understanding he could think aloud, and he proceeded to do so with leisureliness, as he might have breathed rings of smoke into the air.

'I had rather more than that in mind. I had in mind a whole way of life, a life that must really be very agreeable. If it was no longer allowed to be so fantastic – or, to borrow your words, so rotten – you might find it was not nearly so agreeable. I think this is a good example of any change being for some people bound to be for the worse. Now another class of person has little but change to hope for; some people can't get their turn unless things are shaken up. Think of the Napoleonic society.' He smiled; he did not believe that the other would think of it. 'What fun for those people, to have had a new society made for them on the ruins of one they'd had no chance of getting into. They can't have ceased marvelling at their luck!'

'They were also rather clever,' said Kovanski. If a horse had spoken, Harden would not have been more surprised. 'Their luck was that they were given a chance to show it.'

'Oh, certainly, that *is* one kind of luck. There's a better kind that needs neither cleverness nor chance.'

Not caring whether the other would comprehend that he was receiving confidences, Harden elaborated his points about those people who needed no other cleverness than to see that any change would be for the worse, and that they therefore should not provoke it, and those for whom it was luck to come in for a change: a new dynasty, a party to take the place of a caste – anything. But think also of the inconveniences for them! Think, for example, of the company one would be in! The clever ones of a new order! No, not their company for choice. Much better to be all stupid together in the old labelled box – far preferable. Better not to have to do, but only be!

But Kovanski cut him short by looking towards the door, which had been opened. It was shut without anyone's coming in, yet he acted quickly as if he had received a signal. He excused himself having to leave. There was then a lessening of the blankness on his face; he remained in doubt for a moment, and betrayed at that moment some inexplicable vulnerability, before asking, 'And you are going back to Paris from here?'

'I say, like you, I haven't made my plans.'

They parted politely, thanking each other for the pleasure of having dined together.

Afterwards Missy asked Harden if he had got anything out of Kovanski. 'One can't make him talk,' she said. 'What is he doing all the time?'

'He says that he has friends who have a villa at Tremezzo, and that he spends his time with them.'

'Who can they be?' she asked with the appetite of the gossip aroused. 'I can't think of any villa where he would have friends.' She passed the villas there in review. 'He must be hiding something!'

She looked round to challenge Kovanski at once, but he had disappeared, and she forgot him. The little orchestra which came once a fortnight to play at the hotel was tuning up, and she exclaimed that tonight it must be made to play waltzes.

'How do you waltz?' she cried.

'Divinely,' answered Harden, 'but how do you?'

Soon she had the musicians removed from the hall to the Salon de Lecture and all the young people wild to dance. She started the orchestra on 'Valse Bleue' and put herself in Harden's arms without delay. But he did not for long allow her this rapture and began to insist that they must stop, as her 'flirt' was about to make a scene. He forced her to stop and delivered her up, furious, to her young man.

Some of the older people had come in and were dancing too, when, late in the evening, the Urio party made its entrance with all possible effect.

The Marchesa San Rufino had finished narrating to someone the contretemps they had had, when she saw Harden standing beside her. The last time he had been so close she had manifested displeasure by looking through him.

'I watched the "Embarquement pour Cythère" from a window,' he said.

She had never heard of the 'Embarquement pour Cythère', and it held her up for a second. He had thought it would.

'What did the little cupids do – did they all come back again?'

Still at a loss, she found it easier, when he had made the motion of inviting her to dance, to let him put his arm around her than to make any sort of reply. They began to dance.

'Clouds of little cupids,' he whispered in her ear.

It was not in her line at all, but she was impressed by it. He did not keep it up a moment too long, and asked her what had happened to them. At home now, at home with the factual, she repeated the story she had told before while they continued to dance. She did not dance so well that dancing with her could be made to appear a mutual delight, and it was their talking together all the time that was noticeable.

'Let me say good evening to my sister,' he said, and as he guided her there he knew by the willingness of her muscles that no hostility had been set up. With her husband beside Madame Solario in the embrasure of a window she spoke as to a fellow victim of the tiresome episode, and then the brother hoped his sister was none the worse for it, to which his sister said, 'You mustn't exaggerate!'

The music had, though not finally, stopped. Couples walked across the room, and Harden saw, going by, Vivina with Kovanski, frowning, in tow. But the Princess paused to speak to the Marchesa San Rufino, and Kovanski was left suddenly by himself. He then did what it seemed he would not have done otherwise; he bowed to Madame Solario. It was with the formality of an almost military deportment, and she inclined her head in recognition without speaking. As he bowed, his face, anyhow dark in colour, became so much darker, so congested with the blood that mounted to it, that he looked as if he were being strangled. He went on alone, and a few minutes later left the room.

Chapter Sixteen

She was not quite ready to leave her room the next morning when there was a knock at the door. She called out, 'Qui est là?'

'Le Frère Maudit,' he answered pleasantly and came in.

She seemed actually a little embarrassed to have him in her room, and he was amused to see this. After hesitating as to what she should do, she went on with what she had been doing, which was putting some effects, folded, into a drawer. The bed was unmade, the wash-hand-stand had been used, but the rest of the room was already in order. No clothes were lying about in it, only the hat and parasol for that morning. There was nothing intimate to her except her scent that perfumed the air, and the articles on the dressing-table.

'So practical, so tidy,' he observed as he looked around. 'Extraordinary.'

The plane trees of the walk were too close to the windows; they blocked the view. And, as the room faced westwards, the sunlight from which he had just come might have been in another country.

'Nelly, I am ashamed! You have given me a much better room than your own. What true hospitality!'

She shut the drawer.

'But isn't it extraordinary you shouldn't have the finest room – a suite of rooms, a maid, and all the luxury in the world? Can it have happened before in the whole history of woman?'

She still appeared reluctant to have him there, and not only because it might offend convention. He felt it: she wished to keep her privacy, something away from him. Coming upon her as he had, he had seen her being alone, and even from her room he received a fresh impression of her self-containment. Disorder would have given the impression of impulsiveness and haste, of hurrying away from solitude to company; therefore the opposite in her room expressed the opposite of those things. And that was a good reason to impose company upon her. He lounged against the bed-rail.

'I really believe you don't consider luxury as your due, but you know that *I* do. Well now,' he said, 'here is another day, another beautiful day. I've been downstairs, and they've all come out – like beautiful insects that come out into the sun – but what they're going to do, cela ne se dessine pas encore. Everyone is there but the Centaur – the Russian. Nelly, you must tell me about him, for he loves you to madness!'

She sat down before the dressing-table, which was between the two windows, to put on her hat – the hat made up of crisp frills of lilac muslin – and her eyes, looking at herself in the glass, had the same calm thoughtfulness as when she looked at other people. The inquiry was not more interested or acute.

'The other evening when I was alone a man I hadn't seen till then came in out of nowhere and spoke to me – right off, like that, with a story of our having met before.' An unconsciously quick turn of her head warmed him to his account. 'I'm afraid I thought for a moment that I was hearing some bird of doom coming home to roost. I knew at once his story was ridiculous – an accident on the Irish Mail: he almost drowned three fishermen for my sake. Now why did he want to? There was something behind it, but what? Then last night we met again while I was waiting for you; we met in the snobbish bosom of the jeune fille's family, and I saw my chance of finding out why a Count Kovanski – by then I knew who he was – wanted to scrape acquaintance with your unfortunate brother. It was because he was your brother, and I didn't discover it till too late!'

She got up from the dressing-table with her hat on, ready to leave but making no further motion to do so.

'There wasn't a sign of you. I was alone and suggested we should dine together. At dinner I still felt there was something peculiar somewhere, but I didn't guess – Was I a fool not to from the beginning? Now where I *was* a fool –'

He stopped to look contrite and induce suspense.

'I felt he might be a nasty type for some people but not for me. So I talked, just for fun, and not at all as I would have talked if I had known. Will you forgive me, Nelly, for giving your brother away?'

She just perceptibly shrugged. 'It is of no importance,' she said.

'But why isn't it? Everything – anything – may be of importance. Wait a minute. You don't ask me when and how I guessed, because you don't have to. You know. One only has to see him in your presence. It explained everything. But what *is* peculiar is the way you treat each other. One asked one's self, "What corpse is there between them?" as was said of two French politicians.'

He straightened up to engage her not to go out yet. 'I can't think why it was necessary to bury whatever there was so deep. Or is it him you killed? But why? He would be very creditable alive. Bo-Peep was trying to tie him to her sash, and that was not because of his looks.' He saw her repress a smile. 'Don't you think,' he said insinuatingly, 'that he's an interesting variety of *them*? Being who he is, I'm told one knows without being told: Corps des Pages; Chevalier Garde –'

'Garde à Cheval,' she said, demurely.

He was delighted. In that moment they were friends. He was being led by her on this note when he bethought himself, and stopped.

'The murder must have been committed before you came here or I would certainly have heard of it. Why were you so extreme?'

'You say that you didn't know he knew me? He said nothing?'

'I see now what he was after – he was trying to get news of you. It was pathetic! But you seem to feel he might have said something. What for instance?'

'Oh, do I know?'

'Might he say things that are not to your liking?'

She looked down.

'What could he say?' he urged. 'He isn't a cad! Or is he?'

'I don't know quite what that means.'

'Oh. come now, Nelly. But if that is too English, put it into your own words. What makes you uneasy about him?'

It cost her an effort to commit herself. 'He behaves extravagantly. He is excessive,' she said.

'Is he!' ejaculated Harden. After a pause – 'You have aroused my curiosity.'

'Let it be. Don't you want to go down?'

'Yes, we must,' he said, suddenly brisk. 'I'm sure they're waiting, for they can't begin without us.'

Their public entrances together, side by side, were becoming more, rather than less, effective with every one of them; starting with her beauty, the affinity in their looks and their perfect proportionateness to each other had something of a work of art, and that is the more admired for being admired often. And when they came out of the hotel late – the others having already forgathered – with the absence of conceitedness that, being hers, was also his, they were accepted for general admiration as a pair, and for more admiration than ever. It looked to be really true, that they had been waited for.

They parted from each other almost at once, but they came together several times during the day and then he reported to her on what he had seen and done. He was meeting the complications, he considered, adroitly, yet his real interest was in his 'studies', and on a little walk with her he obtained before they went up to dress for dinner the next evening he told her of a piece of news that had got abroad and of its effect, which diverted him. By some indiscretion it had become known that the daughter of the Austrian Ambassadress was going to marry Prince zu Teschau; the betrothal was to be announced in Vienna at the end of the month. A change in the attitude of all the young people to the ugly girl was immediate; she had been hardly human to them, and now they were all looking at her with respect. He told his sister, 'I heard the blonde Wild Indian say in such a tone of envy, "If you're Austrian you need only sit on a sofa and look like a cow, and the most wonderful marriage is made for you."' He laughed very much. 'I like the way she put my point!'

She smiled companionably.

Their walk was past the row of little shops and then the villas on the lake road, and towards a group of cypresses at the bend.

'Do you know, I have never been in Italy before,' he said.

Behind them the sky was clear and green and the lake and hillsides shone, but a large black cloud that hung over the end of the lake they were facing had turned that whole area of water dark.

Madame Solario paused opposite the gates of one of the villas. The villa stood against the steep slope of the hill and had two palm trees flanking the path in front of it.

'There was such a pretty ball here the other week,' she said, 'with a cotillon.'

Enigmatically reminiscent, she looked up at the house. Then a little white Pomeranian dog rushed out of it and down the path, barking at them, as if warning them off, and the two walked on.

He noticed that she now walked listlessly.

'Why did that make you sad?' he asked. 'Was it the dog barking at you?'

'How could that be?'

'Are you ever sad, Nelly?' She didn't answer. 'When?'

'An impression – sometimes,' she murmured.

'Let's not be sad now!'

He knew by this time that he could make her at least want to laugh, and he did not stop trying until he had. They turned at the group of cypresses – seeing another bend of the shore and more cypresses beyond in the gloom of the cloud – and faced the lucent sky.

'I find the décor very enhancing,' he said. 'I would have to make love here even if I had no motives. That *would* be sadness, now, if here, this evening, there were no prospect of making love! But to which shall it be?'

'Have you no preference?'

'Yes, I have – the girl, because of the eloquent shape of her eyelids.'

They were going slowly, no one but themselves on the road.

'But the lady has an advantage, which is over my vanity. I would like to get to the point where I could be sure she wouldn't drop me, at least publicly; she is, of course, a much more uncertain quantity than the girl. Also, Nelly, if I have a real success with her you will be left free to do what you like with her husband. Do his attentions please you? Well, they will *have* to please you; they are part of the minuet we – or I – have engaged ourselves to dance. I admit that my partners are more lively than yours, but yours – the public one – confers a greater social distinction,

I consider. He is the genuine article, and my two are really only imitations. Has there been no one here whom you might have preferred?'

He saw that she would answer and that he had only to wait a little.

'There was an Italian – for a few days – who pleased me rather. I was rather sorry he had to go.'

'Why did he?'

'There was a complication.' Once again a smile looked like some sharing of amusement with an intimate. 'He had a family. That is something you talk a great deal about.'

His delight was again obvious. 'How did it come into this?'

'There was the possibility that something disagreeable might happen, and he could not let it happen before his family.'

They were coming round the curve that brought them opposite the corner of the hotel and the narrow path, between buildings, which dropped down from the mountain behind. A man emerged out of the dark cleft and reached the road as they were going past.

'There he is!' said Harden in an undertone. 'Was he waiting for us?'

The man immediately put the row of oleanders between himself and them and, walking rapidly, got first to the hotel door.

The two said nothing till they were almost at the door themselves. Then: 'Nelly, don't be angry with me, but I'd like to pursue my acquaintance with him! You see, I'm uncomfortable about my foolish talk; and then, you *have* made me curious.'

She gave him to understand that she decidedly did not wish it.

'But I'm here to protect you now.'

Another man's figure – made recognizable by a pointed black beard – strolled out to meet them, and Missy was above, leaning over between the columns of a first-floor balcony. She called down, and Harden stepped back to look up at her. San Rufino said to Madame Solario: 'Je ne savais pas que vous vouliez faire une promenade avant dîner.' In her little pause at the door there was physical lassitude, perhaps; anyhow, that pause without even a look was all languor and reserve.

San Rufino's attendance upon her took from then on an air

of finality. Patronizing in a way, as it entailed less conversation than ever and she did not seem to be consulted, it also established a perfect disregard of everyone else. And she in his case even simplified her usual acquiescence to male attention; she did nothing more than be. She wore that night the large black hat with the black osprey sweeping across it, but he did not try to whisper in her ear and the osprey never brushed his cheek. As the only decoration on her pale-grey gown, two velvet lilies, one white and one black, were fastened against her shoulder. The other couple was in vivid contrast to these two. The Marchesa San Rufino's dress encased her in a close-fitting coat-of-mail of dark-blue sequins, and as she was in constant movement she was always aglitter, and her rough voice was seldom silent; Harden easily kept it going. They did not remain long in one place, but would sit for a while and then walk out and then come back. They and some of the other Romans had been away for some time when Madame Solario and San Rufino also decided to take a stroll.

The night was very dark. 'La lune manque,' said San Rufino. 'Pourquoi cela?'

Madame Solario was seeing at that moment that her brother and Kovanski were talking together. A flush that no one saw rose to her face. It had gone when she received the two men on their coming to speak to her. Her brother spoke; Kovanski seemed to be led by him, to be acting without volition. By a deft manipulation of the strings, Harden got them started with some villa people who were going home, and as the whole company proceeded up the road San Rufino was separated from her, and for a few minutes it was Kovanski who was at her side. He was unable to address her; he could not utter a word. The ones who did not wish to go farther stopped before the embarcadero and dallied there. It was there that Kovanski found his voice.

'May I –' he said. He said again, 'May I –'

San Rufino was back. He took his eyeglass out of his eye and then put it in again, and the contraction of the muscles as the eyeglass was wedged in drew up his lip.

'Yes, of course,' she said to Kovanski nonchalantly.

'N'avez vous pas froid, Madame?' asked San Rufino.

'Oui, un peu,' she said.

Kovanski did not go back to the hall with them.

Harden knocked at his sister's door next morning so early –
so certainly before she would be ready to go out – that she
could not have expected him and said, 'Entrez!' thinking it
was the chambermaid. She was standing in her dressing-gown,
a white silk dressing-gown with long, open, hanging sleeves,
but he made no point of having surprised her before she was
dressed. The surprise it was to her, however, quickened some
process, and he was answered when he began to make excuses.
He knew she was annoyed with him for what he had done.

'But really I had no reason to think you would take it so
seriously –'

'I think it would have made no difference if you had known.'

'Known what? That you would be angry with me, or the
facts? It depends on the facts, and I don't know them.'

After the flash of displeasure, her self-command when she
replied again made that reply the more disconcerting.

'I think it was enough to know I didn't want it. And you may
not like what can happen. You may think one can be sure he
will behave like other people, but one can't be sure.'

'What did he do? If it happened here it didn't come out.
No one has any idea –'

'Something did happen here. No one heard because of the way
it was done. But one person knows, and that is not very
nice.'

'Who?'

'I told you about the Italian.' Though she spoke without
warmth, she had been brought to the point of speaking by
resentment. 'He behaved very well. I told him he must go or I
would have to go, at once, and he went away.'

'Do you mean –' Startled, he put things together. 'Because
of his family – I remember. This man could force you to do
that?'

She indicated that she wanted to go on with her dressing,
but he only came farther into the room, and with resignation
she sat down by the dressing-table, holding her loose gown folded
about her.

168

'How did he do it? You appear not to know each other, or only barely. Did no one see – You must have had some talk with him, for him to threaten you!'

'I had experience of him. He told me what would happen, before I came here. One look was enough – that is, it was the contrary: when he didn't look at me on a certain occasion.'

'You sent the other man away because this one didn't look at you? Without his even speaking to you?' He sat down on the edge of the bed, at the foot.

'He didn't have to speak to me. He had told me what he would do.'

'Haven't you been afraid for yourself?' he exclaimed.

His consternation evoked no particular response from her.

'Nelly, you must be careful!'

'It is I who told *you* to be careful.'

He acknowledged it. 'How long has this been going on?'

'I have known him since last May.' She told him more. 'When I came here I thought it had all been finished with, and that he wouldn't carry out his threat. Even so, I went away for a few days, hoping he would think I had gone altogether and would leave and I would be rid of him. But he must have heard I might be coming back, and he stayed. I was annoyed to find him still here, and – Well, I was unwise. Then I understood – by that, that he wouldn't look at me – that he still meant to carry out his threat.'

'He didn't even have to tell you!' It was this that shocked his imagination.

'The danger is, Eugene,' she said, and an ironical intonation turned it into a warning of the danger to *his* interests, leaving out any to herself, 'that next time it will be someone who will refuse to go away, and there will be a scandal.'

The tone of the warning stung him. 'I've made nothing worse! He would do it anyhow, if you allow anyone's attentions, and not more because you are on speaking terms with him.'

'I didn't wish to be. And if I speak to him, if only before other people, he will have more opportunities. There are other ways of making a scandal than a duel. It was better when he didn't come near me.'

'The main risk is always there. There's not much better or

169

worse than that. I wonder you dared to take it, that you've stayed on, with him still here!'

She warned him about certain dangers, but she had about others a curious unconcern that evaded his logic, unless it were fatalism. He began to think things out, but kept his own counsel. Then he abruptly asked, 'Where did you meet this madman?'

'In the train,' she answered, as if that were quite unremarkable.

'There you met a man you had never known before?'

'I saw him for the first time when I was going down the corridor to my compartment. It was the Rome Express to Paris, and I got into it at Florence.'

'And then?'

'When I came out of my compartment he was still there, standing in the corridor.'

The offhandedness with which she gave him this information did not deceive him. Her other confession was in the mind of both.

'I'm learning about you! It began at once, in the train, I see that. For him, of course, it was love at first sight, the coup de foudre. And what for you?'

'We went back to Italy together two days later,' she said.

'How long did you stay? A mere fillip –' he sneered, in a spasm of his old hatred, 'that's all you can look for now. Counterfeits of the first experience!'

She did not protest against this abuse of her confidence.

'Given that this is your fate, was this experiment more, or less, disillusioning than others?'

Sitting sideways to the dressing-table she straightened several articles on it and the wings of her long sleeve, in falling back, left her arm bare to the shoulder.

'In any case I don't see why, to finish, you had to be so extreme.'

'Because he was extreme,' she answered.

'You made him so by the way you treated him.'

'It was the other way about,' she said with indignation. 'There were no limits – it was too much.'

'You make me blush,' he said as offensively as he could.

'He could spend half the day on his knees. He hadn't another thought, and I couldn't endure it any longer. It was madness. And he would have ruined himself.'

'How?'

The subject was giving her energy of speech. 'When we met he was going to Paris and then Petersburg on his duties, and after a time if he hadn't gone back he would have been left with nothing.'

'Your practicality, even more than a surfeit of adoration!'

'Everything he did made for scandal.'

'Were you openly together?'

Guessing that he feared for his plans, she answered with more than a hint of sarcasm, 'So far there has been nothing open, nothing known. That has been prevented.'

'So what you chiefly had against him was that he adored you on his knees.'

'Adoring always means asking too,' she said contemptuously.

'There is a profound cynicism in that. But why did you keep him on his knees?'

Again she was willing to ignore the offensive meaning. 'He was asking me to marry him.'

The story had unfolded itself so rapidly that he had not yet thought of this. It came as a gratifying surprise.

'What folly to be at the same time ruining his own prospects! What are his prospects?'

There was a movement of impatience to show him he was wasting his time.

'Simply out of curiosity – what are they?'

'Very confused,' she answered, still impatient. 'Sometimes good, and sometimes bad.'

The contempt she had for Kovanski and everything to do with him affected Harden unpredictably; his imagination penetrated to the despair behind all this, and it suddenly depressed him.

He said in a gloomy voice, not looking at her, 'And to think he is here!'

Whether he brought in some of that despair that was so close to them, or because there was some hopelessness in their own existences, and each acted on the other, they both sank into an apathetic silence.

His arms were crossed on the foot-rail of the bed. 'You can't –' he said after a time, 'you can't be so depraved that you took him as a lover – that you went to Italy with him, at once – without any feeling.'

'No. I even thought that for me, too, it was the coup de foudre.'

'Did you? But you see that couldn't last.'

From inertia they went on sitting where they were. A window was open, but the room was not airy and it had kept something of the staleness of the night. And outside, round the corner – if they could but bestir themselves – a bright day was advancing.

'What did he do when you broke it off?'

'I believe he was in a stupor for two days, but I didn't see him.'

'And then I suppose he was violent. You had courage to do what you did! And now we have the consequences on our hands.'

Chapter Seventeen

In the faces – Kovanski's not being among them – turned towards the brother and sister there were only complacent expectations of a day even pleasanter than the one before; not for *these* people, Harden thought, any anxiety or sinking into a fateful past. He asked his sister in an aside, out of nervousness and not as a joke, 'He couldn't be jealous of *him*, could he?' – meaning jealous of San Rufino.

With the serenity of manner suited to their surroundings, she replied, 'We will see.'

He was becoming very definitely accredited to the Marchesa San Rufino; his choice seemed to have been made. Pretty sure she would not drop him now, he saw that he would be firmly ensconced in the Roman circle if all continued to go well. Nothing must go wrong!

In small ways there could be miscalculations, and one afternoon when he came out at four o'clock with a plan, he found she had not done what he expected. No one was in front of the hotel; the place was deserted; she had not stayed behind, he had not even been waited for, and he was depressingly left not knowing what to do with himself.

As he was hanging about, a disembodied mischievous voice spoke close to him.

'Oh, Mr Harden, are you alone?'

He looked up and saw Vivina looking out from the vine-covered arbour.

'Yes, Princess. Isn't it sad?'

'Then come up here and it will not be sad any more.'

He went up the few steps into the arbour and saw that Kovanski was sitting with her there.

'Why has everybody gone away?' he asked, and sat down with the two of them.

It was a peculiar sensation to be with this man for the first time after hearing so much about him.

'Everybody had designs, I think,' the Princess answered with a naughty air.

Her *cavaliere servente*, too, had vanished from the scene. But *she* had not been left at a loose end; she was certainly doing what she wanted, though that could not have been a tête-à-tête with Kovanski; it was probably to annoy that she had remained behind.

'What were your designs?' Kovanski asked her.

The sort of compassion Harden had felt for a short while when hearing about him was very far from what he felt on seeing the hard, dark, in a way primitive face, to which a modern arrogance had been added. This was the man who had a power that had shocked Harden's imagination. It was frightening that he should have that power – but to the fear of him there now succeeded a consciousness of triumph. For *their* power over a man who could look so sure of himself was something to be prized. With the Princess there, the three of them together, Kovanski was not giving Harden the position of advantage that, inexplicably then, he had given him when they were dining together; quite the reverse. Here he was being characteristically himself, and that was somehow impressive; Harden had to submit to being impressed. But in this lay the triumph. A man like that at their mercy! Harden identified himself with his sister: we. We can have this man if we want him.

Vivina was not dividing her attentions between the two men; after her promising reception of Harden she had gone back to what she was saying to Kovanski. If disagreed with she became obstinate, and she insisted on one point for the sake of placing the last word. Harden had to sit by, and Kovanski did nothing for him. So – and it was pleasant – Harden thought: He can look very different at other times. He has been on his knees to my sister. He wants to marry her. From that he went on – And if she married him? There was a shake to the kaleidoscope, a different pattern. He, the brother, would be sitting with these people in a fragment of a family circle.

He did not know the whereabouts of his sister; she might have gone out with the others. It was therefore with a jolt that, his eyes having been caught by two figures coming slowly from the plane-tree walk, he saw that she was one of them. But the man who was with her was the young Englishman.

After the moment of relief he wondered why she was walking with this young man. Had it simply happened, or might she have a motive?

'There is my sister,' he said casually.

'If we had tea up here?' the Princess said to her two men; and to Harden: 'I will ask your sister if she will have tea with us.'

Harden went into the hotel to give the order for tea, and when he came out again Vivina was talking down from her bower to his sister only, as the young man had walked on.

This time Kovanski was in command of his expression, but not of his blood, which again darkened his face and neck when he bowed to her. The four then sat in an apparently reposeful anticipation of tea in the pretty spot overhanging the lake. A beautiful white cloud filled the pale-blue sky between them and the opposite mountain and was mirrored in the water. All was quiet; there was no movement anywhere except when a peasant boat passed down the middle of the lake. With the arrival of tea there was more animation in the arbour. Vivina was made greedy by the sight of rolls and honey, and they drew their chairs up to the table. The surface of this social occasion was all cheerfulness and suavity. Vivina's chair was closest to the railing, and having seen the number of fish just below them, for the arbour was built on rock that went straight down into deep water, she threw out what was left of her roll. The crumbs disappeared in a swarm of fish, and childishly she asked the others for what was left on their plates. Harden told her that these were the little fish she was given to eat between fried bay leaves, and they were called *agoni*. There could be a joke about the name, and then the Princess cried, 'If we fished!'

Earlier she had seen a waiter fishing from the lake-wall, and, their waiter coming to ask if they desired anything more, she ordered a fishing-rod. He might have been the very one she had seen, for in a surprisingly short time he brought a fishing-rod, but no bait. They did not want bait; bread would do. The crumb was rolled into a ball and fixed on to the hook, and the four leaned on the railing while the Princess tried first. The fish darted up and away, and in all that nervous movement below the bread disappeared without result, though there were tremors in the line, enough to keep her excited. At last there was a pull, and she jerked up the rod – but the fish jumped off the hook back into the water. In the instant she thought she had him she exclaimed, 'Oh, Gesù!' – and this released almost hysterical laughter.

While each of them tried his luck, absorption in the game gained upon them. Madame Solario was next to Kovanski. When she needed more bread-balls and when the line got entangled she took his help; enjoyment of what she was doing made her miraculously approachable. Out of prudence Harden shielded Kovanski from Vivina's view, but then Madame Solario landed a fish and the congratulations on her prowess covered everything. She was openly pleased with herself, and her brother smiled across at her and said, 'So competent!' Vivina was determined to have another try and the same success, and other people looked on enviously at the fun – the Lastacoris from their balcony, and guests not in hotel society from tea-tables on the terrace.

The beautiful white cloud that had remained nearly stationary was becoming tinged with apricot when those who had been away returned and found a party of four fishing from the arbour, and one little dead fish to prove what could be done.

Restored good humour after the earlier annoyances was general. San Rufino complimented Madame Solario on her catch, and put his eyeglass in his eye to look down at the fish. 'Magnifique!' he said.

Some of the others wanted to fish, but Vivina did not want them to have her fun; she wanted to have theirs. They had been out in the launch, and now she wanted to go out in the launch. 'Si nous faisions un petit tour du lac?' she said. The sunset promised to be beautiful, but it was the various repaired relations that brought a willing assent to another turn on the lake. Kovanski, however, declined.

Harden and the Marchesa sat alone in the cabin, and Madame Solario was one of those who went forward. San Rufino, who had been offended, rather grandly took his place on the seat beside her; and what was new was a possible welcome from her.

Her white chiffon veil, blown against her face by the breeze, was dyed in a rosy light. The long ends fluttering about blew right into his face and were caught on his yachting-cap, and as she secured them and apologized her eyes seemed to be allowed to sparkle now that they were behind a veil. The chiffon against her mouth moulded it to look fuller than it was. Behind her veil she was not only the poetic beauty and symbol that she had been, and he was all question. There was a colloquy. Her fully moulded lips smiled when she said. 'Non pas.' A little later she turned towards the others to listen or take part in what they were saying. A few minutes after that San Rufino spoke to her again, and she answered with a look that was like a flash subdued. 'It would be best,' she said.

When they returned he left her to her own devices, and she went indoors alone.

Her brother overtook her, and they got into the lift together.

'What did you say to him?'

She seized his arm, and he saw that she was beginning to laugh. And when they had got out and were alone on the second-floor landing they both had a fit of silent, unexplained, irresistible mirth. When the lift was heard coming up once more she broke off and started to walk – with her characteristic indolent walk – down the passage to her room.

The social life of the hotel was a forcing-house for situations; the opportunities to see, meet, succeed, fail, and recover never stopped from morning till night. Every shade of behaviour in public had significance, so that the choice of a seat could constitute a victory or a reverse, and a few words aside change the complexion of half the day. In all this Harden had more and more difficulty in getting private talk with his sister. On two successive nights they dined at the San Rufino's table, and when he tried her door in the morning it was locked and she said from within that she was just coming down. But on the third morning the door yielded.

'Well,' he said, in the best of spirits, 'what are we intending to do?'

As he sat down and went straight on with 'I've got to the point where I should make a decision,' his thought was that a secret contentment was always obtruded upon when he entered her room. It was the atmosphere of her solitude, which he was bound to dispel, that he could feel only as it vanished.

She was still in her dressing-gown, and she put away what was in her hands – a piece of sewing, he thought – into a drawer and rested her elbow on the back of her chair.

'What is there to decide?' she said.

'Something very important. There'll be only another two weeks or so of this – and then? Will it all be over, or do we carry on from here? I say we carry on! But with what – with whom? Don't you see that here in this hotel, by chance – but of course it isn't by chance – we are being given an opportunity to make our future? Part of our future that is – the immediate. Because *our* future, Nelly –'

'What do you mean?' she asked when he significantly but genially paused.

'Well, it won't be all of a piece.'

'What future is that?' she said, quickly for her.

'Oh, yes, for some that can at least be envisaged.'

When her opposition was quick and instinctive he was given something to wonder about.

'Anyhow – Within ten days of linking my fate with yours these opportunities opened up. I don't find it extraordinary – we will always be given opportunities. *But we must take them.*'

'I don't see these opportunities,' she said.

'That's why you need me. *I* see them.'

He smiled at her, making his jollity a blandishment. 'But I won't put anything before you till I've collected a little more information about everybody. I haven't liked to ask too directly – one never should. Are they all just what they seem? Just as rich? Is the Satyr seriously in politics, and might he be going to have an interesting career?'

'I don't see how that can be of any interest,' she said.

He laughed, crossing his legs. 'I see us in politics. Then let's look in the other direction. I haven't given up the girl, you know.'

'No, I didn't think you had.'

'It's difficult to explain to her why we can't have an open flirtation – but just because of all the "considerations" and "obligations" I've talked about, all the nonsense, and having

178

to keep it secret, I've got her to go farther and faster . . . ' He had pretended to hesitate before saying so much. 'It would be a sacrifice, I assure you, to give up the girl. In the evening – or later still – we slip out –' And he pointed to the window and downwards. 'Down there. And it's exciting to come back not knowing if it's been discovered. It's all the mother's fault,' he added in a tone of honest censure, 'for not bringing her up better.'

His sister looked out at the trees of the avenue, so close to the window.

'Whether I develop that, or the other, is what I have to decide. But I don't want to do anything that will part us for long, you and me. The ideal would be –'

'I think we are very well as we are,' she said.

'No, really we aren't! Do you know that I have to ask you for a hundred francs? If it was five thousand, if it was a thousand – But a hundred! Isn't that awful?'

They both laughed.

'Remind me,' she said, not getting up.

'Indeed I must. And now what is happening to you? You did something very clever that day, but what was it? The Satyr is not as he was, and leaves you alone sometimes. Whose feelings did you suggest to him should be considered?'

He was much amused that she wouldn't answer.

'Now you must speak to the Centaur – which will be quite easy after the other day – and do the same by him.'

For several days his mood had been so buoyant that every anxiety was thrown out. 'We must keep them all in equilibrium till I know more!'

It was with an air of promise of a good joke that he came up to her when the after-luncheon *conversazione* was over.

'Let's say we'll walk to the post office before you go upstairs.'

He waited till all the windows of the hotel and the shops had been passed, and only when he safely could – 'I now know that by an extraordinary coincidence you have to do with two *nephews*. *Two* nephews! One of them might so easily have been a son – but no, both are nephews. The Centaur is nephew and probable heir to an enormously rich nobleman with vast estates in the Government of Tula.'

179

He made her stop. Her parasol was open; she shifted it against the sun when he made her stand and look at him.

'The Government of Tula!' He had made her smile.

'Not only that,' he said as they went on, 'the uncle has been a minister – Minister of War, anything you like – which must have greatly added to his fortune. He was too reactionary or too incompetent even for them and was dismissed, and all this fits in with what the Centaur said to me when we dined together, and with what *you* say, that his prospects are sometimes good and sometimes bad. An uncle isn't quite as good as a father, I'm afraid, and galloping about as he does, the Centaur is bound to get sometimes into trouble. There may be anxious moments, but I don't see why the huge fortune and the vast estates should be lost.'

Though not concurring, she listened leniently because he was agreeable to her.

'And the Satyr derives his importance from an uncle, too! His uncle, too, is a minister! It's quite extraordinary. But this uncle is as clever as the devil and is never out of office for long, and the nephew is dug in with him. He doesn't have to be a minister himself. The family's position in Rome is exalted already, and dispenses favours in good old Latin style. Now how much of all this did you know?'

'All of it,' she said.

They came upon a little public garden off the road – a patch of lawn, with a ring of cypresses and a bench – and an hour later they were still sitting there. They were leaning back on the bench, he with his arms lightly folded and she holding up her parasol. She had been talking. Just by chance, by the accident of a remark in a desultory conversation, he had touched a spring and got his first glimpse into her married past. But when he heard her say 'my husband' it was not by way of any intimate allusion to her experience of marriage; it was in connexion with the circumstances of a year of her life while married. Her husband's brother owned a ranch for the breeding of bulls for the bull-ring, and she had lived at the ranch house, taking part in its activities. On the subject of breeding bulls and supplying them to the arena she talked fluently for a little while, and when the sentences began to flow he stared at her in astonishment; he could hardly believe his ears. As she went on he settled back, listening comfortably and pleasurably. His hat was pulled down on one side of his forehead, to shade his eyes, and a smile floated on his mouth under the golden-brown moustache. Like that, he was remarkably handsome.

Gradually she ceased to speak. But the long silence that ensued was not one of constraint, or of something having come to an end. It was in a dreamy state of comfort and well-being that they sat, leaning back on their bench, side by side, without any desire of change.

Chapter Eighteen

The days were still hot, but they were getting shorter, and the Como boat came in just after sunset, after the violet-grey twilight had begun. Its lights were as yet no more than a pale gold lustre on the grey when it rounded the point and came churning up to the embarcadero. On such an evening Madame Solario slowly walked the length of the terrace with Kovanski, but he was half a step behind her and she was not speaking to him. San Rufino, making no advance, was farther back under the trees as the other two went past. And Harden said, on their sitting down to dinner, for the first time in several nights alone together at their table, 'I have seen what no mortal has ever seen before! A Goddess leading a Centaur in subjection, while a Satyr watched concealed in the bushes.'

He laughed the more when she put on her air of not heeding him.

'And I have seen another mythological beast – an attendant dog, a red setter. Can he perform some useful service? There he is. He guards the door, but I've seen him elsewhere.'

He looked towards Bernard Middleton.

'I can't believe he is there for nothing. In short, Nelly, what is this young Englishman?'

Now that their intimacy was advancing, she treated him to sudden capitulations – that is, she would be remote and austere at one moment, and the very next give him his answer with a gleam.

'A young man without a family,' she said.

He put down his soup spoon. 'Am I allowed to think what I like? For family, in one sense, we have deduced that he must have –'

'But not here,' she said.

'Is that it! No scandal to be feared with *him*; just a plop in the water!'

He was looking his surprise at her being 'deeper' than he thought; yet he had already suspected a motive.

'Has he really done duty as a false scent? He's rather young for that, but I suppose he could –'

'Oh, it was not like that,' she said in a conventional sort of denial. 'I have taken one or two walks with him because I like him; he is very sympathique.'

'Ah well,' he ruminated, 'one needn't be sorry for him. He can always go back to Bramblebury Hall.'

She nearly, out of interest, asked him how he knew the name – but of course it was one of his inventions.

'I want you to help me tonight,' he said, forgetting all that and lowering his voice. 'I have been very cautious with my charmer over there and had no more than *verbal* felicities as yet, but the time has come to try to have what one might call a little less talk. I haven't seen enough of the couple to be sure her husband lets her do everything she likes, and that's what I must find out – and I could find out in a very short while, given favourable circumstances. One would think there was plenty of opportunity for getting those, but curiously enough there isn't; too many heads with eyes at the back of them. Well, what I thought I would do tonight was, instead of spending my evening with her and later slipping out with the girl, do it the other way about. Have a nice, gay, open evening – and how pleased the girl will be – and then, if possible, take *her* out, when she's angry – the angrier the better. That voice when she isn't getting her way!' The *non sequitur* burst from him. 'She as good as berated me once – imagine! – because I had kept her waiting. What rights has she got after a week of flirtation? I suppose because it's a condescension to flirt with me. But one can soon put that shoe on the other foot, given the little opportunity. Now, Nelly,' he resumed, his tone altering again in an instant, 'what I want you to do is to keep *him* engaged, not go up until we've come back. And you'll do what I ask,' he said, with his eyes on her half-averted face in a smiling contemplation, 'and I'll know that you are. I'll always be safe with you!'

He changed the subject with a satisfied air and discoursed upon other matters till the end of dinner.

When he went into her room next morning she was already dressed but was still at the dressing-table.

'Thank you,' he said at once.

'It wasn't wise,' she answered, with uncommon directness.

'And why wasn't it? You can't speak for *me*. Certainly you have a right to your own opinion, but you aren't infallible, are you? It came off marvellously, I consider. We'll have to go away tomorrow if you can't have any latitude, not even as much as that – '

'Not even as much as that! It was not something I would do even if I wasn't being watched.'

'That very fact makes the explanation so simple!' he said with bravado. 'You have only to hint to the watcher that you must distract the other's attention from – ' He drew his smiling lips down to the proper sad expression. 'It's very regrettable – his wife – your brother – going decidedly a little too far.'

A movement of her head and one shoulder was half impatient and half hopeless. It cannot be like that, she might have said, but he would not have understood in this mood.

'And I didn't want to stay so long for another reason.' She picked up her hat, aware that she had spoken with asperity.

'What reason?' He begged. 'Explain!'

'I had to listen.'

'So I forced your hand!'

She straightened out some petals of the velvet pansies on the hat, and then, inadvertently it seemed, she raised her eyes and met his eyes in the looking-glass.

'But what a situation,' he said, coming to sit near her. 'You do think it's a situation?'

'Oh, yes, I think so.'

'Shall I tell you what I was finding out?'

'Yes, tell me.'

'I'm afraid she would like to deceive your admirer, Nelly, and it's a thing that can be done without much risk.'

'Didn't you know that already?'

'Appearances of every kind can be deceptive. There's no very settled modus vivendi: they let each other alone, or fight, as it suits them. A pretty life, I gather! Did you gather as much?'

'He didn't speak of her.'

'He's better bred than she is. But then, I had to ask her what the risk was. And I said – for I was humble – that I was no great credit to her, and her husband might object to *me*. Not a Lelio or a Misha, remember, only a hotel acquaintance. This led, all by way of diffidence, to my saying she must let me throw him off my trail a little; and that means I can be more public with the girl, who is about to give me trouble. I have turned my future conduct into a positive virtue! And all this I'm doing for *your* sake, to be taken off your hands.'

He leaned forward to watch her in the looking-glass, and he smiled when she again met his eyes in it.

'I want to see which way would suit us best. But you must remember I'm a disreputable person now, an adventurer. You mustn't be surprised at anything.'

She met the challenge, in the glass, with a front of pellucidness and unsurprise.

'Well, I've not yet seen her this morning, and I don't know if there may not be a couple of second thoughts. That's usual after the first step. As a first reaction she may not like me so well.'

Holding up the hand-mirror, she turned her head to be able to see the side and back of her hat before she said, 'And you – do you think you will like her better?'

He was very pleased. 'I might! I was not left quite indifferent – no, not quite indifferent. You would think even worse of me if I had been, wouldn't you?'

'But of course,' she answered with a little air of reserve, like delicacy, as she got up from the dressing-table.

The Roman ladies were sitting outside, as they always did in the fresh and glittering mornings, for the first meeting of the day. They would hardly interrupt themselves in their endless chatter to be said good morning to, and when the ones sitting with their backs to the hotel were approached from the rear, a hand, generally a left hand, would be raised to the level of the face and be taken and kissed by someone who might not be vouchsafed even a greeting. The ways of those privileged by a cult gave a certain sense of privilege to the cult votaries. Harden was aware of it in himself when allowed some unacknowledged act of respect. The Marchesa's left arm lay along the back of the bench she was

185

sitting on, and he came up from behind, lifted the hand, and clasped it. He felt he was doing it as easily, to the manner born, as anyone; but she, though she had acquired a great deal, did not have the whole *cachet*, and the yielding of the hand and withholding of her attention lacked the natural carelessness and grace possessed by the other women.

She was not having second thoughts. The first sliding glance between them told him so. Place on the bench was there for him to take, and while that was no more than on preceding mornings he took it with a difference. He examined her more exuberantly, a homage she accepted. She had a hard rather than a flowing line, smartly finished, and hair like lacquered ebony with two pin-curls breaking out from the mass, to lie, as flat as pressed leaves, above her eyebrows. Sometimes, as on that morning, she had a little black *mouche*, crescent-shaped, on her cheek-bone below the corner of her right eye. Her husky voice in short rushes gave its only character to her conversation, which was exceptionally humourless.

The affairs of the two San Rufinos were not the only focus of interest. Vivina was losing her cavalier to the less capricious Clarice and finding the loss intolerable. So intimate was that society that she was teased about it, and as her chosen rôle was childishness she was teased like a child, though she was fighting back in earnest. But she was also getting sympathy, and sides were being taken around the three.

On another morning the brother and sister met before the last in the row of little shops, with Georgette San Rufino just inside and her husband reading a telegram that had been handed to him. A knot of talkers provided a sort of screen, and Harden whispered to his sister, 'Come now.' She acted as he wished, and they turned the corner together into the narrow path that was like a crevice between buildings; wanting to run up the cobbled steps, he took her hand and pulled her after him. They had vanished from sight as if a cloud had taken them.

Above house-top level another path branched into the woods, and not till they were in it did he pause; she was not quite laughing with him but yet perfectly in tune.

He put his arm in hers and led her along, deeper into the wood. 'I want to talk about it while it's happening. You can't think how wonderful it is to be having my adventures in luxury and high society! One must have known the waterfront to appreciate it.'

'The waterfront?'

'There are towns that are ports, you know that,' he said affectionately. 'They are the wickedest of all. And where there's a port there's a waterfront; and scum is always thickest at the edge of the water. That's where one drops down to when one has no papers or recommendations – a man without a shadow.'

The pace he had set, with his arm in hers, was rather brisk, and they went lightly up the path under the hugely spanning chestnut trees.

'When one has been down there – lived in places I won't describe, and known only women one can't mention – but what a lot they taught one! – do you wonder that I feel as I do? Dressed like a prince, and finding my bonnes fortunes not in the scum of society but in the cream? I told you I was a disreputable person now, but I don't think it, not at all; I think the contrary. I've *been* disreputable, but now I'm wearing a silk shirt and succeeding with a Marchesa. I want to stop a moment and look on at that.'

He stopped a moment.

'That's the way to savour the experience.' He pressed her arm to draw her onwards again. 'And I don't want it to end here. I'm going to tell you what we might do. We'll go to Rome with them and make the combination famous! No hole-in-the-corner about it; that would hurt our reputations. It will be flamboyant! That will *make* our reputation. It's so extraordinary, the way it has turned out, that it can't be an accident; it's a design. We can see a design in our fate at this juncture. We'll be together, Nelly, and can't you imagine how novel it will be – a mysterious brother and sister arriving upon the scene? Arriving already in possession of the couple San Rufino, the rich and important, socially and politically important, San Rufinos? If *we* were a married couple there would be something scrubby about the combination; but a brother and sister! *We* will be pure. It will be a fashionable sensation, the alliances between us four. And we will be financed in the discreetest way by lucky investments – that's how it's done, and trust the nephew of the powerful minister to know how to invest. I've already asked what is the best hotel, and it's the Grand. We'll live in a suite at the Grand Hotel, Nelly, discreet but notorious!'

She interrupted no more than a spectator at a performance.

'How interesting that it will be Rome! I've never been to Rome. Have you?'

The spectator had been apostrophized from the stage. 'No,' she said.

'I've read – I've imagined it. I could believe I'd been there. Rome, eternal but always dying, full of splendour and corruption! And these silly descendants of horrible people, still bearing their names and housed in their tremendous palaces – won't it be fascinating to see their little spots of fashion and high life in all that antique squalor and gloom? Won't it be fascinating?'

He jogged her arm a little to gain her consent, and then his hand sought hers and he interlocked their fingers.

'When did you find time to read so much about Rome?' she asked.

'I don't have to read much. Half a page will do – I get an impression. The grandeur, and the miasma around it, the sinister streets and the treacherous people – what more does one want? And that'll be the background to our bright lights. But our modern adventure won't look so tawdry, because it won't be out of line. I wish I could have made you the mistress of a pope, Nelly, but one does what one can.'

He tried at last to see her expression. 'You know I'm not joking, don't you? I mean it; it's one of my plans, to form a double alliance with the couple San Rufino. And you know it's possible.'

He could not predict to himself what he would get from her. When he got nothing his mental processes were given a curious twist.

'I don't have to fear you may be shocked by what I'm saying, because you haven't quite the right to be shocked, have you? More's the pity.'

Their hands had fallen apart when they stepped over a root. She simply looked round her as though she were noting what she saw.

'Have you listened to what I've said?'

'But yes,' she answered.

'And you know I mean it?'

It was in his mind that she could have made him say he did not mean it.

'You say that we would arrive as a mysterious brother and sister,' she remarked with her note of irony, proving that she had listened to him. 'How about our family history being known? There might be one of those incidents you spoke of the night you came. You said we would always be at the mercy of incidents.'

'Not if there's been time for audacity!' he exclaimed, lifted to a peak of hopefulness by her oblique reply. 'Not if the double alliance has already been brought off! Then we can carry our past as well. If we are already notorious it won't hurt us to be more so; quite the reverse! All we have to fear is an incident before we're well started – so we must start at once.'

In his elation he continued for a time to talk about his plan, with verve, with – to use his word – audacity, and not a trace of shame. But he had heard of shame; he had a conception of it peculiarly his own, and this he suddenly introduced into the silence in which they were making the last and steepest part of the ascent, up to the rocky shelf above the cliff. As she was contributing nothing, if he paused in his talk there was silence, and while they climbed he had paused.

'Whatever happens we will never be shamed to each other; we cannot be, because we are brother and sister.'

They had not yet got to the top.

'We have everything in common. Every ancestor, every relation – '

They came on to level ground, to the bench placed there above the sunny glades stretching downwards, with the wood spreading up over the hill above. They were lost together in a high, silent, green-and-golden wood.

'Every relation, and all the places and conditions of our childhood,' he said, so slowly and reflectively that he might have been trying to pass them all under review. 'There are no secrets, no ambiguities, and we cannot change ourselves for each other's benefit. Here we are, knowing everything about each other – '

'How long did you live on the waterfront, Eugene?' But this came reflectively too, from further back and not as an immediate point that could be made.

He chose, however, to treat it as a point.

'It doesn't matter if you never know, or that you said, the first moment we were really alone together, "Where have you been all these years?"' He repeated '"Where have you been all these years?" You asked me that. It's of no importance, nor do I even want to know what happened to you after you said "Good-bye, Eugene." We know everything because we know what we are, what is behind us both; because we derive from the same source and by that *we are the same*. One is shamed, if ever, only because of what one is in the eyes of other people. And what one does is judged by what one is – in *their* eyes, in the world, I mean, and that is what we are talking about. That is all that matters to us; or I should say, to me. They will turn on me, if ever they do, because I am not one of themselves; they would shame me for that, but *you* can't, Nelly. You can't look at me with the eyes of other people.' He turned to look into her eyes. She let him do it. 'I am with myself when I am with you.'

He was at peace.

'If I were sitting here with another woman, at some point I would be bound to dissimulate; how and what would depend on who she was. But here we are, not able to dissimulate, even if we told lies to each other.'

'Tell me, Eugene,' she said with that vagueness of manner that was most when her object was definite, 'how long did you live on the waterfront?'

It took him a few moments to go back to that. 'Only five months.'

He would have liked to spin out his ideas, yet the facts, too, were interesting. 'Only five months, but it will always be a measure: how far up from the waterfront?'

He recounted his experiences for the sake of their effect upon her, placed therefore at one remove from their horror. Some dreadful things he described mockingly, and it was more effective in one way to present them thus, though less affecting. But when he reached the end of the worst phase there was a change of key, and he imparted strangely more to that end than to anything that had gone before.

'That very night – such peculiar things happen – a Danish sailor coming down the steps into a bar below the street passed me as I was coming up, and told me he had heard something. Things come through into those places in a way you can't believe, but that Danish sailor giving me a message was the strangest case I

190

ever heard. I thought I was hallucinated. But it was true; the money she had sent me was in the bank up in the town. And I had been found.'

She made a movement with her hand and then smoothed the sleeve upon the other arm. The sign of emotion satisfied him and changed the key again.

'Well, then I was transformed! I wouldn't get on so well with *them*, would I, or know so much about them, if I hadn't had a few periods of the most refined circumstances?'

This change was welcomed.

'And you don't have to read much. Half a page will do,' she said with a tender malice.

'Precisely! It's lucky it's so. For some reason or other, there's never time for more than half a page!'

When she had risen and guided him back to the homeward path, as they retraced their way they came back in another sense, for he returned to the things he had previously said, there where he had said them. He met his plan again, went backwards to the spell that Rome would cast upon them, and came full circle where, just above house-top level, the path branched into the wood. 'You can't think how wonderful it is to be having my adventures now in high society!'

They came out into the road, and, calm and slightly abstracted, so that, though close together, they were not speaking to each other, they approached the hotel and the guests assembling in front before luncheon. The first to see them was the American Wilbur, and they were so much the fashion that he was delighted to connect himself with them by hailing their appearance.

'Here are the Gemini!'

There were then exclamations of 'What happened to you?' 'Mais qu'êtes vous devenus?'

Chapter Nineteen

Kovanski came to the table d'hôte for luncheon, which he had not done before, and sat by himself at a table in the corner that gave him a view, between the columns, of the table for two in the middle of the room. Harden said to his sister, 'Now what does this portend?'

By the next day he felt that it was not his imagination that something was portending. Kovanski spent some time with his Roman friends, and Harden found himself watching for that terrible sign – that he would not look at her. He said to his sister in an undertone, with anger, 'You must see him alone. You must come to an understanding with him. We can't have this hanging over us!'

Two days later the morning dawned in a heavy rain; it was the first rain for many days. When Harden walked into his sister's room he found her occupied, as if the rainy morning were giving her leisure to do what she wanted because there was no necessity to finish dressing and go down. Her hair was unbound – which it had never been when he paid his visits before – and as is done for little girls to keep their hair from falling over their eyes, a ribbon, a blue ribbon, had been passed under it and tied in a little bow above her brow. And she was in *cache-corset* and petticoat – a white petticoat with two flounces of embroidery reaching to her ankles, and a *cache-corset* of embroidery threaded by a blue ribbon. But he was thinking of what he had come to say and was in a state of already-existing though suppressed agitation. He did not even say good morning. She had been washing her gloves, and, without glancing at him again, she laid them, protected by a towel, on the sill of the open window. Close to the window the rain was dripping through the thick foliage of the plane trees, but at some time the weather would clear and the gloves would be dried.

'Why isn't one pleased to see one can get what one wants?' he exclaimed; but it was something that recurred to him at that moment and was not what he had come to say. 'It's nearly as depressing as to see one has been a fool. No, it isn't depressing.' He sat down on the bed, at the foot of it. 'It's very extraordinary and interesting. What's depressing is that there must always be uncertainty, however certain one should be.' He suddenly asked, 'Have you seen this madman alone – have you spoken to him?'

'You make things impossible,' she said – she, too, with a nervous suddenness. 'Because of you, and what you do, I am forced to act against my judgement.'

'And why shouldn't you? Why should everything be according to *your* judgement? I'm older than you, and it should be *my* judgement.' It was like the outbreak of a childish quarrel. 'I *shall* decide, as long as we're together.'

'What now do you want to decide?'

'How you are to deal with this situation. You've had one experience – isn't that enough? I'm sure he's threatening again; something must be done. I won't have your relations with this man publicly exposed!'

'It is you who make that more likely. At every step you do something I could tell you you shouldn't do.'

She seemed to hold her own, and at the same time she betrayed that she was not so independent as before; he was able to impose himself and his mood upon her.

'That's your opinion. Now I know you've spoken to him.' He gave her time. 'What did he do?'

'I thought he would faint,' she said reluctantly; and a current exaggeration became, not to be doubted, a statement of fact.

His disquiet, of a double nature, was in no way relieved. 'I won't ask what you said.' He was both asking and not wishing to know. 'I don't like it – believe me. I don't like him. But we must – '

She silently kept on with her occupation, going from the wash-hand-stand back to the window. He saw her against the wet gloom. Even the change in the weather – the air without colour, laden with moisture, and the drip of the rain – contributed to the nervousness of this new day.

'God, why aren't we able to do as we like! Why can't I take on this affair of mine because I want to – or not, because I don't want? But I've got to go on till I see what it could do for me, do for *us*. And I require a few more days for that. This madman must be kept quiet; an "incident" would spoil everything, would frighten them all off from us! That's why I'd let you give him hope. It would be only to keep him quiet.'

At the window, half turned from him, she said nothing at all.

'I must do what I can for myself. And what else is there to do? – I have a talent, and they feel it a mile off. I've got the artist's temperament, too.' And, with his elbow on the bed-rail, he drew his hand over his face, hard, down from the eyes to the chin.

Looking up – 'Do you think – ' he began. Then he appeared to become aware for the first time of something unusual about her. Stretching out his arm, he caught hold of her – for she was passing close to the bed – and drew her to him. He lifted a strand of her hair and gently put it back over her shoulder.

'Oh, Nelly, your hair! Grandmother used to brush it by the whole half-hour.'

He looked up at her standing before him, and took in this new aspect, not only the wealth of hair but the little-girl bow of blue ribbon on top of her head.

'And to think I want you to further our fortunes with a Roman satyr – of the decadent period!'

She gave an involuntary laugh.

'You see I can make you laugh! You'll see, I'll make you laugh at everything!'

Her attitude was that she was indulging him. She had moved away after her laugh, but came back to lean for a moment, with folded arms, on the bed-rail, sketching the pose of a Latin woman on her balcony. Then when his hand went out again to catch her she slipped her arms through the sleeves of her dressing-gown. She was not getting ready to go down. And the rain that had seemed a disturbing element was now friendly, postponing. The cool, damp, darkened air was providing a respite, a hiding-place – soon he could have said, the happiest morning of all.

'Oh,' was said in their hiding-place, 'if we go to Rome we'll enjoy ourselves so much more than they will! Because we can *tell each other* and they can't!'

'You don't see things as they are,' she answered, but lightly.

'I'll tell you what I can see.' And he began to whisper outrageous secrets. 'There'll be no more of this condescension. By the end of the winter it won't be too much to aspire to Black Juno herself!'

The charm of the present projected him into the future, a far future with all the problems he had brought with him that morning resolved behind them, whose bold, broad picture could entertain him in a present quite different from the one with which he had come. He painted in more and more of the details as he leaned upon his elbow on the bed, while she moved in the room on her little avocations. These he was not interrupting, as he always had before; she was keeping something of what he had felt was her secret contentment, even though he was there.

He reached the peak of his own delight when he was saying, 'Political intrigues! The idea of political intrigues attracts me! Even in Italy ministerial intrigues would have some importance, with international plots round the Triple Alliance attached to them. We must be in politics, Nelly! Tortuous, decadent, clever Latin politics. I see you in the rôle – forgive me! As an asset to the uncle himself!'

He said suddenly in another voice, 'You think those are just my stories, but they aren't.'

She grew still and stood quite still by the window, where he could see her against the gloom.

'You'll come with me, and I've taken the first steps on our way.'

The rain did not cease till the middle of the afternoon; the heavy clouds took another hour to lift up from the lower slopes of the mountains and roll back from the summits, and then the sky shone and the lake glistened. Harden had gone to call on the Lastacoris, as she knew – he had said he wanted to put things on a conventional footing – and he was having tea in their sitting-room when she was asked to join the Romans at tea in the hall. The Marchesa San Rufino was very polite to her, and once addressed her in the most natural manner as 'Natalia'.

Christian names and the second-person singular are the recognition of social equality in Italian society and are universal among men and among women at the high level. With strangers, however right they seem, there is of course a period of reflection.

Madame Solario had not till then been addressed as 'Natalia', and it was the decisive moment of general acceptance. Soon she might be called 'Natalia' by all the women, and the 'tu' would follow. San Rufino's eyeglass glittered with satisfaction, and to commend his wife he spoke to her, which he did very rarely. She did not let this simply pass, but returned a direct and amiable answer.

After tea some of them went out. San Rufino accompanied Madame Solario, and as they walked along the road he every now and then turned his head – not in the unthinking way of other people, but as a deliberate act – and looked at her. She looked ahead, and her perfect femininity was like a sort of delicate suffering.

On the way back, and he and she did not go far – she did not seem capable of the exertion, and there were puddles in the road – they met the other two stepping out determinedly. The two couples crossed each other, Harden wearing a smile, San Rufino blandly disregarding, Madame Solario musing upon it all, and the Marchesa screwing up her eyes.

The company was standing outside the front door while the hotel lights were coming out, when the two couples mingled with their friends. It was being proposed to redistribute the numbers at dinner that night, for the Roman party was large enough to need two tables for itself, but the seating did not have always to be the same.

'Natalia,' said Vivina, 'chez qui veux tu dîner?'

'Dine with me,' said the dark, majestic one whom Harden called Black Juno. 'And you too,' she said to him, and not just as an afterthought.

The brother and sister were invited to accompany the Romans on a day following, to luncheon at a villa about an hour distant; it was to be a picnic luncheon, no precise number was expected, 'and they will be charmed to see you'. Half an hour before they were due to start, the chambermaid brought a verbal message to the sister that her brother prayed her to come to his room.

He was dressed but had not yet put on his coat over his fine silk shirt, and was brushing his hair. The room, unlike hers, was full of sunshine, and the famous view in the open window was striking even from the door.

'I'm not going with you,' he said, laying down his brushes. 'I've got another plan. I'm going to have lunch with the girl and her family and spend the day with them.'

Some exclamation might have pleased him but was not necessary. He was content to do everything himself.

'You're going to make my excuses for me. You'll say I've got an attack of fever, which comes from a bad illness I once had in the tropics; it left me with a weakness, and I'm liable to these sudden attacks of fever, especially after a change in the weather. There's some truth in that somewhere. I *did* have an illness in a very hot country, and I do have fever sometimes.'

He said it all with urbanity and polish.

'You see, I found it rather pleasant sitting with that family, however short of an ideal family it is. I want to get a more complete impression, and when will I have another chance like today? Free and unobserved!'

While putting on his coat he continued, 'There'll probably be somebody left behind to tell my charmer afterwards, so be sure to say, when you're explaining these attacks of fever, that they're very *intermittent*; the temperature goes up and down within a few hours.'

Because in the long run he needed something against which to play the urbane manner, he dropped it suddenly.

'Don't be afraid,' he said with a sneer at the absent, 'that she'll take it out on you today. She's got her next assignation secure, and that makes all the difference; she won't be too bad-tempered. And bear in mind how obliged she is to you. – If you knew how she's managing it – the impudence!'

He re-assumed his complacency. 'Well, there we are, Nelly. These last days must have shown you that there we are! In Abraham's bosom. I suppose it's because we are that I'm taking the day off today. Isn't it perverse of me?'

Before leaving the room she looked all round it, as if recognizing certain things, and it was like something said. He answered.

'You haven't been in my room for many days. Not since the beginning. We had our first talks in here,'

On leaving she said only 'Good-bye.'

'Good-bye. Have a pleasant time! There's nothing to worry about for a whole long day.'

197

He had his door a little ajar and was watching, twenty minutes later, and she stopped for a moment in the passage, just where he could see her; she therefore wished him to get this glimpse through the crack of the door, or she would have gone straight by.

When the launch had started to speed away, eyes scanned the façade of the hotel. Missy and her young brother were standing well forward on their first-floor balcony, and a window almost directly above on the second floor had i⁺ ˉnetian blind dropped to the sill; the slats of the blind were open, and something white behind them waved.

An envelope on her dressing-table attracted her attention at once when she re-entered her room that afternoon. It was addressed to 'Madame Solario', and she studied it before she broke it open. Not only had she never seen herself so addressed by him; she had not seen his handwriting – except in a glance while he was signing his name on arrival – for twelve years. It had changed little from the handwriting of the boy. The letter said:

I can see the launch coming back, and I'm going out by the side door and will walk towards Tremezzo. Do the same, and I'll meet you somewhere beyond Villa Carlotta. Don't fail. Eugene.

She passed through the Salon de Lecture into the plane-tree walk, and to continue as inconspicuously as possible she walked on the inner side of the avenue, along the high wall of the Villa Carlotta gardens. The sharp corner was turned, and soon she saw him waiting for her behind the columns of Capella Sommariva.

'A rendezvous with my sister!' were his first words. 'How original!'

He took her arm and led her into one of those gullies that were the last drop down the mountainside, and he seemed gay as they went up the dark defile.

'How is my sister?' he asked.

He wanted to know all about her day. 'And I thought it would be much nicer to have a good long talk outside than in one of our rooms. All that murmuring that must go on, with people next door! And I didn't know if I could get you away easily. This has been perfect. Now tell me . . .'

198

He was not yet bethinking himself of his own day. And they had first to find a comfortable place for continuing their talk. At the top of the gully a lane to the left was more promising than a climb up through the vineyards, and they came upon two little villas with gardens, between which were a small piazza and a wayside shrine. A stone bench was close to the shrine and looked eastward, towards the finest of the mountains; the lake was hidden by the configuration of the hill. This was a spot that seemed very remote from the haunts of fashion.

A few light clouds were shading the sun from them.

'How much the best part of the day this is,' he observed; whether he meant the afternoon hour or the company he did not say.

'How was it?' she was brought to ask.

His interest in a subject could undergo an eclipse and disappear altogether, but on reappearing it would be instantly vivid. As soon as he began to talk of the Lastacoris he was completely interested. At luncheon the party consisted of the mother and Missy, the young brother, the two little girls and their governess, Signorina Petri, and Pico. The father had left the week before.

'I never had more than two words with him. He seemed very null. Is he just that – a quiet, inoffensive little man?'

'Irritable,' she vouchsafed.

'Ah! that explains! There is a great deal of irritation there. The woman is irritated. I saw that she disliked her husband, but I thought she was unreasonable. She married for money, and with what the little man appears to be she made a good bargain. But something has spoiled her nature. One can see that. She's all moods, and the whole crowd hangs on her moods; even the children are on wires. Even with me there to see it, it happened once or twice – indulgence, kisses, sunshine, then a thunder-clap over nothing, quite unjust, and everyone terrified. They all take her very seriously and worship, as people worship the bad spirits to keep them well disposed. "I adore Mama," the girl says, and it's probably genuine. You've seen all this for yourself, haven't you?'

'I didn't think of the worship of the bad spirits,' she said with a smile.

'But am I not right?'

He had to have the pleasure of a smile of acquiescence before he would go on.

'How much have you seen them? When before this?'

'I met the Marchesa last autumn in Venice, and then I stayed with them for two days at their villa at Vincigliata.'

'You never told me! When was that?'

'It must have been already May, because Missy and the governess were observing the Mois de Marie.'

'But the house, Nelly! What is it like?'

'It is a large, beautiful house, very luxurious.'

'They are really rich, aren't they?'

'They must be.'

He checked himself at the very point of saying something and asked her to tell him how she had met the Marchesa. She became vague about the visit to Venice and a mutual friend, but he did not pin her down on that, as he was engaged in another direction. He ranged over the family's social pretensions. This was the second generation, he had deduced; it was the little man's father who had made a fortune – he did not know in what – in some north Italian town, and the industrial place of origin was exchanged for Florence only when the little man married. In Florence they were severed from trade.

He turned to his sister, smiling, to look into her face and say, 'Nelly, you've seen what's coming. My new plan is to marry the girl.'

'But will they permit it?' she asked conversationally.

'Not at once, of course. It would take a little time. I am not studying the mother's psychology out of a simple interest in human nature, you understand, but to see how it could favour me. If she loves anyone, it's the girl. She dotes on her and is very vain about her, and in everything injudicious. Aren't they an emotional pair!'

'The parents must have ambitions for their daughter,' she remarked.

'Of course. That, you might think, is so big it would block our whole line of vision. But one can look round it. Why haven't they married her off yet? They've had three or four years to do it in. It's because they can't agree among themselves – the mother always opposes the father, and the girl takes advantage of their quarrels to do à sa façon. They won't be able to realize any ambitions at all if it goes on much longer like this. You see, I know a good deal; these evenings, remember. Well, if they go on fighting each other I might get her – for love.'

It seemed that she was so detached from the subject that she would take no part in it. And then she asked, 'How did the mother treat you?'

'She received me most graciously, my prestige very apparent. That I could have gone with our friends, that *she* would give her eyes to be friends with, and that I could say it bored me to go – you can imagine! Wasn't it flattering that I should prefer to stay to lunch with *them*? A triumph for Missy. All that. But it isn't the whole story. Where have I been all these years? That question comes back.' There were signs of the currents under the surface, but not for long. 'So, suddenly, she remembered how we had begun, and without excuse was rather sour! The girl blushed and was miserable, everyone was silent and wondered how long it would last. Then my snob-prestige came up again and remained on top. That's all very well in its place, you don't have to tell me, but one can't do business with it. One must have other strings to pull.' He added, 'I see them dangling.'

After a silence he said, 'I plan nothing without thinking of you. And wouldn't this suit you better? I marry, you marry, and we are respectable instead of notorious! Isn't there really more to be gained by being respectable? You will say, Why decide everything now? But I can see it didn't bring me luck in the past to drop what I had in hand because I thought that if one had one chance one was sure to have another. I won't do it again. If we marry we will be kept apart as we wouldn't be in my other plan, but – Who knows? Anyhow, nothing with us will last for very long; I feel it. And a period of security would be so restful! You won't begrudge it to me? Even in that nervous, parvenu family I felt – actually that I would be glad to sink into it for a while. It's the opposite of what I had been imagining, but each time I imagine something I see nothing but that.'

'Did you ever before think of marrying?' she asked.

'Indeed yes. I got as far as an official betrothal with the daughter of the Chilean Minister of War.' He looked round at her – for they had both been looking contemplatively in front

201

of them – and added very humorously, 'There have been ministers in *my* families too!'

'Why didn't the marriage take place?'

'I'd rather not tell you. They were charming people, in their way – real elegance, and very rich. The betrothal was the culmination and the end of my best period, the most improbable period of all.'

No regrets were to be seen. He was thinking past the event, he was thinking, and he went on, 'Isn't it strange how our destinies got entangled with Spanish-Americans? For it was only by chance. We've got out of that net, but I'm afraid it will be by *chance* again, where we go and what we do. Already there have been so many different countries and circumstances in our history. When you think that Grandfather had an official position in Turkey! A handsome, blond man in a fez! You remember the portrait in Grandmother's room. I said to the French boys I was friends with, "Mon grand-père était dans le service Ottoman" – the way Papa put it – and I was proud of the fact. I said he had a palace on the Bosphorus. You and I went there only once, when you were three, so you can't remember, and I can't very well, but I have a picture in my mind like a memory of the house and garden, partly, I suppose, because of being told about it. And did you know? When a situation had to be found for Father there was a project to send him to Constantinople as Grandfather's son-in-law, to follow him, perhaps – and then, instead, he accepted a very poor position in Cincinnati, proposed by a friend of his. So it might have been in Constantinople, where *she* was brought up, that we spent those years, and just by chance it was Cincinnati! Will it always be like that' – and he made a motion with his hands – 'this way or that way?'

He gave a laugh. 'To show you what variety there has been, I've been told that when we arrived in Paris a rumour went about that we were the children of the King of Sweden, her lover! We know it isn't true; it wasn't even possible; but it shows that mysteries can grow up around us . . .'

Presently he slipped his arm in hers, and his hand sought her hand.

'It was so awful once; the worst was so awful.'

They sat hand in hand.

The clouds had gradually dissolved themselves; the sun, coming through at last, shone fully forth, and the shadows – a little more than life-size – of the two sitting together on the bench spread out before them.

'Nelly, look!' He exclaimed it with such conviction that it was nothing less than a joyful truth that he announced. 'Look! You have given me my shadow!'

He laughed very much on seeing her, first startled by his exclamation, and then pleased as though what he said were in the world of reality. They gazed at their two shadows; he gestured and his shadow gestured; he put his arm about her shoulders to make his shadow follow, and pressed her hand.

'I do assure you,' he said when they were sitting on, without laughter, 'that Peter Schlemihl – that book and the pictures in it, the man in grey rolling up Peter's shadow – made such an impression on me then, when I was thirteen, and gave me such sense of strangeness and fear, that it did return at my worst moment. It added the sort of horror of having stepped into a story I already knew, of stepping into a *story*. But everything I read that summer at Gössefors did something of the same sort, and I still have moments of feeling strangeness – as I did when the Danish sailor spoke to me. Of stepping into a story I have already felt was strange.'

He was talking quietly. 'I could believe that here and now we were in a story, and in it our two shadows would get up from the ground and walk away. We would see them walking away together, and they would stand against the wall' – he pointed – 'and we would sit here and see them *over there*, and see them kiss each other.'

They both waited, as if to see it happen.

'You know I always liked stories about shadows,' he said.

She got up, and they walked away, with their shadows preceding them. In the rich late-afternoon light the shadows were black and rather long and thin, and behaved oddly in the twists of the lane. He was on the side of the low wall that bounded the vineyards, and he pointed as, at the bend, his shadow appeared to caper and jump over the wall backwards and forwards – like that of a 'familiar', or the man in grey.

Chapter Twenty

There was an incident that evening. The short scene took place in the card-room, into which the non-playing Romans strolled to watch the bridge game. As San Rufino paused behind Kovanski's chair, Kovanski said he did not wish to have anyone stand behind him. He said it while continuing to play his cards, without glancing up and without the pettishness that would have given his words a joking turn: with a cigarette in the corner of his mouth, his hands engaged, his face repulsively hard – 'Je n'aime pas qu'on se tienne derrière moi.'

A shock passed through everyone who heard it.

'Allons, Misha, la partie n'est pas encore perdue,' said his partner, a Roman called Lelio, to focus attention on the game, and San Rufino, really dignified, moved on and paused at another table.

The rubber ended almost immediately after, and when the result had been announced Kovanski pushed back his chair. 'Let someone take my place,' he said.

Someone stepped forward at once, but the Italians – though not, of course, San Rufino – talked among themselves.

'Ma che cosa l'ha preso?'

'E un brutto modo di fare.'

'Un caratteraccio,' said Vivina with a shrug.

Madame Solario was at the door with Donna Virgilia. She saw her brother address Kovanski – lightly, casually – when the latter got up from the card-table, and Kovanski allow himself to be drawn a little apart and into conversation. But she saw the Russian speak in his most odious way, hardly a muscle of his face moving, and with a smile and a good night to Donna Virgilia she withdrew.

She was expecting Eugene. She had not taken off her dress when he burst into her room. His anger was febrile; his voice was raised without regard for anyone next door.

'Why should he want to insult me! He brought up what I said when we dined together, when I didn't know who he was. How dare he – your brother!'

She looked not at him but over his shoulder, as though not he but someone behind him were speaking.

'He took advantage of me! I talked like a fool – as I am I'm a fool ever to talk – but I thought *him* a fool. But he stored it all up. I'm not one of those that one can know everything about – in the way *he* means – by simply knowing who they are. He has the advantage of me there!'

'I think he was not very polite to San Rufino,' she said.

The idea of a slight to himself had changed the whole ground. That there was a danger in Kovanski's behaviour to San Rufino was not occurring to him, and she spoke of the incident only by way of a solace to his pride.

'He couldn't insult San Rufino, within their confraternity, as he does me. I am fair game – or he thinks so! But why – why? Why, when he was ready to swallow anything to get news of you, does he suddenly turn on me? As a dog turns and bites!'

'I begged you to have nothing to do with him –'

'Would you have known it was in his character to go against his own interests, like a beast?'

She would not share her knowledge of that character. She attempted nothing more – not even to ask what had been said, in order to mitigate it if she could – from what seemed a sort of apathy.

It was the same next day. He had quickly glanced at the clock – which was not lost upon her – but his obsession had remained unaltered by the night, and she, when she had to meet it again, again met it almost mutely.

'I want you to marry him,' he said.

He did not go on for a moment; he wished to give to this its full effect.

He sat down.

'I will be his brother-in-law. In a day – today, tomorrow, in an hour – everything will be changed. What jokes we can pretend to have about our first meeting! I have one on him, for it was he who spoke first. "How about that accident, mon cher, and the three fishermen you drowned for me?"' He imitated two kinds of ha-ha-ha, a good performance with its overtones of hatred. '"And I took you in when I talked at dinner, didn't I? – though I can't quite remember what I talked about. Just pulling the leg of my future brother-in-law! Now it's all in the family"' – he made a deprecatory gesture of 'don't mention it!' – ' "for I have given my consent."'

'You forget, I cannot marry. I haven't got a divorce.'

'You can get a divorce; you told me so. In France it is quite easy and won't take long. But we don't have to wait even that long. You've spoken to him, and that was the first step. Now, having decided to divorce, you will accept him, and from that hour he and I will enter into the relations I want.'

His gaze was fixed by the obsessional idea. He sat like that for several moments.

'I told you before that you must marry. And you have made it your fate to marry him. You did that when you took him as a lover.'

He recoiled, for the idea had been succeeded by an image. He looked at her with that image in his mind.

'It's no outrage to you to propose him as a husband,' he said, and he walked straight to the door and went out.

As if he wished to visit his complicated ire upon everyone, the whole of society, he abandoned his previous subtle ways and flaunted indiscretion. He gave the morning to Missy and her family, sitting with them as though he belonged there, and he appeared to be ingratiating himself with the Marchesa Lastacori for a purpose. But something, some suppleness, was gone from his manner, and without it there was more than a hint of sarcastically intended exaggeration. The mother saw that – not Missy, who radiated confidence and joy. It was not a situation that the Marchesa could deal with merely irritably, or by snubbing an inadmissible suitor, for this provoking personage, though putting himself half in, was keeping himself half outside the category of suitor. While, therefore, the open attendance on Missy was enraging Georgette San Rufino, it was proving not quite complimentary to the Lastacoris.

And when, in the afternoon, he and Georgette took the steamboat and went off together to Bellagio – she determined to do it in front of her husband, her friends, and the girl – his manner was changed towards her too; the attractive mock-deference was gone, and the humorous questioning look in public, as if he knew nothing was to be taken for granted. Now, if anything was to be taken for granted, it was that she would carry him off. She could if she liked.

On his return he went straight to his sister's room – with the effect of bursting in, as he had the night before – and asked, 'Has he been seen?'

'Not that I know,' she answered. She was dressing for dinner.

'Can he have gone away?'

He said it with such anxiety that she observed, 'So now you don't want him to go away.'

'You know I don't. And it would be ironic, wouldn't it, if he did when I'm no longer afraid of him and see him as your fate?'

Already agitated, he grew more so when he felt her to be less passive than she had been that morning. He came nearer. She was in her evening petticoat of white taffeta, and over her bare shoulders was the little cape of flowered silk that she wore when combing her hair. The moment had come to do her hair, and she sat down at the dressing-table. He stood by the table, where he could look at her, while she looked into the glass, and he was both wrought-up and undecided, not knowing which lead to give himself.

'You haven't taken an abhorrence to him, have you? But would you abhor anyone? I don't think you would. Poor Nelly,' he said bitterly, with a bitterness directed against her fate, 'you weren't allowed to abhor. You accepted – you always had to accept.'

He watched her loosen her beautiful long fair hair and shake it back over her shoulders.

'You have only yourself to blame, haven't you? For why is he here? What put him into my head? Accept just once more,' he said, but he was not quite like himself, saying it. 'Submit again, this time for me.'

When, picking up the comb, she answered, she was not quite like herself answering. 'There are impediments.'

He gave a start. 'What – is he married?' He saw it wasn't that. 'Then what is it?'

'You know I became a Catholic.'

He was at once angered on being reminded of this, but not for the obvious reason, anticipation of conflict – on another score.

'*She* never changed her religion. And we were never asked to; it was understood that we wouldn't. Of course it was only a form that you went through.'

She was combing out her hair.

'When did you do it?' he asked, his anger growing.

'Not long after you left,' she said, almost as provocation.

'I see! You got Absolution, and it was a great comfort to him. I see it all! But that's over now. Religion has served its purpose. Or, if it hasn't, you can join the Orthodox Church. There is even more mysticism in that, but it allows divorce. That's settled!' he said with a rasping laugh. 'The Orthodox Church. Another phase, another religion! But mysticism and you –'

He leaned on the edge of the dressing-table as she gathered her hair with both hands at the back of her head and then, lifting her arms, twisted up her hair and fastened it. But, before going on to the adjustment of the rich wave over her brow, her arms dropped; her hand that held the comb fell, as though it were heavy. He was startled. She looked at him, and he could see that she had something to say, something that should embrace more than the immediate subject. He waited for it.

'You must see things as they are,' she said.

The very meagreness of the message increased its effect.

He went submissively when she told him it was time for him to go, and during the evening the little drama of jealousy was carried on without any direct stimulus from him. The woman he most frequently glanced towards was not either of those between whom he was expected to choose, but his sister. Missy had had a scene with her mother, and then that which had been prepared against, despite her entreaties, did not arise – he never came near them. And she no longer had any young man in tow, her flirt having departed, so that she was left with nothing to bluff with. She was sitting forlorn, with her mother and the hangers-on, not able to keep her eyes from the other circle. When her mother told her sharply not to look so much, her eyes filled with tears. In that forcing-house for situations everything was noticed, and conjecture was lush.

It began to look as though Harden were playing a double game. Supposing he tried to marry? Georgette's *béguin* might make her ridiculous if she didn't pay attention. The Lastacoris were reputedly rich. And if he did think of marrying, what were his chances? What had he to offer? Who was he? What, indeed, were the origins of this brother and sister? That question had not till then been seriously posed; it had not seemed necessary, appearances were so graceful; but it did pose itself when a change in Harden's behaviour began to blur the graceful appearances. It was not, oddly enough, as though he were getting overpleased with himself, which, with his astonishing success – two women throwing themselves at his head – he very well might, but as if his nerves were on edge, put on edge actually by his success, which was really insufferable. Who was he? On the terrace after a luncheon party, guests having come from Urio, he and Georgette were critically observed. He had been restless, but a struggle for the upper hand was going on that it seemed he would not drop, for he would return to her and they would take up all over again whatever it was that was the contention; they then sat down, and she looked dominating and satisfied. But after a pause between them he made, sideways and negligently, a remark that incensed her. She retorted sharply, and he laughed; she snapped again, and he laughed again, sitting with his legs crossed and his hat pulled down on one side of his forehead. To allow this glimpse into their relations was shocking. It gave a little malicious pleasure all the same, but not to Colonel Ross, who looked sad. Harden was a compatriot, though only the day before – that question posing itself – Colonel Ross had admitted that he could not supply any information about these compatriots of his.

'I don't know the name,' he had said with an air of caution – of not going to be drawn one way or the other. 'I don't think I've ever heard the name before. But I do know they have always lived abroad. That may account for it.' In the loyalty of his admiration he wanted to do more than this for Madame Solario. 'She's an uncommonly charmin' woman. I tell her she must come back and live in England now.'

The negative beginning of his answer had been somewhat offset by the positive end, that he would welcome Madame Solario in England. It left her brother with a chance of being welcomed too, if he could qualify as an individual. It was impossible, that afternoon on the terrace, not to speak of him, for he was disturbing.

'A sardonic fella,' Colonel Ross said rather solemnly.

The other couple was so much more to the general taste that the attitude to Madame Solario and San Rufino had become one of almost affectionate approbation. His designs upon her were being legitimatized while the modest carriage of her beauty earned her an ever-increasing regard. In one till so recently a stranger among them, her demeanour in their midst was considered perfect, and Carmine San Rufino had the good wishes of all.

She saw that her brother was ceasing to behave with circumspection, and, thinking she could warn him, she said, turning to him in the presence of others and speaking low, yet with an air of naturalness, 'You don't look where you are going.'

'What do you mean?'

She drew a little apart, and he followed her. He had understood what she meant, for he then asked, 'Why must I treat these people as if they were superior to me?'

She did not dare say more at that time; she did not trust him.

She was resolved on what she would say at the first opportunity, which would be when they were dining alone together. But before she could bring it about he remarked, directing a glance towards the Lastacoris' table in the dining-room window, 'They know our family history.'

The casualness with which he said it was what arrested her most. It was not acting normally to let fall those words with that indifference. She took care in answering.

'You thought they did, the first evening you were here. It is no surprise,' she added, as if saying that also to herself.

'It was a surprise, just the same. As nothing was said all this time, I forgot my impression, the one I had that night – no, *certainty*, by the way the mother treated me, but still I forgot.'

210

'And how did they hear?' she asked with a sort of loneliness and bleakness in her look.

'A Frenchman told the girl. He had left before I arrived, Maxime Guimard – do you remember him?'

Her lips by barely a tremor expressed contempt.

'He was from Paris, so why should we be surprised? The different worlds in Paris do hear about each other. Those other French people, your friends, who left at the same time, don't live in Paris, do they?'

'No, in Nice,' she answered absently. 'I knew them there.'

'You see, I know everything. There was no other channel here but this Guimard.' That seemed all that needed to be established. But then he noticed something. 'You aren't *anxious*, are you? Don't be! It hasn't gone further, as it happens.'

'How do you know?'

'I would have heard, of course. Wouldn't you?'

'No.'

'Ah, no, not you, but *I* would, I promise you.' In trying to reassure her, he came to life. 'It wouldn't matter by this time if it did go further. But anyhow the mother can't tell our friends because she doesn't know them – and even if she got the chance, she isn't such a fool as not to see it would serve her better to be the good friend of their friends; they wouldn't take anything from *her*.'

'Why did the girl tell you that they knew?' she asked after a moment of lonely thought.

'Why didn't she tell me before? you could ask. Why did she keep it from me so long? She could have made a joke of it, in a gale of laughter because I had tried to murder my stepfather. It would have been so like her! But no, it wasn't till last night when it wasn't a joke – nothing is any longer a joke; she confessed to all that is against me as though she were hypnotized.'

It was his indifference again that fixed her attention.

'That plan of yours has not much chance of succeeding, I think.'

'Oh, yes, it might succeed, if I took the trouble.' He calmly developed what could have been a thesis. 'The mother went so much against her nature in marrying for good reasons that she might commit a folly and want her daughter to marry for love.

211

Let *her* be happy, at all costs! She would enjoy a conflict with the father on that line – it would be a revenge. I haven't as yet proved it, it's just an idea, but there was something to put it into my head. Besides, poor Nelly, have you forgotten that sometimes parents have no choice?'

He reminded her of the circumstances of her own marriage without malice, with hardly a change of inflection. But it was not resentment she was moved by, it was another kind of revolt.

'I don't wish it!' she said.

'Of course not. I don't wish it myself.' He looked a little astonished. 'I was telling you how things might be, not how they necessarily will be.'

'I don't want anything to happen!' she said with nervous emphasis, and at the same time there was an unconscious movement of her hand, like a reflex action; she had to find an excuse for it, and her hand closed on the gold-mesh bag that had been laid beside her on the table.

He was still more astonished. These betrayals of emotion were unlike her. 'What do you mean by "happen"?'

'You have put us both in such difficult positions that one can't tell what might come first. I will not wait to see!'

'You told me I must see things as they are,' he said, always remembering criticism as though it were an injury. 'That was so sibylline that I was much impressed. But tell me what things *you* see as they are.'

'That at the very least,' she answered, with her listlessness and sadness that could come so suddenly, 'it might be unpleasant. You have put us "out in the open", as you called it, where we are very conspicuous, and if you make any mistakes it will be in front of everyone.'

'When I said we were "out in the open"' – he was interrupting – 'I meant something quite different.'

'Yes, I know.' And she left it unargued.

'So I don't have to explain. Now what I see, and what is true,' he went on, with the glitter in his eyes that had not been there since their first interviews, 'is that we need your marriage to that man. He won't offend me again when I am his brother-in-law – but let that be; it's a detail. We are "out in the open", in the way *I* meant, still, and until you marry, and he will give you a support – in the way I meant – that you won't lose even when you leave him. I don't know if there is any other admirer, anywhere else, who would do better. Here I see no one but the young man from Beaverdale Manor. This man, this madman, can give you a name that will continue to protect you, whatever happens.'

'Eugene, we can't talk of these things here.' And she smiled about her as if she were amused to make out, in the crowded room, her friends a little way off at their dinner parties. She was wearing, without a hat, the pale-grey gown she had once worn with two velvet lilies, one white and one black, as decoration; tonight, instead of the lilies, two black swallows, exquisitely simulated, nestled, wings spread, against her shoulder.

'Where else can we talk tonight? Would you rather I came to your room, or you to mine?'

'That is true; it's better here. I had made up my mind to say something to you here.'

The people who now had the tables nearest theirs were not acquaintances, and not English-speaking.

'Let me finish first. I want you to marry this man for another reason. It will be less painful to me, your brother, to have him as your husband than to know he has been your lover.' His eyes, with the glitter in them, tried to hold hers. 'Much less painful.' She did not answer. 'And I don't admit your impediment. Morality is of greater value than religion, and you will be returning to morality when you marry him.' He again gave her time to answer, in vain. 'And after that –' He left her marriage behind and embarked upon a vague but beautiful voyage. 'After that we will go back to what we were – together, you know, to what we were. That is my plan!'

Then he asked with mildness and kindness, 'What had you made up your mind to say to me?'

'That we must go away.'

'From here – now? Why?'

'It has become impossible to stay any longer. We are in difficulties on every side. Everything now is unpleasant, and this last thing, that you take so easily, that those people there can talk about our family history – that is indeed the last thing. But that isn't the worst, nor that you are no longer behaving correctly and it is being criticized. There could be worse.'

He looked as though he were being brought from a distance, which was the future, almost the ideal, and came unwillingly back to the immediate, which was her too practical concern.

'You will accept him before anything can happen, and from that moment you will be protected.'

'And where is he now, for me to accept him?'

He turned quickly towards the corner where Kovanski had sat, those significant times when he had come to the table d'hôte. The single place was laid, but the chair remained vacant; it had not been occupied since the incident in the card-room.

'You think he's gone!'

'No, I don't think so. I wish I were like you and it was *that* I was afraid of. He will come back at his own time. And I can't blame him now, because it is a situation he no longer understands.' She spoke bitterly, yet drearily. 'Before you came it was simple; he didn't dare speak to me. Yes, there was always danger, and I had to be careful, but there was never so much as now. You put me in the position where I had to speak to him, and then, to help you, I had to listen . . . to help you, I've had to go too far in that other direction, and then, to prevent . . . I've had to say more to him.' Reluctantly, she who wished to keep everything to herself added, 'He imagined something from what I had to say to him.'

He was bewildered and distracted by too many things that demanded his attention at once.

'That is what I want!' he exclaimed to the last thing said.

'You want not to know what he may do?'

'You can forestall the wrong move –'

'How can one forestall, with nothing in sight?'

He shot another look at the empty chair; it had acquired a peculiar amount of personality.

'We had a warning the other night. I thought he would keep quiet and wait till I spoke to him again, but he won't keep quiet; I'm sure now, just because he isn't showing himself. You had too many plans, Eugene! We must go before you can carry any of them out.'

'This isn't the only place! We can go on to the next and see who follows us. I only hope they won't *all* come.'

'Don't think about that. Think about arranging to go quickly, or I will go without you.'

He did not seem to hear her last words. 'I think further than that, and how to arrange so that in the end we'll be in peace and laugh together about everything.'

He had been too absorbed to notice that dinner was ending, that chairs were being scraped back and people were rising, the noise of their voices growing more strident, and it was with a start that he saw Colonel Ross standing beside their table.

'What a wonderful lot you always have to say to each other! It makes us feel quite jealous, what?' For her sake he was managing to overlook her brother's shortcomings and to be friendly to both. 'It's very different with me and my sister. We'd be sittin' perfectly mum!'

Chapter Twenty-One

The swallows against Madame Solario's shoulder were deemed a
very original idea and much admired. Lelio stroked them with one
finger, but San Rufino did not come so close to look and pronounce his more important approbation – 'C'est très joli.'

His sister had said that they had been made very conspicuous
and Harden might have been trying to make himself inconspicuous, so silent he was. He did not join in the general talk,
which anyhow rolled at first on a matter that could no longer
interest him. A lady who had come from Villa d'Este and was
going back next day had been inviting all her Cadenabbia friends
and acquaintances to a ball that would take place on the following
Saturday night, and the Romans were talking about it, pleased.
The ball at Villa d'Este would assemble everyone on the lake and
be a very agreeable end of the season; but the subject could not
interest Harden, because they had better be gone by Saturday.
He tried to catch his sister's eye during the talk, and while she
was not letting him do it he took notice that she sat at some distance from San Rufino. There must be intelligence between them!
The Marchesa had come to sit near himself, and was holding
forth in a particularly affected way on another topic, a piece of
gossip; it seemed to be a new item, for Lelio declared that it was
her own invention. She argued, a sort of demonstration before
her lover, who was remaining silent. She had a turn of the head,
quick and so extreme it gave her an Egyptian figure, a profile
upon a body seen frontally, that was the acme of conceit, and she
was playing this and her other tricks, at her most mannered and
croaking. And, not speaking to Harden but before him to Lelio –
a practitioner himself at the love-game – she put in the code-
words that were used between them to fix their assignations.

Harden's laugh suddenly grated on a repetition of a code-
word. 'But you are looking tired, Marchesa!' he said.

It might not be understood, but the laugh was not 'correct'. Her answer was addressed to Lelio, who, during the verbal criss-cross, saw Harden look at someone as if he had been unpleasantly cautioned. Lelio believed that it was at the husband, and he was right, but attached the wrong reason to it. Harden had been assailed by a definite suspicion that his sister and San Rufino were in closer collusion than he had supposed, and that the affair was deeper than she was letting him know. He jumped up as soon as he was given the chance. There were other, smaller tensions within the circle, which produced restlessness and the desire for more room to manoeuvre. Vivina went outside to see if the thunderstorm that had threatened was passing over. Madame Solario stayed where she was, a little secluded for a few moments. Her hair was shining fair with the light falling on it from above, and the beauty of her brow and eyes and of her white neck, was of such a sort that in a hyperbolic compliment one could have said that the two swallows were hers in the way doves belong to Venus and the peacock to Juno. He tried to get to her and was prevented, as in a dream.

Meanwhile Missy was being subjected to a long, cutting speech from her mother, one whose nature could be guessed by the Marchesa Lastacori's expression and a trenchant gesture of her hand. With Harden's Roman acquaintances wondering what chances of success his matrimonial projects might have, the Marchesa felt herself observed by people who otherwise over-looked her, and was rattled out of all consistency of action. She visited on Missy both his attentions, which were sometimes mar-ked, and the mortification of seeing him publicly pursue his other affair. On that evening it had to be the latter. Missy too jumped up when she saw her chance – when the Princess's example in going outside was followed. Harden had already gone out, to look back through a window at what was going on within. His sister now had Colonel Ross beside her, and San Rufino had come no nearer; so he had been taken into her confidence; there was intimacy.

But her brother could not spy on them as he wished, for San Rufino's lusting wife, free to do as she liked, had come out too. She stood in a group of four or five, waiting for him to join her and complete their arrangements. The storm was not quite over, and thunder rolled about the mountains, whose shapes leaped into sight when lightning zigzagged down the sky. The trees rustled in warm, moist gusts of wind, and it was a night to disturb a little with its own disturbance even those who were calm. But these people were nearly all uneasy themselves, and there then came out, impetuously, another figure, Missy – not with her old, petulant step, but in a sort of rush. The passionate, spoiled girl would have come straight to him – he had an awful moment of thinking she would ask for an explanation there and then – if the Marchesa San Rufino had not intervened by posting herself in the way. Missy then stamped her foot. She did it easily when thwarted, but to do it to the Marchesa San Rufino was unseemly in the extreme, and she was punished by a burst of unkind laughter from those who were looking on. Harden did not wait to see more than that Pico ran out to fetch her back, and walked off.

He stayed away, furious and aggrieved, for some time. When he returned, many people had gone up to bed. His sister was not there, nor was Missy, nor were the San Rufinos. In the Lastacoris' corner of the hall the Marchesa and Mosca were talking together amiably, with Pico and Signorina Petri in attendance.

Though Mosca had inevitably gravitated to the Roman circle and neglected Marchesa Lastacori, of whom he had been the admirer, he made a point of speaking to her sometimes with the old forms of admiration or even with increased politeness. She must have suffered from his defection in her social feelings, and could not show it but had always to appear satisfied with his punctilious amends. There had not been any of these lately, and the picture of the two of them in conversation – the Marchesa talking with that expectation of incredulity that suited the characteristic *genre* of her stories – could strike Harden as new. It did strike him.

'I forgot there was a connexion between them,' he said to himself as though he were saying it to his sister, 'but there it is! The bridge over which our story could travel!'

It was not travelling then, he could tell. 'Diventai ver-r-rde!' he heard her say, and knew the sort of story it was.

Passing through the hall without stopping, he went up to the second floor. He had just got out of the lift when he saw a figure in a yellow dress turn into the passage at its far end – coming from his sister's room round the corner; there was no other possibility – and it was Missy. He quickly turned to the left, into the opposite passage, and she was too agitated to see him and ran down the stairs.

Not till it was perfectly safe did he retrace his steps. He was intending, not to meet Georgette but to go to his sister, but had she locked her door . . .

He knew at once that it was not in expectation of him that it was unlocked; it was more likely she was so disturbed that she had forgotten to lock it. She gave a faint exclamation on seeing him. She had taken off her dress, and she caught up her dressing-gown, put it on, and folded it about her. In a strange, hurried moment he felt that both her haste and her severity were ambiguous.

'I am so sorry,' he said, as if he were picking up the first thing at hand.

Earlier he would have at once reproached her with secrecy over San Rufino, but for the time being other matters were to the fore.

'I know she was in here; I saw her coming out, but she didn't see me. She must have confided in you, and it must have been embarrassing – painful.'

'Yes, it was embarrassing,' she answered.

Her look of severity now appertained only to the matter of the girl, and the hurried, ambiguous beginning was over.

'What did she say?'

'You can imagine what she said. You have made love to her, she has fallen in love with you, and if you are not in love yourself she thinks you shouldn't have made love to her.'

'How absurd!' he exclaimed. 'She should have held off a little – made a little surer! She isn't an innocent. Naturally I wasn't going to wait to fall in love to do what she asked for. Everything must be the way she wants it, and if something goes wrong – I know these Latins, men and women!' he said hotly. 'Always ready to scream treachery!' His hand went up to his scar, though it hadn't twitched.

'Be careful of Latins, then,' she said.

'Does that come convincingly from *you*? But yes, it does!'

219

'I try to prevent it,' she answered, in a preoccupation of her own.

'We will prevent at this juncture by running away!'

She did not respond to this as he thought she would. The oppression wasn't lifted.

'She's maddened by her mother,' he said, 'and did you know she threw good sense to the winds, in her wild way, and rushed after me this evening and was stopped by the other one? She's suffering because she made herself ridiculous –'

'She said nothing of that. She wasn't thinking of it – she was thinking of something else. You had said you would go with her and some others to Balbianello today, and you never came. They went without you.'

'That place on the point – le jardin d'Armide. I remember.'

'You would have gone if you had been in love with her. She is thinking only of that – whether you are in love with her or not.' She put away into a drawer the two swallows that had been lying with spread wings on the dressing-table. 'She thinks perhaps you may be. That's why she came to me –'

'Yes – why?'

'To ask me if I thought you were.'

'Imagine her coming to you! And what did you say?'

'I said I didn't know. I had to calm her.'

'Her accusation was that I didn't love her –'

'You know how it is – a talk of that sort isn't logical. She accused you of making love though you didn't love her, and yet she hopes you do love her and are behaving as you are for a reason. And I said, when I could, that her parents' wishes for her must be considered –'

'What did she say to that?'

'That is too much in the future. She thinks only of now. She says if she can have one sincere word from you she will be able – in what you call her wild way, she said "able to live".'

He uttered a sound – not of ridicule, the contrary. He had sat down on the bed, though his sister still stood, her arms crossed on her bosom over her long white dressing-gown, and that she stood indicated that she meant him to go soon, but an impression he had received from what she told him produced a painful softening, and, groping for what he felt, coming to it slowly, he said, 'What one would never have thought – there is something tragic about her. One saw her first so spoilt – and always laughing – and a little vulgar. But – do you remember I said I was a little interested because of the shape of her eyelids? Now I see why – her eyelids are tragic.'

'I don't want anything to happen,' his sister said in a tone quite out of keeping with his.

Rather discomfited, he wondered why she could not concur in his moment of sentiment. And why was she not feeling sympathy for the girl? For now he took note of the lack of something in her report of what had been said to her, and it was sympathy. By her choice of words she might have been thought to be taking the girl's part, but in her voice there was no compassion; her severity towards him was, he felt, being dictated by something other than that. She had something more in mind than a girl's woe. Regarding her, thinking about *her*, he tried to remember if he had ever seen her feel compassion. Not in these few weeks of new acquaintance – there had not been the occasion – but in the past, in her childhood? No – though something forgotten came back, that she had liked to nurse, especially to bandage the little wounds and hurts that are the lot of children and animals, and that she had bandaged his – in this so 'practical', and already competent, but not compassionate. When she had told him that she had helped to nurse at her brother-in-law's ranch – terrible accidents occurred there; they had always to be prepared for them – it had been a small detail in her account of life at the ranch, and she described an accident as she described other things, not differently. This extension of his understanding of her merely fascinated him; he could analyse a little more of the absorbing enigma.

She had only just become aware of a silence when she saw the fascinated, helpless smile with which he was regarding her. And he was instantly aware that she had seen it.

'I don't know what you want me to do. It's too late in one way, but not in another – not too late to clear out.'

'Or you could stay and declare yourself.'

'What an idea! I don't wish to!'

He looked his amazement that she should say he might stay and declare himself, and amazement made a kind of confusion with the helpless smile that was not quite gone.

'You were not sure even this evening that you didn't wish to,' she answered.

'How do you know? It isn't true. When did I give you any reason for thinking such a thing?'

'When?' she asked with impatience. 'A very little time ago – at dinner.'

'That is a long time ago.'

'I can't discuss with you if you talk like that.'

'What is there to discuss?'

'At least do not deny what you said only this evening.'

'Will you deny that you were horrified then?'

'Only that you should do it in a certain way. There could be an acceptable way of doing it.'

'Why are you suddenly pushing me?' he exclaimed. 'Pushing me into worse complications?'

'It might not be worse,' she answered.

'Worse than what? What are we talking about?'

'You may not know all the harm you have done in this affair,' she said, faltering a little, 'nor what you could be blamed for.'

'It's not my fault if she's taken it so. It's her nature – ' But he was thinking that he still didn't know the *more* that was in her mind – more than he could see, and what she said to him now was a proof of it. For it was very cryptic, and was said, as she was half turning away, in a lonely murmur.

'Who looks as closely as that? It is enough if one is there.'

He could not wait to understand; he had to rush ahead somehow. He knew that it was after she had caught his fascinated scrutiny of herself that she had adopted this new line; but she was not clear in it, and a complex of anxieties was giving her an expression of foreboding.

'But after all, how lucky we are!' he said. It was an odd tone, drawling and affected, to choose for that moment. ' *We* might be the ones in love, beating our heads against the wall! We're not. They're beating their heads for us. Poor things. Aren't you sorry for them?'

He saw that this, and his tone, were distasteful to her, and so he went on. He wanted to punish her for his suspicion that she had gone further than he knew with San Rufino - punish her for her severity and her foreboding. He chose a strange way of doing it.

'I'm sorry for women, I assure you; they can be so much in love. They are victims! Victims of what – of nature? I don't know, but anyhow, yielded up to men. But you,' he said, looking her up and down as she stood a little way from him, '*you* don't suffer the common lot. No, never you! You avenge the others.' She made the gesture, like a start, of not wanting to listen, but he went on the more rapidly with his strange attack. 'You have from the beginning. At dancing-class you avenged the little girls who didn't get partners by making the little boys you didn't dance with so miserable. You've done that always. If it wasn't for you one would have only pity for women!' He got up to make her listen. 'Aren't you grateful? Because of you and a few others, some men *are* as much in love as women. Even more, to redress the balance a little! It doesn't often happen – aren't you pleased it happens for *you*?'

'If you only knew!' she said, and suddenly began to weep. 'If you only knew!'

She was weeping without restraint while he still could hardly believe he was seeing it. He tried to take her in his arms, and she would not let him. 'Nelly, what is it? What is it?' She confronted him, with tears streaming down her face, and this aspect of her face was one he could not have imagined. 'Nelly, what have I done?'

'If you knew,' she repeated, accusing him, 'what can happen, what can be said to one –'

'Tell me! What can be said?'

Pale from shock, he watched what seemed her aimless movements – going to the dressing-table, to the chest of drawers, touching a chair – and tried to gather words broken by her sobs.

'Yes, it was said to me –'

She was by instinct going through the motions of bringing order to the room, though there was nothing to do, as it was already in order. She opened the door of the cupboard with nothing in her hands to hang up – she merely opened the door and looked at the dresses ranged inside.

'She said to me –'

'Who? Do I know her?'

She shook her head.

'When?'

'About a year ago.'

'Why?'

An incoherent sentence might have been the beginning of an explanation of the circumstances, but they were not circumstances that, as it proved, she ever explained.

'She said – ' She closed the cupboard door she had so uselessly opened and opposed him again. Her sobs ceased, and a deep indignation vibrated in her voice, indignation against an intolerable affront. '"*Mais un drame de plus ou de moins dans votre vie – qu'est-ce que cela fait?*" That was said to me.'

He was stricken by his own despair.

'"One drama the more or the less in your life – what is that?"'

She let the words speak for themselves. The indignation and resentment were so profound that they had dried her tears.

'"De plus ou de moins"' – she put scorn into her voice – '"dans votre vie – qu'est-ce que cela fait?"'

Chapter Twenty-Two

They sat in her room till past midnight, and at first even he was too oppressed to speak; their confidences to each other were fragmentary. What these amounted to was an acceptance, almost tacit, that there was a similarity between their fates, in spite of the differing circumstances of their lives. But after some time there burst from him her words 'If you only knew!' – and on a sudden impulse he began to tell her how he had once lived, not as an example of what had been meant, but simply as that which could not be forgotten. When he had told her before about his worst days, he had spared her a great deal because then there was an elation in his mood that got into the telling, and he was able to compare the present with the past. That night he lost the mitigating present; the present could be illusion, could flicker and alter, but the past was absolute. The squalid houses of the South American waterfront in which he had lived during those five months kept an inalterable reality – all of them, each one; he could give the character and particular loathsomeness of each. The people he had been thrown among could still start up before him and show their faces; the moments of melodrama and abject fear could be relived. The vile smell of degradation could spread again. He wanted her to know all, now that his mood was despair, and his descriptions gained at times a dreadful power – and most when it was not others, not other people, that he brought to life, but himself: like the starving cats, emanations of wretchedness, slinking in moonlight and shadow along stained and livid walls, and up staircases in silence, himself always a silence among sounds that came from everywhere, within doors and without, and sometimes, horribly, worse than brutal noise, when there was nothing to be seen, no one and nothing on that flight of the staircase or that turn of the streets, sounds that came seeping into the ear and

225

sickened the mind. Hunger and fever – nightmare hallucinations, and a lazaret for sailors: night in a lazaret, horror itself. His long narration came to an end as suddenly as it had been begun, and he dropped his forehead on his hand again. All the time she had sat with her head turned away.

The venetian blinds were down on both windows, one of which was open, and the blind over that stirred sometimes, and stirred whenever the trees noticeably rustled. There was this rustling and stirring soon after he had fallen silent, and he looked up. Then he saw, as if newly, her averted face, and he exclaimed, 'I wish I hadn't told you all that! So hideous! I don't know why I did. You are unhappy enough!'

He could not imagine why he had subjected her to those descriptions. His memories had surged up without a direct bidding from his consciousness, because any unhappiness recalled them, as an old wound bleeds from an accidental blow.

'I wish I hadn't,' he went on, exploring regret, 'for now you can always see me in disgusting, humiliating places; you will think of me with disgust.'

'No, I will only think that I should know.'

'But why should you know?'

He asked, yet thought he knew why – by the mournful way she said it, turning her face towards him; she meant that she should know because she held herself partly responsible for what he had suffered – that is to say, for what he had done.

What they had earlier touched upon was the recognition that a certain kind of occurrence had repeated itself in their lives, and, on her experience illuminating his, he surrendered to a sense of fatality. But she – saying so little that he had to use intuition to piece her meanings together – had wished to deny that this recurrence was fatality. She had brought out the little phrase, 'One should be able to prevent.' Not enough had been prevented, and too much had 'happened', and her apprehension that something more was going to 'happen' must have been present when he was not understanding her. It might have been out of very fear of a fated pattern that she wished to accept responsibility for what happened, and it came to him with a deep shock that the dramas in her life that were made a reproach to her included his own violent act.

'But it wasn't your fault! You couldn't help it! None of it was done *by* you, poor child – it was all done for you and to you.'

She had said, 'Who looks as closely as that? It's enough if one is there.'

He quickly brought a chair up to hers. She had been sitting, almost never moving, with her elbow rested on the back of her chair and her loose, open sleeve falling back from her bare arms. She let him take her right hand, and he held it, looking into her face, on which were still traces of her weeping.

'Poor Nelly!' he said, because he had on previous occasions said 'Poor Nelly!' with emotion and so established it as something that he said.

'Poor Eugene!' she answered, saying this for the first time.

'Oh, Nelly,' he said after a moment, 'only you and I can ever know us.'

'Poor Eugene, does that console you?' she answered.

She had not said, 'Poor Eugene!' with pity; impossible to describe to himself how she said it.

He knew, as he sat looking down at his hand holding hers, that he was about to see further into the past. He tried – he struggled not to see; but as she withdrew her hand he saw, he was struck by the vision of a terrible reciprocity. His violent act had been like an explosion, opening the interior of a house to public view, and what could have remained merely guessed at, never certainly known, was displayed for all to see. He had completed her ruin.

'Think what *I* did to *you*!'

The consequences could have been muted without that public exposure, and she knew what he had done to her, but in all their talks she had not said a word that would have opened his eyes. His remorse had been only for his mother's agony and for nothing else.

'It was my fault that it came to what it did! My fault. Partly my fault!' He could not even then take all the blame. 'And your life will never recover from what *I* brought about!'

She was one of those to whom he had brought disaster. His face, which had never expressed so much, could have told her that it was the moment of revelation; but all she said was, 'We mustn't have black thoughts. I have had black thoughts tonight, and I have given them to you.'

She had turned him back upon himself. For a time he struggled – not against seeing clearly, but against the frustration of the little phrases. Then suddenly – 'What your life was never to recover from, before ever it was my fault – ' He saw her prepare herself for what was coming. 'What it was never to recover from, was that the first experience – ' She tried to rise from her chair, and he stopped her. 'There couldn't have been a normal marriage afterwards in any case – there may never be, because nothing may ever touch – '

As some balance about to be lost is retrieved – as a crash is in the last second avoided – they ceased, he from speaking and she from trying to rise and leave him. They reassumed attitudes in which, as before, they could sit perfectly still.

He said at last, 'We haven't sat so late, like this, since the beginning.'

'You mustn't stay any longer,' she said.

The night-hour with the profound human silence surrounding them could remind them of their first talks, and the setting was again what might look like the typical setting of an equivocal situation, an aridly lit hotel bedroom.

'No one in all this place is awake but us,' he said. 'That is – no one talking as we are.'

'We mustn't talk any more.'

'My sister!'

She moved a little, changing her position.

'What are we going to do?' he asked, moving too. 'We decided we must go away. Where are we going?'

'We will talk about that tomorrow.'

She had risen and seemed vacillating with fatigue.

'Yes, poor Nelly.' He had a flush like fever on his cheekbones. 'You must go to bed now.'

She went with him to the door.

'We will make a plan tomorrow,' he said. 'A quite new plan! Good night.'

After he had opened the door and stepped a little way down the passage he paused and listened, and then looked back. His eyes met hers to convey 'All right!' – and the door closed.

But in the middle of his room he stood as if he had been stopped. He stood for some time, then started mechanically to take off his tie. His action was suddenly reversed, and before the looking-glass he tied his tie with such haste that he did not see anything but his hands. He went down the passage with the certainty that he was going to surprise her – but in what, he had not given himself time to think. She had not locked her door. When he was in the room he saw that she was taking out the contents of the chest of drawers and piling them on the top, and as she turned he felt he had startled her in what she was doing. The room had already a look of disorder.

'It is so late. You are so tired. I thought you were going to bed.'

In a moment it was not like the same night, but another night.

'We had decided we were going away,' she answered, 'and it might be tomorrow or next day.'

'So you are already beginning to pack?'

'There is so much to be done; yes, I thought I had better begin.'

'And we don't even know where we're going. Or do *you* know?'

'There was something I wanted to do – I told you.'

'What was it?'

'I wanted to meet Mr Chase before he went back to America.'

'Old Mr Chase! What on earth for?' A warning was instantly set up; he must not show too much astonishment. This was tempered to about the right degree, and she would be reassured.

'He is so kind and charming – very benevolent.'

'That is just what you said before; I remember – "benevolent". And he was Father's friend.'

'He was very kind to us all.'

'What was it about meeting him? You told me, but that part I forget.'

'He asked me to meet him here after his cure. That is why I came here.'

'And then?'

She found it difficult to answer questions that had that shake of emotion in them.

'He fell ill when I was expecting him. Then he himself wrote that he was better, and then I had another telegram – from his niece – that again they had to postpone coming.'

'His niece! I had forgotten he had a niece!' Something else now

229

shook his voice. 'I understand a little better. And where are they now?'

'I haven't heard from them since that telegram. But they are still in Italy, because they were to sail from Genoa early in October.'

'And the niece doesn't know how little you do for money!'

He began to laugh. He sat down and covered his face with his hand as he tried to stop himself.

'And what am *I* to do while you are circumventing the niece? What are you thinking *I* am to do? Or are you taking me with you?'

'Would you like to come?'

'Father's friend doesn't mean as much to me as he does to you. But I don't know why he does – I didn't know you had been so fond of him, of Father. I don't remember it.'

'We had decided we must go away,' was all she said.

He strove against something in the dark. 'Why can't it be somewhere else? Why must it be going after old Mr Chase?'

He thought he was seeing in her face what he had seen earlier that night – that same night, but long ago – a look of foreboding, and what he was striving against affected him with terror.

'Were you going without telling me?'

'No, of course not.' Whatever she answered, he would not believe her. 'I said we would talk about it tomorrow. And I had already told you what I wanted to do.'

'But you don't want to take me with you,' broke from him. 'And I've no money and am dependent on you. When you go to find old Mr Chase you must remember to pay the hotel for me.'

He began to laugh again, and once more covered his face with his hand. 'For a few days ahead. I'll find some means after that.'

'I have enough for both of us, poor Eugene,' he heard her say.

'I must find some means of supporting myself, as I'm not going to carry out those plans, but remember – no papers or recommendations!'

'There's the money I consider I owe you,' he heard her say. His laughter let him off, and he looked up.

'How can you hand it over to me? Where is that money?'

'In the Crédit Lyonnais,' she answered, as though they were discussing business. 'It was transferred there.'

'Will you give up meeting old Mr Chase and let me come to Paris with you – go to Paris with you now and get it? I'll need that money at once.'

'We don't have to go ourselves. That is foolish. I can write to the bank.'

'But that will take time. Where will we be all that time?'

'Why must we talk about it now? It is so late.'

'Though it is so late, you were beginning to pack.'

'I won't do that any more. I will wait till tomorrow.'

'You want me to go,' he said, and he sprang up and went out.

What brought him back were his old terrors, which were his memories of the worst turned into fear. He could not be alone with them. That had become associated with the worst – to have to be alone. But her door was locked. He found it locked; he knocked several times and it would not open, and he sat collapsed on her big dress-trunk, which stood in the passage beside her door, because he could not go away and be alone. She was on the other side of the door – and did she too not have her terrors? Not like his, nothing like his, but she too must have felt terror when that occurred, his violent act that exposed their lives to public view, and though the door was between them they were together at that hour, living through the consequences of the same past.

When it had gone on too long – the night silence of the hotel pressing on him while he sat alone – he knocked again. The key turned in the lock, and he went in. What she saw at once was his fear, and, seeing it, she moved away so that he could come farther into the room. She held her dressing-gown closely folded around her, and he glanced down and saw the edge of her nightgown below it and the blue mules on her feet. With the idea that, now she was undressed, she must be protected against intrusion, he locked the door. She made no objection. She had about her – in her manner, at once, as if she were receiving him socially – her most perfect composure, and he gazed at her, knowing he was entirely in her hands.

'I have been thinking, Eugene,' she said, 'about what we ought to do. I was going to tell you tomorrow, but now that you've come – that you can't sleep – I had better tell you tonight.'

Her composure made him feel faint with dread. He noticed

231

how airless the room was, with the blinds down, and that her scent seemed heavier than before in the atmosphere.

'May I draw up the blind?' he asked. 'I'd like a little more air.'

The wind had dropped, and when the blind went up over the open window he looked into a dark stillness, a sullen stillness, sullen after the storm.

'Sit down, as we must talk,' she said. There was no chair for him – the other chair had her clothes on it – and he went to his usual place at the foot of the bed, and sat turned so that he could face her.

'I was thinking,' she began again, 'that we must carry out one of your plans. That is the solution.'

'Why?'

'What will we do if we do nothing? We can't live together in my apartment, it is too small, but I can't leave you to yourself, poor Eugene.'

'Which plan shall we carry out? The one' – he used a tone of execration – 'in which we take possession of the couple San Rufino, and have our little share of the grandeur and decadence of Rome?'

'Not that one. That wouldn't last long enough.'

'The other plans were for marriage.'

'Yes, and they were yours, not mine.'

He could only gaze at her. 'Neither marriage is thinkable to me. Why is it thinkable to you?'

'Because to do nothing is not thinkable either. And you will see, once we start thinking about it, it will be thinkable.'

'Which?' he asked with a grimace of loathing.

'Could yours come about without your bringing great blame on yourself?'

'The foolish mother might give her consent –'

'But not the father.'

'But yours!' he exclaimed. 'That you wouldn't hear of! What about your new religion? So,' he said, seeing no change in the steady regard that met his consternation, 'religion – that one – was only a phase after all, as I told you!'

'You want always to prove yourself right, Eugene.'

'I had to be very brave – or crazy with rage – to put forward that marriage –'

232

'But you put it very well. Have you forgotten?'

'You wouldn't consider it for a moment then. Why do you now?'

'Because I see it now as a solution,' she answered, at her most unemphatic.

Here was something specific to struggle against, a frank issue – or one that could appear so.

'I won't consent! I will refuse to let you sacrifice yourself!'

'I don't think one ever sacrifices one's self,' she replied. 'It may look as though one does, but really one can do only what one wants.'

He was surprised into a forlorn sort of laugh by that. 'That is positively philosophical. It may be true. Then you want to do this thing? But why?' He could make it sound frank.

'Because,' she said, with a little pressure now on her words, 'I think, after what I did, that I should marry him. You said so yourself. Don't you remember – "morality"?'

'What we were brought up on – but it didn't have much effect on you and me.'

He had a glimpse – a fleeting one – of unhappiness.

'It wouldn't be so much like marrying him as like going back to your husband,' he said bitterly. 'But one doesn't always advise one's sister to go back to her husband, does one?'

'You did once. You saw advantages once.'

Calmly, when he tried to argue, she placed the practical advantages before him. She must have seen them and mapped out the future in that little space of time between his going and his coming back. But that space of time, too, seemed to belong to a night that was past, and this again was like another night. They instinctively spoke in low voices after he had once or twice glanced round at the door, though the room next to hers was no longer occupied, and the service stairs were on the other side; they did not have to think they might be overheard, but it suited their subject to speak low. She having taken command of their destinies, he let her tell him that, when she would go with her husband wherever she must, she would leave her apartment to her brother, and her income too, or part of that, for as long as he needed it; that should keep him out of adventures, she said with her first smile; that was a great advantage. About the very immediate future she could not be

233

quite precise. *He* – the name of Kovanski was never spoken – had to appear. The momentous interview first had to take place. *He* had not been seen for several days, and his next appearance must be imminent; in fact she was rather surprised that he had stayed away so long. She had felt very uneasy that evening – she had expected, she could hardly tell why, some unpleasant intervention. Her brother remembered his own misgivings, but his recollections of the first part of the evening were blurred.

He must be given a sign before he could make a scene, and Eugene must be on the alert the whole time they were downstairs. He must remember that there were, perhaps, excuses to be made for *him* and she looked aside as she added 'I told you that he imagined something. Then he had reason to be suspicious, and that may have upset what balance he had.'

'As it turns out, his imagining was prophetic,' said her brother sarcastically.

But they were collaborators, partners in an enterprise, and not, as they had been in the earlier night-hours, nerveless and fate-haunted companions. The enterprise would require his cleverness – to avoid mistakes and bring about the dramatic solution artistically – and he suddenly foresaw the excitement of playing a tricky game. She needed his cleverness. She had always resisted his plans, and there had never been this partnership till now, when he was acquiescing in hers. And he was helped to acquiesce by the large fact that the future she mapped out was not tomorrow or next day, for they would very soon have to part from *him* – they must carry the matter through with all care for her reputation – but not yet from each other. He tried to make her suggest that he and she should go to Paris together, at once, after the momentous interview, to get her divorce started without delay, and she at least did not make any other suggestion. There was no more thought of meeting old Mr Chase, for which he was as thankful as if old Mr Chase had represented some occult power. Her decision to marry was extraordinary and strange in every way: in itself, in its suddenness – like inspiration, or conversion, or madness – and in its effect, for by it they had come into another atmosphere, as on a journey one passes out of one kind of landscape into a different one.

'You aren't preparing to go tomorrow, at any rate. It was a

nightmare when I thought you were. And all that packing to be done! Like the nightmare in which one has to pack, and one packs and packs against time. How will you ever pack them all?' he said, thinking of the number of her dresses and hats.

'I can engage someone who will help me do that very well – the wife of the under-concierge, who was a ladies' maid before she was married. She is very good.'

Talking of packing and the good ladies' maid was a little excursion in the new landscape. They were carried on, as down a gentle slope, and came to a reminiscence, and, hardly knowing how they had got there, he examined her on what she remembered about Gössefors. He had never done it before because of the baleful shadow of what was to come, but now he wanted her to look back with him on those summers and see them bathed in their own light, as he could.

'Couldn't we go back there together some day? Stay somewhere near enough and drive secretly past the house? Be up there again on Midsummer Eve! – Won't we be able to take a holiday together sometimes?'

'I think we could permit it to ourselves, after a time,' she answered. 'But,' she said, 'we weren't so very fond of each other as children. Don't start inventing a fairy tale about two children and then say it's a story about us.'

They laughed.

They had laughed, and there were holidays for them in the future, as well as a period of security, even the 'withinness' he so envied. With that laugh he became as lightheaded as though he had been drinking.

'Oh, let's laugh tonight,' he said, 'for it won't be the same even tomorrow! Everything will be changed when you have a future husband. And I've earned something, haven't I? For, tell me, am I not behaving very well? Giving you no trouble in any way, not putting forward any ideas of my own – not one, observe – asking only that you should say you are pleased with me!'

His elation was genuine; of that she had to take some moments to convince herself, but she was then convinced.

'What more can I do to please you? Make a few promises?'

'Would I believe them?'

'At least you could judge my good intentions by them.'

'Have you got good intentions, Eugene?'

'Yes, I have. I'm going to be a credit to you, not a discreditable appendage! I must be a brother you can get recommendations for, mustn't I? A brother who can be given a position in – a bank, for instance, a director or something, from which he can start rising to the top.' He glanced quickly aside, and if he thought he had heard something it was nothing, but from then on he was yet more irresponsible. '"Do you know my brother? C'est un garçon très sérieux. We are expecting him to join us here."' A brother who can pay his own journeys and meet you whenever you go abroad. Oh, come and sit over here and listen to him, won't you?'

She yielded, got up from her chair, and came to sit on the bed – the other side of it. It was wide and put some space between them.

'And one you can invite to come and stay with you – for you will, won't you? An irreproachable brother who will come to stay with you on the uncle's enormous estates in the Government of Tula.' He bent double as he laughed, which he did in the equivalent of a whisper. 'The Government of Tula!'

'You are crazy,' she said.

'Because I do exactly what you want – fall in with all your plans and never reproach you? Ready to follow you wherever you go! So closely that I may be received into the Orthodox Church on the same day as you.' He knew he could say anything he liked. 'We'll make such a pair that day that we may figure afterwards in icons – for you are so beautiful you must be a saint, and I – Don't ask me to say it. They'll put our two faces side by side, in thick gold haloes. Two saints in the Orthodox Calendar! But under what names? Under our own?'

'Why not just Saint Brother and Saint Sister?' She said it with demure, not open humour, and he was transported.

'That's what we'll be famous for! At last I know. And you will have done everything for me –'

'You must do some of it yourself,' she said.

He straightened up from leaning on his elbow and listened. He had heard an odd rustling, but when he began to listen he heard nothing more.

'We don't hear the bells on the fishing-nets tonight, do we? I think we are saints already, and those would be –'

There was an inexplicable noise of something happening

just outside on the same level as themselves – a leap, and a man had landed, squatting, on the window-sill; he almost lost his balance, gained it by taking hold of the frame of the open window, and then jumped down into the room.

Kovanski stood squarely before them, breathing hard at first, his head a little lowered, bull-like. His eyes went first to the man, to learn instantly who he was, and plainly it was not the one he had expected to see. When those strange, prominent eyes were turned on her, they looked as though they would never look away. The contrast between the intruder and what was intruded upon, between the jesting that was sparked off by his passion and the passion itself, imposed a few seconds of silence.

Then Harden brought out what the situation required. 'How dare you break into my sister's room like this?' He and she had both risen, one on each side of the bed; she had not, he noticed, exclaimed, as he involuntarily had done when the startling leap was made. But the situation was extraordinary, because this was the man they were prepared for; it was the dramatic moment, though not as they had imagined it. Coolness was needed to meet its complications. And Harden's anger suddenly shot up, the like of the anger he was bound to feign at the start.

'What right –' but that wouldn't do, and with a quick step forward, the more furiously because he had to weaken his demand – 'Is there any excuse for this?'

'My jealousy!' answered Kovanski.

What came through 'jealousy', as he said it, caused another moment of silence. He had her before his eyes, and what it had been when he did not have her there came through the word. But it was of the past. The suspension of jealousy, when he had her there before his eyes and not the man he had expected, was a suspension of all else, an end, with nothing more to come.

She moved forward from her side of the bed. 'Tomorrow –' she said.

Her brother turned on her. 'Not yet!'

'What was that?' asked Kovanski hoarsely.

'This isn't the time to ask questions. I must protect my sister. How can she be safe from you?'

'By not having a man in her room,' said Kovanski, veering to him.

'Where's your apology for your mistake?' asked Harden with his most rasping laugh. 'It's overdue!'

'What did you mean by "Not yet"?' The state of suspension was over, but he gave an impression of animal bewilderment. 'You couldn't have said it for nothing.'

'You flatter me!'

'Natalia!' said Kovanski, looking again at her. 'What did you mean by "Tomorrow"?'

They were both looking at her – Harden in evening dress and Kovanski in a blue suit – and she was in her white dressing-gown, which, gathered up by her hand and pulled close about her waist, let her nightgown be seen falling below it to her feet.

'Didn't you mean,' Harden interposed, 'that you would ask for an explanation of this tomorrow?'

'Let her speak. Natalia, why did you say "Tomorrow"?'

'I said "Tomorrow" – meaning not tonight.' In order to evade and postpone she put forth seduction, not as an entirely conscious act but in an instinctive summoning of natural aid. Without motion or deliberate provocation, simply by what emanated from her, her form, her look under slightly arched brows, she set logic at nought. 'I think we shouldn't explain anything tonight.'

The effect upon her brother of her evasion was that of a narrow escape. Resting his weight on the foot-rail of the bed he was brought nearer to her, and they stood drawn together as a pair, facing Kovanski.

'Will you explain what you meant – what you said – the other day?' Kovanski asked, hardly articulately.

'It couldn't have been much, or you wouldn't have had to come through the window,' said Harden, able to avenge, on this creature deprived of its wits, what the contemptuous, privileged man had once forced him to swallow. For others he might be a dangerous man; *they* could treat him as they liked.

But she thought this too strong to be safe. Glancing down at herself, as if to point out her predicament, she said hesitantly to Kovanski, 'My brother must have been very much surprised. He had no idea. You should understand . . . the first moment . . . and put yourself in his place.'

She gave him his status of a former lover. He was bemused

by having her acknowledge it, but her brother reacted quickly to fear of her intentions, and said to her, 'This surprise has altered my feelings very much. I think they are quite changed.'

'They may change yet again,' she said. 'Let that be a consolation to you.'

The irony was the last touch to seduction. With a smile of which he was quite unaware he leaned nearer, searching her face for her meaning. When Kovanski's voice broke in he heard it without seeing him.

'Now he has understood, and we can speak in front of your brother and not wait till tomorrow.'

'End it now!' burst from Harden.

He doubted her, though she had evaded when she could have secured the previously desired climax; she might have decided merely to defer it, and his suspense and her overpowering seductiveness were one.

'What is he doing here?' Kovanski asked in a loud, hoarse voice.

The dangerous man, the man who fought duels, was before them. Harden's scar twitched viciously, and then he laughed. It was everything together.

'Oh, don't ask me,' he said. 'I'd rather not tell you.'

'Make him answer,' Kovanski said to her.

'I'm afraid –' An instant's thought, and with a consummate mixture of regret and humour he brought out 'I'm afraid I was here to try to borrow money from my sister.'

There was a moment like a beat dropped.

'My brother is rather wild,' she said. 'I'm sorry you have to know this.'

'Then he is not the one to protect you,' said Kovanski. 'I should protect you from him.'

'I didn't threaten her – not as bad as that. But just the same, perhaps *I* should now apologize to you. My position was rather weak.'

'I can lend you money,' said Kovanski. He said it with his gambler's face and voice.

'That is too good of you, but really –'

'My brother isn't in any serious difficulty,' she said with a little laugh of embarrassment.

'And now that we have made our confessions, isn't it enough for tonight?' said Harden. He stood up, having been inclined towards her. No longer reckless in manner, he seemed to have come under some physical stress. 'Don't you think we ought to go?'

'If we go together,' said Kovanski.

'Of course – but please, you understand, we must go very quietly. No noise at all.'

He went towards the door. Kovanski still stood on the spot from which he had never once moved. His face had an absolute impassivity and hardness, and his eyes, with sallow whites bloodshot, were as expressionless as marbles. She had grown very pale, and while her brother was turned away she seemed to waver.

'Are you coming?' said Harden in a whisper.

'Good night,' she murmured.

Kovanski gave her a moment to say more, and then he bowed to her formally, as he would have done at a ball.

Harden was unlocking the door.

'Will you go down the stairs just here?' he whispered, showing a nervous hurry. 'Very quietly. I will go to my room by the corridor.'

He shut the door upon them noiselessly.

In a few minutes he was back. He shut and locked the door behind him, and the stress he was under was so great that in crossing the room he came not straight but stumbling.

'*Comme votre papa est bon pour vous,*' he gasped out.

Part Three

Chapter Twenty-Three

Kovanski walked slowly the whole length of the terrace next morning with his hands thrust down into his coat pockets. None of his Roman acquaintances, but a few English visitors, were in front of the hotel, and Bernard Middleton, who had been out rowing, crossed from the water-steps to speak to Colonel Ross and two ladies on the other side of the road. The trees hid Kovanski from him till he was nearly in his path. Normally a man with whom one had almost collided would stop for a second, not arrogate to himself the right of way as Kovanski did. Having held Bernard up, he turned his head to look back at him, and then grinned his beastly grin; and in an upwelling of rage Bernard did what he hadn't done before under this provocation – he grinned back. Kovanski walked on, apparently laughing, and Bernard answered Colonel Ross's 'Good morning!' across the road.

The bitter part was that Kovanski's vindictiveness was founded on a mistake, but he would not forget that he had once been put in the position to think Bernard was in great favour, and his way of getting even was to point out, as he did with his grin, that he knew what a mistake he had made. To do it once would have been enough.

And it seemed a bad portent that Kovanski, whom he hadn't seen at all for a week, was back and looking ugly. In spite of the lapse of time, Bernard felt him to be a menace to Madame Solario's peace, capable of doing something that might suddenly cause her to leave; and he would get very little warning, or none at all, and simply find one day that she had gone. But the sense of menace had deepened his absorption in everything to do with Madame Solario, and through it, as a consequence of it, he had had his nearest approaches to her. For it was not only what she had let him understand about Kovanski; the arrival of her

243

brother had made a less explicable but more sinister impression of menace than anything else. He was sure she was not expecting her brother, and he was near her when she first saw him; his acute awareness of her picked up what others might not have noticed – small evidences of unpreparedness and even fear. He knew the brother's story – her own, indeed; he had heard Guimard tell it to Missy. And it was a shock-like moment when the brother whom he knew had been twelve years in exile was recognized: when a man stopped in front of her and Bernard saw her expression and heard her in an altered voice say, 'This is my brother.' He watched them at dinner that evening, and after dinner when she came out of the door and her eyes met his – he was standing outside – she did not smile, though she looked straight at him. It seemed to him that she singled him out, and he believed that he was the only person there to whom she could betray herself even to that small degree. He had to try, while thinking about it afterwards, not to make too much of it – that in a moment of tension something had passed between them. Very soon everything changed, and her life was calm and brilliant; her relations with her brother – in public – were ordinary and even affectionate, he could see nothing whatever to suggest the contrary. But that evening, together with the story he had heard, had shown him a dark side, and also made a claim, that held his imagination.

Her world and his were completely divided, but there were chance encounters when she could say a few words in passing, or even stop to speak to him for a few minutes. On the first occasion after that evening there had been a sort of absence of denial, but later she always spoke so tranquilly and lightly that he could think she wished him to relegate the dark side he had seen to oblivion. She reminded him again, laughing as at a real joke, that she couldn't remember what the red oleander flower was to mean and what the white in their agreed-upon signal. Twice he walked with her for about half an hour – Kovanski had seen them come back from one of these walks but had probably not repeated his mistake – and they talked on what seemed to him afterwards oddly random subjects, nothing that corresponded with his thoughts about her and yet immeasurably adding to them. His life in his own little world went on, with her –

not often more than glimpsed – giving it its significance, so that his life had a surface and a depth quite different one from the other.

He was ostensibly enjoying himself, for he had been drawn into the young society, which was very gay. He saw a good deal of the Leroy girls and their friends, the villa people, and the Americans called him 'Belle's beau'. He couldn't help noticing that Martha, the younger sister, always blushed when she first saw him, but Belle, he knew, preferred someone else. Sailing was in great vogue, though it wasn't always the weather for it, and they would be becalmed for hours while he was impatient to get back. He went for a couple of long walks with an English visitor of his own age, a man recently come down from Cambridge, and once it was over the mountains that separate the Lake of Como from that of Lugano; but in those beautiful woods he could think of nothing but Madame Solario and her love of woods, and thought of himself at moments as being in the one of which she often dreamed.

When he felt unhappy and foolish, which he sometimes did, he made excuses to himself for staying on much longer than he had originally intended – such as that his friend Charlie Trevor might even yet turn up here, or that he couldn't leave sooner than he must any more than he would leave a play before the end. It was an interesting, queer turn of affairs when Missy fell in love with Harden. He and Missy had heard of Harden for the first time together, when Guimard told her the story out on the Leroys' veranda, while he stood inside the house hearing their voices; their laughter had suddenly depressed him. He wondered sometimes if Missy remembered that scene, and how she had first heard of the man she was to fall in love with to the twanging of Guimard's guitar. He himself had disliked her for knowing something about Madame Solario's past and for being able to spread the story if she wished. It seemed more likely that she would after the brother arrived. And then what might have been a leak was stopped up. That was how it presented itself to him one evening, early on, when he saw her dancing with Harden. That's stopped up, he thought. She wouldn't talk now. The affair was watched by all her contemporaries with interest and a sort of awe, because she was so much more showy and daring than any of them could be. She could make even un-requited love look exciting.

There wasn't much time left. The season was drawing to a close. After he had nearly collided with Kovanski and had spoken to Colonel Ross and the two ladies, Bernard went on into the hotel to see if there were any letters for himself. Every day now that he didn't get a letter summoning him home he felt reprieved. But here it was at last! – the letter from his father, giving him his instructions. He was to meet his father and mother in London on the following Thursday, stay with them at his uncle's house in Grosvenor Place until the Saturday, and then proceed to the northern town where was the branch of the family bank in which he was to start his training. So it was all over, bar three or four days; Kovanski wasn't needed to bring it to an end. Of course it was coming to an end anyhow, but common sense couldn't deal with the immediate blow. And what he was going to was so dreary: the dreary northern town, the dreary work. For the rest of the morning he kept thinking – if his parents hadn't decided they wouldn't put him into the Diplomatic Service, that his uncle's offer was too good to be refused, he would have had a life abroad in which he might have come across these people again and heard what happened to them; he could have hoped to meet Madame Solario again, when he wasn't so young, so much at a disadvantage. He felt bitterly regretful of the opportunities he had so narrowly missed. He could see and hope up to next Tuesday or Wednesday, whichever day he must leave, and everything that was to come after that loomed through a dense, depressing fog.

Late in the next afternoon he walked back alone from a villa on the far side of Tremezzo. Sunset was near, and the reflections of the shore were stretching, beautifully quiet and mellow, over the water. The Angelus bells were beginning to ring. So quiet was this bay-like part of the lake that there was, at the moment, only one boat to be seen, far out, a row-boat with two people in it. He was being given a particularly lovely evening on purpose, it would seem, to increase his regret. How extraordinary to think that he would have been here less than a month – for certain incidents were already like things that had happened long ago. When he walked past the plane trees he thought of poor little Ilona, and thought of her with amazement that he could remember her so well when it was so long ago. As he came up to the door through which she had disappeared, he heard Missy singing inside the room. Her thrilling voice had enhanced the romantic atmosphere on many occasions, but at this moment he was startled by it, it had timed itself so perfectly to affect him. He stood outside to listen, having looked in and seen she was alone, sitting at the piano, accompanying herself. She had no audience for the poignant melody. He thought how he and she were both alone – and how nothing had gone right for any of them. And if anything had gone right, in this place how wonderful it would have been!

She stopped, there was a silence, and then he heard her go out of the room. In front of the hotel he met Colonel Ross, who entered at once into friendly talk. Everyone had gone to tea with Duchessa M—— at Bellagio, the big villa (She will have gone, thought Bernard) but he, Colonel Ross, had had to stay behind as a man had come to see him, and he explained who this man was and his business, Bernard meanwhile looking across the lake to see if the launch had started on its way home.

Colonel Ross paused rather abruptly. 'I think you know Count Kovanski,' he said with entire irrelevance. 'Don't you?'

He had seen, of course, that morning, if not Kovanski's grin, Bernard's own, so ridiculous and full of hate. Bernard wished Colonel Ross wouldn't bring it up, but he had evidently been struck by it, and his type couldn't beat about the bush.

'Oh, I've met him once or twice,' Bernard answered. 'I can't say I know him.'

To turn the matter off he had spoken too quickly; Colonel Ross was now definitely mystified.

'When I say I've met him only once or twice – Once we fell slightly foul of each other, and that's about all the acquaintance we've had. I've seen him since, but not to speak to.'

'Ah!' said Colonel Ross, who had looked triumphant when he heard they had fallen foul of each other. But then his expression became kind in a worried way. 'One had better be careful with foreigners. We don't quite understand them – they don't play to the same rules, you know.'

'Yes, I do know,' said Bernard. It was perhaps because the

shadow of paternal authority had just fallen on him and he was going back to England so soon that he felt irritated by Colonel Ross's paternal, proprietary attitude. 'But I don't see why we should play to theirs.'

'Oh, I don't say –' said Colonel Ross. 'But it's better to remember one mayn't always know what one's lettin' one's self in for, you know.'

In his irritation, Bernard noted very particularly at that moment Colonel Ross's whole appearance, tall and upstanding – and his face, with big nose and grey moustache, and an odd sidelong glance that was his own, not generic, and that he gave as he went on, 'This Count Kovanski doesn't look a pleasant fella, what?'

'I haven't found him so,' answered Bernard.

'Did he – did you –' Colonel Ross wanted, it was plain, to be told how they had fallen foul of each other, but didn't like to ask the straight question. Bernard was not going to enlighten him, and he began again on another tack. 'Even his friends say he's an unaccountable sort of fella and would pick a quarrel as soon as not. The other evenin' when he was playin' bridge he went out of his way to be rude to someone, and they were all quite jumpy for a bit.'

'Who was he rude to?' asked Bernard.

'The Marchese San Rufino, as a matter of fact.'

The man with the black beard – of course. Another Ercolani incident, possibly. More menace. Colonel Ross saw that he had made an impression on his young friend.

'They say he's fought several duels – Kovanski, I mean – and they seem to think he's a bit mad.'

'Do people still fight duels?' asked Bernard genuinely.

'Oh, yes, of course they do – abroad. In some countries more than others – Russia and Germany most, I believe – and in France they do, of course, but there it's generally over politics. In Italy I'd say it would be more likely over a woman, what?'

'Yes, I suppose so. And in Russia?'

'Over anything, as far as we know – we can't understand them.'

He then added, but with a humorous intonation – not to be

too heavily admonishing, one could see – 'I wouldn't fall foul of him again, if I were you.'

'It's all right, sir, he won't challenge *me* to a duel,' answered Bernard, as though he had private knowledge. 'Besides, there's hardly time. I'm leaving next Wednesday.'

'Oh, are you? We're going on Thursday, I think, unless the weather breaks before. Are you going straight back?'

They talked of routes and times – Colonel Ross knew of bad connexions with hours lost here and there – after sitting down on two little iron chairs facing the lake to wait for the return of the party from Villa M——. Bernard was getting an exceptional opportunity to meet her and be in her company for a while. His eyes were fixed on the point, the big villa, from which at any moment the launch would detach itself and be seen speeding towards them. The expanse of water it would skim over was rosy, for it was one of those sunsets when the whole air is flooded with colour, and lake and sky were in the flood. From the right, presently, the sound of oars became audible in the quiet; a rowboat was coming in along the terrace-wall. Colonel Ross got up to look over the parapet, and exclaimed, 'I thought you were with them!'

Bernard got up too, and looked down into the row-boat, and there was, as always on seeing her, a leap within him. She was looking up from the cushioned stern, and the man with her was starting to ship his oars. It was her brother – not San Rufino or anyone else! The relief!

Colonel Ross and he went to the top of the water-steps to meet them, and Bernard remembered that Colonel Ross had done the same thing when he and she were returning from their row. The boat bumped against the stone, the lazy water lapped the step, the oars clattered in, and the hotel boatman ran down and seized the side of the boat. Her brother gave her his help, and she took it and rose to her feet. They both stood in the boat for a moment, together, looking up, and their two faces were singularly irradiated.

'Where have you been?' Colonel Ross called down.

'To Balbianello,' answered her brother.

Ah, what a waste! thought Bernard with a pang.

Chapter Twenty-Four

The Bellevue guests were to be transported to Villa d'Este for the ball in various launches – that of the hotel and those of neighbouring villas, which would call for them – and Bernard was to go with Belle Leroy in a Tremezzo launch. He had to start for the Leroys' house, which was his place of rendezvous, before he had seen who was going from the Bellevue, and therefore he could not be sure, though it was probable, that he would see Madame Solario at the ball. He had to start without having had a glimpse of the grand world in which he had no part, and pick up, if he could, the eager mood of his own friends. But poor Martha was too young to go to a real ball, and her face when they left her behind made him smile and wish she were coming too. She had helped him out on the night of the cotillon.

The journey was a long one, down to the end of the lake, and before they had got to Villa d'Este the evening was, to him, as good as finished and over; but the spectacle on arrival there changed all that had gone before. It was so operatic – more so than anything at Cadenabbia, on a finer and larger stage – that it seemed certain that something fantastically better than real life was going to happen, to one's self just as well as to another.

After landing, he and his party pressed on. The hotel had once been a princely villa that had – surprisingly – been so little altered and spoiled that his ball had very much the setting it would have had in the time of the d'Estes. The pillared hall was in the best eighteenth-century taste, and the large ballroom, to which the young people were drawn as rapidly as they could make their way, was a lordly painted and decorated eighteenth-century room. The music, which had briefly stopped, began again, loud and sudden, just as they entered it, and those moments of waltz-time before a well-known tune triumphantly broke forth had in them the excitement of all the possibilities of the ball.

Bernard had become more proficient since the cotillon, and he started off quite confidently with a good partner, an American girl. Soon he saw, among the many heads of strangers, people whom he knew by sight, and then the strangers were rubbed out, and only faces he knew met his eyes. The first of those he was looking for was Missy. She was dressed in white, which he had never seen her wear before, but she looked very well. When he next saw her she was dancing with Harden, a long white drapery attractively floating from her shoulders, and it occurred to him on seeing them that she might be in for a good time. A little later his partner was taken from him, in the foreign way, and he went out, having made sure that Madame Solario was not in the ballroom. He saw her at once in the corridor, standing by the arch that led to an inner hall, and he stopped where he could look at her without her noticing him. The man with the black beard was with her. Her gown was so beautiful that even if it had been worn by someone else Bernard would have thought it beautiful, and it took his eyes from her face. It was composed of fine black lace over pale-pink satin, and had a black velvet sash; her diamond stars were on her shoulders. She and her companion came forward while he was looking, to the door of the ballroom, and he thought that there she exchanged a glance with someone in the room; he couldn't think who it could be. Her smile might have been escaping involuntarily, and he was reminded of the night of the cotillon. She must love dancing, or she would not so glow in the anticipation of it; success at a ball was the only kind she appeared to enjoy.

There was no object in getting her to recognize him, as he could not ask her to dance, and he walked through a yellow Empire salon and out on to the terrace. The full moon had just topped the opposite mountain, which was dramatically near and black, and stood above the scene at its centre; it was almost too perfect to be true. Everything else, boats and lights and terrace and figures, was, as it were, low down in a frame, insignificant, the moon upon the black mountain so dominated the human part of the scene. The terrace at the water's edge lost itself in dark wooded gardens, and he wandered through moon-

251

light and shadow, hearing the sound of a small waterfall. Down a little ravine a stream cascaded from one baroque basin into another, and glittered in the moonlight, and he thought again how wonderful it would have been ... and that after three days he would be gone.

Returning to the ballroom, before he got another partner he discerned Madame Solario, on the other side of the great room, dancing with one of the Roman men. Harden was dancing with the Marchesa San Rufino, who was turning her head from side to side, as though no part of her could keep still, and talking. It became difficult to pick out individuals, the crush was so great. Some time later he danced with Belle, and in a pause he told her about the moon and she said they must go and see it. It had moved on and was no longer poised upon the highest mountain, but the effect was still marvellous. They were joined by three of their friends, and the night itself was the entrancement. No one wanted to go in again, and presently they were playing childish games on a little lawn half in moonlight and half in the shadow-mass of trees – 'Sur le pont d'Avignon' and 'Still Pond No More Moving' – and from that they invented 'attitudes' beside the ornamental basins into which the stream cascaded down. They took the attitudes of statues, singly or in pairs, on the balustrades, or perched upon the baroque rocks, the girls very daring and pretty, attitudes becoming more extravagant and comic, yet all of it ghostly in the blanching moonlight. But the distant music never stopped for long, the ball was going on without them, and when they went back to it they did it in a hurry, to see what, after all, they had been missing. The others paired off into couples in a waltz, and Bernard was free to look about.

Madame Solario was dancing with her brother. They came down the length of the room towards him, were close to him, passed, were lost among other couples, and reappeared to his sight far away, the whole room between him and them. From sheer humility he felt he would remain invisible to them, and that they would never see him, however long he watched them. She had produced that feeling in him before, at the cotillon; however unapproachable she could be at other times, it was never so much as when he saw her dancing. She and her partner became another

252

order of beings from himself, not only as he was now but as he always would be – lacking in some quality, some element. Her chosen partners had it – Ercolani, and now her brother, so that it was a quality not dependent on other kinds of attraction, an element that belonged to an order of being.

And she and her brother made an even more harmonious couple than she and Ercolani. They were better suited in height, for Ercolani had been rather too tall, and from a likeness of proportions, and probably their relationship, there resulted an even more perfect attunement, a more freely flowing motion. His jealousy of Ercolani was allayed. He knew that it had been to some degree needless when he saw her dancing with her brother and it was proved that the harmony she and her partners could attain was godlike. There was that element in them that was not in him, but, even though invisible to her, he could feel a satisfaction, which was that she danced more divinely with her brother than with Ercolani.

The couple disappeared and reappeared, and at each reappearance he saw one thing rather than another, one thing at a time. When they were in a moment of clear space not far from the door he saw her whole figure, and her beautiful dress captivated him afresh. The fine black lace over pale-pink was something by itself, till he imagined having her form pressed against one by one's arm about her. Then, when her back was to him, it was the line of her neck and shoulders that he saw, and then her fair hair, and, in a sudden reappearance, it was Harden's face – for a few seconds only Harden's face, almost fully turned to him. He was very handsome, one had to acknowledge it, and the more so – more than usually so – because the something that was always peculiar to his expression, difficult to define – at the worst subtly false, or a mock mockery – was gone, and it was extraordinarily happy.

But Bernard was drawn into dancing again and seemed to himself to be at it for a long time. He saw only intermittently in the crowd, while time went by, the people who interested him. The Bellevue people, with all the high society of the lake, kept together in the midst of the *hoi polloi*, and, after they had danced, would return to a part of the ballroom they had made their own; but Madame Solario was always dancing, and he knew, without often being able to see just what was happening, that she was having the success she enjoyed. He did see her and what happened at the time when, one could feel, the ball was at its height. She and her brother were dancing together again, and as they passed that appropriated part of the ballroom they were exclaimed at with amusement, perhaps for dancing with each other so much. Several people clapped. The momentum of the ball could be felt collectively and in everyone, and the familiarity and amusement, and the clapping, and the couple's acknowledgement, the way they laughed back, were all in the spirit of a ball at its height. When the music stopped, as the main crowd was making for the door a small, separate crowd of high society formed itself at the other end of the room, below the orchestra. The conductor was called to, and he leaned down to hear what was evidently a request. He spoke to his men, and about half the orchestra began playing a South American tune, and Madame Solario swept into the first pose of a Spanish dance and clacked her fingers as though they held castanets. Then it was over, being only the flash of a movement and one moment of gaiety. Her brother beat his hands together and cried, 'Olé! Olé'. The sense of menace was entirely absent, and all was brilliance and applause.

The height of the ball could be felt and heard in the hall and on the terrace. The moon had slid farther and was shining into the basin that had the lights of Como brightly clustered on its rim. Bernard stayed outside till it was no longer the smallest satisfaction to be by himself, and when he went in again he walked through all the beautiful rooms open to the public as if he were expecting to meet someone; he did not know who it could be, but there floated in his mind the idea that something had been intended for him and he would come upon it. In the farthest rooms and the big hall there were only strangers; a little flirting was going on in the yellow Empire salon; in the inner hall some chaperones were sitting, and among them was the Marchesa Lastacori. He was reminded of Missy, whom he hadn't been aware of for a long time. He went back to the ballroom as though he were going to look for her, and Harden was just taking his sister from another partner. Then they came in his direction, moving to 'Valse Amoureuse', and he had been through the whole thing before: the tune, a couple, a man's masterly guiding of her, and her ineffable compliance. When he had gone through it before – and this was what the tune and the couple suddenly reinvoked – the drama in her past had been so newly present in his mind that there was still a touch of Elizabethan horror about it. The mother died, he had remembered. That came back with a waltz-tune and some other similarity, but in the most curious way the drama seemed to break up into pieces, so that what he was seeing was another piece of it. This must be the final reconcilement. They were in such perfect accord that it seemed an intrusion to watch.

They passed from his view, and Missy happened then to come into it, and unreasoningly he would rather have seen Harden with *her*, playing his rôle of flirt or fortune-hunter. He had thought the beginning of the evening augured well for her, and he was proved wrong thus far, but she had picked up somebody here, at any rate got herself a new partner, not quite young but not bad-looking. While watching out for the other couple, he saw enough of her to know that she was running through the scales of her laughter from the low, throaty vibration up to the top peal – dancing with verve, stopping abruptly. Her white dress made an unfamiliar effect and not a girlish one – on the contrary, rather stagey, like herself at the moment. Somehow none of it boded good. Belle signed to him as she was leaving the room and told him that they were going to see what sort of supper there was, and he attached himself again to her and her party.

They could order what they liked, champagne included, if they paid for it, and could be served in the open-air restaurant, which had an awning over it – stretched rather low over many little tables with shaded candles – only the sides being open to the night. Darkness was close around, trees brooded in the stillness, the night-air hardly stirred. Stimulated unusually quickly by the champagne, Bernard thought this supper party was going to be as good a send-off as he could wish. He wouldn't be in better company than this – the seven of them together with their jokes and allusions – not for a long time, and he might have been challenging someone to find him better. Belle looked so fresh. she was so *piquante* and her preference was such a lighthearted

255

affair – that was such a relief – and already everyone was beginning to get silly. Champagne pushed far back in time the operatic début to the evening, which had promised something larger than life – back, too, though not so far, something that had been like experiencing it, really only imagination. It was pretty under the awning, becoming crowded, nearly all the tables occupied. With the buzzing roar of talk in various languages, it was foreign, Continental, attractive, and soon terribly to be missed. All of them at his table would soon be dispersed to different countries, but it seemed to him that all the others would be staying together and always carrying on like this, and that he alone was going away. Another glass of champagne all round, another bottle ordered, and someone asked how much money did they have between them? Would they be able to pay for their supper? That was the final letting-loose of merriment. They didn't have enough – they couldn't pay! The girls had no money with them, of course. The men had brought very little. Bernard thought of his financial situation – having paid his weekly bill that day, he knew he had just enough to pay for the remaining few days and his journey – but one couldn't worry here, and he suddenly felt himself to be quite tipsy in an extraordinary release from everything that had been possessing him. He was perfectly free to enjoy himself, drink and laugh as much as anyone else, and he laughed so loudly that it caused surprise. This freedom and independence, with which went a queer and conscious sense of gratitude, were exuberantly keeping themselves up when he saw Madame Solario making her way with her brother to a table by the railing that separated restaurant from garden. He saw her against the darkness that hemmed in the scene under the awning, and even through his tipsiness he felt what he always felt on seeing her: the world of difference there was between the moment when he was not seeing her and that next moment when suddenly – it always seemed suddenly – she was there for him to see. He was obliged to watch and know what she was doing, and she and her brother were not joining their Roman friends, who were all together at a large table, but were sitting down with a much smaller company. Bernard knew these people by sight, and that they were lake society, but he was so used to seeing Madame Solario always with the same people that it seemed wrong that she was not at the other table. The effervescence of enjoyment had subsided.

The problem of paying for their supper resolved itself; one of the young men could borrow what was needed from a relation of his he espied in the distance. The music was not playing; this was a long lull for supper. Bernard's vision of Madame Solario was sometimes interrupted, but her table was the fixed point of his attention; its candle against the darkness of the garden was the one he could immediately pick out again whenever he had looked away; it was the focus of regret for the night of the ball. The shaded light was always on her white neck and the bodice of her dress, not on her face. He had glimpses of Harden's face, and it seemed to him that the expression of it was excited rather than happy, and he wondered if he, too, was getting a little drunk.

Their emissary threaded his way to the table of the relation from whom he was to try to borrow money, and came back waving some large notes above his head. These were a gift! It became a triumph to be able to ask for their bill and to pay, and the munificence of their tip – because they had to spend the whole amount given them – was the crown of it. They thought they had better go, for they had been among the first to arrive in the restaurant, and as the orchestra was still absent and the ballroom empty they went to sit on the terrace. Guests were beginning to depart, were soon departing in large numbers, but they themselves were not intending to go for a long time yet. Bernard lapsed into a sort of dreaminess. There was a bush of *oleo fragrans* near that gave out in the darkness its marvellous scent; he had never met this scent until he came to Italy, and it was stronger and more delicious than any he had known.

The music began again within: those heart-catching first bars of waltz-time! The others went off in couples, one after the other, and Bernard followed the last. The departure of so much *hoi polloi* made a great difference; this now was more like a private ball, and the fine, painted ballroom, by being much less crowded, looked the finer. But something had gone – the *entrain* of the ball at its height. Without the crowd it would of course not stay the same, and the absence of liveliness might be only in himself, because for him there was to be nothing more. Yet he could still see Madame Solario, in her beautiful dress with the black velvet sash round her waist and her diamond stars on her shoulders. She was dancing with one of the men who had been at her supper-table; but her glow and sparkle had gone. Those brilliant moments when, swirling into a Spanish pose, she had clacked her fingers like castanets and everyone had applauded were like the spirit of the ball at its height, quite in the past. It was no longer having her success to look at that changed the face of things. There were no longer the same things to watch. There had been a change. But Harden and Missy were dancing together, and that, for some reason, he was glad of. Madame Solario and her partner came to rest near the door – near himself, but she didn't notice him – and, able to see nothing but her, he was not conscious of her brother till Harden had walked up to her as if to ask her to dance. Then Missy was between them, and Bernard instantly knew she was going to make a scene. Something that didn't happen in a ballroom, some break-out of unbridled excitement, was going to happen. The terror of a scene was all Bernard knew for a moment. Then – Why, why? If it had been another woman, the Marchesa San Rufino, one would have known it was jealousy, one would have understood, but to make a scene to *her* – Was Missy mad? Madame Solario placed her hand on her former partner's arm and turned her back on the two, and what Missy wildly said – covered by the music – was said to Harden. They must both be mad, Bernard had time to think, as Harden caught hold of her and the two precipitately left the ballroom together.

This had taken place near the door, and Bernard could not see that it received any attention except from those two or three who were before the door and were pushed aside. Madame Solario's partner spoke to her – jokingly, he thought – and she smiled. But still aghast Bernard looked into the corridor, and a little later – not to follow too patently – he went on to the big hall. The couple were not anywhere to be seen in the crowd. It was relatively quiet on the terrace, and he could see at once that they were not there. But he stopped there. The moon was low over the hills behind Como, and the lights of Como were almost all out, only a very few winking here and there on the crescent-shaped shore. The ball would soon be over . . . He did not know someone was coming up on his left until Missy, running, was upon him. As though encountering an obstacle she had not yet seen she spun round, and said as she did, 'His sister! His sister!' Then she ran on, so quickly, with her long white drapery streaming out, that it looked like flying – flying from pursuit. Yet who was pursuing her? No one. He let her white figure go flying on and disappear into the wood.

He wanted now to get back, and he went in by the yellow Empire salon that was a thoroughfare to the ballroom. When halfway between the French window and the door into the corridor, he saw that two people were sitting on the sofa, one of them talking with extraordinary ... They were the Marchesa Lastacori and Count Mosca, and Mosca was listening with something more – much more – than the amount of interest the Marchesa's stories usually commanded. It might be the story that Missy knew, which had never been spread but which the Lastacoris might now want to spread out of revenge for Harden's treatment of them. But that was an old story. Why was it worth what she was making of it? Bernard stood between window and door in the garishly bright room, with them sitting on the yellow Empire sofa not taking any notice of him. She was talking in Italian, and he could not understand a word she said, but time and again he caught the name – Missy. Mosca said nothing, till he threw up his hands and exclaimed 'Dio buono!' Bernard turned, turned tail. They were going to make a great deal of it, all for revenge. He could not face seeing her, unconscious of the venom the Marchesa was letting out – letting out perhaps more than he knew. A feeling almost of panic was on him, and he imagined the people in the ballroom, all Madame Solario's acquaintance, in dream-like numbers with malign but imprecise potentialities. What would they do? If Missy came back fairly normally, much less; and while he hoped against hope to see her white figure emerge from the wood, the lapping sound at the water's edge had to be listened to. How present the sound of lake water had been throughout these weeks, and what a curious character it had in moments of suspense. With various weathers went different sounds, and this was the soft, insidious one. They must, must soon be going home; but he would then see those people again to whom Mosca had probably communicated

259

what had made him throw up his hands. And supposing Missy created more trouble by having to be searched for? On the other hand, she might have got back, and nothing might be as he imagined.

He turned to go in, and along the terrace a man's figure was slowly coming in his direction, away from the hotel. The black of the pointed beard with the white shirt-front struck the eye even from some way off. The two men crossed each other. Bernard had never been presented to the Marchese San Rufino and did not bow. San Rufino had his eyeglass screwed into his eye, and his lip was lifted up on one side. He looked at Bernard, the eyeglass causing the look to seem very concentrated, piercing – indeed almost like speech. But he passed. To Bernard's immense relief, his own friends were all together inside the main entrance, ready to go. He saw a group of the Romans at the back of the hall and averted his eyes – just in time, he felt. Their launch was called, and the young people hurried down to embark; they were getting away ahead of a number of launches. Bernard's suspense was not over, for as they settled themselves in the cabin he expected that they would at once start talking of what had been taking place. But soon he realized that they had heard nothing at all; they did not mention Missy. And all talking gradually ceased. Before the long journey was half over, everyone but Bernard was asleep. Belle's head had dropped against the shoulder of her young man.

In that lake-and-mountain region storms come up quickly, and sometimes one end of the lake is having different weather from the other. When they landed, clouds were blotting out the stars and bringing premonitions of rain.

Chapter Twenty-Five

Bernard heard the rain when he woke, and it seemed fitting, for he woke to deep depression. He got up much later than usual and no one was left in the dining-room; but no one of interest ever breakfasted downstairs. Though the rain had been stopping for the last half-hour, there was still no rift in the clouds. He was looking out at the gloomy prospect when the concierge came up to his table with a letter – simply handed him a letter and went away. It had not come by post; it had only *Monsieur Middleton* on it in a rather foreign handwriting, and it felt lumpy. The envelope contained no letter at all, not a scrap of writing; it contained only two oleander flowers, one white and one red.

She was going, and she had remembered her promise. The where and when he was to meet her were not indicated, and he at once took up his post in the hall, pretending to read the newspapers of the day before, which were neatly spread out on a table. Now and again somebody passed through. But for the accursed rain they could have gone out, but it was too wet underfoot, too cheerless for a walk, and he might get no more than a few minutes' talk with her here in the hall. The night before was a dark background to her departure – yet he might have imagined too much, and it was conceivable that she was not going and had some other reason for wishing to see him again. In any case, she was treating him as a friend. Would they have a little time free of interruption? People would be coming down before long, and with an awful sense of the necessity for hurry, about which he could do nothing, he studied the headlines of the *Corriere della Sera*. Then it occurred to him that she was already gone, and the oleander flowers were not a summons but her only way of saying good-bye. There sat the concierge, busy at his desk. The concierge was the person who could tell him, who knew everything, and to whom he couldn't speak.

Some English visitors, recently come and quite strangers, three of them, stopped before the desk, and one of them inquired the way to the English church. The two ladies held prayer books, as Bernard noted in the throes of thinking that he was never going to see her again. The next minute he saw her, and she was dressed to go out, with her hat on and an umbrella carried in the crook of her arm. He did not start forward on seeing her; he waited. She saw the English strangers and paused to let them go ahead of her, then followed them. On the way, she acknowledged Bernard's presence with a slight bow, and while she bowed she looked straight at him. As once before, he received intelligence from her. She went out with the English visitors, and when, not too quickly, he went out too, he saw her walking at the same pace as they, so that they and she appeared to be together. From a distance they made one group on the road. Her figure detached itself from the others at the end of the row of oleanders and turned into the narrow opening between houses that was the way up to the woods. He ran up after her.

The steep cobbled steps were so slippery with wet that he put his hand under her elbow to help her. She let him. He wasn't thinking clearly, and what he said, when they were almost at the top, above the roofs, was, 'Did you go out in the rain to pick the oleander flowers?'

'No, the wife of the under-concierge picked them for me,' she answered.

He had a better view of her face when they were in the stronger light above, before they took the path into the woods, and all his fears were confirmed. Her face had become marble, that was the impression. So definite was the impression that any impulse to bring up their little joke, or her promise, died, and he could only wonder why she had remembered him. Over the vineyards stretching away up the hillsides, with the clouds rolling back, there was a look of brighter weather, but in the wood it might still have been raining, for the trees dripped. One could see how many leaves had already fallen when they lay wet, soddenly covering the ground, and here and there they were coming down in the showers of collected drops. So late in September one heavy rain could bring autumn, and even the smell of autumn was now here. That she should come out on a morning like this was in itself a confirmation of his fears, and with it was the gloom of the end, made visible in the wet wood once beautiful and golden-green. He was the first to speak, but not to remind her of anything that had been between them.

'I think you are going away.'

'Yes, I am going this afternoon. And you,' she said, 'when are you going?'

'Terribly early on Wednesday morning. But now I'd just as soon go before – go on Tuesday, or tomorrow.'

'Would you?' She was not yet, he thought, dressed for travelling, but her bolero and skirt of finely striped blue and white flannel were different from her summer attire and suited autumn and the end. 'Tuesday, or tomorrow?'

When she turned her face to him he was not surprised that it didn't smile. It did not express tenseness or anxiety – nothing exactly, except that, like marble, it couldn't change.

'You wouldn't be sorry to go as soon as tomorrow? There is nothing you particularly want to stay for?'

'No, nothing.'

'But you have been having a pleasant time?'

'Oh, yes.'

'Isn't it still pleasant, and you would miss something by going sooner?'

'There's so little time left – no time for anything more. It's all over, really – '

'There was nothing pleasant you were going to do tomorrow?'

'No, nothing. Nothing I had particularly thought of doing.'

'Then you wouldn't be sorry to go even today?'

From almost her first question he had felt every question leading inexorably on.

'Not at all sorry to go today.'

They were keeping steadily on the upward path, she helping herself with her slender umbrella.

'But could you be ready?'

When she reached the last question, when they were there, he had to get his breath. Was it really true – incredible! – that she was asking him to go with her?

'Of course I could be ready.'

Till then nothing had delayed her – not stones or roots; she stepped over or round them without noticing.

'I must explain,' she said, pausing then, at a turn of the steep path. 'My brother can't come with me. He has to go in the opposite direction.' Bernard had not had time to think directly about her brother. 'I won't be able to have his company, and I don't like to travel alone.'

At last she smiled, faintly, with that inquiry that was one of the first things about her that had affected him. With this look she had asked him if it would bore him to take her out in a row-boat. But his unspecified apprehension of the dark side intervened, just because of her attempt at that moment to dispel it with the look and smile he knew. Her face chilled to marble again.

'I am asking a great deal, I know.'

'You're asking very little. You want me to travel with you. Of course I will. Where are you going?'

'To Florence.'

He thought of his father's orders, and that he must be in London on Thursday.

'Travel with me to Florence, and there I will be with friends, and you can go back to England from there.'

I'll do it easily, he thought.

She looked round with a start, looked down the path by which they had come up, down into the depths of the wood.

'Listen!' she said.

He listened, and heard perhaps – a footfall below, the echo of one, what he would have heeded no more than the drip of the rain. Madame Solario looked up, up the path by which they were going, and seized his arm. He responded to her influence so quickly that she did not need to draw him away from the path and up over some stony ground. A little way off the track, the cave opened at the foot of the crag. He had a moment of thinking, as he followed her in, that it was not so deep as he remembered. She went as far as she could, and the cave had irregularities that yielded most depth in one corner. When she was backed against its rough rock wall he stood in front of her, but he could barely make out her face, it was so dark there. He had noticed the cold damp as they went in, and then, as they stood close to each other, it was her scent, familiar and yet belonging to the farthest realm of romance. Breathing in her scent, he could hear her breathing; he was almost touching her, but other senses were on the alert, and it was not as he would have imagined. The sounds grew unmistakable – footfalls, though muffled by the wet leaves, small loose stones sent rolling down on the steepest part, sent by someone climbing hastily, one person, and that a man. When that person was at the turn of the path where they had left it – as near as that – Madame Solario seized Bernard's arm again. Her fingers held it gripped. The man was passing by, and it could only be Kovanski, as she was reconciled with her brother. He saw the glint of her eyes just before he turned his head to look over his shoulder towards the opening. And he had what was like a fleeting glimpse of Colonel Ross's face, big nose and grey moustache and sidelong glance, and Colonel Ross's voice was saying, 'One mayn't always know what one's lettin' one's self in for, you know.'

The man would have to come back and pass them again. And he might go a long way up, and they would have to wait a long time. Kovanski did not come into what Bernard had feared the night before, he did not come into the story, but he was a menace that was concurrent with everything that happened. And it might be that what Bernard had feared had not happened, but something else had, and the reason for her departure was not the dark side but only Kovanski. All this went through his mind while they stood as far back in the cave as they could, in its deepest corner, and her hand still gripped his arm. Her hearing was very acute, for she seemed to know when the man was coming down again – but they soon made out that he was taking the other path, the one that at the top led away from the cliff, more windingly and less steeply down. She took her hand from Bernard's arm and held up her finger; he could just see it, and just hear the footfalls a little way off and going away. He would have gone to the opening to look, but she shook her finger, quickly, several times to stop him. The sounds quite ceased, and that sense of a presence that one can have without hearing. Though the man had gone the other way, they would have to wait some time before they could be sure that they would not meet him at the bottom of the hill, and when they came out of their corner they still stayed inside the cave. But he could feel the fresher air of outside, and could see Madame Solario's face before him.

'I can't explain everything,' she said, 'and it may seem strange to you, what I am doing and asking you to do.'

He shook his head, meaning that it wasn't strange. Her face was before him in this cave in the hillside where they were imprisoned, and an hour ago he had been in the hall, in a fever thinking he would not have more than a few minutes with her, if he saw her at all, if she hadn't gone. He could hardly pay attention to what she was saying.

'I, also, was going on Tuesday or Wednesday, but then something happened and I must go today. What makes it more complicated is that I mustn't let my brother know I am going. That is what I cannot explain. But if he knew, he would be glad you were coming with me and I wouldn't have to travel alone.'

It was all said in little above a whisper, as if she might be overheard. From what they could see of the wood, there was no life there at all, not a bird or a squirrel, but she whispered.

When she said 'It is a rather complicated journey, and we don't arrive till very late. I am taking the half-past-three-o'clock boat to Varenna, and there I take the train. If you come with me that is what we will do. It's a slow train, and we stop some time in Milan and don't arrive in Florence till midnight' – the rapid speech was given a character by her whispering it, so that its prosaic matter was not out of keeping with her face, the face of a statue in the dim light, the statue of some classic mythological person – a Medusa perhaps.

'I don't want to be seen leaving, and I will take only a small amount of luggage with me.' Luggage! It wouldn't take him long to pack. 'I must leave my big trunks behind.' He had once gone to the end of the passage on his floor and looked round the corner, and seen the huge dress-trunk with the initials N.S. outside her door. 'The wife of the under-concierge will pack everything I leave behind – I must trust her, I think I can – and the under-concierge will send on my trunks when I let him know. The under-concierge will see that our luggage is taken out to the boat at the last moment. Now if you come with me, will you also please not be seen leaving? Will you meet me on the boat, coming down at the last moment? There are stairs, I am told, at the end

266

of your corridor' – so she knew where his room was – 'and one can come out a back way and not have to go through the hall. Are you willing to go away like this?'

She had already worked it out to the last detail. This practical ability was like another force, and he could not have countered her plans even if there had been no irresistible wish to fall in with them. She had come out with them formed. He wondered, one part of him detached and amazed, how she would have put it to him if things had not gone just as they had – if there had been a different beginning, something else said; with her plans already formed, there had been no hitch; it had all gone forward as she intended it to. But she could always have put it to him; she would have known how.

She was still whispering. 'I am not going to ask for my bill till the last moment, when I am ready to go. One should, of course, announce two days before that one is going. Had you told them you were going on Wednesday?'

'Yes, I told them yesterday.'

'But you shouldn't pay more than for one day beyond today.'

It broke upon him that he might not have enough money to get back to England if he went to Florence and had the much longer journey home. She seemed to guess it.

'Have you enough money?'

'Yes, plenty.'

'Because I could lend you – You could pay me back later. You are doing what I ask, to please me, and are very kind.'

She took his hand and pressed it. That caused him utter surprise. She wore a glove, a soft glove, and he couldn't feel her hand. He caught at it when she had let his go, and then he let it go again.

'You are very kind when I can't explain everything.'

It was true, he didn't understand the situation. The pieces he knew about, or thought he knew, didn't fit together, or there were too few to do anything with. And because he was at this point – had come to this moment – without the least preparation, he was, though so deeply excited, able also to feel oppressed.

'Then you understand,' she quickly began again, as if she had had to interrupt herself. 'It will be at the last moment that you pay your bill and your luggage is taken down. And you won't tell anyone – anyone you may meet before – that you are going today, will you?'

'But the manager will guess at once, when I pay my bill within a few minutes of your paying yours, that we are going together. It can't be by chance that we both go like this, taking the same boat.'

There was just a little silence before she answered. 'Yes, of course, but if he says anything it will be afterwards, when we are gone.'

It wouldn't do them any harm, she must mean, if it was said after they had gone. They would never see any of these people again.

The peril that made her whisper her instructions so urgently lay in her being seen, being prevented from going. She must not be prevented, and he and she would have to escape without his knowing what they were escaping from.

He was recognizing the sort of claim he had felt upon him ever since the evening of her brother's arrival, almost awestruck by having it thus proved to him that he had been right – something had passed between them and constituted a claim. He again could hardly listen to what she was saying, but he looked at her face, upon which there was still no play of expression, no softness to its beauty.

'Will you be all right,' he asked, 'all right when you get to Florence?'

'Oh, yes, when I meet my friends. Do you remember, I told you who they were? An old American gentleman, who was a friend of my father, and his niece?'

Of course he remembered. He remembered everything she had ever told him. And she had told him this – and he had heard with surprise that it was an old American gentleman she was expecting – when they were sitting on the bench above where they now were, on top of the rock at whose foot they were hiding.

'I think,' she said – he couldn't be sure how long they had stood silent – 'I think we can go down now. I will go first, and if I meet anyone I will have been for a walk alone. No one who may meet me will see you if you come down some time later.'

But she seemed as loath to go as he to have her go. She hesitated at the mouth of the cave.

'I would like to see you again before we meet on the boat,' she said, whispering. 'Don't go down to lunch till a quarter past one, and leave your door open. I will go past your room.'

He nodded. She stepped outside. When he saw her walking away she was a different person from the one she had been in the cave. She was a fashionably dressed figure, carrying a slender umbrella in the crook of her arm, and all that was unusual was that this figure should be walking alone that morning under the dripping trees. But, stepping down the path, going away from him, she was something else again, going down to unknown perils through the sad, autumnal wood. It was dreadful to let her go alone. And then he thought, supposing this had been their last interview, and that as he looked after her he knew he would never see her again? The reality could scarcely be taken in.

The last thing he could see of her, her hat, had been out of sight for some time when he followed. On the way down something struggled through into his excitement: regret – actually regret that he was leaving like this without saying good-bye to anyone. And possible developments – Kovanski, in short – were not, to his shame, something to be quite ignored as being of no importance. Reaching the road he hesitated, and turned to the left. He could not say good-bye to the Leroys, whom he so much liked, but he could see their house again and say good-bye to that. Just where their garden wall began the scent of *oleo fragrans* met one, and he knew it so well, the spot where it was like something palpable across the road. He always noticed it, and it had associations. He walked past the big iron gates and glanced up the path to the covered veranda with the two palm trees in front. On his other hand the lake was lead-coloured, and the water was heaving up and splashing back from the lake-wall. It was the moment of a sort of good-bye. But he had to walk on at least to the bend in the road before he could turn back – and the Leroy girls came bicycling round the bend with their little white Pomeranian trotting in their rear. They jumped off their bicycles, and Belle said she hadn't waked up till half-past eleven.

'I believe you're only this minute up yourself!' she said.

'Oh, no, I've been up a long time,' he answered lamely.

'Wasn't it the greatest fun? Middleton was positively – I told you,' she said to her sister. 'Heavens, you were gay! One could see it was good for you. My mother must never know about the

269

champagne and our running up that bill. I'd never be allowed out again!'

Something seemed odd to him; it was that Martha hadn't blushed when she first saw him, as she always had before.

'Whose guardian angel sent us that uncle, do you suppose?' said Belle, and it seemed to him that she was talking for talking's sake.

'Where have you come from?' he asked, putting his hand down to the little white dog that had capered about him.

'We've been just for a spin, to freshen me up. We were afraid of meeting the people coming out of church – they'd think us godless – but they must have got ahead. Is it very late?'

'Then you haven't seen anyone this morning?' he said, having had a sudden fear that they had heard something.

'No, we haven't seen a soul yet.' And then he thought they would think it odd that he had asked. Did one usually ask people if they had seen anyone that morning?

He thought they were looking at him with their clear eyes as though they knew that everything was different. It was only a few seconds since Belle had spoken, but those seconds were like a silence. Martha hadn't blushed, and it seemed to him that both girls were looking at him with sympathy. He couldn't understand it.

'Neither have I,' he said, so that they'd think afterwards – He couldn't work it out.

They were getting on their bicycles. He minded very much at that moment that he wasn't going to say good-bye to them and 'Perhaps we'll meet again.' They started, the little dog frisking about their wheels.

'Middleton!' called Belle, and he turned. 'Come round to tea this afternoon!' and he waved.

Again he had to walk on a little way, as if he were going somewhere, in spite of a fearful conviction of wasting time. When he hurried past their gate they had gone in. Approaching the hotel, he saw a whole party of people boarding the motor-launch and recognized the Romans – the Romans going out to luncheon. He wondered if their going would increase the chances of Madame Solario's getting away without their seeing her, or add a risk. But what these people represented was more weighty and baneful than a chance that they might come back at the wrong moment. He had felt a kind of panic the night before, thinking of them in the ballroom being told something, malignly repeating it and talking, talking as they always were, but suddenly with something to talk about, all coming together to talk – or so he saw them in his heated fancy after Mosca threw up his hands, and of course it was at the end of a long evening, when one's fancy could run away with one. But when he saw them he again felt afraid of them. They were powerful in a way, the way of the world. For him they were also shallow and malignant, fortunate and despicable – all because they might have been told something about Madame Solario and her brother. Here they were, showing by everything about them their luxurious habits, and going off, absolutely fortunate and cruel – their boat cutting the water into two sharp, white-edged, lengthening waves – and leaving him with a heavy sense of reminder of the dark side.

He went up to his room and began to pack. Then he had to try to believe that this was really happening, and his familiar clothes became endowed with a human consciousness on being packed under these circumstances; when last worn, they never would have thought it. He had sent a trunk home before coming to Cadenabbia, and his luggage now consisted only of two large suitcases; one of them, packed with his flannels and what he would not need again this year, could be forwarded from here if there was time to arrange it, for he must not be encumbered with two great suitcases on their complicated journey. At five minutes past one he opened his door, his heart beating harder. Soon after quarter past he heard the rustle of a silk lining, and there she was at the door, in the act of passing.

'The under-concierge will come for your luggage at a little after three o'clock. Go down now.'

'Yes. Your –' He could not any longer call them her friends. 'The whole lot of them went off in the launch before luncheon. Did you know?'

'Yes, they are lunching at Villa Serbelloni.'

The day before she would have gone with them, he was sure.

'Mightn't they come back just as you are setting out, which would be awkward?'

'No, they won't be back till four o'clock at the earliest. This is very lucky, on the contrary.'

To his fancy, *they* were all together triumphantly *in front*, in the light, while she was in a rather dark passage at the back, alone but for him.

'You see the door of the escalier de service down there?'

'Oh yes, I know it.'

The pathos with which he was investing her was different from every other aspect under which he had seen her till now.

'We won't meet until we are on the boat. Good-bye,' she murmured, and was gone from his door.

He would not have gone down if she had not told him to. That the Romans would not be there made it easier. The Lastacoris, too, were not at their table. He hoped that no one would speak to him before he went and that he would never know. But Harden was in the dining-room, and he had joined a man who had lately come, and was sitting at his table. Bernard sat in his usual place by the door, from which during these weeks he had been able to see her generally twice a day, so that he had come to know her clothes, her attitudes and little ways, her face, as well as if he had a close acquaintance with her – he had had more opportunities of seeing her than he would have had in a year of ordinary acquaintance – and he had best been able to observe her when she and her brother were alone at their table in the middle of the room. He had observed her brother too, and he had never got over what he had felt the first evening after seeing her recognize him. He had not, if he were to be frank with himself, been glad when they came to be on affectionate terms with each other, and when he had seen her brother make her laugh he had always felt unhappy. And on this day, in the dining-room, from which all the other people who interested Bernard were absent, leaving empty tables and areas of silence, Harden, talking jovially, in good spirits, with a stranger, was as sinister as he had been on the first evening, or rather more.

He went out before the two men had finished. Harden hadn't bothered to look his way. He changed into a brown suit, concluded his packing, and counted his money twice in the hope of making it come out a larger sum. The suspense was getting extreme, for if she was prevented from going he would never see her again. He ran downstairs at a little before three. That, he thought, was the 'last moment' for paying his bill. As it was Sunday, the manager was absent and his clerk was functioning – a youngish man who gave Bernard a lively look when he heard he was leaving that day and wished to pay his bill tout-de-suite. He had paid his weekly bill only the day before.

'Vous avez réténu votre chambre jusqu'à mercrédi, jé crois?' he said with his Italian accent.

'I will pay till Wednesday,' said Bernard, to get through as quickly as possible.

A deprecatory gesture was like 'Figurez-vous!' or 'Si figuri!' and the man wrote something in violet ink with a pen like a pin. Bernard pulled out a note and waited for the change, trying not to show his hurry, and the other moved rather slowly but looked very sharp.

He asked the concierge as he tipped him if he had settled up everything the day before, the boat-hire and all, and was told that he had. He half expected to find Colonel Ross beside him, hearing and asking questions, but no one was there. Colonel Ross had been very kind to him and would be surprised. He wished he could leave a message, an excuse – he could have invented one, but there wasn't time.

Waiting in his room, he thought the under-concierge wasn't coming – it was all up. Then the man came in and looked for the luggage; it must be all right. The under-concierge was Swiss, and though he was being treated confidentially was not looking interested. Bernard asked him if it was possible to have a suitcase sent to England and if he could attend to that, but agreeing to *petite vitesse*, which would be very slow but cheap, and writing out his home address, and giving the money that would cover the expedition, were almost too much of a strain. He twice went to the window because he thought he heard the boat.

'We must go!'

The most perilous moment for Madame Solario was going to be when she crossed the road to the embarcadero, and anyone looking that way would see her. Bernard and the under-concierge reached the embarcadero, and the man set down the suitcase beside some luggage that was already there and started to go back across the road, five minutes before the little white steam-boat came sliding in. The sailors threw out ropes with cries of 'Cadenabbia-a-a!' and the little gangplank clattered down. Two or three peasants went on board, and Bernard followed them but looked back with one foot on the gangplank; he would have been speechless if anyone had spoken to him then. Trees and a wooden shelter blocked his view of the road, and he did not see Madame Solario till she was across. The under-concierge, carrying several pieces of luggage, called out 'Aspetti! Aspetti!' Bernard went on and paid for the tickets, knowing she was behind him; the under-concierge handed all the luggage up to a sailor, who deftly seized the pieces and dropped them on the deck. The ropes were thrown back, the gangplank was pulled up, and the paddle-wheels began to turn.

Chapter Twenty-Six

They met in the cabin. She sank on to the bench, and he sat down on the bench opposite and, not to observe her, steadily looked out of the window at the receding shore. They were not past pursuit, for if her flight were discovered in time someone in a motor boat could get to Varenna ahead of them. But for a little while they were, in a sense, nowhere – out of the world.

When, after Bellagio, the boat was in the middle of the lake again, he said, 'I'll go and have a last look.'

'Yes,' she said, 'have a last look.'

They hadn't spoken before.

The familiar landmarks had been changing their positions and scale, and the villas he knew best, strung along the road, were already small at the base of the wooded ridge. As he stood on deck, hearing the thrash of the paddle-wheels and the wash of the water, past occasions in these romantic weeks formed themselves into a chain that from his meeting with Ilona, which was the beginning – the very beginning – he could see had been leading all the time to this unimaginable conclusion. The whole scene was for the last time before his eyes, and it was dully overclouded, as it so rarely had been. Just in one spot behind them a beam of light, coming one couldn't see how, struck the water, and a round patch glinted white in a sheet of grey. After his last look he had only to step back into the cabin to see her, who had usually been only in his thoughts.

'We should not have more than a quarter of an hour to wait at Varenna,' she said.

'And no one has got ahead of us yet,' he said. 'I've been keeping watch.'

She was travelling in dark cornflower blue, jacket and skirt, with a small blue hat that had a pair of bird's wings for trimming, and the shirt she had worn that morning; he recognized the cream silk cravat. A sailor had brought in, after they started, her morocco dressing-case and a travelling-cushion buttoned into a leather cover, and put them on the bench beside her. If, Bernard thought, he had seen her for the first time on that journey, would he not have been bowled over by the elegance and mystery of this lady travelling alone, and would he not have remembered her all his life as *l'Inconnue* whom he had once seen in the cabin of a little lake steamboat, and would he not have wondered all his life about her?

The boat stopped at Menaggio – the name shouted out, and tension in both of them because it was conceivable that someone had got here by road. But the paddle wheels began to churn, and no one came in.

The next stop was Varenna. He went out on deck again and watched the shore once more coming nearer; and he suddenly and clearly remembered his surprise at hearing a cry of 'Middle-ton!' and seeing the group of young people standing there at the end of the jetty, the girls in their white dresses, when he was alone, going anywhere because he was so unhappy about Ilona. 'Middle-ton!' – long-drawn-out – had had something in it like a call from much farther away. Now he had to see to their luggage, and hers was only two suitcases and a little hat-box, so they had a very manageable amount. The station was but a short walk from the embarcadero, and a porter wheeled the luggage to it on a barrow, and though it was not likely that anyone had got there first Bernard could not deny he had a horrid feeling of running the gauntlet as they walked across.

In the grimy, rather empty station he saw a window marked *Prima Classe*, and they went towards it.

'Get the tickets only to Milan,' she said to him. 'We will have time in Milan to get the tickets on from there.'

That would throw someone off the scent, he saw.

She stood beside him and took her handbag from her arm. 'You must let me pay,' she said.

'No.' But he couldn't hold out; he had no margin at all. 'Only for yourself, then.'

She heard the cost of *due biglietti per Milano* and gave him the notes that approximated to half – they overpaid him by a couple of lire. He thought someone might be seeing her do it and would know this wasn't a real elopement, and that was very painful.

They followed the porter to the trains, and it was nearly as agitating as catching the boat, just because they were on the home stretch. A waiting train bore the words on a white board: *Varenna – Lecco – Milano.* All their luggage was put into an empty first-class carriage, and she took the seat by the farther window, going forward. He tipped the porter, who looked scornfully and embarrassingly at the money lying on his open palm before he shut his hand and went away. There was then what seemed a very long wait, and they didn't speak. When the train began to move she leaned back and put her hand up to her brow.

The train gathered speed and went rattling along; they were away. No one would catch up with them now.

After a time she turned to the window and said, 'What is this? What are we seeing?' in a tone of conversation.

'It's the lake of Lecco, the other arm of Como. Bellagio is on the other side of the promontory, over there.'

'Ah, yes. I don't think I ever came to this lake. It is wilder and sadder, isn't it?'

'I've sailed here. Once we nearly ran on to those rocks. There's rather a strong current along there.'

'I've often seen the white sails of the little yachts. Haven't there been races?'

She was going to make conversation; she was now like a hostess putting a guest at his ease. He wished her to see that he was quite at his ease. Then, when she had established ease and the tone of their journey, she took the fawn silk cushion and her book out of the leather cushion case and settled herself in her corner. In all her motions there was that absence of haste and purposefulness that was one of the secrets of her grace. He knew it so well. He had not felt it that morning when she was walking, when she was questioning him, not when she was urgently whispering. But it was there again, the secret, in the way she loosened her veil and raised it so that she could read, placed the cushion behind her, took the paper-cutter out of the book and cut a few pages; a little more and it would have been languorous, but it was not quite. Seeing her do these little things stirred something like fear – the question to himself: if he so felt the grace of every little thing she did, what then?

He took out his own book and opened it; it was still the romance by H. G. Wells that he had brought to Cadenabbia. She looked over at him and asked what he was reading. He showed her the book and told her he had been reading it for a month.

She showed him her book, a novel by Colette Willy. 'I have had it a month and not even begun it!'

Then they both pretended to read.

The train stopped at Leccò and after that dawdled, occasionally stopping suddenly as though it had sat down. And the scenery changed, for they had left the mountains behind, the mountains that were like a rampart about the lakes, and had come into the plain. She looked up from her book and saw the change and spoke of it a little. He longed for her to speak a little more, and he also, to his shame, began to be hungry. He would very much have liked tea. Daylight was going. The train stopped in a fair-sized station and stayed stopped for so long that he thought it might stay very much longer.

'If I could get something to eat – a bun or something – would you like it?' he asked her.

'I think it would be very nice,' she answered.

He asked a station official in a braided cap who was passing, 'Quanto tempo?' The official said, 'Ancora –' and held up both hands with all the fingers spread to denote ten minutes. Bernard jumped down and saw *Ristorante* some way off. He would have loved to buy a bottle of Chianti in its straw coat, but they had no glass, and he bought only buns, the kind called *maritozzi*, and half a kilo of black grapes. He ran back, thinking the train might have started, but of course it hadn't, and running back to it he was ecstatically happy.

She smiled, took off her gloves and broke a bun in half, and ate, leaning a little forward so that crumbs and sugar shouldn't fall on her lap.

'It's very good,' she said.

He was so happy, seeing her eat, himself being hungry, that it was like shooting lights, singing and jubilation.

'Will you have some grapes now?' he said, and he flattened

out the paper bag to spread on her lap. 'I've never anywhere eaten grapes like this kind they have here – the whole inside popping out of its skin in one go.'

He was meant to know by the way she did it that as she pressed one grape after another to her lips the insides were popping out of their skins into her mouth. His laugh burst out. He offered her his handkerchief to wipe her fingers on.

'We will have time to dine in Milan,' she said.

He watched jealously for further evidences of a lighter mood, thinking that now that she had got away she should be carefree. But perhaps relief itself was intense and exhausting. When the light had been turned on in the carriage she opened her book again, and he tried not to look at her. In spite of the reflection on the window he could see that white mists were rising from the plain, and lights in the distance didn't twinkle. After a time Madame Solario looked out too, and they looked together at what they could see of a ghostly country.

The conductor put in his head and said, 'Milano!' Bernard moved a suitcase into the corridor, and the moon was on that side, out there on the low horizon – the harvest moon, full as the night before, when he had seen it hours later than this because it had had to top the high mountain. Nothing in his whole life had been so extraordinary. Only the night before, when he had seen the moon above the mountains and the lake all was about to happen but he had believed all was over, and now, the very next night, as he was seeing the moon over unknown, flat, and misty country, Madame Solario in a railway carriage was putting her cushion and book into the fawn leather case he had come to know; and when he went back into the carriage he would take the rest of their luggage down from the racks.

Milan station was seething with people – all talking at once, by the noise. Bernard led the way for her to the ticket-office, and he could see when he looked back that her fairness was like an illumination in the midst of the drab, plebeian crowd. He asked for their tickets but he did not quite understand the reply, and she translated, opening her handbag again. It was just as painful as before to take her money. Though their train had been late they still had nearly an hour, and they crossed the squalid central hall to the station restaurant.

279

The restaurant did not look too bad, and they ordered soup, a veal dish that was said to be ready, and a bottle of red wine. The muffled din of the station grew acuter whenever the door was opened, and when it opened she would glance up. He was in a state of double-consciousness, being with her and yet thinking about her, thinking what he could say to her and wouldn't say. He was not with her because it would interest her to hear that he couldn't believe it was true, after all these weeks of watching her, that they were dining together. But they *were* dining together – it was she, *her* face a little shaded from the harsh light by the brim of her hat – and he could tell himself what he couldn't tell her.

It seemed to be established that they did very little talking; they had so far spoken only about the things that came up, but he did not have the embarrassment he would have had if he had been taking her out and failing to entertain her. That their time for dinner was limited was a reason for not talking much. As he suddenly felt the quickening passage of time, it was of the end of their journey that he began to think.

'Will we – or will you go tonight to the hotel or wherever it is your friends are staying?'

There was one of her hesitations before she answered. 'I thought as we will get in so late we would go to a hotel near the station tonight. My friends are at the Grand Hotel.'

She added – to his great surprise, as something quite new was introduced – 'I'm sure they are still there.'

He nearly said, 'Then you aren't sure?'

To his continuing surprise, he felt uneasiness when she went on, a little as if she were going over it to reassure herself, 'I saw in the *New York Herald* last Wednesday that they were staying at the Grand Hotel in Florence, and I telegraphed to say I was coming.'

'Then they must be expecting you,' said Bernard.

'But then I telegraphed after that that I had to postpone coming, and I have done nothing since.'

'Have you heard from them since your two telegrams?'

'No.' She said again, 'But I am sure they are still there. They were staying there.'

As it would have been better for him if they were not there,

Bernard felt sure that they would be. And whether or not she would find her friends in Florence was so unimportant, relatively. She had got away from whatever was menacing her, and he could have reproached her for not being entirely thankful, out of the woods and lighthearted. She was not – no, she was not – and he had to consider that this doubt might reasonably be important to her.

'Would it matter very much if you did not find your friends?'

'Yes,' she said. She let the waiter pour coffee into the cup beside her, and then she lifted the coffee-cup to her lips.

After a few moments his very silence made her speak. 'If I could see Mr Chase again, I might arrange to go with him and his niece back to America.'

All Bernard's double-consciousness had gone, and his whole attention was focused on the word 'America' The parting would be more terrible if she were going much farther than Paris – to America.

'Do you want to?'

'Yes. I lived there as a child. One likes to go back to where one was at home. For a little while. Mr Chase is old,' she said. 'He is very kind and –'

She drew down her veil and picked up her gloves. 'I think we should go.'

What struck Bernard as being one of the salient features of an Italian railway station was the predominance of men – a quite Oriental absence of women, and great numbers of men. When they boarded their train (*Milano–Bologna–Firenze*) they had to push past men, and, to Bernard's dismay, there was no empty carriage, even first-class. He found one with only two occupants and took a window-seat for her, but while he was getting the luggage disposed the place opposite hers was taken, and also the one beside her, and there was nothing left for him but room in the middle of the seat; at least it was on the opposite side, and he could see her. He was as dismayed as if he were being denied wonderful opportunities of conversation that might prove to be the last he would ever have.

Their fellow travellers were professional men or businessmen with brief cases, and when the conductor came in for the tickets three of them showed passes. Two began talking to each other, and Bernard gradually became familiarized with these circumstances – the movement of the train, which was not like the dilatory train from Varenna; the noise and rattle; the light in the ceiling falling full on them all, yet making hard shadows; the men talking in the foreign language, sometimes both together, in a sort of rhythm raising their voices each to drown the other; and Madame Solario sitting by the window with her elbow on the cushioned rest, looking out.

Unhappiness entered and filled him in a rising tide. This was the last lap of their journey, and she would join her friends next day, because of course they were there, and he would at once go back to England. He might be back sooner than was required. Tomorrow week he would be starting work in the bank in the dreary northern town to which, for several years anyhow, he was doomed. There was no hope to grasp and keep hold of in the tide of unhappiness.

There had been a long stretch of time when she moved, turning from the window, and raised her hands to loosen her veil and push it up to her brows. She then leaned her head against the back of the seat. But while she exposed her face for them to see, she was not seeing them. Bernard did not think she was conscious of her action or of where she was; and her face, fully revealed, was even more enigmatic to him than it had been behind her veil. He wondered what she was seeing, for her eyes were not, as they might have been, vague with fatigue, nor did they have the soft, musing look he knew so well. Her eyes under the beautiful sweep of her brows, by being fixed ahead of her but on something only she could see, some inner sight, gave her an expression he had never known before. He had once or twice felt that those eyes and eyelids, and that classic line of nose and brow, had a sort of impersonality of beauty – but now it was not impersonality that was baffling, it was what was personal, the look of seeing with those eyes what no one else could see. The word 'fate' came to him, for her beauty even now suggested what it could represent, as it had suggested marble, a statue, a Medusa, to him that morning. But it was not herself as fate – what was so personal to her in those moments was the look of seeing her own fate.

The deep disturbance caused by this was a cross-current

with his own unhappiness. Something then provided a sort of relief. He saw that a man in the corridor was peering in at her, now through the inside window of the carriage and now through the door, and though at first he was given a start, he encountered after a time the black eyes of an unknown Italian. They were then withdrawn, but ten minutes had not gone by when Bernard saw them again, looking in more circumspectly, from the side and not the middle of the window, and he jumped up. The man did not stop to challenge his right to advance so aggressively and wandered away. It might be ordinary Italian male behaviour and an acceptable compliment, but Bernard couldn't stand it. He sat down on his suitcase, which was in the corridor, prepared to guard the approaches. Those rather nice men in the carriage, with their wedding-rings and their briefcases, hadn't openly looked at her after the beginning, and he could glance in on them from time to time, keeping watch. She turned to the window again, and he thought she had not noticed anything, not noticed that he had left the carriage. He was quite by himself, and he could see through the window the moon in the sky and something – sometimes – of a moonlit landscape, and houses and cypresses, and a square with a palazzo and church close to a station. The train rushed on and on, and it was going through Italy – that occurred to him; he was going through Italy in the night, never having seen it, only its mountain edge. Italy – the desire of poets, of everyone. The train had not stopped for a long time when it pulled up with a great deal of choo-chooing and he came to, wondering where he was. They were in a station, and on a large hanging board the name of the town was big and clear – *Parma*. Why did it seem strange to be there?

What did he know about Parma? The Duchess of Parma – but who was she? Parma violets. And in the long pause there were hollow, clanging sounds of iron on iron. The train choo-chooed off. The black eyes had not dared show themselves, and he went back to his seat in the carriage, where the men had ceased talking and two were asleep, and Madame Solario had opened her book.

When, after a long time, the train stopped again, he read on the hanging board *Bologna*. Bologna – one of the oldest universities in Europe. Three of their men got out, bowing politely, and only one was left, asleep, and Bernard could move into the window-seat. She was ivory-pale. She must be very tired, for she could have got no sleep the night before, not after the ball and what had happened. He had had little sleep himself. The moonlight when they went on again made him think of the ball and remember playing statues around the fountain. It seemed so long ago. Gradually all his thoughts and recollections became confused, were blotted out, and then suddenly he saw Madame Solario in a quite different place and quite different situation. She was sitting in a chair, a little inclined forward, in what might have been the hall of a fashionable hotel but was not the Bellevue, and she was wearing a pale dress with a large bunch of Parma violets in her belt. She was directly facing him but not seeing him, and no one was with her. He woke with a start, and she was sitting opposite him, her head leaned back and her eyes closed. On thus awaking and seeing her white eyelids dropped over her eyes, on seeing her asleep, he felt a commotion within himself as if he were surprising her when he had no right to see her. He did not see her thus for long. Her eyes opened, were at once widely open. She looked at the door, at the man asleep in the corner, and back at him. The deepest night-hour of their journey had a moment of eeriness. But she would not have it so. She said, 'We should soon be there' – and put her book into the cushion-case.

'I don't know what time we ought to be there,' he said.

'I will get ready.'

She went along the corridor, and he mounted guard. When she came back her veil was down and locks of hair that had strayed a little were smoothed. Finding him in the corridor, she rested her arm on the window-rail and said, 'I am sure those are the hills round Florence. Have you ever been to Florence?'

She asked him this as if he were coming to Florence in an ordinary way as a tourist, and not entirely on account of her.

'No. Have you?'

'Yes, I was here last spring.'

He remembered – the nightingales in Italy that sang night and day.

'We are seeing the hills by moonlight. Those must be the

lights now. If you opened the window and leaned out you might see the Duomo and the Campanile in the moonlight.'

He didn't move. This was what she was saying to him, and how she was saying it, at the end of that day, at the end of their journey. He was too miserable to speak. Before very long the conductor appeared, said, 'Firenze!' and passed them, and Bernard went in to get down the luggage.

It was nearly one o'clock, and the station, though there were some travellers and porters, had the look and the echoing sound of a station late at night. Madame Solario spoke to their porter, who understood and said, 'Albergo Baglioni.'

'Si, Albergo Baglioni. It is right here,' she said to Bernard.

The porter went ahead, and they followed, Bernard carrying the bandbox and the cushion, and she walking at his side in silence, without the step or any air of fatigue. Indeed, he had to keep up with her. Now that she had almost reached her goal, her resolution was more apparent than at any time that day.

They came out of the station into a piazza, and while they were crossing it, bearing to the left, he saw a mass of building before him – a church, the back of one, with cloisters or something of the sort; and on the walls, black and white marble in geometric designs were very striking in the moonlight. The swing-doors of an hotel opened to them, and they entered an empty lobby.

A concierge who had been napping stood up.

'Have you a room,' she said in French, 'for me, and also one for this gentleman?'

'You are together?' asked the concierge, with an Italian accent and without the French forms of politeness.

'No.'

'I have a fine room on the first floor,' he said.

He called, 'Beppino!' and a sleepy boy answered the summons. The concierge gave him a key and instructions, and Bernard indicated which was his luggage and which was hers. While her pieces were being taken to the lift she held out her hand to Bernard.

'Good night,' she said.

Shaking hands with her was so unreal to him that it might have been another dream he was having about her.

'You will go out very early tomorrow morning, I suppose,' he said.

'Not before eleven o'clock,' she answered. 'Will you go out before that?'

'I shouldn't think so.'

She followed the boy, and he was left with his suitcase and the station-porter to tip. The man looked at his palm in the usual way, as though he couldn't believe his eyes he had been given so little, but the concierge spoke to him sharply, and he went off.

'And my room?' asked Bernard.

'There is one on the first floor, and one on the second,' said the concierge.

While Bernard was not saying which one he would have, the visitors' book was pushed towards him.

'Will you write your names, please.'

He wrote his name and *Angleterre*, without an address. Not everyone, he saw, gave an address.

'Et Madame?'

Bernard was silent, and the concierge said, 'You are not here for long?'

'Only one night.'

The concierge shrugged as though the question became negligible, but when Beppino had reappeared and been given another key, Bernard, as he was turning away from the desk, saw the concierge write on the line just below *Bernard Middleton – et Madame*.

Beppino and he went up to the second floor, and into a rather small single room in the front. The hotel was an old one, of a provincial sort, but it seemed to be clean; it would not be a hardship for her to spend the night in it. He would see her in the morning – whatever was to happen afterwards, he would see her before she set out to meet old Mr Chase. Resolving to go with her and be with her till the last possible moment, thinking only of that, he stood at the window and looked down into the piazza. It was very irregular in shape, and now completely deserted, but he hardly noticed what he was looking at. Then a pair of carabinieri emerged from the far side and slowly walked across the square diagonally towards him. The moonlight was so brilliant he could see them plainly, throwing long shadows: their fantastically large cocked hats surmounted by tall plumes, their big epaulettes and white cross-belts, even a glint on a dagger. They were shoulder to shoulder, but their walk was so slow that it seemed affected and dandified. At last they were under him, and he looked down on their plumes. They had no significance, they represented nothing; they were the detail that, when the mind is desperately absorbed, sometimes impresses itself on the eye, and on the memory for years.

Chapter Twenty-Seven

He had so little trust, indeed he had a belief that she would set forth without his knowing, if she could, and he was downstairs before half-past ten. He went out to look at the day, and it was cloudless, the sky bright blue above the yellow-ochre buildings. At a quarter to eleven he met her just as she was coming out with the concierge, who hailed one of the waiting cabs for her, and while she was being helped into the cab – a little victoria – without a word Bernard went round and got into it on the other side.

She said, 'Grand Hotel!' to the driver and nothing to Bernard, and he formulated no hopes that she wasn't tired and had slept well. The horse trotted along the street upon which the cloisters abutted, but when they had come into another piazza she said, 'Fermate!' and the cab stopped.

'Look,' she said, 'that is Santa Maria Novella.' And he looked. It was a façade, all in white and coloured marbles, like nothing he had ever seen before, but he was not going to examine it now. 'I think you should go in and see the church. There are beautiful frescoes in it, by Ghirlandaio.'

'No,' he said, 'please don't ask me to.'

'You really must not go past like this. Over there, in that arcade, is a beautiful Della Robbia, very famous, of Saint Benedict and Saint Dominic kissing each other. – The frescoes are behind the altar; a custodian will show them to you.' And as he did not move – 'You must especially notice the woman in the golden brocade dress.'

Her indirect method defeated him to the extent that he could not be direct himself; he had to be as indirect as she. She did not want to arrive with a young man who had to be explained to Mr Chase and his niece, but he could be an anonymous young man who did not have to be explained. He got slowly out of the cab and stood a moment, not yet quite complying, with his hand on the hood. He saw that she was wearing the white flannel with the fine blue stripe that she had worn for the walk in the woods, and the small blue hat with birds' wings of the journey, and her travelling handbag was on her arm. He felt she was tense, longing to be rid of him and on her way. He stepped back, and she said, 'Avanti! Grand Hotel!' up to the box.

He let the cab get some way ahead before he started after it, running now and again. He lost it in a crowded part, but he could ask the way to the Grand Hotel. He had a view of the river traversing the town, hills in the distance upstream, and the Grand Hotel was not far, its side to the river, its doors on a modern square. He went in without hesitation, but without any idea whom he would ask for and what he was going to say. It proved unnecessary to ask anything. He had followed at such a pace that she had not long finished her business at the concierge's desk, where she might have been kept waiting. She was walking slowly away from it towards the chairs and tables set out in a large foyer. He went straight up to her, and he did not have to excuse himself, because he did not exist, or only as someone to whom she could say, 'They left yesterday.'

She chose an armchair and sat down. 'The concierge may still have something to tell me,' she said.

Bernard sat down facing her. A strange smile, one he didn't know, was on her mouth; it even twisted her lips a little and gave them an expression of contempt. That passed, but not her smile, which stayed, ironic and for herself alone, like some knowledge she might possess – not for him. He wondered very much. Why was this such a blow to her? Why had she set such a great hope on meeting Mr Chase? It was a mystery in spite of what she had told him in Milan. And it was a mystery that, when these people meant so much to her, they should not have waited till she came.

'Do you know where they have gone?' he asked.

She shook her head.

'They haven't left an address?'

The enigmatic, contemptuous smile appeared again on her lips. 'She will send it later.'

He noticed that she said 'she'.

She became so abstracted, was so deep in thought, that he could not ask more. But he could think about himself. She might have been sitting here with Mr Chase, and all would have been over, and he felt he had dizzily seen and been drawn back from the brink of a precipice.

The concierge, a very grand one, was coming towards them, and she looked up.

'May I have your name?' he asked in good English.

'Madame Solario,' she answered.

'Mr Chase and Miss Armstrong used the American Express,' he said. 'They might have left their address there. You could inquire.'

'Yes, I could inquire there,' she said, and got up.

'The American Express is in Piazza Santa Trinità. If I hear anything myself I will inform you.' And as they walked away together Bernard saw her take her handbag off her arm. He did not follow till the concierge was saying, 'I know the names of two or three of Mr Chase's friends. I will telephone and ask them if they know where he and Miss Armstrong have gone. Will you call again?'

'Yes, I will come again this afternoon.'

'I will not be here in the middle of the afternoon, just today. Could you come at five o'clock?'

He accompanied them to the door, reiterating his assurances that he would do what he could, and signed to a cab. As she stepped into it Bernard got in on the other side.

She said, 'This is the Lung' Arno.' She might have pointed it out to be kind, or because it gave her pleasure to be seeing it. The pale green, smoothly flowing river, and the radiant paleness of the town, and the hills from where the river came, and the towers and the bridges, made up, with her looking at them too, the most beautiful picture he had ever seen. The horse clop-clopped along the Lung' Arno, and she looked across the river. The American Express was not far. He thought she would prefer to pursue her inquiries alone, and he looked over the *New York Herald* until she came back.

'They do not know,' she said.

It seemed very odd to Bernard that Mr Chase and his niece should wish to vanish without trace. Whether it seemed merely

290

odd to her, or whether something confirmed a fear that had already suggested itself, he could not tell. He didn't know whether he should appear sympathetic or still confident.

'You telegraphed that you had to postpone coming – but only postpone?'

'Yes.'

'If they didn't telegraph – if they wrote to Cadenabbia,' he said with a sudden inspiration, 'you mightn't have got the letter! It might have missed the post.'

'That is true.'

It disposed of Mr Chase's and Miss Armstrong's having been rude, but it did not help her to find them.

'The concierge at the Grand Hotel may have news for you this afternoon.'

'Yes, he may.' He felt that she did not wish her anxieties to press upon him – nor bring him deeper into her affairs – and when she said, 'What shall we do now? Shall we go for a drive?' he knew it was a way of putting him off. But the prospect was marvellous.

They got into another cab.

'It is Monday morning,' she said. 'I think that everywhere there is more life on Monday morning than on other mornings.'

He could feel at once that the town was bursting with life, and he was bursting with life, beside her in a little cab that pushed its way through narrow streets – people everywhere, joyous noise, the sky bright blue overhead. He had to keep from speaking, not to show his happiness too much.

They came out of a street suddenly into a piazza which he knew was famous because he seemed to recognize it – that tremendous, gloomy pile and the tower with the battlemented top, he had known them and terrible things about them without ever having seen or heard of them for a first time. The cab stopped.

'The Uffizi are there,' she said. 'Wouldn't you like to see the pictures? Don't you like pictures?'

'Oh, yes, quite, but not this morning. Not on a *Monday* morning!'

She smiled, a smile he knew.

'Do *you* like pictures?'

'Yes – yes, I like pictures very much,' she said.

'Oh, but then you ought to see them this morning.'

'No – there are other things to see.'

He knew that with her powers of self-command she could deceive anyone as to what she was feeling, but if she wanted to deceive him with a semblance of interest for sight-seeing, when she might be feeling only the blow she had just received – well, he had to take advantage. She disregarded a beggar-woman who, with her hand out, had thrust her body into the cab, spoke to the driver, and they started off again.

'Do you like pictures best?' he asked, to try to get her to tell him something personal. 'Better than music and poetry?'

'Pictures and music best,' she murmured.

'Do you like music very much?'

'Yes, very much – a certain kind.'

'What kind?'

'Mozart – and the earlier music, too: Scarlatti, Pergolesi,' she said, looking away to what was on her side of the cab. And, while still looking away – 'The operas of Glück – I wanted to study music once,' she said a little later, surprising him; everything he heard about her surprised him. 'I wished to be a pianist.' He could hardly have been more surprised. 'I studied for two or three years, and I was sorry I could not go on.'

'You were prevented?'

'Yes. And you,' she said, turning her head towards him. 'What do you like? Music?'

'Only tunes.'

'And poetry?' And a little over her shoulder she smiled at him.

'Yes,' he said, and knew he said it sheepishly. 'But nothing very high or deep.'

A man with a barrow suddenly uttered his cry close to them, a cry that rose, executed a little dance of notes in the air, and sank, trailing off into nothing. Another barrow almost collided with their cab, and their driver shouted instant abuse; the other man replied simply with an 'Ah-h-h!' that was abuse itself. There were so many street-cries, the noises were so varied, spontaneous, dramatic and diverting, that they would have interrupted any conversation, and those vital activities provided both a topic and a substitute for talk. He and she looked on, and he would want to say, 'Oh, look!' – and sometimes did. The eaves of the houses were very deep, jutting far forward, which gave a special character to the streets and narrowed the lane of sky above; the Florentine streets, wouldn't he know them anywhere? – which was a silly thought. And there were glimpses of famous things as they went along; 'Very famous!' began to be something he said. His delight was so great that he was in a sense alone with it and not with her. They came out of the area of streets and were near the pale green river again, and in open-ness and sunlight; the sun was hot, but the air was fresh and the shade purplish – a perfect September day.

'We could have lunch soon,' she said, which was also delightful – the intimacy of it, and the idea of luncheon.

The restaurant to which she took him was on the ground floor – a little below ground level – of an ancient and sinister palazzo, and was of a make-believe and probably expensive simplicity. But it was authentically vaulted and pillared, and foreign. She chose a table beside a huge pillar, and he could tell she had been there before.

He asked her, 'Were you in Florence long last spring?'

'About six weeks in all, here and in Vallombrosa.'

Their dish of scampi was brought, and he poured out the wine.

'Two days ago we did not either of us think we would be in Florence today,' she said later in the meal.

'No.' He could not say more.

'But you mustn't stay. You must go back to England at once, isn't it true?'

'Oh, not for a few days.' By great good fortune he had not told her he must be in London on Thursday; it was better she should not know that he was under orders, but, he calculated quickly, he could still do it by leaving on Wednesday. He was silent, thinking about it.

'Really you do not have to go this evening?'

'Of course not!'

'The Rome Express stops here late in the afternoon, and I thought you would have to go by that, today.'

'But we have an appointment for five o'clock!'

'You need not come with me. Why should you?' she mur-mured.

'I won't go till you have met Mr Chase,' he said – or rather, it said itself.

Her eyes offered their beauty, as once or twice he had felt before, offered their beauty to his gaze, and then, not consciously lowered, turned a little away.

'And after that,' he said, 'you may go to America.'

She nodded her head a very little.

The vaulted place in which they were had no windows and needed electric light, which was used sparingly; but it had a wide door that was open, and his eye was caught by the door with the sunshine outside, for it was like the mouth of a cave. They were in another kind of cave. He remembered, what he could forget – as he had done during the whole of their drive – and should not forget, that something had driven her away from her former friends and he had felt panic himself. What she was doing was seeking protection – old Mr Chase – and she wasn't finding him. She had no one but himself, who was no protection at all, only someone with whom she could hide in a cave, and all this rolled over him like a wave of the sea.

She was no longer eating, and she put her elbow on the table and her hand up to her cheek. She was again thinking deeply and not pretending that she was not. They had ordered cheese, and he ate some; it was strange that he could go on eating, but he could. Then coffee was brought, and she rested her two elbows on the table to drink and drank slowly. They sat on, for they had nothing to do. She made a little effort after a time and spoke of the ancient palazzo in which they were, told him its name and something about it. At last she moved to go; she let him pay for the lunch, and they went out and took another cab. She told the driver, 'Hotel Baglioni.' They were driving along to the accompaniment of warning cries with which he was now familiar, when she said, 'Always in Florence one sees the hills at the end of a street; I like that so much.' In another minute they again passed a street with jutting eaves that had far blue hills at the end of it, and the charm of this connected itself with her.

When they alighted at the Hotel Baglioni she said, 'Now you must go off and see more for yourself. What a pity you haven't got a guide-book.'

He thought he could not leave her: it was not that he would not, but that he could not, as if some ominous physical symptom had declared itself.

'I will go up to my room and rest,' she said, 'until five o'clock. Let us meet downstairs at five.'

She left him. When she had gone indoors he took one of the first streets he came to. This led him to the piazza of Santa Maria Novella, and because she had spoken of this church and told him he must go in and see it, a star was over it and he went in. But as he entered, a suspicion pierced him like an arrow. She might have a new reason for getting rid of him – she might be wishing to get in touch with someone when he was out of the way. He pressed the suspicion home as if he must. He was not going to see her for nearly three hours, and something worse than itself had to be attached to the waiting. He, who three days before could not be sure that he would have even a distant glimpse of her that day, now was sure he would be with her in three hours and was far unhappier.

She was punctual, downstairs at five o'clock. There was no greeting each other, just meeting and getting into a cab. He had to try not to think of himself any more, but think only of her, resuming her quest and her hope.

This time he was by her side when she asked her question at the Grand Hotel.

'I am sorry, Madame Solario,' said the concierge. 'The friends of Mr Chase and Miss Armstrong didn't even know they had left Florence.'

'Ah,' she said. She did not turn away as though the matter had been finally settled, and that seemed to be a proof that this blow was so severe she could not at once rally from it.

'Where are you staying?' asked the concierge. 'For I might hear tomorrow morning. Miss Armstrong must give us Mr Chase's address, as there are already letters to be forwarded.'

'I am at the Hotel Baglioni till tomorrow,' she answered. 'Please telephone me in the morning. And now,' she said to Bernard, 'shall we have tea?'

'I will send you the waiter,' said the concierge. 'Where would you like to have tea?'

'Can we go in here?' she asked.

The foyer was lighted from above and had no view, but a writing-room by the front door had windows on the Lung'Arno.

'Certainly,' said the concierge, doing the honours, and she went in. 'Will you order tea?' she said to Bernard.

A waiter appeared in the foyer, and on being given the order asked, 'Avec pâtisserie et citron?'

Bernard went back to ask her and found her sitting near the window, looking out. He had to use her name to attract her attention.

'Madame Solario,' he said with an effort. He had never used her name before, and he did not like to use it. 'The waiter asks, "Avec pâtisserie et citron?"'

'Yes, both,' she answered.

When he returned to her and had sat down, she said with a little smile, 'You must call me by my own name, not "Madame Solario", because I told the manager of the Baglioni that you were my cousin.'

An extraordinary inner hush was created for him in which to hear her say this.

'Shall I call you "Natalia" as your friends do?' he asked after a moment. He had not forgotten that her brother, on first seeing her, had said, 'Nelly!'

'If you like,' she said.

'But it is your name?'

'Well, yes. I took it when I became a Catholic. It was the name of my godmother, and so I took it.'

'You hadn't been called that before?'

'No.'

'Then I don't think I will call you that. What were you called –'

'I had the same name as my mother,' she said in a new, touchingly simple way. 'When that happens one hasn't got a name of one's own, as one can't very well be called by it.'

'But what *is* your name?'

'Ellen,' she answered.

He was vaguely taken aback. The only Ellen he thought he had ever known or heard of was a nursery-maid he and his brother had had. They had been very fond of her.

'It is a Scottish name,' she said. 'I mean, it comes from Scot-

land. You know many Scottish adventurers went to Russia and
Sweden and other countries in the seventeenth century. That is
how the name came to Sweden, into my mother's family.'

He had remembered! His preparatory school, and himself standing up on a platform, feeling dreadfully shy, and reciting
'Young Lochinvar':

> To wed the fair Ellen
> Of brave Lochinvar.

'Ellen Douglas,' she murmured. 'She brought it.'

'But I can't call you Ellen,' he said, having thought about it, 'if
you say that was not like having a name of your own.' He would
not tell her that he had heard her brother call her 'Nelly,' and
she did not tell him that, with her brother at least, she had had
this pet-name.

'It has sometimes seemed to me,' she said, 'that I haven't got a
name.'

The waiter came in and set out the tea things on a little table, but
this did not break the spell. Nothing from the outside world could
penetrate to the inner hush. And yet a sound from outside was
continuously there, but it was lulling – the sound of a waterfall.
He had noticed that morning a little waterfall in the river, and it
was below these windows.

She poured out tea. It was very strong, and she wished to weaken it and took up the metal jug filled with hot water. But the
handle of the jug was loose; the jug tipped forward, and the hot
water was poured over Bernard's hand. She exclaimed with concern, but he didn't know what she meant. He felt nothing.

'It must have burnt you very much!' she said.

As they drank their tea they seemed to be in the same mood;
and to the sound of the waterfall he thought in a vague way of a
boat that has gently slipped its moorings and is gradually carried
down a gentle stream. They were the boat, or they were in the
boat, he didn't know which.

He could see out of the window, and the town on the other side
of the Arno was getting a lovely light, like the villages at this hour
on the lake. He thought of the lake, and for the first time wondered what they had left behind them – what, that is, had been
said, and what certain of those people had done when it was dis-

covered that she was gone; and he with her, it would have to be said. He thought of it in this spellbound safety, where no one would find them.

The waiter came back and took away the tea things.

'We will think tomorrow,' she said, as though the clatter had recalled her to the need of that.

'If you go to America – ' he said, for the idea of America had dug in.

'It doesn't look as though I would go,' she replied, contemptuously rather than bitterly.

'But you still may – and if you go, it would be back to the same place?'

'Yes, where we lived.'

'You've never been back?'

'No. And Mr Chase told me, when I met him again last summer, that my father had left his books with him.' To Bernard's surprise she told him this as if it were something very interesting; she never, one might say, spoke as though she thought that what she was saying had any great interest, but she did now. 'My father was unfortunate,' she said, and he knew she was making an unprecedented confidence. 'Nothing went well for him. He lost a great deal; but he kept his books, a good many, and took them to America. They were in our house in Cincinnati. He was going back to England, he hoped to go, and he asked Mr Chase if he could leave his books in Mr Chase's house – he has a big house – until he knew where he was next going to live. But he died that summer. No one ever claimed the books. I didn't know about them – I didn't ask. I had forgotten them – I didn't know until Mr Chase told me. It would be giving him a good deal of trouble to have them packed and sent to me – there are so many. If I go, I can bring them back.'

Bernard knew she had told him something very important, but he could not see why it was so important. And telling it worked a change in her. She must have been reminded of something, and under its sting she suddenly moved. But he did not want her to go and impulsively put out his hand to stop her from getting up.

'Do tell me – would you go back to that place where you went every summer, that you told me about?'

'What did I tell you?'

298

He thought of it as something to say that might hold her back for a minute.

'Those woods and lakes that were like Sweden. And do you remember you told me that you sometimes dreamed of being in a wood like those?'

'Did I tell you that? And just the other night I dreamed it again. But there was something different that time – I came on a church in the wood.' He wasn't sure it was true; the way she said it, it might have been a sudden invention, an invention cruel to herself – to him – to someone. 'Yes, a church was in the middle of the wood, but I couldn't get in; it was locked.'

He thought it might be true.

'You never got in?'

'No, and I couldn't see in, either. There were shutters inside the windows.'

'But then it was like Cappella Sommariva!' he said, still trying to keep her another minute. 'Do you remember – when we first met, in front of Cappella Sommariva, which was locked?'

'So we did!' she answered. He thought she was going to laugh. 'Yes, I remember!'

She would not stay any longer. She walked quickly, and on their way out the concierge said to her, 'Hotel Baglioni! I will not forget.' Once more they stepped into a cab. But soon she said, 'Fermate!' A kiosk, at a corner was covered with coloured bills, and she leaned forward to read something. A church's bells were ringing, and their reverberations within the narrow street made a terrible din.

'Look,' she said, 'you see.' And he saw a woman's name, a Spanish name, in large letters under *Sala* something, on a bill. 'She was very well known fifteen, even ten years ago – one of the best known. I think I would like to see her.'

They drove on, and she said, talking with unwonted liveliness, 'I noticed her name on the walls this morning, and it made me curious. She must be very much on the decline, to be in a café chantant in Florence, after what she was! I don't know why we shouldn't go to see her. It is quite out of season, there would be nobody to see one, and I won't have a chance like this again. It begins at nine o'clock, didn't it say?'

The whole day had been like a stream carrying a boat, carrying him from one new scene to another, one experience – emotion – to another, always on a totally unfamiliar course. Now it was evening, the pale street-lamps were being lit, and with sudden vivacity she was wanting to go to a café chantant.

Before going up to her room she said, 'Shall we dine here in the hotel? It won't be very good, but that doesn't matter. Shall we say eight o'clock?'

He got through the time somehow. She must have friends in Florence, as she had stayed here in the spring, but she had not mentioned them till she said there would be nobody to see her at this season, or rather out of season. He didn't know what it was, or was not, possible to do abroad, but that she wanted to go to a music-hall disconcerted him.

She had changed to the blue jacket and skirt she had travelled in, but a lace blouse and a hat composed of blue flowers – he thought of the bandbox it had come out of – produced another air. The hotel dining-room was very second-rate, and so was the dinner, and so were the two or three diners. By her questions she got him to tell her something about English politics, a subject in which he was very little versed, but he could tell her what he had heard said, and it was something to talk about. She put in no comment or opinion of her own. Soon after nine they went off again in a cab; the evening was not chilly enough for the hood to be raised, and it was still in a little open victoria that they drove. Down the middle of a long modern street, with trees on both sides, the lights were hung on a cable overhead, so that the shadows of the trees were thrown over the fronts of the stuccoed houses and decorated them fancifully. He noticed the look of the evening because it was the evening of that day.

Arrived at the Sala something, she told him to get *une petite loge*, and she took a chair at the back and asked him to sit in the front of the box, which was very small – just room for four chairs. Six young women were doing a dance on the stage, with high kicks – in long black stockings and short spangled petticoats – and it was poorly executed, the orchestra tinny, and the house was a tawdry provincial theatre, half filled with, he could see, a mostly common audience. When the dusty velvet curtains dropped and the lights went on in a big chandelier, the men below immediately got up to look about and up into the boxes, and the staring of black eyes began. Bernard tried to screen her from view, and he was so awkwardly placed that to see her himself he had to turn his head.

'It is very boring,' was all she said for some time, 'and when we have seen her we will leave.'

But the interval was long, and a mixture of the tedium of it, the resentment that she should be there, and their relative positions in the box, played on his nerves. Then the curtains parted and the orchestra crashed in, and the Spanish woman marched on to the stage attired as a female matador and acknowledged the applause with gestures that embraced her whole audience, and even with winks. The song she then sang was in Spanish, but intelligible words were not needed, or even a tolerable voice. Her voice could never have been good, but she turned its harshness and cracks to comic account; she displayed the redundances of her figure to coarsely suggestive account; she turned everything she had to some sort of account. Her self-assurance was so impudent and her conceit so brazen that one could imagine her being the same before a large audience as before a meagre one like this, or a hostile or derisive audience – she would always be the same. No longer beautiful – and her face must always have been too long and her eyes too close together – she still had a certain vulgar magnificence, and by the end of her song her male audience was feeling its effect.

Bernard tried to look at his companion.

'I saw her driving in the Bois – oh, more than twelve years ago,' she said. 'She used to create a sensation.'

That was all for the moment. But when the Spanish woman, having made a quick change, came back, the voice behind Bernard let fall, 'I knew something about her that interested me.'

'Something about her that interested me.' He believed it had to do with the dark side. The Spanish woman was putting on a lion-tamer act – with imaginary lions – cracking her whip and singing a song in French at her audience of men, which turned them into lions she could tame with her whip and her ribald laugh, and they were responding to her. Bernard felt Madame Solario lean forward to look over his shoulder, and, moving his head, he had her face close to his – her face as she

301

looked down at the audience to judge the effect the singer was having upon it. The mental part of the surge of sensation was jealousy. Her expression was one he had seen when she listened to Ercolani whispering in her ear, and what was associated with Ercolani set him on fire. But jealousy had no present embodiment. He had to go back for a figure, back to her recollections – not anyone here, and not *his* proximity, he knew bitterly, had roused in her what was communicated back to him. She was thinking of someone; he knew it. Yet she was resting her arm on the back of his chair, and her face was close to his as she looked down, and then again at the stage and the professional animal of a woman she regarded so equivocally.

The velvet curtains dropped, sweeping out dust, and she got up at once.

'We've seen enough,' she said. 'Let's go.'

They were out before the lights were on, and only a few pairs of eyes in the foyer stared as they went by. Bernard wished to have the hood of the cab put up.

'You will be cold,' he said, almost roughly.

'No, it isn't cold at all,' she replied.

They were silent all the way. The tumult in him was atrocious as he watched for a single half-sign that she would entertain something for him, if only for a moment. While he was helping her out of the cab he saw he hadn't the remotest chance. She said, 'Good night!' and went towards the lift without a second's pause. But in his room he twice started for the door before he gave in to his own conviction.

Chapter Twenty-Eight

There was no appointment for the next morning, and after the dreams he had all night he could form no idea of the coming day. What amounted to nightmare in his dreams was that he did not know what to call her, and so she stayed always out of sight. He could have called her by one of two or three names – he knew three names – but yet he could not, for unseizable reasons, call her by any of them; at one time he could not remember what any of them were, and that produced something so sinister that he woke up. He slept again and dreamed in new circumstances of this dire thing, that he could not give her a name. Books began to divide them, and books were sinister too. Books fell on him, and then he heard the clang of iron on iron. He tried to find a wood, and in the course of his search he went through a rambling, empty house, and at the end of a passage his old Monkey – a dirty white toy monkey – opened a door that was the door of the old nursery at home, cautiously peered out, and ran away. He went after Monkey, but soon his feet were rooted to the ground; he *could not* move them, and he tried to pull himself along by his arms. He saw Monkey calmly walking into a pond while he could not move forward and again he woke up.

Though he was on the watch from ten o'clock on, he missed her when she came downstairs and saw her first as she was coming out of the little room in which was the telephone. He saw at once that there was momentous news.

'The concierge of the Grand Hotel telephoned me,' she said. 'He heard this morning from Miss Armstrong. The address is Poste Restante, Milan.'

He thought only of himself; wasn't this against him?

'What are we going to do?' he asked. To him the important word was *we*.

'We will go to Milan. It's on the way – to England, to Paris, one has to go by Milan.'

She was playing down her quest. Milan was just a town on the way somewhere else. But seeing her again decided him. He was not going back to England on the morrow.

'When do we go?'

'I will ask now about trains.'

He listened to her getting the information. The *direttissimo* went at two o'clock, and a station porter would be sent for to take the luggage across.

'Shall we have luncheon here at the hotel at a quarter to one?'

He agreed. 'But there's two hours now before luncheon. Won't you come sight-seeing with me?'

'I think I will not go out,' she said.

She would not say anything so direct as that she was tired, but it looked to him as if she too had had a night of badly broken sleep.

He went out – walked off, anywhere. He seemed to be acting in anger, to have come to his decision in anger. He wouldn't – he would – It was a small symptom that he wouldn't go to the Uffizi because she had told him that he should go, and he went into a number of churches instead.

At luncheon it gave him a hard satisfaction when she said that they would stop at the Palace Hotel in Milan that night, and that he would go on next day, to think how little she knew she wasn't going to get rid of him. They paid their bills separately, but then he took charge, counting their pieces of luggage, announcing when they should go, and in the station he asked her to go on and reserve the places while he got the tickets. She could seem guided, too feminine to be anything else. He bought the two tickets and hadn't the courage then to count the money he had left. Never mind – never mind. He walked along the train (*Firenze–Bologna–Milano*) and she was at a corridor window, looking out for him. Her fairness was again an illumination – one saw beauty like a light.

She had got the two window-seats facing each other, but other seats had since been taken. Then she said, 'I forgot how much the ticket cost. What was it?'

'Never mind now,' he answered sullenly.

The people who had taken the other places came back; they were a middle-aged married couple, very nice, the sort of people one knew. They glanced covertly at Madame Solario, recognizing her elegance, ready to recognize her but not able to. They glanced at him when he asked her if she would like the window a little more down, and it was easy to guess that they wondered what the relationship was.

She settled herself against her cushion, with her book. The train started. He took up his great decision again, but not in anger any more, looking at it with grim determination. That his money was as good as all gone certainly presented a frightful problem, as he could not now apply to his father. He could not borrow from her, for it would look like asking to be paid for his services, and besides, she would try every means to force him to go back to England. But he would have to borrow from someone, to keep him till he knew what she was going to do. She might find Mr Chase in Milan, and the immediate future depended on that, but what he must prepare was a sort of long-term working out of a mode of life.

By sitting sideways he could look up from his book high enough to look at her without appearing, he thought, at least to the couple, to be doing so. He could not give up seeing her. He must have a life in which he would see her constantly. Wherever she lived when she came back from America – if she did go there – he would get a job in her vicinity, and she would become quite used to seeing him.

The motion and noise of the train imposed after a time a rhythm on his thoughts, which would go round and round and then slacken, and for whole periods be dulled almost to a state of comfort. They had stopped at Bologna surprisingly soon, and then there was nothing to measure time by. He looked out sometimes. Italy was going past the window beside her, and her eyes turned sometimes to gaze at Italy. The brim of her hat, with the pair of birds' wings above it, curved down over her right eyebrow, and that was an added allurement.

The man of the couple had fallen asleep and the lady was playing patience with a tiny pack of cards, a few at a time, on her handbag. He didn't have to consider his family. Hugo, his brother, was all that they needed; a younger son could do as he liked. Younger sons were always going abroad – in fact they had to go abroad as a rule. He might do very well – in the long run – in something he found for himself, but he would take anything to begin with, the lowest position – a menial position.

She wasn't reading. At last she ceased to turn the pages and leaned her head back. He knew that gesture and that look. He would not admit that her mood was despair, but, like a reflection of her mood, he had a despairing thought of his own, which was that she was older than he. She was about five years older. That had dire implications, as in his dream that he couldn't call her by any name. In his pursuit she would always be ahead by five years. He got up suddenly, without thinking, and took the seat next to her.

'May I?' he said. 'I would rather go forward.'

There was nothing any more but the sensation of being beside her.

The lady playing patience was on the same side, and the man opposite. No one was speaking. She let him be close to her – but then she could not prevent it, and there was no further movement on his part, nothing on the part of either. After a time he had to speak, he had to break something. The train ran into a town, and into a station to a stop.

'It is Parma!' he said. 'We were here the other night. I thought – the Duchess of Parma. But who was she?'

'Wasn't she the Impératrice Marie Louise?'

'I wonder if I would ever have remembered that.'

As they went on again he saw a russet dome, a town of russet roofs with cypresses on the edge and mountains not far off. One day they would come to Parma.

For the rest of the journey he sat beside her with a little space between them and watched to see if by a change of position, a movement of her hand, she would bridge the space between them and touch him. Her hand held her book closed with one finger in it to mark the place, or opened the book, but it never dropped into the space between them. He knew her stillness; this was her characteristic stillness, and not an abstention of movement because he was so close to her. She did occasionally change her position, she readjusted her cushion, but a fugitive touch had no meaning. Time went fast in this way; the night journey had seemed long, but this journey was over all too soon.

The evening was coming on misty, and a big town spread out, patterned in little lights. This was not to be their last journey together; there would be another in a few days, and they would go through these now familiar actions, she putting the silk cushion into its leather cover and he taking the morocco dressing-case down from the rack, because they had to go on from Milan, and it wasn't conceivable he would let her go without him. When she got up, as he was taking down a case, both standing together, they were almost against each other. The noise of the station broke out with cries of 'Facchino!' He got a facchino, helped her down from the train, collected the luggage. She said as they started off, 'We walk across to the Palace Hotel.'

The old Milan station was much farther down the hill and was on the upper side of a large piazza that sloped downward a little, planted around its sides with plane trees; a modern statue stood in the middle. The Palace Hotel was on a corner and was handsome and orange-coloured. They went in. It was she who inquired about rooms.

'You are together?' she was asked as their luggage was unloaded from the barrow.

'We want separate rooms,' she said.

The reception clerk consulted his lists. 'Madame can have a room on the second floor. There is a room also on the second floor, if you do not mind it is at the back,' he said to Bernard.

Then the visitors' book was presented. Bernard could see that she was strongly disinclined to signing it, but there was nothing to be done. He saw her write. He moved away so that he was not on hand, and the clerk, his attention momentarily distracted, did not ask him to sign. He heard her say to the concierge, 'Are Mr Jefferson Chase and Miss Armstrong staying here?'

'When would they have come?'

'Yesterday – or on Sunday.'

After a short pause he heard the answer. 'No, they are not staying here.'

He met her on her way to the lift, but she then drew him aside, to the door of a *salone*, and said, 'I am not coming down again this evening. I will tell you – there might be people here who know me.' They became aware of two men sitting in the room; it took a few seconds to see that they were strangers. 'It might really have been better not to come to Milan – people are just now passing through – but if my friends are here – But I will stay in my room.'

'And what will *I* do?'

'There is only this evening to get through,' she said with a pale smile. 'Go out for dinner – go to a restaurant in the town – and afterwards – The season at La Scala may have opened. Ask if there is a performance tonight. Then you could go to the opera.'

'I might do that,' he answered, knowing very well that he wouldn't and couldn't. 'But how will I see you tomorrow?'

She tried to think of something to say. 'We will have to see, tomorrow morning. Oh, I won't be in prison, I will be able to come out! – Let's go up and see where our rooms are.'

They went up together and came out of the lift into a long passage with doors on one side and, on the other, windows giving upon an inner court. It was the sort of good hotel one would get in a big town, but this part of the building must have been old, and there were unevennesses of floor and wall. The chasseur stopped at a door half-way down and opened it with his key; it was her room, a good room.

'One hundred and fourteen,' said Bernard.

'And yours?' she said, having a look at the other key. 'A hundred and twenty-five.'

Her luggage was carried in. He had a last look at her face – behind the fine mesh of her veil, under the alluring brim of her hat.

'Good night.'

He followed the chasseur on and round the corner, and, left alone in his room, he sat down, feeling a great sinking of the heart. The prospect of his solitary evening and his decision, which affected his whole future, had about equal weight. He struggled up under it, washed, and left his room. The door of Number 114 had its effect on him, but he could not pause for a moment before it because a stout old chambermaid was waddling down the passage. Downstairs, the clerk who had received them came out of his little office and stopped him.

'I think you did not give us your name,' he said.

The book was open. Under *Madame Natalia Solario – Paris*, in a foreign, feminine handwriting, were two names of still more recent arrivals, and *Bernard Middleton – England* came three lines lower than it might have done.

He walked for some time and got the impression of a more ordinary, modern, commercial city than anything he associated with Italy; there was even a northern fogginess about it. The very streets, which were still busy, made him feel his lonely and peculiar situation. At last he was hungry enough to look for a restaurant, and he chose one of modest appearance. In a rather small, warm, cosy room five men were sitting together round one table, talking business or politics he conjectured, and there were no other customers. He accepted the waiter's suggestion for dinner and, while waiting, got out his money and counted it. He had forty-three lire left. He thought he must have lost some notes, but there was no use thinking about that – he must think what he should do. He sat trying to think. During the time he had been abroad he had received his allowance each quarter by banker's draft, and the final quarter was exhausted; he had always spent everything that came in, and now he had nothing to draw on. The talking of the five men got in the way, and then eating got in the way, but the problem had to be faced. He knew no one in Milan. Then *her* affairs got in the way, and it did seem very strange that Miss Armstrong should have given their address as Poste Restante, Milan. Why not a hotel, or a house? Had it struck *her* as strange? He thought of her now, tonight, writing to Poste Restante. It gave him a queer stab that she should do anything – She couldn't get an answer for a couple of days at least, and they would be in Milan for a couple of days. The Palace Hotel was obviously expensive, and his room and breakfast would come to about twenty lire a day. What was he to do? The waiter was listening to the conversation of the five men and putting a word in now and then, and it occurred to Bernard that he might take a job as a waiter when he hadn't a penny left. But something had come into his mind and was held off for only a little while. He could go to the British Consulate and try to borrow from the Consul, with the legitimate excuse that he had to get to Paris and his money had – Well, some money had been stolen. By giving his father's name and address he might easily borrow enough money for a journey – four or five hundred francs – but of course that was the painful thing, using his father's name. He looked ahead in the indefinite, not definite, tense, and thought how he would later write to his father and explain that he had behaved as he had because he simply could not stand the idea of the bank. Anything was better than that. He hadn't been consulted in the matter, and he had felt justified in deciding for himself and taking a different course. There were openings of all sorts for young Englishmen, and he had his Oxford degree, a third, which was some advantage. The coarse red wine he was drinking conferred an inestimable benefit; the future was not next day, but next month, or even next year. The present was no more than this little warm Italian restaurant and the five men at the next table – like all Italians in a discussion, talking with passion and listening with indifference. He was glad he was going to live abroad. He would be a great deal by himself, of course, have to spend many evenings alone, but there would always be entertainment in the foreign scene. And she would suggest things for him to do – as this evening she had suggested the opera – and it would be delicious to know that she knew what he was doing.

With a huge effort he put a brake on his imagination, paid – and had a few lire the less – and went out. The next turning but one brought him before La Scala, in a piazza called after it, and it had a pale, classical portico with columns, and great charm. But it was silent and unlit; nothing was going on that night.

He found his way back to the hotel, and as he went in he felt uneasy because he had been away for several hours, and half expected to be given a message. He paused for only a few seconds before 114; the stillness within made him giddy. And in his own room his heart sank again, as though that had something to do with the room – his heart must always sink in it.

He saw in the morning that the room had a poor outlook, a back street of dingy houses and no sun. After breakfast in it, he sat thinking. There was nothing else to do but go to the Consulate, see the Consul, and borrow as much money as he could. He had to have money at once. He wrote on a sheet of hotel paper he found in a drawer: *I am going out for an hour or two. Is that all right?* – rang for the chambermaid, and waited for her in the passage. It was the fat, waddling one. She took the note in and was soon out again, saying it was all right. 'La signora dice che va bene.'

Having obtained the address of the British Consulate and instructions how to get there, he started off down the hill. In one of the busy streets it suddenly came over him – why should the Consul believe him? What proof could he give that he was who he said he was? He hadn't a single document on him, though he might still have his father's last letter in his suitcase, with one or two other letters addressed to himself. That might be sufficient. The idea of producing his father's letter for his purpose was loathsome; but if he had been going back to England he would have had to borrow money just the same, in the same way, and that took him on. After some difficulty in finding the street he saw the royal arms on a shield over a door, and by that time he felt only fear that he would not succeed.

The Consulate premises were not imposing, and a shabby, gloomy little Italian let him in.

'Se si vuol accomodare,' he said, and left Bernard in a dismal waiting room in which some nondescript persons were sitting against the wall, under a pair of large photographs of King Edward and Queen Alexandra. The gloomy little doorkeeper came back after a while and handed a sheaf of papers to one person, who got up and went away, and spoke to another, who, with his companion, also went away. He then said to Bernard, 'Se vuol passare.'

Instead of the middle-aged man, the age a Consul should be, that, in his nervousness, he was keyed up to meet, he saw a slight, unprepossessing young man who bowed coolly and did not get up behind his kneehole desk.

'You asked for the Consul, but he's out of town today, I'm afraid. I am the Vice-Consul. Is there anything I can do for you? Won't you sit down?'

'I wanted to see the Consul,' answered Bernard. He did not immediately sit down.

'You couldn't explain your business to me?' said the Vice-Consul.

He could indeed not explain it to this young man, who would have to refer the matter back to his chief and yet might put on patronizing airs.

'Do you think the Consul will be in tomorrow?' he said for all answer.

'What is your name?' said the Vice-Consul for answer.

'Bernard Middleton.'

He knew the phrase, 'I felt as if I had come to borrow money.' He was knowing what one felt. The Vice-Consul sharply glanced up before he wrote down the name.

'Where are you staying, Mr Middleton?'

'At the Palace Hotel.'

The Vice-Consul wrote it down.

'And how long are you in Milan for?'

'Two or three days.'

'I'm sure the Consul will make an appointment to see you, and he can ring you up at the hotel. Will you be in tomorrow morning?'

'Yes, certainly till eleven o'clock.'

The Vice-Consul got up and conducted him to the door politely. 'I'm sorry I couldn't do anything for you, but I may see you again – tomorrow. Good-bye.'

The delay was very upsetting, but he had not been rebuffed, and he would go back next day and take his father's letter with him. He started to walk back to the hotel, back to the treasure that was there, and he thought of her up there in her room and walked faster and faster. He cut across the piazza towards the orange-coloured Palace Hotel at the corner, and the old leaves fallen in the dry summer from the plane trees rustled under his feet. He had not got clear of the public garden in the middle of the square when his eye was caught by the figure of a man who was still some way off, who must only a moment before have walked out of the station, and who was followed by a porter carrying two bags. He did not get into a cab, but continued to walk as if making for the Palace Hotel. He among all the other people in the piazza, with cabs both coming up and driving away, caught Bernard's attention even at a distance – someone recognizable, and something already experienced. The man carried a fawn overcoat over his arm, wore a brown Homburg hat, and walked lightly – a distinctive walk. It was her brother.

Consternation pounded through him. He would not be alone with her any more. He sat down on a bench in the public garden and watched Harden walk across the whole width of the piazza in front of the station to the door of the Palace Hotel. He had not thought of her brother, and he could now wonder why. He hadn't liked to think about him, but that was not a good reason. She could not want to see him, or she would not have departed from him so secretly, but her brother had a right that she had not denied when he had come before. He had come again, and there would be no more journeys.

Later he too entered the hotel, and he saw that, giving off the lobby, the inner court was partly glassed in; chairs and little tables were set out, and sunlight came down into it. He established himself there, with a newspaper he picked up, like any other guest. How would he and Harden meet? What line would Harden take? What would she do? It could be said that he had 'gone off' with her. She hadn't turned to her brother as a natural protector in whatever had happened – quite the reverse. When she saw him again – this morning – had she looked as she had when he stood before her on the night of his arrival? The past – the story he knew, with its sequel, the twelve years' exile – and the return; and these last events in which he himself had played a part; what he had seen – her marble look – and their flight together: nothing had ever stirred Bernard so much as the sum of these things. Because it was the latest thing, it seemed one of the most potent and the worst – Harden coming into sight that morning and walking across the piazza.

But she might need his help again! He understood so little about the first flight that there might well be a second he would understand no better. She might at this moment be trying to reach him, and he was down here and she didn't know where he was! He rushed upstairs. He came into their passage, and not a soul was about. He stood before Number 114, and then he knocked; he knocked again, and a third time loudly. He ran down to the lobby. The concierge was engaged; people were coming and going. Bernard asked when he could, 'Has Madame Solario gone out?'

'What number?'

'A hundred and fourteen.'

The concierge glanced at the board on which the room-keys hung.

'The key is not here. She must be upstairs.'

Bernard ran up again. He again knocked at her door and got no reply. He went on to his room and sat down on the bed. It didn't mean anything – she hadn't gone – she was with her brother, and he might be wrong about everything. But if all was well and she didn't need his help, then his part was played, and here he was with nothing more to do. They might go off and leave him that very day. While he was thinking – or not thinking – his eyes were fixed on the little card, nailed above the electric-light switch by the door, on which was printed an admonition in two languages. *MM. les Voyageurs sont priés* – he could read, and never tried to read further. But whenever he thought something new, or his heart sank lower, he read again *MM. les Voyageurs sont priés* –

He sat till he saw it was half-past one. They might be down-stairs, having luncheon. That would be the way to meet them, doing something naturally. He quickly smoothed his hair; he felt that he was going to meet them. When he passed her door he knocked again, and, getting no reply, turned the handle. It gave; the door wasn't locked. He wouldn't open it more than that and ran downstairs. They were nowhere to be seen, and he had the awful thought that he looked like a lost dog running about. He went into the dining-room, sat down, and ordered something; people came in, but never they. He was out again before long and ordered coffee to be served to him in the court, from where he could observe what was going on through the open glass doors, and where he could linger in a natural way, smoking one cigarette after the other. He was sitting there when he saw the hotel manager come through the glass doors and straight towards him; he knew he was the manager, as he had caught sight of him that morning in his office, a professional-looking man, rather tall.

'I think you arrived with Madame Solario last night,' he said, and, being in no doubt about it, he went on at once – in English, which was made to sound pretentious by strong Italian inflections. 'Doctor Novachek was just in the hotel, attending to one of our guests, and I asked him to go up.'

With his Italian quickness he saw what brought a change into his tone. 'Didn't you know that Madame Solario's brother had arrived this morning from Como?'

'Oh, yes, I knew –'

'Did you know he became suddenly very ill?'

'No, I didn't know.'

'The chambermaid of the second-floor came down and told me. As Doctor Novachek was just coming to the hotel, I thought, simply as a matter of prudence, it was better he should go and see.'

'Did Madame Solario ask to have a doctor sent for?' She had not sent for him.

'No, we do not know that she wants one. The chambermaid reported as a matter of duty. It may not be serious,' he said; his whole manner was indefinably unsympathetic. 'But you understand the hotel has a responsibility. Doctor Novachek has been many years in England, and is very well known. He attends our guests when there is occasion.'

'Is he up there now?'

'Yes, he went up some time ago.' Together they were going back to the lobby. 'I imagined you would know this gentleman was ill.'

'On what floor is his room?'

'Also on the second floor.' The concierge prompted him. 'Room a hundred and three.'

Bernard was taken up in the lift, and Number 103 was pointed out to him. It was not in their passage. It was not far from the staircase, round a corner, and he waited at the head of the stairs where the doctor would have to pass. When he had waited what to him seemed a long time, the doctor turned the corner and stopped abruptly on seeing Bernard posted there. He looked like a man of abrupt movements and uncompromising character; he even had a ferocious air, which was helped by his moustaches and his eyebrows.

'Will you tell me –' said Bernard.

The doctor rapidly considered him, up and down. 'What do you wish me to tell you?'

315

'Someone is ill in room a hundred and three.'

'Are you the young man I am told arrived with that lady last night?' His accent was not Italian, but, like his general appearance, Germanic.

'Yes.'

'And you are associating yourself with this pair?'

'Yes,' said Bernard after a moment.

'Is it a necessity? Are you a relation?'

'No.'

'But you have relations?' The doctor, having impatiently looked him up and down, was now observing him, taking him in. 'You have a family somewhere?'

'Yes,' said Bernard after another and longer pause.

The doctor seemed to come to a decision, and he first manifested his decision by putting his case under his arm and pulling on his gloves. They were grey cotton gloves, and Bernard gazed at them as if fascinated.

'I don't know what your studies have been, but you may know that geologists speak of *faults* when they mean weaknesses in the crust of the earth that cause earthquakes and subsidences.' Having pulled on his gloves he was energetically buttoning them. 'And I will tell you something out of my own experience. There are people like "faults", who are a weakness in the fabric of society; there is disturbance and disaster wherever they are.'

He gave Bernard a fierce look beneath his bristling eyebrows.

'Young man, go away from here! Get on to solid ground as soon as you can!'

Under the impact of the doctor's words Bernard had, instead of a clear understanding of them, a confused recollection of mountain-climbing, and of the worst moment he had ever experienced, when a crevasse opened just ahead of him.

The doctor plunged downstairs, and Bernard's first steps towards his room were unsteady, what had been conveyed to him was so powerful.

He had not long been back in his room when he thought – he would find Mr Chase. Mr Chase was in Milan; one could find him! He must go at once. He had to ask the concierge what other big hotels there were – 'I have friends staying at one of them and I can't remember which' – and while he was standing there the manager came out of his office but ignored him; the intention and the look of annoyance were unmistakable. He set forth on a quest that was not hers any longer but his own. He was impelled to look for something, and as he hurried along he formed a picture of Mr Chase – rather small, with snow-white hair – and imagined the benign smile with which the old gentleman would receive him. When he went into the Hotel Grande Bretagne, the sort of hotel at which Mr Chase would stop, he so longed to hear the words 'Will you go upstairs?' that he was certain he was about to hear them.

'Is Mr Jefferson Chase staying here?' he said, as a preliminary to being asked to wait and then to hearing those words.

But still another concierge with the crossed keys of St Peter on his collar answered, 'No, he isn't staying here.'

This time he couldn't believe it.

He went to two more hotels, but they were so uncosmopolitan that the porters spoke only Italian and made nothing of the barbarous name.

Milan was a large town, completely unknown to him; there was a good hotel somewhere that the Palace Hotel concierge would not tell him of, but he would come upon it only by chance, and he could not range over the whole town. He had to give it up. One saw hotels, as a rule, frequently, but on the way back he didn't pass a single one. There *was* another in the station piazza, the Nord, but it was inferior to the Palace and he tried it without hope. Not looking to the right or left in the Palace Hotel, he went up to the second floor.

He had got to the corner at his end of the passage when, feeling a presence, he turned. She was at the other end, coming towards him. They walked towards each other, and in the last seconds before they met at her door he was aware of details, like the rustle of her skirt and the poise of her head a little tilted back. She opened the door and drew him into the room, but she didn't shut the door, she left it half open. Behind it, she put up her arm in a beautiful gesture while he stood transfixed, and pressed his head down to her till his lips were pressed against hers. Then she disengaged herself from his arms and drew him out of the room.

Chapter Twenty-Nine

He was in his room again, having stood in the passage as long as he dared – someone went by – to see if she would open her door. Life had come through his lips in a flood that reached every part of his being. But he wondered how his arms could have let her go. The amazement of the moment had been too great; he had been robbed of his power of action. It was only when she was gone that he could live the moment as it might have been lived. Yet he lived it again and again even as it had been, only a moment, and a flood of life pervaded him.

Not a word had been said. He knew nothing more. But he would hear, he would know certainly within a few hours – something, and what it would be he need not try to imagine. He knew that a strong element of surprise would be in whatever he was going to hear. He had to continue to wait; that was all he could do. He could wait, feeling his lips pressed to hers.

But he did not have to wait the whole time in his room, and he might learn something, pick up some scrap of information, by going downstairs. He sauntered through the lobby with an entirely new demeanour. Seeing that the manager was in his office, he went to the door and said, to assert his position, 'You will have heard that Mr Harden is better.'

'It is not an infection,' answered the manager, scanning the papers he held in his hand. 'It was probably a crisis of nerves.'

His intention was still unmistakable – to withhold the proper courtesy from certain guests.

That meant nothing to Bernard now. He walked over to the stall where newspapers and cigarettes were on sale and bought four packets of *tre centesimi*. Then he sauntered back, not knowing what he was going to do next. The visitors' book was open on the concierge's desk, and he was drawn to glance at it and see those signatures. He did not get so far. The name of the latest arrival was written so hastily – or with such arrogant carelessness – that it sprawled over two whole lines: *Comte M. A. Kovanski – St Pétersbourg.*

It did not come as a shock. He was instantly braced to meet the challenge; he could have smiled.

He gave Kovanski plenty of opportunity to meet him downstairs before he went up again, and in his room he did not sit down; he stood, as if ready – at the window, ready to turn if anyone came in.

This, too, was going to develop quite unforeseeably; again no need for him to try to imagine. 'Foreigners don't play to the same rules, you know.' Some dramatic but sketchy visions hovered about his mind and caused him no real trepidation. In his state of excitement everything contributed interestingly, pleasurably, to a razor-edge of time just before something was bound to happen. He was looking into the street, and at this sunset-hour here, too, in this poor sort of street, there was more noise and life than earlier in the day. A church-bell started to clang. Opposite his window a woman threw open hers and called down 'Gina!' with incredible nasalness. An answering cry came up. Children were playing in and out of doorways. Everything was alive.

It must have been nearly an hour before there was a knock on his door, and he was over to it in an instant, saying, 'Come in!'

The chasseur stood outside. 'I signori L'aspettano giù, se vuol scendere,' he said.

He didn't understand – that is, he understood the words for 'waiting' and 'descend', but *i signori* was in the plural: gentlemen.

'Abbasso. En bas,' said the chasseur.

He followed mechanically. They passed her door, and he lived again the moment behind it half open, and went on, ready for any encounter.

The chasseur took him to the door of the *salone* downstairs, and he went in. Kovanski and Harden were standing together. They might have been a pair of inquisitors having him brought into their presence.

Kovanski was facing him. Harden turned and saw him. 'How do you do, Mr Middleton,' he said.

319

Kovanski said nothing. Bernard walked forward, and Harden took a few steps to meet him and shook hands.

Bernard could believe that Harden had been ill, but he had recovered from whatever his illness had been, and a sort of ravage was only in his face; the rest of him was fully charged, like an electric battery. Bernard then looked at his enemy, straight in the eyes. Kovanski had a curious expression.

But while Bernard was expecting something to develop, Harden turned back to his fellow inquisitor to go on with what he must have been saying just before. Movement and words were quick.

'Meeting under these exceptional circumstances, don't you think we should take the opportunity to bury the hatchet, as they say?'

'Yes, we can bury the hatchet, as they say,' the other replied.

'And act together?'

Bernard saw that Kovanski's hand was being forced, and that he did not like it.

'Yes, we can act together – for the time being. If you wish. How are you, Mr Middleton?'

A little of the old accentuation was on that.

'*I'm* very well, thank you,' answered Bernard.

It was the best he could do to show he was ready. 'For the time being' were words surely full of meaning. It struck him, after Kovanski had spoken, that the man looked exhausted – for all the hardness of that exterior, it was possible to see it. And Harden, on the other hand, was electrically charged, and said at once, actually with jocoseness, 'Well, then, will you dine with us this evening – both of you, with my sister and myself?'

To Bernard it was a fantastic development. It might have been to Kovanski, too. He said with his old hoarseness, increased by his exhaustion perhaps, 'Are you sure this will be acceptable?'

'I can answer for my sister. She will think it a very good way of resolving the problem – of putting a good face on the matter.' He used a little emphasis in his turn, of a different sort, *his* sort. 'Don't you think yourself that it's the only civilized way of treating this multiple rencontre? – But would you rather I went up and asked her, and brought you an invitation from *her*?'

'Yes,' said Kovanski. He stopped Harden suddenly with 'No. I invite you to dine with me. Say that I ask – will she – with you – and Mr Middleton – dine with me at Cova's tonight.'

'I will,' answered Harden and left them with that incomprehensible, light, jocose air of his, which went with the ravage of a recent illness.

'You heard,' said Kovanski to Bernard. 'I invited you too.'

Bernard got a full impression of his hatefulness – round bullet head, opaque eyes, hard mouth under a line of coarse dark moustache. But he wasn't showing his odious blunt teeth in a grin. It would be an odd sort of game if a man could invite another to dinner first and challenge him after, but it looked to Bernard as though Kovanski might play it. The very idea raised him – while still feeling his lips on hers – to exalted superiority.

He could answer carelessly. 'Thank you.'

Kovanski turned aside to a table on which illustrated papers were spread out, picked up a paper, opened it, and stood examining a page full of pictures. Bernard knew the look of his back in a blue serge coat, and he thought he particularly hated Kovanski's back. But his hatred was no longer of the raging sort, for he was in the superior position – as at their first meeting, walking with her in the plane-tree avenue, and how much more so now!

Harden was away some time. Kovanski never looked round, turned all the pages of one paper, and picked up another. Then at last Harden came in, buoyantly, and something in him or about him seemed to have been heightened, and Bernard most unwillingly conceded him his remarkable good looks.

'My sister accepts your kind invitation. She thinks it an excellent idea that we should all meet like that.' Bernard knew he was lying about her, and that he didn't care if they knew he was lying – might even want them to know it. But why did he want to be devilish?

Kovanski had thrown down the paper he was holding. 'I will order a table.'

They all three went into the lobby. The manager came out of his office with a very changed manner – something very smooth. Kovanski, speaking surlily at the desk, ordered dinner for that evening in a private room at Cova's, for four.

'Vous allez retinir un salon particulier pour Monsieur le Comte chez Cova,' the manager said to the concierge beside him. 'Et pour quelle heure?'

'What time do you think?' Kovanski said to Harden. 'Half-past eight? Nine o'clock?'

Harden left it to him.

'Shall we say half-past eight? Huit heures et demie. Please let me know if –' Bernard saw that he could not speak of her, and as an excuse gave his attention to the concierge, who asked, adapting himself partially to their English, 'Would Monsieur le Comte like to order dinner now?'

'Tell them the same as last time.' And to Harden – 'I was here with my colleagues before manoeuvres. We were given a very good dinner. Where shall we meet? Here in the hotel, or at the restaurant?'

'Why not here?'

'Certainly. Shall we say here at half-past eight? Cova's isn't far.'

They could now part – going their several ways, not up together. Harden went first, and some ten minutes later Bernard, Kovanski having disappeared.

He was in his room again, and it had been as he had known it would be – impossible to imagine. He at once unpacked his evening clothes, and then there was nothing to do but wait again, and think. He would see her for the first time after their kiss at a sort of ceremonial feast with the very two from whom he had helped her escape. During the evening she would find means to let him know what she wanted, what they – he and she – were to do after that; what plan she had. But there might be an encounter with Kovanski that would upset her plan – and did she know it? The prospect before him was amazingly mixed. There was first to be dinner at Cova's – and he had heard of Cova's, Missy had spoken of it, pleased to have dined there; it was a very smart restaurant, internationally smart. He was to dine there in her company with those two men a good deal older than himself, both about thirty, who had to treat him now as their equal in age and who probably believed – He couldn't let himself think of it. But because that was believed, the dinner party might end in a duel. And this was happening to him!

He must send a telegram to his father first thing in the morning, and he didn't know what he would have to say when the time came.

He gave himself plenty of time to change. He knew that he could look very well turned out in the evening, but unfortunately his hair had begun to need cutting; he brushed it hard to conceal this.

Kovanski, alone, was ahead of him. Well turned out himself, though his physical type was not best suited by evening dress, he had put on the manners of a host; the only flaw in them was that when he asked his guest if the grouse-shooting had been good it was with an unpleasant effect of speaking without moving the muscles of his face. Bernard replied that as far as he knew, it had been good. Then Harden came running down the stairs, and Bernard thought that the only thing missing was a white flower in his buttonhole. His dislike of her brother was at two levels, one deep and obscure on her account, and one superficial and insular. But as Harden came up to them his cheek had a spasm in it, and the superficial impression of him was shivered.

He at once found something to say. 'Is there opera tonight, by the way? Has the season begun?'

The manager was there again. 'The première at La Scala is on Saturday. We will have many guests arriving for that.'

The door of the lift, at the back of the lobby, opened, and she appeared to their view.

In spite of his confusion, meeting her like this after all that had happened, Bernard was aware of a shade of difference in her carriage of herself. She moved towards them with a more apparent exercise of charm, a more definite smile on her lips, a more self-consciously slow, swaying, feminine walk – more, that is, than had been characteristic. She was wearing a white lace dress that he knew, and the hat composed of blue flowers that she had worn for the café chantant, but to that was added a swathing of blue tulle whose long end was thrown round her throat and over her shoulder. During her slow-timed approach he could feel that she was undergoing an ordeal. She was pale. He now knew that when he had seen her in the passage she had been very pale.

She gave her gloved hand first to Kovanski and then to himself

with the smile and the murmured greeting of a charming woman –
celebratedly charming. Kovanski had ordered a coupé to take
her to the restaurant, and she was ready to go. Kovanski asked
Bernard to follow in a cab; the swing-doors were opened for
them, and the manager bowed to them all because Count
Kovanski's guests were personae gratae to the hotel.

Cova's was not at all the sort of smart restaurant he had
expected; the establishment looked small and old-fashioned,
and the entrance was restricted and not even well lit. Bernard
did not see the dining-room, but a hum of voices came from
somewhere, and a party of very well-dressed people was going
in that direction, on the ground floor. His own party was already
on its way up the unimposing staircase. They were received
above by a maître d'hôtel with a 'Buona sera, Signor Conte!'
and bowed into the *salon particulier*, which was a smallish room,
entirely one could say perversely, old-fashioned, not refurbished
at all. It was dark, with red velvet curtains and red flock wall-
paper, and had two great gilt looking-glasses opposite each
other. The table laid for four was not in the centre but to one
side, allowing a fair amount of space before a massive sideboard.
The attendance, at least, corresponded to the reputation of the
establishment. The men's hats and coats were at once taken
from them, Madame Solario's light wrap laid on a chair, and the
maître d'hôtel had two waiters under his orders. Hors d'oeuvres
were handed as the members of this incomprehensible dinner
party stood before the sideboard. The maître d'hôtel said, 'La
signora prende Marsala?' – and she took a glass in her hand. 'Il
Signor Conte prende Marsala?' He went round to the four of
them, and when Harden, who was the farthest away and the
last served, had his glass, he raised it a little and said, 'Our first
toast should be to our Italian detectives, eh, Kovanski?'

He looked only amused. Kovanski betrayed nothing, and
raised his glass a little and briefly before setting it down. The
blood rushed into Bernard's face. Harden was diabolic – now
he was sure of it, and now he knew how it was that the two
of them had turned up on the same day. He hadn't asked himself;
he had taken it as the thousand-to-one chance; he hadn't thought.
It was infinitely worse than chance. He gave her a quick, stricken

look. But she seemed to have heard her brother's toast without indignation, and, in the time that had elapsed since she had undergone her ordeal, to have become indifferent.

The maître d'hôtel brought the prepared menu of the dinner to Kovanski for his final approval, and he in turn submitted it to Madame Solario. She barely glanced at it and smiled. Even the wines were already chosen, but Kovanski consulted Harden about them in the sense that he announced to him what they were to be. Bernard was not consulted.

'Posso far servire, Signor Conte?'

They moved to the table and Kovanski placed his guests, Madame Solario on his right and Harden on his left, and Bernard opposite. The table was large for four people, and, seated on heavy red-velvet-upholstered chairs, they were rather far apart. The light came from a pair of brackets on the wall – the old gas-brackets electrified – and from candles in candelabra on two consoles and the sideboard. But the dark red walls absorbed some of the light, and the room remained gloomy.

She laid her gold-mesh bag on the table, and, while the soup was being served, slowly pulled off her long gloves and drew the blue tulle scarf away from her throat.

Harden began as he unfolded his dinner napkin, 'Do you remember, Kovanski, that the first time we met you said you thought you had seen me before? Did you ever decide when and where that had been?'

Kovanski didn't answer.

'You thought first it had been on the Irish Mail when we – it should have been we – were involved in an accident – a tragic accident, I think it was. Didn't you?'

'I said so.'

'But you were mistaken, because I never *was* on the Irish Mail. So where could it have been? I would so like to get it settled. We can't often have been in the same place, our activities were so different. That's what makes it intriguing. What year do you think it was?'

'Shall we say five years ago?' said Kovanski, wiping his mouth.

'Now where was I five years ago?' Harden's soup-spoon

paused. 'In New Orleans, with an English firm of exporters. We can't have met over business! You didn't need cotton for the Army, did you?'

It was pretty clear that Harden was trying to score off Kovanski, though he had willingly accepted his invitation. It was strange conduct, a most strange dinner party. Kovanski said, 'There is a simple explanation. You reminded me of someone,' at the moment that Bernard was letting himself look at her. The horrid thing he had just learned was another tie between them. But when his eyes could at last, once more, rest on her face, it was only her kiss that he remembered. She too must, must be remembering!

Her incurious glance dropped under her full white lids and was not lifted again. And she did not think it necessary to speak – to say one of those little conventional things he sometimes found so baffling or mysterious, he didn't know which, but which, whatever it was, would have made this first meeting pass off more easily. Thrown back into confusion, he too continued to swallow the turtle soup. He did not listen to what the two were saying to each other – had not heard Harden's reply, though reply there was. Then something made him look up, and Kovanski was staring at him across the table. It was the stare that had been the first thing he had noticed about this man, so repellent, and yet in a way without meaning – no expression other than hardness in the prominent eyes, only a stare. This was it – not an intelligent scrutiny, just a repellent, meaningless stare. Bernard met it with his head high and the blood rushing to his face again. Looking at Kovanski, he put himself once more into possession of what had been given him, and was the one who had triumphed and who could defy.

Harden was saying with a peculiar humour, 'Actually I am sorry I am not that man. I think it would have suited me to be he.'

Yes, he was the one who had been the chosen companion of her journey, and those two had needed detectives to find her. But for that, he and she would still have been alone together, dining as they had – in the station restaurant here in Milan, so near. He saw it again, coarse tablecloth and crockery, coarse food and wine, when the maître d'hôtel presented a beautiful trout on a silver-plated dish to Kovanski for his inspection before giving it to a waiter to serve and himself pouring out for them what was probably a fine Sauterne. In recollection, the dinner in the station restaurant had been marvellous with the intimacy of her confidences, and luncheon in the cave-like restaurant in Florence also had had a marvellous intimacy. The difference of every sort between that and this sinister dinner party – The difference in her. Her composure now, even her way of helping herself to the dish – and the way she didn't listen – had an absence in them: the absence of the preoccupation and tension he had often been aware of during their journey, the absence of her resolution. At a definite moment he felt it. She must have abandoned her quest.

'. . . a nice, labelled box,' he heard Harden, who had been talking when he hadn't listened, say. 'Nice because it was labelled. Do you remember what we said about the people who were in labelled boxes?'

'You remember a great deal,' said Kovanski.

'Only what has interested me, and the talk we once had interested me.'

Kovanski was about to say something, and refrained.

'It interested you too, because later you reminded me of it, and *you* had remembered so much I was surprised.'

'As well, you don't forget,' said Kovanski.

'I was too much surprised. Do you know that thing called a Jack-in-the-box? It jumps up in its box and startles one. I had thought the Jack was in *his* particular box with the lid down – but up flew the lid, and up jumped the Jack, and *I* jumped!'

Kovanski was willing, Bernard thought, to let Harden score, but as he couldn't address her – he seemed incapable of doing that – he had to answer Harden, and he said with his hoarseness, 'You must have pressed the spring.'

'Oh, no, *I* didn't set the thing off. I was just someone who stood too near and could be made to jump.'

Kovanski's colour had darkened. Bernard turned to her, for he was able to speak to her, and Kovanski wasn't.

'I didn't do any sight-seeing today,' he said. 'It's very ignorant of me, but I don't know what there is to see here.'

'Didn't you go to the cathedral?' she said, her conventional tone ready, but not the soft look that so often went with it.

'I saw it at the end of a street, but I didn't go out of my way to see it.'

'It hasn't much charm, I find.'

He thought of what he had really done when he had gone out that day, and then: What was he to do on the morrow – if there was a morrow – if she didn't find the means to tell him what she wanted? And would there be a single minute when she could evade the lynx eyes of those two, and would she try? A fearful ding-dong battle was beginning to take place – between the memory of her kiss and the sight of her calmness and indifference.

'Is there a picture-gallery here?'

'Yes, the Brera. And in a convent there is Leonardo da Vinci's "Last Supper".'

'Very famous,' he said with a shaky smile

He couldn't carry it further. Nothing they could say was suitable to being overheard, for everything he could think of contained some reference or allusion to their journey, which wouldn't do. Their journey – while she was being driven forward on her quest.

Kovanski had wanted to hear every word, but Harden, who seemed to be a very accomplished talker, went on forcing his attention, as if deliberately tormenting him. It might have had a connexion with his mysterious illness, but certainly something was working in him, an abnormal state that needed as an outlet the peculiar insinuations of his talk to Kovanski. For a time his subject was a certain race in South America whose ridiculous customs and inexorable codes he described – or invented – picturesquely, and clever analogies could be made, so that the insinuations came through. Bernard could see his malice in his very looks as he talked, a sort of glitter. In his different way he was as detestable as the other – at the moment, more, for Kovanski, strangely enough, was submitting, was downed for a time.

Bernard listened only by fits and starts. But when Harden had got much nearer home than South America he heard Kovanski say, 'Isn't cleverness a good fortune too?'

'Not of the most superior sort. Cleverness has often – in our world – only a posthumous good fortune,' answered Harden. 'Clever people, who have nothing but their cleverness, may be *remembered* as superior, but they weren't allowed to feel it at the time. Stupid people can say the most devastating things!'

Kovanski turned his meaningless stare upon him.

'But then good fortune puts on another face, and there's another kind of injustice,' said Harden.

'Another set of labelled boxes?'

'Not always. Sometimes everyone is out in the open.'

Bernard noticed that Harden never looked at his sister as he talked. His intentions kept him fixed on Kovanski, but his victim could not be entirely held down; Kovanski was more conscious of her than he was of the malicious raillery, as Bernard could see, because they had her sitting between them. Bernard was reminded of the triangle they had made, they two and she, that other night at dinner, and – how strange! – this dress of cream-white lace was the one she had worn that other night; a picture in his mind was still actuality, and she was wearing this dress with a rose in her belt, and a large open window, trees and an evening sky in it, was behind her. Now she had a blue posy in her belt, and the blue of the hat and tulle was like pallor beside the rose-and-white of the other picture, the more melting softness of that rose-and-white.

'Another thing to see is the Certosa of Pavia,' she said very unexpectedly to Bernard. 'I haven't seen it, but I believe it is interesting.'

'Yes?' he said with an eagerness that the subject of her remark scarcely warranted.

'It is outside Milan, but not far, I think.'

'How does one get there?'

'By train,' she answered – negligently, which might be a blind.

'You don't know the time of the train?' he asked, as low as he dared.

'Oh, no. Perhaps they go often.'

He didn't know what it meant.

After a rather long wait the little, lean maître d'hôtel came in with the next course – *filet de boeuf à la Béarnaise*, according to the menu – and the wine that went with it, red Burgundy; he left the waiters to do the serving and went away again.

The wine-waiter was very assiduous in keeping the glasses filled.

While his tormentor was talking about the Napoleonic period – humorously, it seemed – Kovanski cut him off and turned at last to Madame Solario. His face was darkly flushed.

'This is a funny sort of place, isn't it?' he said to her. 'It is so ugly and small, but people won't go to the new restaurant here that has much better rooms.'

'I think it has a certain cachet, being like this,' she answered and looked a little about, at the red velvet and gilt.

'We have a restaurant like it in Petersburg – also ugly and small, and people go to it, it seems, for that reason.'

The other two were silent while these two were speaking to each other. Their speaking, especially because it had been so long postponed, could not pass naturally. Kovanski's manner was strained, as one would have imagined it would be; but Madame Solario's did not have the little, exquisite embarrassment it sometimes had and might so well have had now. Ever since their arriving at Cova's Bernard had felt the absence of something, and in the absence of it an emptiness and even coldness. Even when it was towards Kovanski it chilled him.

Harden looked away from those two, and did it as if he was devilishly pleased about something. 'And is there a place like this in London?' he asked.

'I don't know. I don't know London restaurants,' said Bernard shortly.

'And why not?'

'Partly my age. I haven't had time.'

'There is nowhere to go after dinner here,' said Kovanski. 'Not even the opera tonight. In Petersburg we would go to the islands to hear the gypsies sing. Would you like that?' he asked her, his constraint of manner relaxing with a sort of recklessness, as though he knew it was no matter what he said. 'Do you like gypsy music?'

'I know only the music of the Spanish gypsies, and that must be different. It is for dancing, not singing.'

'It wouldn't make one want to drink and dream as our gypsy singing does,' said Kovanski, as though it didn't matter to himself what he said.

330

Harden heard, and laughed. Bernard remembered the peak of the ball, when she had swirled for a moment into a Spanish dance while everyone applauded, and he felt a sharp pang, as though he thought a peak had been passed for ever.

'You laugh because you are too clever for that,' said Kovanski.

'You know I don't want to be clever. You don't flatter me by telling me I am.'

Bernard let the waiter fill his glass again. He would drink as much as they did.

'I don't mean to flatter you. And we don't do so well, at home, for not being clever.'

'In spite of everything, you may still have a good run for your money!'

Kovanski turned to her again. Having spoken to her at last, he could not easily be brought back. He had succumbed to looking at her. But there was nothing he could say.

'What is it you are destined to be?' Harden asked Bernard.

'I don't know what you mean by "destined". I'll be what I like. I'll be a waiter if I like.'

'Oh, no you won't. You'll fall into your place like a billiard-ball into a pocket.'

Bernard saw that there was a good answer to this, but he couldn't frame it well enough – he was reminded that his future had been entirely changed and was blank until she gave him a sign – and he didn't answer at all.

They were all silent, far apart at the large table.

When a waiter came in to clear away for the next course, Harden said, 'How were the Italian manoeuvres?'

'Not very impressive.'

'Your present duties don't interest – or occupy – you very much, do they?'

'My present duties are very light. I think I told you why I was sent to a post abroad. But I am at liberty to give my demission.'

'Wouldn't you be sorry to do that?'

Kovanski's face looked engorged, and his eyes were not so expressionless. 'You have never been in the army, any army, have you?'

Harden was going to be annoyed by that, and Bernard saw a chance for himself.

'What do you want to see in Milan?' he asked her abruptly, almost roughly. 'Isn't there anything you want to visit again?' By a look, an inflection, she could convey to him that they would be able to meet. 'The cathedral? The picture-gallery?'

They were having their chance – he was straining towards it, nearly there – and he saw a little arching motion of her brows, as though she were surprised by either the importunateness or the triviality of a question.

'And is there no one in Milan you want to see?' he asked, with something of his soul in the question.

When he saw that arching motion of her brows again, heard her say 'No one', he was incredulous, as when the concierge had answered, 'No, he isn't staying here.'

The maître d'hôtel bustled in, accompanying the pail of ice in which stood the champagne, and imparting to this entrance a little extra satisfaction, to be felt by all.

The champagne was poured out before the course arrived. Bernard drank his first glass of it while he was still astounded. Then, facing Kovanski as he was, across the table, he conceived the wild idea that he would do the challenging himself – fight a duel just because there was nothing to fight over. He brooded on it as, with a roast duck and a salad, the champagne went round again. He was Kovanski's guest, an intolerable position, but the usual obligations were not being – nor need be – observed at this dinner party. It was outside ordinary experience. If it was not to end in her giving him a sign that they would meet again, it must end in another way, with a crash of some sort: an end that one could see and hear, not an end that one could only miserably feel.

She drank a glass of champagne very slowly. Kovanski, desperately engaged with Harden, kept turning his eyes on her, the turn of his head becoming almost mechanical. The twitch in Harden's cheek came more often, baleful evidence of his excitement. For Bernard, the voices began to have the near-and-far and what they said the clarity-and-strangeness that can be pleasurable, but in this situation was even frightening. The animosity between the two men had a dark underside, he knew it. Harden told Kovanski that, born into *his* box, he could never know real life. Real life was the lowest common experience, and that he would never know. They must be drinking more than at an ordinary dinner party; but it was a Russian party, and the waiter poured out gleefully. There was nothing, no general talk or enjoyment, to temper the effects. Those two were pitting their experience of life each against the other, which was unbelievable – that they should. Making light of it, in *his* way, Harden had known the depths in a South American port, but Kovanski said that the most degraded conditions anywhere were not so disgusting as the sights of war and defeat. That brought back to Bernard the scene in the card-room and the Russians laughing themselves speechless, and, fitting into the incredulity with which he listened now, was Kovanski's tone of having suffered outrage. Harden answered, and his tone was that of talking, or rather sneering, brilliantly, that war, if he didn't get killed, was bound to be a brief incident in a man's life and didn't touch his pride unless he ran away. It was an incident in a career he had voluntarily entered upon and could not be compared with the experience of inescapable circumstances.

Kovanski stammered something, not too clearly, about his adversary's circumstances. 'Be that as it may! Be that as it may!' said Harden. 'Circumstances have a way of fastening themselves if there are no fathers or uncles standing behind!'

Within a few minutes he seemed to be taunting them both with having fathers and uncles – for Bernard was brought into it, and, on being taunted with having a father, he thought of his visit to the Consul and was too angry to know what to say. Having brought him in, Harden wouldn't drop him. As a witticism, but sneering too – 'I don't expect circumstances will ever separate you from Barleyfield Park!'

This invented name for his home made Bernard want to throw something at him.

Harden's line led deviously, like a marsh-fire. At one moment he maintained that Kovanski had been so fortunate he was not to be allowed to speak, and at another he himself, because of those recent, sad events all over the world, was the fortunate one.

'Who knows if, in the coming time, men like *me* won't be the men of the future!' he said, laughing so much that one couldn't know how he meant this to be taken.

A tight-rope was being walked. A balance was going to be upset. But suddenly they looked at her and stopped talking. It was the agonizing effect of her beauty and her silence that made them drink and talk, to forget. Her silence was not simply that of abstraction or disdain, it was not a silence one knew – there was so much distance in it that one could not come close enough to give it a name. And she would even let them get drunk in her presence. Kovanski looked at her desperately, but all he said was, taking up his own glass, 'Will you have another glass of champagne?'

With her left hand she put back over her shoulder the blue tulle, which had fallen forward; she inclined her head to him, lifted her glass when it was filled, and sipped the champagne. Her coldness, grace, and distance were, together, not like that grace of hers that was all softness and languor. The three of them had been looking at her. Happening to turn his head, for the first time Bernard saw her brother looking at her.

Harden began to laugh and talk again, but one would have said it was with a violent effort.

'But I am *not sure*, so you still have something over me, Kovanski!'

He gave his attention to Bernard, and rallied him on having listened to them, knowing he was the luckiest of the three.

'Isn't it true, Kovanski, that an Englishman of this sort has always a calm and lucky look? But he *is* lucky, isn't he?'

'You can't say that,' said Bernard – or it said itself. 'You don't know what is in store for me.'

He felt, after that, an awful depression, and didn't listen for some minutes.

From hearing nothing, he heard suddenly, spoken loudly by Kovanski, 'Why are you saying this?'

'Because we are never going to see either of you again.'

Before he had fully taken the blow, Bernard heard Kovanski's breathing.

'But we wanted to see you once more to settle some misunderstandings,' said Harden.

'What misunderstandings?'

'You may have got a number of false ideas.'

'What false ideas?'

Harden laughed.

'Don't let people get false ideas!' said Kovanski, so thickly that the words barely got through. 'Be more careful!'

'More careful! What do you mean?'

'You say too much!' said Kovanski.

'Oh! When have I said too much?'

Kovanski fixed him with his bloodshot eyes, and the lines of Harden's flushed face altered to an extreme discomfiture.

'So you heard the gossip? An hysterical girl – '

'Say nothing! You have said nothing!' Kovanski pounded the table, and his eyes veered towards Bernard, who felt a panic fear.

'*You* say nothing, then!' Harden reached for his glass, and his trembling hand knocked it over. 'Leave us alone! It has nothing to do with you!'

Madame Solario, with her most feminine, slow, swaying movements, rose from the table. The waiter, who had served *glaces* and fruit and was about to leave the room, at once stepped forward.

'La signora desidera qualcosa?'

'Non, grazie.'

She moved to the window and stood with her hand laid on the red velvet curtain. The two older men sank back into their chairs, and the waiter gave them all a look and went out.

'Don't say you are never going to see me again,' said Kovanski. 'I could be of some service to you.'

'We don't need you!' screamed Harden, springing up. 'We need nothing in the world! I said too much, did I, to that fool of a girl? *You've* said too much here. It's you, who threw in our faces what you'd heard. Come, Nelly – come, dearest!'

'Stop!' shouted Kovanski, beside himself. 'Stay where you are!'

'She's mine, only mine. *You* won't have her – she's mine!'

Bernard lurched to his feet, and his action arrested Kovanski even at that moment.

'Not before this child! Don't say it – spare him that!'

'It's you who told him, not I!'

'Child'. He had said 'child'.

Something connected with the words of Doctor Novachek came back to Bernard – words, and a sensation that the ground was giving way under him. The crevasse opened, and this time he lost his footing and fell to the bottom of it.

Chapter Thirty

'But it isn't true!' he heard. 'You are a clever man and it seems to you clever to say terrible things. We will make it all right with those people. You could have made it right even that night, and you shouldn't have let it go an hour – '

'Who's been spreading it now, you madman?'

'No, this isn't spreading it. Here we are friends. We have been dining together. If you had told me – next morning wouldn't have been too late – I could have made it right. But I didn't hear till the evening, when you had all gone. But everyone was confused because she – she – had gone away with this young man – which was very lucky, though I didn't like it so well when I heard, and we must thank him that he was there. Look, I thank you.'

Bernard raised his head. Kovanski was making him a low foreign bow.

'Who heard the story? Only a few people. But it mustn't go further. You – you mustn't stay with her – '

Bernard saw her brother then – saw Kovanski, frantic, on his way to her, push him back so hard that he reeled. Then Kovanski took her hands and led her to a chair. He knelt down in front of her, still holding her hands, and prayed to her to make this thing not true. He told her that this terrible thing that had been said – because of the accident of a moment of excitement, at a ball, anger, a crazy girl – need never be said again and could be forgotten. Would she marry him and let him take her away to his country, where it would never have been said? He had to ask her now – at a terrible moment – because she had refused to see him and he might never again have the chance. He had to ask her now. He asked her, not as he had before, hoping she would love him, but to give an answer to the world that this thing was not true. He didn't blame her or reproach her – she could see he didn't reproach her. It was for her to forgive him for having persecuted

336

her – could she forgive him his jealousy? . . . and the utterance of love passed the bounds Bernard had believed every man preserved for himself. It was so appalling here – this sense he had had before that there were no limits to what Kovanski was willing to say – that it became the horror. He couldn't look at her – he couldn't think of her – but he could think that he must stop Kovanski from saying more, as it was this he could not bear. He got to his feet again, he started forward as if to pull him away, he went forward and then back; he looked to Harden even – though what help would he get from him? Harden had let himself be pushed aside and had dropped into a chair at the table. The scar in his cheek twitched continuously, but he had begun to build up appearances and was putting on airs of disdain.

Madame Solario freed her hands from Kovanski's, and Bernard felt the fall again, inside himself. And then Kovanski was turned to her brother, imploring him to act towards her – towards the world – so that this thing could never be said, and he was again between Bernard and what could not be thought of, because he should be held back, if he could be, from the absolute sacrifice of himself. He took the blame that this had come up that night; it was his fault – it proved how fatally easy indiscretion was, when one had drunk too much, perhaps – and he saw how one could fall into the trap of saying too much. Wouldn't the other believe that he saw this – and believe he blamed himself tonight?

'Don't, don't!' Bernard entreated.

This generosity towards the man who had earlier been so insulting – and a lawless and guilty man – and one who was incapable of meeting him generously – this, too, was passing all bounds.

Harden had built himself up again. 'That's all very well, but from what I've heard I'm to be shuffled away as if I no longer existed.'

'No, no!' exclaimed Kovanski. 'I've done you a wrong if you think so! We must be friends –'

'Not to him,' burst from Bernard, of all he was saying. 'Oh, not to him!'

'Yes, to him. In time this will be forgotten and we can all be together. We will be happy –'

'Do you mean I will come and stay with you? I will come to stay –' With that Harden was mastered by febrile laughter, and that was ghastly; whereas with Kovanski everything, the excess of emotion and its physical aspect, went together, and it was his sincerity that appalled.

'Yes, you will come!' he exclaimed, as if he had been promised.

'Oh, don't you see?' said Bernard. 'Can't you see?'

'How do I know you won't change your mind?'

'To show you I mean it, I will give you a toast!'

He seized the bottle of champagne standing in the pail of ice beside his former place at the table, and poured out a glass for Harden and one for himself. He said to Bernard, 'Bring me your glass.' Then he held up his own.

'It is a Russian toast. *Vipiem na ti!* It means "Let us drink to becoming 'thou'." Drink, drink! *Vipiem na ti.* Let us be brothers!'

His glass ceremonially raised, he looked from one to the other with a kind of distraught but almost happy confidence, and Bernard glanced sharply at Harden to see if he would drink. He did, with his smile of disdain. Kovanski's hand shook so much when he was drinking that some of the champagne was spilled.

'And now,' he said, 'what we have seen here will be forgotten by all of us! We will hold together – we would say "thou" to each other.'

'We must go; this is too painful for her.'

'How did it happen? I don't know. But now we will meet tomorrow. Natalia!' he said, going back to her. 'It *will* be tomorrow?'

Bernard brought himself to look fully at her, and it was in his mind that this was the last time he would see her beauty. What look did it have now? Not of marble – not of a statue, or fate. Fatalistically, only fatalistically, she saw what was happening, and for her there seemed no choice or conflict, only submission to the compelling force.

'Come,' her brother said to her. 'We must go.'

She moved to the chair on which her wrap had been laid.

'We must go together!' said Kovanski, again terribly agitated. 'Wait – one moment!'

The door opened, and the maître d'hôtel came in with the waiter bringing coffee and liqueurs. Through the door, left open, could be heard the good-humoured voices of people close outside. Harden tried to take advantage of the interruption, and Kovanski saw him do it.

'Wait until those people have gone past, and we will go together! We don't know who those people are. I beg her to forgive me, but you must try to understand!'

'Un bicchierino di Tokay, Signor Conte?' the maître d'hôtel said coaxingly.

While the waiters were trying to serve them, Harden went to get her gloves and bag which were lying on the table and Kovanski tried to prevent him.

'L'addition!' he said at the same time to the maître d'hôtel. 'Et vite! Wait till I have paid the bill, and we will go together!'

The maître d'hôtel went out – so did the waiter, having given up trying to serve them with coffee – and Kovanski walked up and down before the door. Harden had given his sister her bag and gloves, and he whispered something very brief to her; they both turned a little away, towards the window, when Kovanski opened the door to see if the maître d'hôtel was coming back, and Bernard saw her put her gold-mesh bag into her brother's hand. It sickened him to see it. When Kovanski looked round again her gloves and bag were in her hand, and Harden was putting his hand into his pocket.

'We asked you to dine with us,' he said with something of a grand manner. 'And I would rather that you had dined with us. Please let me have the bill when it comes.'

Kovanski's face, forehead, and neck became a dusky red, and his mouth opened.

'I am – humiliated!' he said.

'You are humiliated! Out of snobbishness you'll say you are humiliated!' A malignant passion was suddenly, extraordinarily released. 'What do *you* know about humiliation? What do you?'

Kovanski looked utterly bewildered.

'What do you?'

'I told you. I saw our men running away – from the Japanese – '

'And you?' Harden said to Bernard, with contempt both for what he had just heard and for what he was about to hear. 'What do you, an Englishman, know about humiliation?'

Bernard had come to the end of what he could understand.

When he heard 'humiliation' he thought he had never heard the word spoken before. He had seen it written, but he had never heard it said.

'No one can speak who doesn't know what it is!' As if he only then realized what he had been saying, another expression leaped into Harden's face, but able in a trice to shift his attack – 'No one who hasn't been a young man who tried, and just failed, to murder his stepfather! No,' he said, having returned to his diabolic humour, 'we don't meet on the same ground, you two and I!'

Then the maître d'hôtel came in with the bill in his hand. Confusion followed. Harden put the wrap over his sister's shoulders and kept his arm about her to lead her away, and Bernard saw her perfect compliance, as when she yielded to her partner in a waltz-beat. Kovanski, having pulled a handful of notes out of his pocket and thrown them on the sideboard, started after the pair. The maître d'hôtel ran down the stairs after him, saying, 'Signor Conte, Signor Conte! Sarà troppo!' Bernard was separated from Kovanski by the maître d'hôtel on the narrow stairs, and when he reached the bottom of the staircase he was held up by a dinner party going out, laughing and talking. The maître d'hôtel turned back. Bernard pushed his way on and to the street, where the three were together on the pavement and the coupé was moving up.

'Do you swear to me I will see you tomorrow?' Kovanski was saying. 'Do you swear to me?'

Bernard saw her figure with the long end of the blue tulle fluttering in a gust of wind – he saw her face and thought how his lips had been pressed to hers.

'Do you swear I will see you tomorrow?'

Harden turned as she was bending to get into the coupé. 'Yes, I swear.'

He got in after her. They were gone – together – like this.

'Did you hear – he swore. Did you hear him say, "Yes, I swear"?'

'Yes, I heard.'

'We can get to the hotel as soon as they do. Quick –'

Two carriages were coming up to the door of the restaurant. People were laughing and saying good-bye to one another.

'We'll walk to the corner and find a cab. Kovanski–let's walk to the corner.'

'Call me Misha,' said Kovanski, looking completely distraught. 'We are brothers.'

They had come away without hats and coats, but Bernard couldn't go back. The street led into a piazza – and there was La Scala, the pale, classic portico with columns, and something going on there tonight, for lights were in some of the windows. A few people, a few cabs, were in the square, and moonlight was in the sky with scudding clouds. He saw what it looked like – what it could look like when one felt one was in hell. He helped Kovanski into a cab, and on the way – the horse clop-clopping – Kovanski said over and over again. 'Will we get there in time?'

The long yellow front of the station appeared behind the trees of the public garden, and the orange-coloured Palace Hotel on the corner. There was no sign of the coupé. Bernard paid and ran in after Kovanski, who, not seeing them in the lobby, instead of becoming more excited was dazed. He must be got upstairs.

'Do you remember the number of your room?'

The night-porter didn't know the number of the room, but, given the name, was able to look it up and took the key off the board. They got into the lift. Bernard thought that the night-porter and chasseur would simply think Kovanski was drunk.

The room was on the first floor, in front. Bernard went in first and turned on the light.

'May I stay with you for a while?'

The room, a large one, was in some disorder, things having been pulled out of a bag and left lying about. Kovanski came to himself a little, took the clothes that had been thrown over the armchair and threw them on to another chair.

'I didn't bring my servant,' he said, with a sort of surprise at being there. 'I sent him back to Rome.'

Bernard remembered – 'My orderly, Pavlusha.' This, now, was surely a dream.

Kovanski began to walk up and down between the corner and Bernard's chair. He had gone to and fro only twice when he stopped.

'I will send up and ask to see him!'

Bernard was at the door before he got there. 'I wouldn't tonight, if I were you. You can't very well see him again tonight.'

'No?' He walked away, to the corner. 'But tomorrow morning! Early tomorrow morning!'

In the silence between them Bernard was able to sink to the depths of his knowledge. It was her brother – it had been her brother. But when the horror was too great to be borne Kovanski would be back, in his walk to and fro, and would fix him with his bloodshot eyes, and they would look at each other. Then Kovanski would walk away.

His loss, his loss – however it had come about. The life he was to have led – it was no more. What he had had – the night journey, the deepest night-hour and the moment when he had seen her white eyelids dropped over her eyes, the moment of sleep – he felt it would burst his breast . . . but Kovanski was going backwards and forwards more quickly. He was talking to himself.

The effects of drinking had passed, but moments were cut off from reality, hallucinatory. The room in the Grand Hotel was there, with the lovely light and the sound of the waterfall. 'What is your name?' 'Ellen'. 'My father was unfortunate . . .' Then, very clearly: 'Is Mr Jefferson Chase staying here?'

He jumped up, and as Kovanski was just turning away he went with him. He needed someone to help him bear it.

'You heard him, didn't you? You heard him say, "Yes, I swear"?'

'Yes, I heard.'

'So I can go to see him early tomorrow morning. We drank *na ti*, and he swore. He shouldn't stay with her, and I can make him see it.'

'Yes, you will.'

'He will let me explain it all to him, because we drank *na ti* and he understood what it meant.'

His anguish increased. He must have had a thought of what might be taking place, and he went quite mad for a few minutes. But Bernard was able to hold him back from the door because his very wildness weakened him. After a struggle he partly submitted.

'Let me go now!'

'It would do no good. He wouldn't let you in.'

'I will knock on his door and hear his voice!'

Oh, God, thought Bernard, is he in his room?

'He might not answer, and you wouldn't know if he was there. He may be asleep, and he'd be angry. We mustn't wake up other people in the hotel. Misha, don't you see? There may be people you know – and you'd make a row, knocking on his door, and they'd ask what it was all about.'

'I must –'

'I beg you!'

'– hear her voice!'

'She wouldn't answer.'

'Come and sit down,' he said after a time. 'Misha, there's nothing more you can do tonight.'

He got him at last to sit down. Watching him, as if he shouldn't take his eyes off him, Bernard thought only that he himself did not now, and never would, he never could suffer as much as that. His own experience dwindled and paled, and he was only the attendant on one whose capacities for experience and emotion were so much greater than his.

He walked up and down with Misha when he wanted to walk again. But a crisis had passed and he was much more rational.

'You understand – it was only talk!' he said, abruptly stopping and facing Bernard. 'He likes to talk.'

'I know he does.'

'But it is dangerous. Because then others talk, and *there* they are talking. No time must be lost.'

Bernard knew what he meant and wanted to do – he wanted to marry her – and he felt, all in a second, amazement that he should want to marry her.

'You – you –' Kovanski said as they faced each other. He couldn't, from delicacy, speak of Bernard's case, but it was evident that he would try to touch upon it. He had drunk *na ti* with him too. '*You* will be glad, if you know she is well and protected from talk?'

Bernard suddenly, passionately, didn't want him to marry her, for *his* sake; he was revolted by that sacrifice. But Kovanski might think a hesitation meant that he didn't want it on his own account, out of regret or jealousy.

'I'll be glad,' he said at once.

Kovanski smiled – a tentative, almost shy smile coming with difficulty on his hard face.

A little later he sighed deeply, looked down on the ground, and shook his head. 'I don't know – I don't know,' he said.

'Let's try to get some sleep,' said Bernard. 'We still have a number of hours to wait. If only we could sleep and pass them that way!'

But what was there to wait for? Once more, he couldn't imagine. He felt such dread when he thought of the morning that he wished the night-hours might never pass.

'Lie down on your bed,' he said. 'I'll go back to my room if I want to go to bed, but I would really rather stay here. That chair's quite comfortable. I might fall asleep in it.'

Kovanski gave in. There was something ominous and mournful about his quietness, about everything at the moment.

A lamp was on the bed-table, and Bernard thought he would turn it on and turn off the overhead light. On the table was, too, what from a distance looked like a book, and as Bernard turned on the lamp Kovanski picked up this object. It was not a book but a small, dark icon in a silver-encrusted frame.

'I wouldn't take my servant with me,' he said, one part of him saying it and another part not heeding what he said. 'He begged me to take him. The tears were running down his face. "Mihail Alexeitch," he said, "then take this".' He put the icon back under the lamp and stretched himself out on the bed.

Bernard sat down in the armchair across the room. It was Kovanski he was looking at, and of all the amazements this was the greatest. But he was not going to sentimentalize. He was not going to think that he had been mistaken and that Kovanski was never what he had appeared to be. Bernard was sure he was always what he appeared to be. His absoluteness was, in some way, in everything he did and in every moment. The only occasion on which, one might think now, he had not been absolutely sincere was when he laughed in the card-room about the war; but one could say there was a sort of absoluteness in that incident too. He could be brutal; he *was* brutal. – But had he really fought duels? Was that true, or perhaps only a reputation that had grown up? It might be true. Some absolute anger or contempt, or an outrage to his sincerity, might make him challenge a man. If things had turned out differently he might have killed an inoffensive young man – Bernard himself – in a duel, and he wouldn't have liked that but, looking at it in an odd way as though it had happened, Bernard thought it was something that, given Kovanski's character, couldn't be helped. If it had happened he would never have known the whole character and another face of that absoluteness – the frenetic magnanimity.

He had found it so distasteful and painful that the charming Ilona loved the cruel-looking man that he had tried hard not to think of Kovanski when he was with her. He should have trusted Ilona. That was not to say that Kovanski hadn't been merciless when his sincerity made him tell her the truth, but all of it went together, and Ilona probably loved him still.

He got up after some time to see if Kovanski mightn't be asleep. The dark, round head he had so hated was back on the low pillow so that the face was slightly upturned, and his mouth was a little open; Bernard thought he saw the edge of his teeth. His eyes were closed. Bernard went back to his chair. The olive-green curtains were only half drawn, and some street-light came into the room, also sounds from the piazza and the station, a train being shunted and the whistle of an engine. What was he going to do? What was he going to do with himself?

He was waked, for he must have fallen asleep, by something terrible, by terror. Kovanski was in the middle of the room, talking, shouting almost, in Russian. Bernard was up in an instant, and Kovanski went on, talking, talking, wild-eyed, telling him something in Russian.

'I can't understand!' said Bernard. 'Speak to me in English!'
Kovanski grasped both his shoulders.
'What is it? Misha, what is it?'
Kovanski stopped talking and looked at Bernard's lips with a frown.
Bernard said, 'Misha, try to tell me in English!' He said it twice.
With both hands on Bernard's shoulders Kovanski looked intently at his lips, like a totally deaf man trying to lip-read.

Then, as if understanding had come to him thus, he said, 'I must have dreamed.' He turned away.

Bernard hardly knew it himself, but when Misha was trying to read his lips he had never cared for anyone so much in his life.

He was now too tired to know what happened; he found that Misha was pulling him out of his chair, saying, 'Go to bed!' He still wanted to stay there, and if there had been two beds he would have suggested it.

Misha smiled – his difficult smile – at the door, putting him out. He didn't even say good night, and shut the door.

Bernard ran up the flight of stairs to the second floor, passed the spot where he and Doctor Novachek had stood, and went on down the passage – past her door – wanting only to reach his room and sleep.

He did not sleep very much, deadened though he was. 'Early tomorrow morning' was always in his mind. Whenever he woke he turned on the light and looked at his watch. It was at last a quarter past seven. After that he was very realistically, exactly as though he were awake, in a strange, rocky country with not a tree in it, only very large rocks. He was trying to find a way somewhere when he saw Monkey's face peering down at him – just his face, over the top of a rock. The next thing was that he saw the whole of Monkey ahead of him, and he was almost as tall as a man, almost as big as himself. Bernard was trying to get nearer to him when suddenly Monkey screamed in terror and ran gibbering away, round and among the rocks, and Bernard tried to run after him, though he was terrified too. 'What is it? What is it?' and someone said, or he simply knew, 'He saw Misha's dream.'

He must have been in a very heavy sleep before he dreamed, for when he woke he didn't know at first where he was; he struggled up, turned on the light, and it was twenty minutes past eight. But he was not able quite to rouse himself till his eyes were drawn to the small white card under the electric-light switch. He read: *MM. les Voyageurs sont priés . . .*

He washed, shaved, and dressed – quickly, but it was still 'early tomorrow morning'. In the morning light of a sunny day he left his room, not fully determined on what he should do.

He had not got far along the passage when he saw that a door halfway down it was open – and he had time to think that it couldn't be. But it was 114. He stood for a moment before the open door, heard someone moving inside the room, and walked in. The fat chambermaid was making the bed. It was an ordinary hotel room being prepared for the next occupant. The chambermaid flipped the top of the sheet over the blankets, glanced at him, standing looking at her, and said, 'Partiti.'

His immobility seemed to require something more from her, and she jerked her thumb in the direction of another room. 'Partiti tutt'e due.'

That meant 'Gone, the two.'

'Quando?'

'Stamattina, presto presto.'

Did that mean 'early early' or 'quickly quickly'? Either would do.

He moved slowly to the door, and pictured there her luggage being carried out. The travelling-cushion! He felt an ache in his hand and looked at it – he had struck the frame of the door hard with his fist.

But Misha. He must go at once. He was going to run, when the manager appeared at the end of the passage, and he had an expression of such severity that it lifted him out of his former category and put him into another one. Bernard thought that if he could get round him – past him – everything would be all right; but he couldn't.

'I must speak with you, Mr Middleton.'

'I'm in rather a hurry –'

'But if you were going to see Count Kovanski, you will not be permitted to go into his room.'

'Why? Has anything happened?'

'I am afraid, yes.'

'What?'

'I am sorry to tell you – the worst that could happen.'

'Is he dead?'

'Yes. He did it himself.'

'When?'

'A quarter of an hour ago.' He might so easily have been in time! 'Count Kovanski rang the bell about a quarter of an hour or half an hour, before that, and asked the sommelier to take a letter to the other gentleman's room. The sommelier found out that Mr Harden, with Madame Solario, had left the hotel, and he went back and told Count Kovanski. Soon after, a shot was heard. I heard it myself. Mr Middleton, I would advise you –'

'Please don't.'

'I must tell you it would be better for you to leave before the police arrive. We are only just now notifying them. As it is a suicide – there are no suspicions – they may not be here just yet, but soon. You were a friend of Count Kovanski. You would evitate for yourself a painful interrogation if –'

'Please let me be alone for a few minutes.'

'Certainly, a few minutes.' As they parted Bernard heard, 'I offer you my sympathy.'

Bernard did not get as far as his room; he was obliged to lean against the wall. He could have been in time! He reconstructed everything – hurried a little more – got there ...

It mercifully came to him that, though he could have prevented it a quarter of an hour ago, at *that* moment, he could not have prevented it at every moment, for, given Misha's character, it would happen. He need not think he could long have stood between.

This was despair. Misha's life was over, and all that he could still have done and enjoyed was not to be. But he thought of himself, too. He was now alone. With Misha alive, even if he never saw him he would have known that he was in the world and could have thought about him, and someone else would have known about that night; now he would always be alone in knowing about it, and the loneliness of that was for the rest of his life.

He turned. The chambermaid, who had been away, was coming back, waddling, with towels over her arm, her key on a long black tape swinging over her white apron. She gave him an inquisitive glance as she went into the room. In his mind he went into the room with her – and then he thought with stupefaction that *she* would probably not remember that room or this passage and what had happened here. In the lives of those two, what had happened to the others during these weeks would, he believed, not be particularly rememberable. They were a few

348

weeks in those lives, that was all. But in *their* lives . . . He had seen Missy flying as if pursued by the furies, and Misha was dead, and Ilona's heart was broken, and he – Well, no matter. Those two were gone, gone leaving all that behind them – and what else would they leave behind them ?– on their way.

It was the concierge, not the manager, who came for him while he was still leaning against the wall by the window in the passage.

'A gentleman is downstairs who has asked to see you.'

He could not think of anyone in the world. There was no one in the world, as it couldn't be Harden or Misha.

The manager was at the door of his office, talking to a young man who had his back to Bernard; the manager saw him coming and made a sign to the young man, who wheeled round, and it was Charlie Trevor.

'Oh, hullo,' said Bernard.

'Oh, hullo!'

'Did you just happen to come here?' asked Bernard after the moment it took to begin speaking again. 'You didn't know I was here, did you?'

'Yes, I did.'

'Really? How?'

'Colonel Ross told me.'

'Colonel Ross! How did *he* know?'

Trevor didn't answer.

'How did *he* know?'

'I think he heard through the Consulate.'

Resentment of this supervision flared up in him. And then, very far away, a corner of an arid waste was softened by a sort of dew, the thought: My own kind.

The manager was talking again, in a low voice, to Trevor – saying it to Trevor, not to him.

'The Russian Consul will be coming with the police, and it would be much better if all the persons who had dined with the Count last night were gone. There were three, and two have already gone. Because it was a personage a great case will be made if possible – you understand – and it would be better, I confess also for the hotel, if there was no one to interrogate – very little to be said.'

'I understand,' replied Trevor.

'Mr Middleton and the Count came in alone together at midnight and went up to the room where this morning – You understand. Mr Middleton would evitate having to remain here perhaps some time while the investigations proceed –'

'I quite understand,' said Trevor.

They were talking about him as if he weren't there, and though he resented it, he was not quite able to take the matter into his own hands.

'We could go at once,' said Trevor. 'Can we catch the train to Paris?'

The manager, much relieved, glanced up at the clock above the porter's desk.

'The train for Paris left unfortunately twenty minutes ago, and there is not another till the night train. But you can get to Switzerland by a train going in about half an hour, and from there you could proceed very easily –'

'Shall we go?' said Trevor to Bernard. 'I came late last night from Cadenabbia and left my luggage in the station, all but a bag. I spent the night at the Nord, opposite.'

'We will send for your bag,' said the manager. 'There are two trains, the Simplon and the St Gotthard' – he kept glancing up at the clock – 'going one a little after the other. You might get the first. Then from Lausanne or Lucerne –'

'Have you packed?' said Trevor to Bernard.

'No. And I haven't enough money to pay the hotel bill, let alone my ticket.'

'That's all right.'

'Oh,' said Bernard, making it sarcastic, 'did Colonel Ross know that too?'

Trevor didn't answer.

'I haven't much to pack,' said Bernard.

'Shall I run up and do it for you?'

He could perfectly well have acted for himself if they had not started by taking everything out of his hands; now he would let them go on doing it. The manager opened the glass door into the court, and he went and sat down in the sunshine, like an invalid. It was the manager who fetched him when they were ready to go.

'I couldn't find your hat,' said Trevor.

'I know – I left it at Cova's.'

'You can buy a hat in Switzerland,' said the manager.

He was in the lobby to see them go, and the concierge, and the two chasseurs, and a waiter out of the dining-room, and a porter, and two or three people – they all seemed to be coming round to look, like cattle round a dog in a field. He was leaving Misha. But he mustn't leave him! He stood still. He should stay by him to the end!

For a few seconds he stood still; for a few seconds Trevor's hand was on his arm. Then they went forward again, the swing-doors were opened for them, and they walked out into the piazza.